The 10th Province

Of Jaryar

A tale from Ragaris

by

Penelope Wallace

A Mightier Than the Sword UK Publication

©2017

The 10th Province of Jayar

The Tales from Ragaris

By Penelope Wallace

A Mightier Than the Sword UK Publication

Paperback Edition

Copyright © Penelope Wallace 2017

Map of Marod by Stephen Hall

Cover Illustration by Ian Storer

Cover Design by C.S. Woolley

ISBN 978 198 146 139 4

All rights reserved. No part of this publication may be reproduced, stored in a retrieval system, or transmitted in any form or by any means, electronic, mechanical, photocopying, recording or otherwise, without prior permission of the publishers.

"There was a little city with few people in it; and a great king came against it and besieged it, building great siegeworks against it. But there was found in it a poor wise man, and he by his wisdom delivered the city. Yet no one remembered that poor man."
(Ecclesiastes 9: 14-15)

"It is in truth not for glory, nor riches, nor honours that we are fighting, but for freedom – for that alone, which no honest man gives up but with life itself."
Declaration of Arbroath, 1320

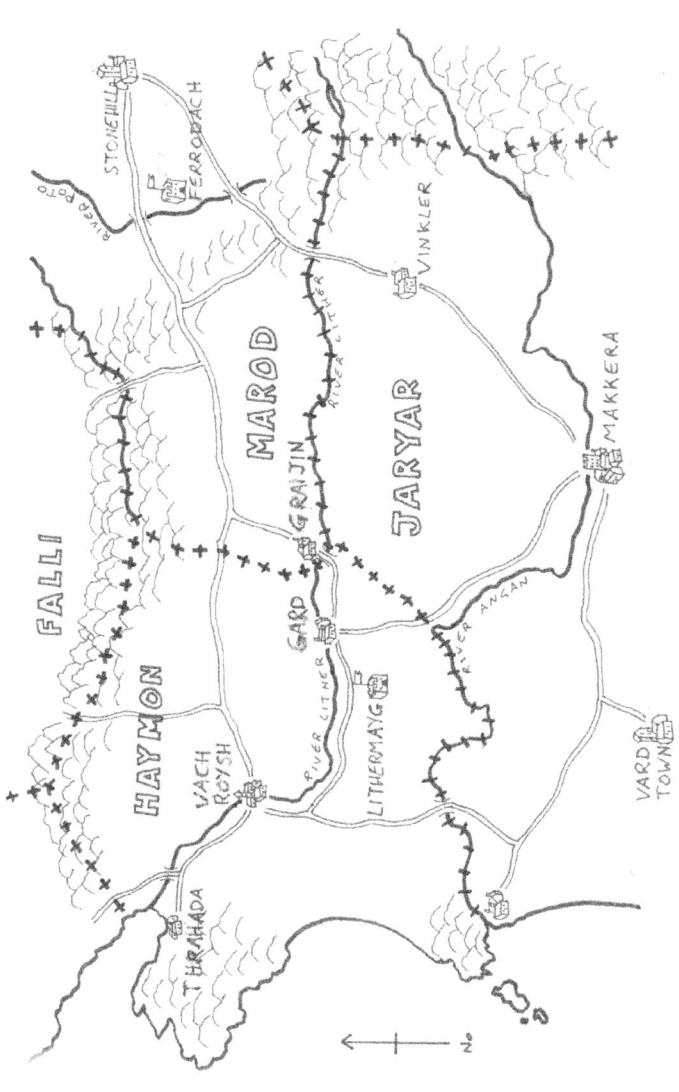

Characters

<u>The rulers:</u>

    Osgar, King of Jaryar and Overlord of the West, residing in Makkera

    Nerranya, Queen of Marod, residing in Stonehill

    Invildi and Jaikkad, Ruling Consuls of Haymon, residing in Vach-roysh

<u>The two delegations:</u>
<u>For Queen Nerranya</u>

    Barad, her husband, King of Marod

    Braidoc, her brother, Prince of Marod

    Fillim Queensister

    Paul, Abbot of Lintoll

<u>Accompanying them</u>

    Lida, Prince Braidoc's squire, aged 14

    Fric, Fillim's squire, aged 9

    Jeppa, King Barad's servant

    Yaif, Prince Braidoc's servant

    Brother Jude, the Abbot's attendant

    Draider Queensbrother

Kalla, a secretary

And seven other servants and guards.

For Duke Haras

Haras, Duke of Vard

Antonos of Tayn

Errios of Girifay

Elizabeth, Archbishop of Makkera

Accompanying them

Palla, Dowager Duchess of Vard, the Duke's stepmother

Illi, his lover

Justar, Antonos' squire, aged 17

And twenty servants, guards and others.

Natives of Haymon:

Talinti of Lithermayg

Meriden, her steward; Kariam, her maid; Brod, her groom

Her children: Araf, aged 12, Mritta aged 8, Yerdin, aged 6

Demis of Arring, her uncle

Tormenas, her kinsman, residing in Vach-roysh

Lady Madigam, King Barad's sister

City guards, tavern-keepers and others.

Natives of Jaryar

Upali, an exile

Lady Yairil of Qasadan, and her ship's captain Ardas

Electors from all the nine provinces, with their servants

Other

Mary, Prelate Peter's envoy to the Council from Defardu

Lady Jeriet, visiting from Ricossa

The Call to the Council

I

1st April 619 After Landing

It was an ordinary morning, until the strange woman came.

Meriden was standing among the rigs with one of the Lithermayg farmers, trying to forget that Sametta was marrying another man, and discussing this year's crops. "Our lady insists we need the beans, so very wholesome, and pretty in flower. And after all, I've been arguing with her for ten years or so -" he shrugged concedingly - "and she's often right." Garren grinned, and they both looked around.

The humped rigs of greening earth lay between them and the village road and its cottages – *that roof still not fixed*. Beyond, cattle hungrily grazed after the winter fast, and up the sloping pasture they could see the distant hall, and the church off to the left.

And the sky was pale blue - patched with blowing clouds, for the day was breezy - and an occasional lark soared and fell, soared and fell – like its own music, their lady would say. She had odd fancies.

A pleasant dull scene. Meriden didn't love it, but it was home.

But then there were shrill shouts. On the road, an unfamiliar old woman leant swaying on a stick. Three children were dancing backwards before her, laughing and calling, "Get away! Plague! Plague!" A stone, or a clod of mud, soared and fell, unmusically, and struck the woman's shoulder.

"Leave her, you brats!" Meriden strode towards them, putting all his lady's authority into his voice. "Shame on you! Shame!" The children scattered. He jumped the ditch, and hurried back along the road to the woman, praying *Not plague*. She took a slow step forwards, staring at the ground.

Meriden saw stained brown travelling clothes, a cheap newish satchel, and a figure that swayed. An elderly wandering pauper. His lady would want him to be charitable, within reason.

Then she looked up, and he found someone he didn't expect. Surely she was younger than him - perhaps twenty-five. A thin brown face, with no rash and few marks of weather; ungreyed hair. Her breath was shallow, and her eyes dark-rimmed, but as they met his, he saw pride and anger. He saw her superiority over this place, and certainly over him.

"Greetings, madam," he said.

"Good – good morrow, sir. Is this being the road to Vach-roysh?"

A foreign voice. His puzzlement grew. "Vach-roysh? Yes, but it's several days – many days away on foot." She was rocking on her staff. *Exhausted – she's going to weep.* He dared to stretch out a hand. "Madam, you need to rest."

"No. I must - I have a message -" But she gasped, and was falling forward, and he had to catch her.

He called Garren, and they carried her to an empty barn, roomier and fresher than those children's homes would be. She was starved-light, and her skin hot. "Go and tell the mistress. She'll want to help. But she shouldn't come herself – there may be fever." Garren hurried away, and Meriden found a blanket, and water.

The woman lay on the straw, eyes wide, shoulders shivering. She revived a little to drink. Kneeling beside her, he noticed that her teeth were sound.

What is such a woman doing, deep in the Haymonese

countryside, without servants?

"You're safe here, madam. Please rest. I am Meriden, steward of this estate. What is your name?"

She swallowed, staring upwards. A pigeon sat on a beam above them, jerking its head and fluffing feathers. "Upali. Upali of - it doesn't matter."

"Where have you journeyed from? D'you have friends or kindred near here, to help you?"

"Kin." A grunt. "Curse them, all of them."

Meriden blinked. She turned her head (with pain, he thought) and stared at his pale-skinned but otherwise very ordinary face. Her eyes were dark.

"I can see your soul," she said. "You have a sad soul."

You are a strange woman, Upali. This is going to disrupt my whole day.

"I need a priest, or someone who can write." She stopped to cough, and her body rattled. "There are words. Words for the great ones at Vach-roysh."

"I can write for you," he said soothingly, and drew out parchment and pen, to prove it. But she wasn't looking at him; she was staring at the pigeon.

Then, softly, "I saw their deaths, Abbos and Rosior.

I saw it, and I spoke it, and they died. And now - I have seen. Write," and she was commanding a servant.

Meriden was a servant, and so he wrote. Her voice was slow and thin, and sometimes she stopped to cough, but every word was deliberate.

> *"To the hall with six flames*
> *Call the great of the nine*
> *For an heir to the King;*
> *They will seek for a sign.*
> *From the north see a wife,*
> *From the south see a son;*
> *And the second will rule*
> *When the counting is done.*
> *There is hate, there is death,*
> *I feel fear, I see blood,*
> *But one has stooped low,*
> *Raised a bloom from the mud.*
> *Bowing down to be raised*
> *For the Dream, and God's law.*
> *But the sheep, they all wait*
> *For mild peace or grim war."*

The voice stopped. As he was writing the last of this nonsense, he heard the door open behind him, and the light was blocked by shadow.

His lady pushed gently past him, knelt, and took the woman's hand. She spared Meriden a glance, and he tried to say *She's very ill, and perhaps mad,* without words. Aloud, "Her name is Upali."

"Madam, I am Talinti of Lithermayg. I'm sorry to find you sick, but I've sent for a physician. Can you eat?"

Upali stared at the other woman, perhaps a decade older and glowing with health. If she saw Talinti's soul also she didn't mention it. She lifted a weary finger and gestured to his parchment. "The words. They must go to Vachroysh. They must -" Her breath wheezed.

"My lady," whispered Meriden, "I think we may need a priest."

His mistress nodded sadly. Then she too looked over at his writing. For a moment, he wished he'd hidden it away. But that would have been a betrayal of duty, and now in any case it was too late.

He was fairly sure that those words would be trouble.

II

From "The Great History of Jaryar in the Seventh Century"

All of Jaryar mourned for Prince Abbos and his son, but King Osgar's grief was the most bitter. From that time his health began to fail, and by the next spring it was clear that he was fading towards death. Then there was great consternation in the land and in the capital, for he had neither child nor grandchild, nor sibling nor nephew nor niece. His nearest kin were the grandchildren of his cousin once removed Igalla, who had married the Prince of Marod in the year 571.

Of these grandchildren, one was Nerranya, Queen of Marod; and the other Haras, whose father had returned to his native land, and who was now Duke of the Province of Vard. There were some who said Jaryar could never endure to be ruled by a foreign queen; but there were those in other provinces who did not love Vard, and did not wish to give its duke the crown. And all agreed that warfare within the kingdom was to be avoided beyond everything, looking to and fearing the example of the seven-year War of the Throne in Ricossa, in which it is said ten thousand died.

And at last it was proposed to gather the great of Jaryar, both of the nobility and of the church, to a Council, and there present to them the claims of the two Competitors, the Queen and the Duke, who would send delegates to speak for them. And the selected people would hear all the arguments fairly presented, and weigh matters before God, without malice or strife, greed or selfish ambition, and would elect one or the other to be King Osgar's heir.

This was agreed, and then arose the further question, Where should this great Council be held? For the rulers of Makkera city feared the incoming of so many, especially barbarians (as they said) from the north and from the islands; while others argued that Makkera would be a hostile city to the Marodi Queen, where she would not receive a fair hearing. The solution came unexpectedly from the King's vassals in Haymon in the west.

And so messengers rode and sailed out in the winter of 618 to all the nine provinces of Jaryar, calling lords and ladies, bishops and abbots, to attend in April 619 in Vach-roysh, to hear what the Queen and the Duke had to say, and then, by God's guidance, to choose between them.

The Setting Out

"The wife from the north"
The Castle, Stonehill, Marod

Her master was in the Small Chamber with the Queen and Council, making the great decision, and so Lida was hopping from foot to foot in the anteroom. It was an airy and well-windowed place, with gleaming shields hanging on the walls, so when hopping tired her, she bounced over to stare at her reflection. She twisted what she knew was a pretty face into grotesque shapes, and awarded herself points out of five.

There was an occasional murmur from the Chamber, but she couldn't distinguish words. Surely the Queen would select her brother the Prince for this most vital mission, and so surely - There was no one about to check her, so she turned a cartwheel down the room, and almost crashed into the stone king.

He was more than life-size, carved in stone and brightly painted, dressed with grand robes and crown, and in his rather large cupped hands he managed to hold three tiny babies. Such a thing was called a "statue", Lida knew, and she liked looking at it. But this was idleness. If she wanted God's favour — and today she desperately did — she should use her time in holy fashion, practising swordplay or reciting psalms. So she unfastened her jacket and stood on tiptoe to drape it carefully around the king's shoulders. Before turning away, she gave it a fond stroke, and sighed happily. New, blue wool with red piping, and actual horn buttons, the latest thing, so that it opened all the way down. Bought for her by her parents, for the journey to foreign lands that she *might* be sent on. Lida sent up a little hope to God in the direction of the beamed ceiling, drew her sword, and leapt forward to attack an imaginary enemy. (Every time she met someone she looked to see if they had buttons, and ranked them accordingly.)

Forward. Back. Side. Slash. Block. (And always Watch.) Back -

Suddenly the voices shifted, the door ground open, and she had just time to scamper over, sweep her jacket from its irreverent place, and stand by the wall - chin up, arms by sides, eyes lowered.

The guards and the Queensbrothers. Queen Nerranya, in blue and silver, and a lovely white fur cape.

The King. The Marshal and the Warden. And next in line, her own master, who jerked his eyes at his squire to fall in beside him, and then led her away from the others towards his own chamber. He didn't look disappointed. *I hope I hope I hope.*

They reached the small dark square room, wall panels portraited (Lida had invented the word) with past kings and queens and saints. The Prince tossed his hat to her without looking, and walked over to kneel before the crucifix, head bowed. Lida poked the fire into life, and then waited, feet and fingers itching for news.

He rose and sat down, instructing her with the flick of a finger to pour a cup of wine. Prince Braidoc didn't resemble the Queen his sister; his long nose, heavy brows and medium stature were inherited, people said, from their father. His hair and short beard were neatly trimmed, his manner quiet and considered, and his knee-length gown and hose were in sober black. Buttons, but only because the Queen insisted. ("An absurd extravagance," he'd said, half-frown, half-smile; and so she'd had to give him new clothes at Christmas, and order him to wear them.)

He sipped his wine.

Please!

And his face crinkled at her in his unexpectedly warm smile. "Yes, we are going to Vach-roysh. I am to be one of the four delegates. And you will accompany me."

Yes, yes, yes! It was the most wonderful news in her fourteen years, and she couldn't stop herself grinning.

"I am not surprised you are excited," he said, but then the smile vanished. "Lida."

"Yes, my prince?" *I, Alida, daughter of Arrada, I am going with the Queen's delegation!*

"*Lida.*" He stared at her, plainly waiting for her to be ready to concentrate. "This is a holy work. We must win this contest. It is God's will, and it is necessary for Marod's safety, and that of all our people. No mistakes, no carelessness. You will be well-mannered and correct, you will keep your eyes and ears open, and report anything of interest to me. And if anyone at the Council asks you who should rule Jaryar, and why, you will know the answer."

Lida nodded obediently. "Queen Nerranya should rule."

"And why should the Council choose her?"

All the arguments that the other squires had been discussing had flown away. "Because – because she is the true heir?" was all she could think of, painfully obvious.

"Exactly. She is the true heir – the eldest child of the eldest child of the next line of descent. That is the only thing that is relevant. Do not be distracted into arguing that she would be a better monarch – although she would – or that Duke Haras is a fool – although he is. She is the lawful heir."

"Yes, my prince."

"Tomorrow I will fast, and attend confession and Mass to prepare myself. You will also do this, I trust."

"Of course, my prince." *Not again!* But she'd been his squire for two years; she'd learned to endure a day without food.

He leaned back in his chair, staring upwards. After counting a long enough pause not to be disrespectful of holy rites, Lida asked, "When do we leave for Makkera, my prince?"

His eyes left the ceiling. Silence. *Oh.* "I mean Vach-roysh."

"Yes, you mean Vach-roysh. You know the difference between Makkera, the Green City, the capital of *Jaryar*, and Vach-roysh, the capital of *Haymon*?"

Yes, but - "Forgive me, my prince," she said humbly. "But why Haymon?"

"That is what has been agreed. There are reasons. The Council to choose a monarch for Jaryar is to take place in Haymon, which has no monarch at all."

*

They fasted and prayed accordingly. Lida confessed her sins of inattention and frivolity, which were all she could think of, chewing the skin next to her finger-nails – *filthy habit* – while waiting to be given her penance. She always liked the moment when the priest said, "I absolve you. Go in peace," and all her badness was suddenly gone, and she could skip away from the Castle chapel, fresh and innocent and clean as a newborn lamb. Although of course she didn't actually skip. And the newborn lambs at home weren't really clean. She pictured herself with a baby lamb, washing it and combing it, and cuddling it in a soft blanket - and then she was back at the squires' dormitory, and she had to pack, and to commiserate with her friends, and tell them how sorry she was that they weren't also coming. In many cases, this was even true. She ran a score of errands for her master, and tried to remember – or at least look as if she were remembering – all his instructions.

And at last it was the *day before*, and she was standing in the White Hall, crowded with a hundred others, every eye fixed on the dais. It was a plain, bare-plastered room. They said that when the foreign Queen Igalla arrived from the south long ago, her husband and father-in-law allowed her to make what changes she liked elsewhere (installing the statue of King Tristar in the anteroom, for instance) but not to touch the Hall, a place for simplicity and awe and (sometimes) boredom.

Not boredom, today. Queen Nerranya, tall and majestic, black hair piled up and studded with pearls, sweeping red gown cut wide to cover her pregnancy, stood, and so did everyone else. And Bishop James of Stonehill read the Declaration, issued jointly by feeble King Osgar of Jaryar, and Peter XXIII, Holy Church's Prelate of all Ragaris.

A Council will commence on the twenty-fourth day of April of the year 619 or shortly thereafter, in the Theatre of Debating in Vach-roysh.

Burble burble burble.

Each of the Competitors may bring a delegation of four people, who may include themselves, to put forward their claim.

As the Queen named her delegates, they walked to the centre of the room.

"I am not going to speak for myself, so I shall send

my bone and my flesh. Barad." The King kissed his wife's hand before stepping down from the dais. Unlike most of those present, whose skin was brown, of varying hues, King Barad was very dark, almost black. His hair was short and soft, covering his head neatly like moss (Lida thought) except of course black instead of green. It was a style that many tried, and failed, to imitate. Middling in height and broadish, he stood relaxedly, smiling at the Queen as if sharing a private joke. Lida had been in his presence often enough to know they would have no shortage of conversation on the journey.

"Braidoc, my beloved brother." Lida's heart swelled. Her Prince made no gestures; he simply stepped forward. They said he was the most learned, and the most devout, prince Marod had ever had - and no slouch with a sword either. The centre of every eye, he stood as always very still.

"For the Church, Abbot Paul Tommid of Lintoll."

"Who?" muttered a few voices. "Lintoll?"

Lida, silent and smug, knew the answer. The Abbot was her master's suggestion, and she'd heard him explaining to his lady. "The Bishop is too infirm for the journey, and Vard will doubtless manage to send an *Arch*bishop, who would outrank him in worldly terms anyway. So we have chosen solid worth. The Abbot's learning and piety are respected abroad, and if people do not know him here, that is because he stays in his Abbey, attending to his duties, rather than pleasuring himself in the city."

"I see, of course," Lady Mella had agreed.

And here was the Abbot, stumbling forwards and almost tripping on his robe. Lida suppressed a giggle. Solid worth indeed – wide-shouldered and with a waistline to match – not fat, perhaps, but certainly well-fed. And old. He was dressed in full-length black, with hair cut as short as possible, like all monks. Once before the dais, he stood with his hands clutched and fiddling behind him, eyes flicking around the Hall, and large lips quivering. He looked out of place.

"And Fillim Queensister, for the Queen's Thirty." Everyone had known one of the Thirty would be sent (*"They don't have a Thirty in Jaryar"* - *"Or Haymon"* - *"They don't have a Queen in Haymon"*) and there'd been much hopeful speculation among the squires as to which. On the whole, Lida approved of the choice. Fillim was tall and graceful, and the greatest swordswoman in Marod. Her long brown hair, coiled into a point on her head and barely covered with a small simple cap, was almost (oddly) the same colour as her skin. Her nose was snub; her mouth rather large. How was it, then, that everyone called her beautiful? She wore a green jacket (buttoned) and hose, and her hand rested on her swordhilt as she bowed to the Queen.

About her there hung the aura of interesting tragedy. Fifty years ago all her mother's family had been slaughtered in the Ferrodach massacre, leaving only one five-year-old child.

The drawback, for Lida, was that Fillim's squire was a dull nine-year-old, no fun. Whereas if the Queen had sent Jasser Queensbrother, his squire - However.

The four delegates bowed, and were applauded.

"The Bishop will now bless your mission."

"By your gracious leave," said Prince Braidoc courteously. "The mission is not ours alone, but depends in part on all who go with us. May Bishop James not bless us all?" He looked across at Lida, and smiled, and she was warmed by his kindness.

The Queen had no objection, so Lida, Fillim's baby squire Fric, and the various servants and soldiers and miscellaneous people who were to leave for Vach-roysh next day (eighteen in all) stood in the centre of the Hall to be stared at and gloriously envied, while the Bishop made a long prayer to which probably not everyone listened.

*

Lida had had a terrible problem deciding what to wear for the farewell feast that afternoon. Along with the jacket, her parents had provided a wonderful new gown, rose-pink with gold-embroidered sleeves, and plainly that one must go with her to Vach-roysh. (Surely there would be a celebration of some kind. And surely Prince Braidoc wouldn't deny her an opportunity to dance.) But to wear her second-best blue, which had a wine stain on the sleeve that probably no one would notice, and was really too tight for her – "You are *growing*," the Prince's servant had said, almost disapprovingly – to wear that tonight before the Queen and King, and all her jealous friends - But if she wore the rose and, horror unbearable, tore or stained it, she would have *nothing*.

She pondered and re-pondered as she combed her hair (all the rest of her family had interestingly curly hair, but hers was at least thick and long), and scrubbed behind her ears and under her arms. Out of pure vanity – impure vanity, Sour-Faced Jeppa would say - she ran her fingers over her face, tracing her little pointed chin and poking the dimples in her cheeks. In the end she selected the rose, reminding God hopefully that she was a clean lamb, and it would be desperately harsh of Him to spoil things for her.

The Great Hall, much more lively than the White, was full of tables, flickering flame and candle-light, the most beautiful clothes, and the sumptuous smells of roast meat – and Lida was too busy waiting on her Prince at the High Table to think of anything else, except her own hunger. Dimly along to the right she heard the King grumbling merrily that this was the last good meal he'd have for a month, foreign food being so uneatable, and the Queen laughing at him, and the Bishop putting in a good word for the Haymonese cheeses. And her Prince was deep in discussion with his uncle the Warden – something about relations with the Jaryari province of Vendor. *("Name the nine provinces of Jaryar," as her tutor would've said.)*

When the great people had finished, or almost finished, the squires and servants behind the table could feed themselves, and the lesser musicians gave way to storytellers. Tonight it was the familiar tale of how King Tristar had united three warring kingdoms into Marod two hundred years ago - and Lida suddenly understood for the first time why the King's statue was holding three babies. It was a parable, or something.

And at last the tables were pushed back, and the dancing began. The Prince dismissed Lida with a pleasant nod, and withdrew aside – he rarely did anything so frivolous as dance, and especially not on a Sunday. But Lida longed to, and found her foot tapping as the music started up. King Barad left his wife, whose condition didn't permit it, and offered his hand to the Warden's lady. And all over the Hall couples swept into the line, and colours started to swirl, and feet to stamp, and the music of pipe and rebec curled and trembled up through the air. Lida saw her friend Jima approaching the handsome squire she liked, and joining hands with him. She saw the solid Abbot Paul sitting alone, plump hands folded in front of him, a vague smile on his face as he watched. Fillim Queensister was talking to her friend Lady Yaffet, but she gave her hand graciously to Draider Queensbrother when he came up with, "Do you dance, madam?"

Fillim was now dressed in a silver overgown with scarlet beneath. She wore no jewellery except – Lida had noticed this before – always on her right wrist a simple bracelet made not of metal or jewels, but of black human hair. There was much gossip about whose hair. Draider, whose hair was also black, like most people's after all, was going with the delegation, in charge of security. He danced Fillim down the line and back, and then all the couples peeled apart to swing other people. Fillim looked bored, Lida thought. *I wouldn't be bored, dancing with Master Draider! Or with anybody.*

She found the man Yaif standing next to her. He was Prince Braidoc's new servant from his country estate – employed for this journey because he knew Vach-roysh, and would be more useful than the regular man. Yaif was about forty, she judged, tall and broad-shouldered with curly hair, a cheerful face, and a laced blue jacket. He bowed to her politely, and said, "Madam. Do you know everybody here?"

"Well, nearly everybody."

"The woman over there talking to the musicians?"

Complaining about their choice of tune, probably. "That's the King's servant, Jeppa, daughter of Anam." *Sour-Faced Jeppa.*

"Er - she will be coming with us tomorrow?"

"Oh, yes, I believe so." They exchanged a rueful look. So he'd been in the Castle less than a day, and had already been flayed by Jeppa's tongue. "She's very frank in

31

her opinions," said Lida, quoting Mistress Fillim, and grinning.   Yaif looked encouragement.

"She once pushed a woman into a corner who'd made a joke about the King, and threatened to gouge her eyes out with her own comb."

But her comments are entertaining, when the victim is someone else.

"The King will be well served, then. And is Mistress Fillim taking anyone?"

"No, only her squire, Fric."

"That's an unusual name," he said, raising his eyebrows.

"It's short for Fejederic. Everyone calls him Fric. He's only a child – he's over there, the one in the green jacket." She pointed to a corner where a few youngsters were playing marbles and comparing play-swords.

She was so desperate to dance that she almost said the words to Yaif. But he was two or three times her age, and a servant, and one day she would be the lady of Dendarry, so her mother would say she was lowering herself. She looked away, and Yaif bowed politely, and wandered off.

Lida bit her lip. And suddenly, "Do you dance,

madam?" and it was King Barad himself, twinkling down at her, and the night became wonderful. "Oh, yes, Your Grace!"

"I thought so," said the King, whirling her gently into the double line. Another couple twisted between them, and on. "I noticed you this morning, Lida, and thought that you looked happy."

Lida wondered if this were a bad thing.

"We're departing tomorrow on a very serious expedition, aren't we? Oh so serious and important, as it is indeed. And I think you and I are the only people expecting to get any pleasure out of it. I'm looking forward to seeing Vach-roysh again." They joined hands, and danced down the line and back in their turn. "You haven't been to Haymon before?"

"No, never."

"Not even to see your - was it your great-uncle's tomb?"

"My grandfather's cousin, Your Grace." She sighed inwardly. *Please, no more conversation about Dendarry's hero.*

"Ah. He will have died before you were born?"

And then they had to part to swing all the others in the line, and Lida slid her arm against Master Draider's, and

Jima's squire's, and Lord Layn's son's, and the man Yaif's, and many others', and then back to standing opposite the King, who continued as if nothing had interrupted them, "You're fifteen?"

"Fourteen, Your Grace."

"I was nine when I first came to Stonehill with my family, for King Jendon's funeral. It was all very solemn and mournful, but also exciting, for a curious lad. I hope you enjoy the Council, Lida."

*

Between dances, there was entertainment. A visiting troop from the neighbouring kingdom of Falli danced. Lida thought her master – or her mother, for that matter – wouldn't have approved of what they wore. Falli had a reputation. The men were bare-chested; some very hairy, and some not, making her feel a little odd down below her stomach. And the women's dresses were low-cut, and the skirts slashed with not even a smock beneath, so that a bare shin or even thigh could occasionally be seen. Lida thought some of the men watching were particularly interested – Abbot Paul didn't glance away once. He sucked his lips in, and then wriggled them around, chewing at nothing.

The dance itself was very fast, almost tumbling, and

the applause tumultuous. And then, at the Queen's request, Fillim Queensister stood in the middle of the Hall to sing. It was a ballad Lida didn't know, with a tune that got inside her head, and wouldn't get out - a strange and sinister story about someone called Marbali, who vowed to kill the men who raped her sister, and discovered too late that one of them was her own son. Fillim sang well, and shivers ran down Lida's spine at the blood-soaked conclusion.

"I hadn't heard that tale," said someone.

"It's from Tell, in Jaryar," said the Queen. "They're fond of tales of divided loyalty there. It was my choice. I thought it would do us no harm to learn about our southern neighbours. Thank you, sister."

"'Neighbours' is a friendly word for them," Lida heard Master Draider mutter.

And the next song was a comic one, "The Wolf and the Buttercup", and then a sweet love story, "The Tale of Jovi's Mill."

*

The delegation was leaving early next day, so the evening couldn't go on late. Lida, tired and exhilarated, came meekly over to ask Prince Braidoc if he had any last instructions. He was sitting in a corner with Lady Mella, shy, learned and pretty, to whom he was almost betrothed. As Lida approached, she saw him slip something into his pouch, and say, "I will not need this to remind me of you every day. But I thank you." He kissed his lady's fingers, and smiled gently, and Lady Mella's body gave a happy wriggle, and Lida looked away in embarrassment. Then the lady rose, curtsied, and departed.

"Are you ready for tomorrow, Lida?"

"Y – yes, my prince." *Except for packing the rose gown, and a thorough wash.* There wasn't enough time for a bath.

"I will be sleeping out. You need not wait for me. Be ready before Prime," he said, and walked off. Lida watched him march through the courtyard, speak casually to the guards, and be let through the gates into the town.

He was going to his rented house on Pigeon Alley, to the woman who waited for him there. Lida had twice had to fetch him from her bed.

Once, in the early days, when she still thought a winning smile could excuse impertinence, she'd asked, "Does Lady Mella know about this, sir?"

He had looked up abruptly, across his little candle-lit room. "Come here, Lida," in a quiet voice. She came over to where he was sitting with a book, and he put a gentle hand on her wrist.

"No, she does not know. And, Lida, if she finds out, and finds out through you -" He paused. "I will send you home to Dendarry. And I will send you with your back bloody, and your face will be rather less pretty than it is now. God hates disloyalty." His hand gripped her so hard that the tears pricking were of pain as well as fear. "Do you understand?"

But most of the time he was kind to her.

*

"The son from the south"
Castle Vard, in the province of Vard, northern Jaryar

Old Errios and the woman who waited on him reached the door of the Sky Chamber. The guard recognised him, bowed, and knocked. The door opened. Errios walked slowly in, leaning on his servant. There were constellations painted on the ceiling of this room, but he could no longer straighten his neck to look at them. He advanced towards the three people standing in the centre.

Time to think again, *What's my grandson done now? How much trouble is he in?* There could be no other reason for such a summons. From the Duke himself.

Errios was sixty-seven years old. He had buried two wives, and four of his seven children. He needed help to climb stairs, and a secretary to read and write for him.

People called him – he'd heard – "the most distinguished warrior in Jaryar." The one with the most distinctive scars, they meant. Two fingers missing from the left hand. A red ridge down the side of his face, from the useless right eye to the edge of the mouth. But still his hair was long and thick and white, plaited down his back in the soldier's way.

With difficulty he went down on one knee before his lord, who was twenty-one.

The Duke was growing a beard. It made him look more like a king, which must be the point. He was compactly-made. His arms were muscled, and his dark-red gown spotless. He'd pulled off the matching hat, and was fiddling with it.

By his side stood his stepmother, the Duchess, a middling-sized woman dressed in yellow. She was looking at a parchment in her hand.

"My lord," said Errios. The Duke nodded. His attendant stepped forward to help the old man rise.

"Welcome," said the Duke. He gestured to the

Duchess, and she smiled up, waving her parchment.

"Your information was most illuminating, sir," she said. "The Duke and I are grateful."

Errios' mind jerked in surprise. She was holding the report he'd been asked to prepare a month ago, *"What is Known or Suspected About the Royal House of Marod."* Finding the facts, ordering and dictating them – it had been a more enjoyable task than he'd expected.

This wasn't about his dissolute grandson, then.

"Thank you, my lady." His voice grated, and he coughed.

"Are you in good health?" asked the Duke suddenly.

"As good as I could hope, at my age, by God's grace."

"I believe you can still ride? Long distances?"

A strange question. "Yes, my lord."

"Good. Your report has impressed us, as the Duchess says. It will be most useful in Vach-roysh. *You* will be most useful."

"My lord?"

"Tomorrow I am naming you to the delegation," said the Duke. "You will leave in a week's time, with myself, the Archbishop, and Antonos of Tayn."

Errios stared. The Duchess added, "All expenses will be covered by the royal treasury, thanks to our King's kindness. Please advise the Marshal by tomorrow how many servants you will be requiring to bring." She smiled.

He was dismissed, and took his astonishment away with him.

*

The Duchess invited the Vard delegation to take spiced morbah and fruit pancakes in her private rooms. On the way, Errios passed a young woman in the corridor. Her hair was short and covered with a kerchief. Her kirtle was plain and grey, like the lowliest of the Duke's maids. But Errios knew enough to bow to her as he passed. He didn't approve. But he wasn't an utter fool.

The Duchess was laying out papers on a table. Some looked like maps, or so he thought. She greeted him, and took his arm to guide him to a chair. *That's how feeble they think me.*

A moment later he had to push himself up to greet the tall woman who arrived next. The Archbishop of Makkera – nearly his own age, but standing straighter than he could. Her cropped hair was a dull grey, pale against her black skin. He'd seen her in the distance before, but they'd never met. He didn't often visit the capital.

"You'll be knowing of Errios, son of Broxos, of Girifay, Your Reverence?"

"Indeed. His deeds go before him," said the Archbishop. Her voice smeared butter through the room.

"The honour is mine," he said, and was able to sit down again.

Antonos of Tayn came in with the Duke. Errios knew him as the Duke's friend, but not well. It seemed that he was related slightly to the Archbishop through his wife. At last the six of them were sitting round the table, sipping the disgusting morbah. Four delegates, the Duchess, and the Duke's secretary. A servant stood behind each chair except the secretary's.

"We'll be thirty-three in all, then, if we include your brother and cousin, and their servants. Are we agreed that ten soldiers will be enough? For the journey, and in case of any trouble while we're there?" Antonos asked.

"Do we expect trouble?" The Archbishop patted crumbs from her lip.

"It's the *un*expected trouble that fills coffins. We've had centuries to teach us not to trust the Marodi. Nor do they trust us."

"It's not the Marodi I'm expecting trouble from," said the Duke. "It's the treacherous bastards from Vendor and Indesandu. They called this Council, and for one reason – to destroy our house."

The Duchess softly tapped the table. Her stepson went on, "Don't fear, mother – I will be polite to them. But all this waste of time and money is their doing. I am the heir, and no one said otherwise until Voros stuck in his finger, and whispered to the King, and the priests."

The Duchess coughed. The Archbishop said, "My lord, your grandmother Igalla and her Marodi husband had two – no, three – children. Queen Nerranya is the daughter of the eldest -"

"Yes," he said, looking away and tapping in his turn.

"If the Duke of Indesandu hadn't pointed this out, others would have done. *She* would have done. If one traces by strict law, she has a claim."

"If one is tracing by common sense, of course it should be you," said the Duchess briskly. Perhaps not for the first time. "But the War of the Throne in Ricossa lasted seven years. By agreeing to the Council you show that you're confident enough, generous enough, to meet any argument and trust to God's leading, and your people's wisdom. They will be flattered. And don't fear, my son, most of the nobility of Jaryar agree with us. They're not wanting a foreigner to rule over them."

"Yes, my lady. Although I've heard the argument that the Marodi would be less trouble on our border if we had the same Queen," said the secretary timidly. "The electors from the northern provinces may think this, and the delegation should be prepared. I've even heard it said that this could be a bloodless way for us to conquer Marod at last."

"By giving our throne to that sanctimonious bitch!" the Duke cried angrily. "Oh no, there's one way to conquer Marod, and I will do it. Make me King, and give me soldiers, and I'll sack Stonehill."

It was absurd, but Errios felt a thrill at the words. The space where his fingers had been itched. *Marod has been trouble for too long.*

"I must protest, my lord," said the Archbishop, of course. "War between Christians is a terrible thing, hateful to the Almighty."

"Queen Nerranya is your first cousin," said the

Duchess. "And the Marodi are less aggressive than they used to be, leaving aside the Haymon war. Even that was nearly twenty years ago. We hope there'll be no need for bloodshed." Errios' eyes were a little dim, but he thought she looked hard at her stepson. "Do not fear, Haras, we'll ensure that you win. You know the preparations are in place. Now, can we turn to the immediate matters? Here's the route that's been suggested to me." She waved at the maps.

Errios rose with the others a quarter of an hour later. He had said nothing. He was better informed about the travel arrangements. No word the wiser as to why he was wanted.

He was to be part of the highest possible delegation. It was a great honour. It was absurd. *I'm not an ambassador, or a speech-maker. I'm a plain soldier, who's been studying history, now I'm too old to wield a sword.*

He had done good service in battle against Ricossa – against Haymon – against *Marod* – and the nobles of Jaryar might remember that.

It didn't seem enough.

But then, "May I speak to you privately?" asked Antonos. Errios and his servant remained behind after the others left. They remained in the Duchess' room. So plainly she knew what this was about.

"Sir?"

Antonos picked up a mug from the table. Tracing the pattern on it, and not looking at Errios he said, "There are a few points that we're not sharing with the Archbishop. The Duke wants me to tell you that, if we succeed in Vach-roysh, as we intend to, *after* we've succeeded, yes, Marod will be ours. Most of Marod."

Oh. Duke Haras' boast had sounded childlike, but not completely wild. There had been cream in his voice.

"In the meantime, the Duke wishes you to speak at the Council. And to do something else for him. Agreed?"

Errios looked at the man before him. Youngish, pale-skinned, slim, smooth-looking and well-dressed. Not built for fighting. *I don't expect to know as much as the Duke or the Duchess. I am happy to know more than the Archbishop. Why should I know less than you?*

But he said of course, "I am at his disposal."

Antonos explained. Errios went back to his own rooms, and sent his servant out to get a message to a man he'd once known, on the Marodi-Haymon border. His old contacts with spies could be useful, then. It still didn't seem enough.

They were leaving in three days. At least it wouldn't be a Friday, or any other kind of unlucky date. He made his way to the chapel, managing with a stick rather than a shoulder. There he sank down on one of the few seats, next to the statue of the Duke's royal ancestor, King Rajas the Old, and stared at the altar. From inside his gown he drew the tiny phial that hung on a chain round his neck. On it he traced the etched image of St Michael the warrior-angel, his own name-saint.

He thought of Haras, the child he'd watched grow up. Errios had served his father and mother, and his sister. He'd known his grandmother, Queen Igalla.

Igalla of Arabay. She went away long, long ago. Not beautiful. Sweet, and brave, and beloved by everyone in Vard, and one day he'd seen her crying. As he strolled past an open door with his sweetheart, they glimpsed and heard the young woman weeping in the arms of her maid. "To live there forever, with *them!* I can't!"

Someone had shut the door.

Igalla's marriage had been arranged for her, of course. She was the King's granddaughter. Next day she rode away with a smiling face, to marry the barbarian prince and become in time the Queen of Marod, and she never came back.

Errios had seen her ride out. He did not forget the agony of watching her go, or his fierce desire to save and protect her.

Of coure he could do nothing.

No complaint came back from Stonehill. Errios married his sweetheart, and fought for his lord, two kings and a queen, and time passed. And he learned many things about Marod.

Whether it was Duchess Palla or Heaven who had chosen him he didn't know. He knelt before the altar, and kissed the phial of holy water, and prayed, asking St Michael to intercede for him. He prayed that he would be strengthened to do whatever was necessary to keep the Marodi woman off the throne of Jaryar.

*

The bearers of the prophecy
Lithermayg, County Bard, in Baymon

"Well, niece," said Demis of Arring, lifting a goblet to eye-level and inspecting it for flaws, "I must thank you for an adequate meal." He smiled at Talinti, and then let his gaze wander up and down the table, past the five other people who had dined with him. Possibly he was thinking *My great-nephew gobbles his food, my great-niece is far too young to join the company, their tutor's Latin is poor, the steward does not show proper respect, and does Talinti really think that collar is the latest style? How standards have fallen at Lithermayg since my day.*

Talinti gave him time for these silent criticisms, and then she said, "I'm very glad you could come, uncle, with so little notice."

He set the goblet down. "Yes. And I didn't expect a feast in Lent, so you haven't disappointed me. I did expect some entertainment, however. What have you to offer?" And he glared at the minstrel Jaira, now playing her second-best tune for the third time, and that rebuke was justified. But Talinti could rarely bring herself to dismiss anyone who was at least willing.

"No entertainment. I was seeking your counsel. Shall we speak in my room?" As they all stood, "Children." Twelve-year-old Araf and eight-year-old Mritta knelt for her blessing, and allowed their tutor to usher them upstairs, not disgracing her by arguing in front of Great-Uncle Demis. "Meriden, bring the wine, please. And a cup for yourself."

They turned away from the table, Meriden nodding

reassuringly to the nervous maid and man waiting to clear, but Demis looked back. She watched his eyes rest on the huge hearth behind the chairs, with the friendly gargoyles carved above the flames, one on each side, named and renamed by generations of Lithermayg children. Above the fire hung the great banner of Lithermayg's liege lord, Foros of Gard - boar on a green background. There'd been no live wild boar in this part of Haymon for more than a hundred years.

Talinti walked and her uncle limped towards the door in the end wall, and she heard his scornful sigh. *Honour your father and your mother, which means all your elders,* she told herself. *And remember he's been in constant pain for eighteen years, ever since the Battle.*

He was her mother's younger brother, and therefore she outranked him. But he was a wealthy and distinguished-looking man, and he dressed so. His gown was deep scarlet, reaching below the knees, the sleeves decorated in silver thread with a pattern of birds. His pointed shoes were also scarlet, the hose and hat contrasting black; but the hat sported a dyed-red feather.

Together they entered her chamber, where the kitchen-boy was reviving the small fire.

She beckoned her uncle, leaning heavily on his stick, to the best seat; but he preferred to stand against the chimney-piece, staring at her. She herself sat down by the hearth, while Meriden arranged the candles, poured wine, and retreated to stand by the door. Her bed with its green and blue hangings, her maid's cot in the corner, her shelf of precious books, her chest of clothes and the other locked one of documents, all faded into shadow.

The kitchen-boy bowed and left.

"And so?" asked Demis. The knuckles on his brown hands clenched white on his stick. Talinti rubbed one hand over the other in her lap. He made her nervous.

"Yes. A few days ago, a woman with a Jaryari accent and the name of Upali walked onto my land, without companions. She was trying to reach Vach-roysh."

"She got as far as Lithermayg, then? I heard of a crazed beggar harassing the people all through the east. We threw her out of Arring fast enough."

"She won't be harassing anyone else. She's dead. She spoke words to my steward before she died."

Demis gave Meriden an unfriendly look. "What was your steward doing meddling with such a one? Dead, you say – what infection has he brought into your house, to harm your children?"

"Not only Meriden. I spoke to her, and so did Sister Salome for the last rites, and she's buried in our churchyard."

"And who paid for the funeral? I've told you before, Talinti, your people and your heirs will not thank you for wasting Lithermayg's substance on evey stray rat you can find."

"I don't think it waste," said Talinti. She opened the box on the table and drew out a folded parchment, her movements a little larger than necessary, to make it clear that they were moving on to what mattered. "She spoke words, as I said." She held the document out, but Demis shrugged, so she read it aloud.

To the hall with six flames -

When she'd finished, "That's correct, is it not, Meriden?"

"It's as I remember, and as I wrote, my lady," he said, in his flattest voice.

Then there was a pause. She met her uncle's eyes.

"A king, in Vach-roysh? In Haymon we have no kings," he said. His mouth curved tormentingly, which meant she was right. There was something here, which he was waiting to tell her. That was why she'd needed Uncle Demis. Meriden had many excellent qualities, but his lack of normal curiosity meant Lithermayg was never well-informed. Whereas Demis knew everything.

"She mentioned people called Abbos and Rosior," she said. "I've heard the names, but I cannot recall exactly where."

"Can you not?" Demis raised his eyebrows, and took a step towards the table. He swayed forward with a soft grunt to pick up the parchment and hold it close to the candle to read. "Doubtless there are many men called Abbos, but the one you've heard of was King Osgar's brother." *Of course.* "He died two years ago, I believe, lost at sea. His son and only child died with him. This is why there's a succession crisis in Jaryar, or will be when Osgar dies."

Although he seemed to have finished, plainly there was more to come.

"That would fit," said Talinti slowly. "She said she predicted their deaths."

"So she's a prophet? Do prophets often come to Lithermayg?"

"And then - choosing between two. A wife from

the north, a son from the south. The nine, perhaps the nine provinces. The Dream. King Asatan dreamed his Dream over a hundred years ago, did he not, but it could still come true." She paused, having perhaps made enough of a fool of herself. "It may be nonsense," she said, but she didn't think so.

"Indeed it may." Demis laid down the writing. His face was close to hers, and he was smiling. "Truly, I'm amazed. Do none of your servants listen to news at the markets? You don't know what our great Consuls have been doing?" He flicked his eyebrows at Meriden, who stared stolidly back. With some effort, Demis reached across the table and picked up a goblet. "Here," he said, waving and then setting it down, "you have a madwoman raving about 'seeking an heir', 'the north and the south", and being raised up. *Here*," he picked up another goblet, "you have a dying King with no children. How do these things come together?" He placed the second goblet next to the first, and pulled himself upright. "The Jaryari nobility want to argue between rival heirs, and they needed a place to talk. And our Consuls thought they would please King Osgar and the Holy Church by offering their helpful interference, and their Theatre of Debating, the one you've never been to, for this purpose.

"It all comes together at Vach-roysh, in three weeks or so."

*

The next day, having prayed herself into a panic and out again, and then taken a ride singing defiantly in the blowy sunshine, Talinti marched into the steward's room, tucking a stray hair under her cap. She was thirty-five, and thanked God for good health, three still-living children and a thriving estate. And now for a new duty, one which both daunted and intrigued.

Meriden rose as she entered. He'd been sitting at his desk, assessing stocks of physic. All the little phials were arranged in a Meriden-tidy row. Talinti curbed her usual childish urge to flick one over.

"You recall what my uncle said last night about the Council in Vach-roysh?"

"Ah. I fear I don't remember the whole, my lady."

I thought so. You didn't listen.

"The Jaryari Council to choose their next monarch needs to hear the words you took down from Upali."

He glanced down at his parchment and pens. "You wish to write a letter, my lady?"

"No. We're going to Vach-roysh. I'm going, and you will accompany me." His my-lady's-whims-will-make-more-work-for-me disgruntlement, hastily wiped from his face, was all that she'd anticipated, and she grinned to herself. "We'll need Kariam, and one or two guards. Think about the preparations, and we can discuss tonight -"

"We are to travel to Vach-roysh?" he said slowly. There was something unexpected in his look, something almost of distaste. Any normal servant would have been at least a little excited.

"Yes, we are. I shall visit my kin, and pray at the shrine of Jaddi and Lumia, and Kariam may also have people to see. And the Council starts on the 24th, so there's much to do. Consider, please, who we should take, how much money we'll need, and who can best manage in your absence. Arro, perhaps, or Salome?"

Long pause. "Yes, my lady." She turned away briskly, but he spoke again. "My lady -"

"Yes?"

Slowly, "The great matters of foreign kings are nothing to do with us. It isn't - you don't have to do something just to annoy your uncle."

Demis always said, Izzan had always told her, that

her servants were allowed too much freedom, and Meriden in particular. But this was insolence. "How dare you?" she asked quietly.

"I ask your pardon."

"You do not have it. See that you make the preparations." She swished out of the room.

Holy Week started, and no work could be done on Good Friday or Easter Sunday, which made the other days even more frantic – packing, letter-writing, formal farewells. Best clothes were checked, brushed, and repaired. Sister Salome, Lithermayg's chaplain, consulted Meriden nervously, and made list after list – "Things to count every day"; "Tenants whose excuses should be treated with scepticism"; and the like.

And now it was the Tuesday after Easter, and they were leaving in the morning.

Talinti had to choose between farewell respects to her dead in the churchyard, and spending time with her living children. The children won, of course, for mothers are soft-hearted. She was crossing towards the stairs with Mritta when her daughter darted away to the man at the door.

"Meriden! Please tell me if you've started making

plans for the Christmas entertainments yet? Will you be looking for new ideas in Vach-roysh?"

"Christmas is eight months away, Mritta."

"Yes, but, when you do start arranging it, *please* may I play the Fool?" She pulled back her eyes with her fingers, and twisted up her face. "I can do it."

"I know you could be an excellent Fool if you tried. The difficulty is that so many others here are excellent fools without trying. Such as myself, for example." He made an even more contorted face.

"Please, Meriden!"

"When I come back from Vach-roysh, I will ask Sister Salome to tell me how foolish you've been in my absence. And if her report is satisfactory," he said ambiguously, "I will consider you for the part." He looked round. "I'm going outside, if I may, my lady?"

Talinti nodded, and Mritta said, "Are you going to see Sametta?"

"Mritta!"

"No. Not any more. I will take a walk to the Stranger's Hill."

"To the Kingsbrother's grave? In the dark?"

"Come, Mritta," said her mother in a tone of

displeasure, and they let him go.

Upstairs, Talinti played Fox and Chickens with Mritta and five-year-old Yerdin, using the cherished and battered pieces Izzan had carved for Araf's birthday long ago. Her eldest was far too old now to tolerate such a game, so she listened to his recitations of Latin verbs, and the Kings and Queens of Jaryar, right down to Osgar. And she was tucking Yerdin into bed, and preparing to sing, when Mritta said, "Mother - someone said Vach-roysh is very beautiful, but the roads are dangerous. You - you will be safe?"

Who was "someone"? Probably Araf, which was not kind.

"Of course we'll be safe. We're not carrying cases of gold and jewels, so no one has reason to rob us. We've no enemies that I know of. And we have Brod. No one would dare to attack Brod."

"Or Meriden. Or you."

"Or us." She struck a warlike pose. "Don't be scared, Mritta. We're all in God's hands."

Mritta nodded, a little reassured, and Talinti settled down to sing. Some time later, hoarse-voiced, she came down the stairs to the dim hall. No one was there except her maid. Kariam was a pretty slant-eyed woman in her mid-twenties, and rather uncharacteristically she was sitting curled by the fire with a borrowed book of poetry - which she dropped as she jumped up.

"No, don't worry. I can manage myself tonight."

Talinti felt a great fondness for her home. She almost went over to stroke the fireplace gargoyles. But instead, sober and sensible, she retired to her very quiet and empty room.

She was going to the capital, and she was going without her husband.

"She has her oddities," Izzan's father had told him how many? sixteen? years ago. "But in her bones Talinti's a sensible, good-humoured lass, healthy, and comely enough. And your children will inherit Lithermayg. What more d'you want?"

Izzan had told her this in bed, the morning after their marriage.

Talinti's own father, shrivelled by all the deaths, had said, "He's a decent lad, of a decent family, and the estate needs heirs. Don't be difficult, young woman."

So they were betrothed, and after the traditional six months' wait they were married, and it had worked out well enough.

He'd died five years before, and she no longer missed him, except in bed. But he would have revelled in an expedition to the capital, for whatever reason, and her eyes pricked as she sat by the fire studying maps before she took down her hair, undressed and prayed, and lay down.

Would the world be changed by the time she got home?

Suddenly she felt as excited as a child on Christmas Eve.

The Journey

The Duke's party rode over the New Angan Bridge, and were in Haymon. They were a much larger group than had set out. As they travelled west and then north, nobles and clergy from various provinces had joined them. Electors on their way to "this greatest event of our lifetime", as some idiot put it. The Duchess and Antonos were pleased to talk to these people, doubtless praising the Duke, and pointing out that like them he was a native-born Jaryari.

Errios wasn't skilled at such work, and he kept alone, looking about him. The road was wide and well-paved, and the land fertile and neatly-farmed. Much like the Vard countryside. *It should be different*, he thought. *But no, this part of Haymon ought properly to be part of Jaryar anyway.* That was what the war in 601 had been about.

When they passed through villages, people stood and watched. Respectful, tidily-dressed, clean. A prosperous land. As the old Song of the Peoples said,

From the green land of Haymon comes cheese and comes bread.

The flowers are fragrant, the people well-fed.
They vote for their rulers, a rare sight to see –
But they'll lick any arses if that 'has to be.'

He hadn't known he was whistling aloud until someone else joined in. He looked round and saw Antonos on his fine chestnut, his young squire and servant trotting behind. The three were sharing a tent at nights with Errios and *his* servant, but so far not much had been said.

"So you've returned in peace, sir," Antonos said, pointlessly.

Errios grunted.

Antonos tried again. Perhaps making sweet talk to the old fool was his task for today. "Was that the bridge you crossed in 601?"

"That bridge is new. They threw down the old one before we got here."

Antonos widened polite eyes in his milky face.

Errios continued, "We built rafts in secret, distracted them with arrows here, and floated across at dusk further up."

"Oh, of course, I remember." *Remember?* Antonos looked down at his reins, and nudged his horse closer. "My aunt fought with you on that campaign."

"At Lithermayg?"

"No. The Battle of Rodrerlan."

"Uh. What's her name?"

"Vinaril. Vinaril, daughter of Mildi."

Errios screwed up his eyes. "Aye, I remember."

Yes, he remembered Rodrerlan, barely a battle. After little more than an hour, the half-slaughtered enemy line had broken, and fled squealing. Errios and his warriors rode after them, shouting as if at a hunt, cutting down those they overtook. He sent riders ahead on both sides, herding the fugitives, driving them forward.

Into a village, where he stopped. The enemy had vanished.

"They ran into the church, my lord," his second reported. "Barred the door on the inside. Shall I fire it?"

Errios looked at him with scorn. The church was the only stone building in a village of wattle and mud and thatch. He hadn't known its name. He learned it later, and then forgot it again. "Burn the houses."

"W-with people in them?" asked Vinaril, fair hair hanging loose, blood on her face.

"Get the rats out first."

There were more rats than he'd expected. Children,

old folk, a crippled youth, two pregnant women. A bunch of perhaps a dozen.

Somehow in his memory it was snowing, snowing and dark, like that other village. But of course that wasn't the way it had been. The Second War of the River happened in early summer, and the day had been cloudy but light.

Errios scooped up a little boy, three or four years old, and carried him kicking under his arm to the church. He thumped on the door.

"Hoy, cowards in there! You left your families outside. Come out now, and I'll spare their lives." Pause. "You have till the count of ten." He nodded to Vinaril, and she lifted her horn. One blast. Two. Three.

On the sixth note the door opened, and the Haymonese fighters walked slowly out. Sullen, defeated. Errios gathered them in a clump – the rats off to one side. He separated out the two who looked worth ransoming, and had them disarmed and bound. But he let the others keep their weapons. That would have told them what was coming.

Everyone was staring at him.

"You," he said. He drew his sword and stepped

forward to face the one who'd come out first. "Cowards and rebels. Kneel and swear fealty to Queen Emeli, and I will let you live."

The woman glared back. "We're no rebels. She's not queen here!"

So Errios killed her, very easily, and then stood back to let his soldiers finish the rest.

When it was over, he turned to the villagers. They were too frightened to weep. "Take what you can carry, and get out of here," he said. "Run to your city without walls, and tell your treacherous Consuls that Errios of Girifay is coming. With fire."

He was no good at making speeches, but he'd had time to plan that one.

But he never got to Vach-roysh, the wall-less city. Just as they were setting a torch to the last house, a messenger arrived from the western army. *Jendon of Marod has sent soldiers and many of the Thirty to support Haymon. Help is needed by the river, in Gard. Come at once.*

All those years later, Errios remembered his anger. The war could have been over in a few days. How many men and women had died because of King Jendon's meddling?

But he obeyed orders. He divided his forces, and sent some north, including Vinaril, but he and the majority rode west. To Lithermayg.

And sometimes he remembered *We're no rebels. She's not queen here.* A fair argument, one that he'd had by the fire with his wife and brother-in-law before setting out.

But in war a soldier's enemies are chosen for him, and he kills them.

Eighteen years ago. He looked around him now, at Vinaril's nephew. Who said, "My aunt told me of the battle, and the soldiers who hid in the church. She wondered, she said, if they hadn't come out, would you have killed the children, and the others?" He raised an eyebrow, as if the answer couldn't matter.

"Of course not," Errios grunted. "We left barbarism to the Marodi."

*

Eighteen years ago at Lithermayg, a crowd of youngsters clustered around the man sitting on the hill in the sunshine. Later it would be renamed Stranger's Hill, but then it was Boundary Rock, with a good view in all directions, and that was why Talinti had been asked to bring him here, the hero that King Jendon of Marod had sent to save them from the approaching enemy. He didn't seem to mind that all the children from the estate flocked around, and clambered up with them. And after looking north towards the river, and east towards the distant mountains, and south and west over the farmlands of Gard, and considering, he sat down and held merry court, answering all their questions, and telling of his adventures, until they almost forgot their fear.

"Show us where you were branded!" begged one of the youngest, and he laughed, and opened his shirt to show the mark burned onto him years before, the mark that made him who he was, a Kingsbrother of Marod. And not just any Kingsbrother. The greatest in a generation, the legend. Gormad the Lucky.

He wasn't young. "It takes time to make a legend," their priest had said. His conker-coloured face was creased with laughter and years, and his hair, long spiral curls, was greying. And hanging among the curls fluttered ribbons of blue and red and white and green.

"Do all the Kingsbrothers have them?" Talinti's brother dared to ask.

"No, only me." He grinned. "I started wearing them to annoy my old master, and never stopped."

So they talked, and then they took sticks, and he

sparred a little with her and her brother and her squire Ros, and generously found things to praise in their swordplay. And sat down again, and tried to learn all their names, and then asked, "What do you youngsters wish for, when you grow up?"

"To be a warrior," said Ros at once. "If only there were Kingsbrothers in Haymon -"

"A Consulsbrother," said Mojjer.

"I want," said the littlest girl, and then turned shy, and the Kingsbrother had to coax her to say, "I want to be able to swim like a fish," which made them laugh.

And the quiet giggly errand-boy Meriden, sitting hugging his knees, said, "I want to travel, and see all the world." In those days he wore his brown hair tied absurdly on top of his head, so that Talinti's mother said he looked like an onion.

"Oh? Where d'you want to go?"

"Stonehill," he said, with surely innocent flattery. "And Makkera -"

"To see if it's really green -"

"And to the Old Stones, and Saints' Landing, and maybe overseas to Jerusalem, and I want to explore the Jattamans, and climb Moonladder Mountain -"

"Go and live in the moon, good riddance," teased Ros, and they punched each other's arms, in best-friend manner.

"And you?" The man from Marod turned to Talinti. "What do you want to do?"

She was no longer a child. She was preparing to fight in her first battle. "I suppose I shall stay here, and manage Lithermayg."

It wasn't quite an answer, but he didn't ask again.

None of them had said, "If I survive."

*

Talinti jolted out of her reverie to realise that nothing had changed – Kariam was still describing the wonders of her home city, Brod was still listening in fascination, and Meriden was looking bored.

And the sun was shining. There was a single cloud shaped like a bearded man above them, and distant church bells were tolling the hour. They were riding to Vach-roysh to try to prevent a slaughter like that eighteen years ago.

The sheep, they all wait

For mild peace, or grim war.

She thought again, *Why us, O Lord? Who are we for such a task?*

She was missing her children. Yerdin's slobbery farewell kiss planted on her cheek, Mritta's cry, "Come back safe, mother! And bring us lots of presents!" and Araf standing sternly, hands on hips and feet apart, to remind everyone that in his mother's absence he would be master of the house. It was a pose he'd copied from what he remembered of his father, she knew.

But she was in good company with her servants. She liked Brod; she felt sorry for Kariam, even if their minds seldom met; and Meriden, for all his maddening lack of ambition, was the most trustworthy person she knew.

Brod and Kariam rode in front. Brod was burly and bearded and bushy-browed, and had been chosen in part for the calm almost-scowl with which he could confront the world and deter any trouble-makers. But now his eyes were happy, drinking in the detail of where, beyond his dreams, he was travelling to. Perhaps he was also enjoying the company of a woman as young and attractive as Kariam; although the lover he'd left at home was male. Kariam gestured with delicate fingers, lifting her face and seeming perpetually on the edge of laughter. Had three years in Lithermayg been such an exile, that she was so very pleased to be going back, even for a few days? She was the least accustomed of the four to riding, and her saddle was padded under her wide skirt, but she would still be sore before the day's end. Her hair was plaited and coiled and fastened firmly around her head with pins, so she could show off her best dark-blue cap. It matched her gown, Talinti's from last year, taken in for Kariam's more slender figure.

Talinti had dressed plainly for travelling, with a simple brimless hat and a long veil down the back. She hated veils generally, but they were very respectable, and could be wrapped round her neck and shoulders, for it was only April, and the wind blew. Her sword thumped disconcertingly at her side. She hadn't had time for everything before leaving home, and had had to sit up late the night before to polish and sharpen it in the common room of The Bishop's Disgrace Inn in the little town of Vach-renn. It wasn't the best or cleanest inn she'd ever stayed at, but they'd brought their own sheets, and at least no one had slit their throats in the night, as Meriden observed.

Her steward came last, riding his sturdy Leo, and leading the two pack-mules. He also wore a sword, just in case. On his face was his customary expression of amiable boredom with the world, although he'd been cheerful enough yesterday and the day before, taking his turn at story-telling and riddling. Brod's New Year ghost story was less scary in the sunlight, they'd discovered, than round a stormy fireside, and Talinti had forgotten a crucial detail in "The Tale of the Prince and the Ploughman", but the time had passed amicably enough. Just as well, for there was a long way to go before they reached the city, and hopefully the hospitality of Aunt Falina and her son what's-his-name.

"The Nobles' Assembly meets in the Palace, and that's where the Consuls live also," Kariam was explaining. "And they're buried with the old kings and queens in the Cathedral. Only the Last King isn't there."

"Doesn't he have a grave?"

"He couldn't be buried in consecrated ground. He lies in the King's Garden, very beautifully kept, in a street near the Cathedral. People go there sometimes, to view his grave. Or to spit on it.

"Most of the city buildings are very tall – three, four storeys high." Brod stared upwards, as if trying to imagine it. "The houses are joined together in rows, streets, like in Vach-renn. Where the streets cross, there are little plots of earth for flowers or herbs to grow, or small trees." Kariam smiled suddenly. "They're good places for people to do business in summer, or for lovers to meet."

"Or dogs," Meriden muttered, for he and Kariam never got on. Which of them had tried to seduce the other, and failed, when she first arrived from the city, Talinti didn't know.

Abruptly there were rapid hooves behind them, and they shuffled over to the hedgerow. *Give way to those going faster, unless you're much more important than they are.* "Keep it out of the ditch," Kariam fussed unhelpfully, as Meriden struggled with the more awkward of the mules.

Two clerics, a middle-aged man and a young nun, and a servant, cantered up and stopped. "God's peace on you, madam," said the servant, dark-faced and beak-nosed, with the very short hair of all the Jaryari poor, "is this being the right road for Roysh-town?"

"Vach-roysh," hissed the nun.

"And on you also," said Talinti. "Yes, it is. A few miles further on, the road will run closer to the river, and you need only follow the river to the city. But it's three days' ride."

"We thank you," said the older man, blessing them formally with the sign of the cross. Possibly a bishop,

Talinti thought; and then the strangers rode on, slightly less fast than before.

"The Jaryari," said Brod, as one who has seen a strange thing.

"Yes. And I should have said, if we meet any more, it's best to keep your eyes lowered. In Jaryar, for a servant to stare is insolence."

"To look at them!"

"To look above their waists," said Meriden.

"Thank God we beat the bastards in 601! My lady, you brought me to protect you. I can't do that looking at the road."

"I brought you in case of trouble. There's less likely to be trouble if we don't annoy guests in our land, even arrogant guests."

"You must allow me to keep watch on strangers!"

"I 'must', Brod?"

She made it icy, and he dropped his eyes. "Your pardon, my lady." There was a moment of silence.

"Your lady knows you meant no offence," said Meriden. "When the fighting starts, you can look anywhere you think best. Before the fight, courtesy." And as Brod nodded, he went on quietly, "Perhaps - there are only four of us, and the journey is long. It might be permitted, my lady, for your servants to speak more freely as we travel together than would be right in your own hall."

"It might. You can speak your thoughts, Brod, so long as you don't use the word 'must'."

"Yes, my lady," he answered, but he seemed to have no further thoughts to speak.

She hoped her directions had been correct – it was many years since she'd been this far from home, and her map was old; but Kariam hadn't contradicted her. And indeed they soon came to the banks of the River Lither, and the road, slightly muddier, ran alongside as she'd said. A little later, after silence broken only by the lilt of the water at their side, Talinti nudged Dragon up next to Meriden's Leo. "So - speaking freely, in your impertinent way, you believe this journey to be a foolish waste of time and money. Do you not?"

She wouldn't have blamed him for looking wary, but he said straight-faced, "It is a visit to the holy shrines of Jaddi and Lumia. That cannot be wasted time."

"I have wished for years to pray at those tombs, yes," she said, which was true. "And we're to bring God's message to the Council. It may indeed be God's message."

"This Upali," he said.

"Do not despise her for having no money or home. What do you or I know of what prophets look like? She said we're waiting for 'mild peace or grim war.'"

Or at least the Jaryari are.

War. Oh, God, please -

Meriden was silent. Then he said, "It's the Jaryari throne that they're disputing over. You believe we have a duty to help them?"

"We have a duty not to hate them. Don't be dull, Meriden. I know you want to preserve my money for me, and so you should. But this matters."

To choose a ruler by talk and prayer, seeking the best, the most legitimate, person, not just the most powerful. That must be godly.

Meriden looked away, and smiled a little. "And you've brought me with you, my lady, to persuade me of this?"

He was incorrigible. "I brought you, because you are the witness," she snapped. "She spoke to you. You may have to swear to the words. You may be named in future chronicles."

"Jaryari chronicles," he said, and she laughed.

And I brought you in case Sametta broke your heart, and you needed distraction. Fourteen months of visiting her fireside – and I dare swear doing more than that – and now all of a sudden she's to marry her innkeeper. That must have hurt? And I brought you because on a good day I enjoy your company -

She didn't want to say these things, so, "Years ago, you said you wanted to travel."

"Did I, my lady?" For once he looked truly surprised. "*Makkera, and the Old Stones, and Moonladder Mountain.*" In all his life, she thought, Meriden had never journeyed even as far as Vach-renn, two days' journey. Nor for many years had he seemed to want to. What had happened to the boy who had sat on a hill listening to the tales of the greatest hero of the age?

She had no way of answering the question.

*

The first inn they passed looked very dirty, and the second was over-full. "We can find a place to camp - and test our stitching. If the tent holds up for the journey, we can use it for the fair in June." "Indeed, my lady," but for a whole mile there was nowhere suitable. They couldn't pitch a tent on mud. Kariam was clenching her face and fists with pain. At last however they came to a riverside copse with a pleasant flattish and dryish space in the centre. Meriden and Kariam set off, walking stiffly, to the nearest farmhouse, to seek permission and offer a guest-gift of wine, while Talinti and Brod, anticipating a favourable answer, watered, tethered and rubbed down the animals, and prepared a space for a fire.

"I am truly sorry, my lady, and I will remember," he muttered. "But we're not slaves, and this isn't their country."

"There are no slaves in Jaryar, or even Ricossa, any more. They have different rules, that's all."

The others returned successful, and the tent they'd all been frantically stitching for days was unpacked from its panier, and spread on the ground.

Such things are less easy to erect than one expects, and the light was fading.

Kariam was inside holding a pole, and Talinti was stretching cloth one way, and Meriden the other, and Brod was pointing and saying, "That's twisted there, my lady, I could go in, I'm taller," when it must have occurred to him that he should be on guard, and he looked over at the animals. "Hey!"

Talinti's eyes jerked across, and saw the woman

who'd crept up at the water's edge to untie Dragon.

Dragon! One of Lithermayg's most valuable possessions, and very dear.

Brod was running, and drawing his sword, but suddenly two – three? – more people leapt out at him.

"Thieves, thieves!" Talinti shouted, dropping the cloth, and drawing as she ran, and Meriden followed, calling, "Stay back, my lady!" - and Kariam squawked as the tent collapsed.

Meriden clashed swords with a big bearded man. Brod was fighting two of the robbers at once. A third turned to Talinti - a wiry woman with wild hair and a sword too big for her.

Steel screamed and jarred as the blades met. Talinti wasn't a great warrior, but she thought she was better than this woman. Her opponent squealed, and there was blood on her hand. Talinti pressed forward. But at the edge of sight, a huge cudgel swung at Brod's leg, and he screamed and fell.

"No!"

Someone else was coming at Talinti – *oh, dear God* – as quick as that, everything could change – there were five of them - Meriden was still fighting, but he couldn't -

Behind her there was a high ululating yell, and hoofbeats.

*

Lida was leaning against the side of the boat, talking to Jeppa and Fric, and watching the King and the Prince fight. A fresh pale sky was beginning to darken, and she was thinking that the journey to Vach-roysh was proving even better than she'd hoped.

Two days' riding from Stonehill had brought them to the lands of Ferrodach, Mistress Fillim's childhood home, where they were welcomed and feasted by her elder brother and his wife. Fillim herself didn't seem happy to be there, and walked out into the grounds, but everyone else found it an impressive and comfortable manor. Lida was much more reconciled to young Fric after she'd taken him to the little room by the hall – now a library – where murdered children were said to walk, and had told him the whole gruesome story, by the light of a single candle. At the right moment, she scampered her fingers down his spine, making him shudder, and cry, "Get off!" and then demand another tale.

The next day they rode on, and a week later came to the town of Graijin at the border, where the River Lither lay before them, and a large flattish cog, freshly painted with the name "Queen's Messenger." The pack horses were unloaded and sent back home, and so were some of the others. For the King and his friends were really to travel through Haymon on the water.

Once cautiously up the gangplank, Lida found her feet on wood that bounced gently as she walked. Some people – Abbot Paul for example – plainly didn't like this at all, which only made it more fun. The cog wasn't boarded over completely – there was a wide space to walk all round the edge, a flat decked part at the front ("the bow," the Prince's servant Yaif told her), and another at the back where there were cabins for the great people. But in the centre was a square hole with a ladder down. Next to it the mast reared up, carrying the enormous sail, with the Marodi pine trees and chi-ro symbol on it, which was going to capture the wind, and make it push them "downriver" to the city. Sailing, like in a ballad.

The only disadvantage was that there was nowhere to sit down, but then squires were not lords or idle layabouts, and couldn't expect to sit much, except when riding. When Lida was not learning lists of possible Jaryari electors (*Duke Yivas of Lefayr is nearly eighty, and unlikely to come himself, but his children will*) she walked springingly up and down, or leaned over the side to watch in fascination as the cog's front edge cut creamily and endlessly through the water. And all the time the land was passing them by, without any effort on their part, and at night those not privileged with a cabin camped in tents on the shore.

It was now the second day on the river, the nondescript Haymonese town of Gard behind them, and the banks on each side were flat and green. The trees and distant houses were much like those at home, but the sky was bigger, as they left the Marodi hills behind.

Some of the horses were walked about the deck, but most were ridden or led along the shore, or along roads not too far away. They were all collected at night and guarded on the land. "Why do we need horses if we have a boat?" Lida asked, and her Prince answered, "In case the wind fails us. God expects us to be prepared for such a chance."

A few of the party, therefore, were riding beside them, and conversation occasionally passed between boat and shore. Abbot Paul had been helped with some difficulty onto his strong mare, but Mistress Fillim had leapt up with her usual grace.

("Is there anything she cannot do?" the royal

secretary Kalla asked wistfully.

"Sit still," Draider Queensbrother responded, his face twisted.)

And now King Barad and Prince Braidoc had thrown off belts and jackets, and were sparring with wooden swords on the deck, and all except the dullest were watching them.

"They should be careful," Lida heard, and she looked round at one of the crew, a small pale man. "If they misstep into the hold, that'll be a broken leg."

Sour-Faced Jeppa curled her mouth, as if to say that there was no danger of that with her master. She'd served the King since his marriage three years before, a round little dark-brown woman. "Why are they fighting?" the man went on. "Are they not friends?"

"Excellent friends. It's a game."

"It's an entertainment for us," said Lida. "They were talking about God, and they argued, and the King said, 'Mere words will not settle this. Are you bored enough to accept a challenge?'"

The two men were darting around the deck, sticks clunking cheerfully. The Prince was an excellent swordsman – so good his sister had offered him a place in the Queen's

Thirty. He had refused, claiming to be unworthy (so it was said with awe) and the place had gone to his younger brother.

Lida hadn't often seen the King fight. He was grinning, throwing out casual comments, mostly praise – then backing away, skipping to the side, and leaping forward fast. The Prince was silent and steadier, almost but not quite smiling. The white shirts dazzled.

"They're fighting about God?"

"The King's been reading the book Abbot Paul is writing about the blessings of poverty," said Jeppa.

"Oh," said the crewman, with respect. After a moment, "Do they disagree about religion, then?"

"Certainly not." Jeppa's voice was a snap. "What is there to disagree about? They're passing the time in practice, that's all."

And indeed the two were suddenly face-close-to-face, swords crossed, and the King said laughing, "Enough?" There were beads of sweat on his dark forehead.

"As you will. I concede defeat, Your Grace." Prince Braidoc smiled then, and the King smiled back, for plainly there had been neither defeat nor victory. They slapped each other's shoulders, and the watchers around the deck applauded. Jeppa and Yaif turned away to fetch water and towels.

"Is Abbot Paul truly writing a book?" Fric asked.

"I don't know." It certainly seemed an odd thing to do. Lida had never read the whole of a book. But monks, she understood, did nothing but pray and teach, and perhaps they wrote books for a change. Or a penance.

"Why did the Queen choose him as a delegate, and not her uncle the Warden?" mused the crewman.

"Why are you standing here with nothing to do?" Jeppa looked back abruptly, and glared at him.

One of the sailors was stretching up to light a lantern at the bow.

Then - "What's that noise?" asked someone.

They all heard then, ahead on the path, the clash of steel. And footsteps running back towards them; a youngish woman, alone.

"Help in God's name, please, help!" she gasped, as she came level with the riders. "We're attacked – horse-thieves – murdering my mistress -" Her voice rose. Fillim glanced up at the boat, and then away. She spurred her horse forward, and several soldiers followed her, and so (to

Lida's surprise) did the Abbot.

Dimly ahead through trees, they could all see a fight. Not many people – at least one on the ground -

"Bring us in alongside," called the King. He gestured, and one of the remaining soldiers scooped up the panting woman onto his horse. "Who is your mistress? Are you travellers?"

"She's Talinti of Lithermayg. We're going to Vachroysh for the Council." There was a stir of curiosity, and the woman must have heard it. She said, "She has words of prophecy for the Consuls and the electors." And turned her head anxiously forward, as they all heard Fillim yell, and more swords clashing.

But King Barad swung round to look at his brother-in-law. "Prophecy?" and one of those grown-up conversations-without-words seemed to pass between them, with no more than raised brows from one, and a half-nod from the other.

Then the boat passed the group of trees, and Lida could clearly see a crowd of people on the shore, and Mistress Fillim waving energetically at them. The fight seemed to be over.

The captain threw a rope to a soldier, who was

unused to boat-life and caught it clumsily. The sail had already been brought down, and the cog slithered to a stop, a little beyond the trees.

Everyone looked back. There were a number of people on the ground – one (Lida thought uneasily) seemed to be dead, still and bloody. She hadn't been expecting bodies on the journey. Three more were plainly badly hurt and groaning. A man knelt by one of them. Another man and woman, poorly dressed, were on their knees, with their hands on their heads, and Abbot Paul was standing over them swinging his staff. And a strange woman was standing by Fillim panting and looking confused, holding a lowered and bloody sword.

"Fillim? What passes?" asked King Barad.

She approached the water's edge. "No need for fear, Your Grace. These travellers were being attacked by horse-thieves, and we arrived to give a little help."

"Jeppa!" the King called. The gangplank had been swung over, and Jeppa wobbled across, carrying a large satchel, and made for the nearest of the wounded.

The King looked over at the woman on the horse, and back to the one on the shore. "Talinti of Lithermayg?" She was quite well-dressed in a plain gown, about thirty or forty, Lida thought.

She curtsied, and said, "Yes, my lord. Thank you in God's name for your people's assistance. We're travelling to Vach-roysh, and were preparing to camp when we were attacked."

"Lithermayg? Where the battle was fought. Where Gormad the Lucky fell."

"Yes, my lord. He is buried on my land."

"Ah. Are your people badly hurt, madam? Have any been killed?"

"Not killed, but this is my guard." She indicated one of the wounded, and Jeppa looked up to say, "The leg is broken, Your Grace. A blow from a cudgel, it seems."

Perhaps the woman didn't take in all her words. She was looking back at the groaning man, and the other beside him, whom Jeppa had elbowed aside. The King turned from them to Fillim. "Well done, sister, you and your soldiers."

"And the Abbot," she said, grinning. "He rode up behind us, and knocked one of them down with a single blow. I had no idea, Brother, that you were so warlike."

"I wasn't always a monk," said the big man, with a shy shrug. "As a boy, I squired for one – no, two, one after the other – of the Thirty."

That sounded like a tale, Lida thought. Prince Braidoc said, "There must be some lord or lady nearby whose officers can take charge of the dead, and do God's justice on such rogues. Do you know whose land this is?" he asked the woman Talinti.

"I believe, my lord, we're in county Fenert. We passed the village of Drem a few miles back. The lady of these lands lives beyond that hill." She pointed.

"Excellent," said the Prince kindly. "Is your business in Vach-roysh urgent?"

"We're going to the Council that is to be held there. We have a message to deliver."

"What message?" demanded Secretary Kalla eagerly.

Lida shared everyone's annoyance when Talinti replied, "By your leave, my lords, my lady, they are words for the Council, and not before."

Fillim and several others looked at her with disapproval, but the King said, "Indeed. Madam, ah, your man won't be riding anywhere for some time, I think. We also are going to Vach-roysh. Do you and your party – how many are you? – care to travel with us?"

Draider said, his face shocked, "Your Grace, we know nothing of these people. It's a risk to you."

"Charity to strangers is pleasing to God," said Prince Braidoc.

"I don't think they arranged to be attacked and have legs broken in order to beg transport on the Queen's Messenger," said the King. "And I'd welcome the chance to speak to my fellow-countrymen. It's long since I left Haymon."

And Lida, looking down, could see Talinti at last realise who she was talking to. "Your Grace!" she exclaimed, and knelt.

King Barad of the Marodi, who had been born Barad, son of Lord Adgor, in the northwest of Haymon, smiled and said, "Get up, madam. Gather your people and your possessions, and come aboard."

*

Lida thought Talinti was a nice name. She didn't succeed in learning the others', and had to identify them to herself by description, as was her way. The Not-Quite-Dead-Guardsman, the Dainty Chatterer, and the Smiling Short-haired Steward. (She was proud of this title, and only wished he looked Sinister as well.)

It was the next morning, cooler and cloudier than the day before. The King strolled round and round the deck, talking to his guest, and a few paces behind them followed their personal servants, the Chatterer and Sour-Faced Jeppa, arm in arm. These little groups passed Lida, Fric, Yaif and Master Draider, lounging by the side, as Talinti said, "I was only there once, some years ago. For my cousin's wedding to the son of Lord Admant."

"Not that wedding? Ah - I wasn't there, but that was the one where the priest was too drunk to perform the ceremony, and they had to send out for someone from the next parish, no?"

"Yes, Your Grace. We were kept waiting hungrily for her for half the afternoon, and the feast couldn't begin until it was dark. We were tempted to eat the bride's flowers."

They walked on past, and in a few moments Lida heard the Chatterer say to Jeppa, "I had to spend my first six months in her household remodelling all her clothes. She's a virtuous lady, but doesn't really know how great people dress, or behave."

"She does you credit," said Jeppa, unusually generous. Then, "Is her conduct odd, then?"

"Well. She rides round the countryside singing, sometimes indecorous songs." The two women giggled together. "She worries everyone with her cheerfulness in the mornings. And although she's very devout, I cannot deny it, well, a few years ago a priest in one of her villages fathered a child on a local woman, and refused to acknowledge it or marry her. My lady walked into his house with sword drawn, and threatened to denounce him in front of his congregation if he didn't make the proper provision for maintenance. His servant told me that he – the priest - asked her if this were her respect for Holy Church, and she said, 'It's my respect for hypocrites.'"

They'd passed on before Lida could hear whether the priest had paid.

"Like all prophets, then, she may be uncomfortable company," murmured Draider.

"Are you remembering to pay maintenance for your bastard children?" asked Fillim, strolling up to Fric's alarm.

"Oh, of course, all five of them."

Lida hadn't known he had any.

The King and Talinti had gone round the boat, pausing for the King to stroke his Silverfoot's nose and feed him an apple, and were now back opposite them again. "My father would be shocked by such an attitude, madam. Haymon is the only nation on Ragaris – perhaps the only nation in the world – where the rulers are chosen by the people they rule, or at least some of the people. Do you not feel honoured to be given this responsibility?"

"Indeed, I do, Your Grace," she said smiling, "and you make me ashamed. But it's a long way to go to vote every three years, when I know little about the candidates for Consul."

"Unless they've served several terms, like Jaikkad? He is finishing his fourth, I think, and Invildi her second."

Five paces behind - "I fear not, Jeppa. My lady hasn't told me what this Upali's words say, only that she thinks they may be important."

"No one else knows anything?"

"Only she and the steward. And he, if I may say so, is tiresomely close-mouthed."

One of Fillim's plaits had come down, and she was twisting it back up under her cap. Several of the men on board were watching her deft movements, including, Lida saw, the close-mouthed Haymonese steward. But Draider's eyes tracked the King. This Talinti, for all she seemed awed and charmed by her high companion, and had laid aside her sword, was still a foreigner, and probably carried a knife.

Fric shifted from foot to foot.

They were coming round again. "I surrender, then. I ought to make the journey each election. After all, the Jaryari are travelling to Vach-roysh for *their* vote."

"Aye, from as far south as Tell and Lefayr. A long journey indeed, discovering their land as they go." He began to sing softly, "*Riding through the lands, riding high, riding low.*" They smiled together, and then Lida saw the King's eyes gleam. "And what will they hear when they arrive? From you?"

The Haymonese woman's smile wobbled, but she rebuilt it. "It'll be for the Consuls to decide, I suppose, whether the words I bring have any relevance. Until they have ruled, the words can be no help."

"Brother, may I speak to you? The captain thinks the weather is threatening." It was Prince Braidoc. Both men nodded politely to Talinti, but she was plainly dismissed. She marched to the side, out of the sailors' way, and produced a small piece of sewing from her pouch. The Chatterer joined her, perhaps reluctantly, and Jeppa walked over to Lida's group.

"The maid knows nothing. As if anyone would tell secrets to that disloyal tattletale."

Guilt prickled in Lida's stomach. "Disloyal." She had said far worse things about her prince. But not to complete strangers.

Jeppa went on, "Only the lady and the steward know."

"Hmm." Fillim grinned. Then she leaned back against the ship's rail, stretching her arms to the sides, and arching her neck to stare at the sky. Perhaps she knew how many men were watching her. "Fric," she said lazily but clearly, paying some rare attention to her squire, "the King mentioned Tell and Lefayr. Name the other seven provinces of Jaryar."

*

The King and the Prince quietly gave their instructions. Without alerting or alarming Talinti or her people, everyone was to learn as much as possible about her – her loyalties, her weaknesses, her family. And so Fric was sent into the cabin to play Fox and Chickens with the wounded Guardsman, and Lida hovered around whenever the lady talked to her maid, and Fillim placed herself where a youngish man could look at her. (And he did.)

But most of the information was gathered by Jeppa. Talinti had no connections with Vard, or anyone in Jaryar, later than the Battle. She was unrelated to the Haymonese rulers, and hadn't visited Vach-roysh since her youth. She'd been widowed for five years, and although her husband hadn't been thought much loss by the neighbourhood, she'd wept for him, and as far as anyone knew had lived chaste since. Her people's main complaint about her was that Lithermayg criminals were punished in private, so that anyone who wanted to watch a good flogging or hanging had to travel to Fenert or Ludi, which most, of course, couldn't afford to do.

"A woman of tedious virtue, in fact," murmured Draider, and winked at Lida, as the Abbot and the Prince both frowned at him.

Late that afternoon it began to rain, tickling heads, and greasing the deck blackly, as it grew heavier. And since (according to Yaif) they were ahead of time, the captain consulted the King and the Prince, and ordered the wet sail folded down, and the boat halted.

The horses were taken ashore. Huge oiled cloths were (with difficulty, and many shouts of "Out of the way," and "Move, pighead!") fastened to the sides and the mast.

This made a kind of tent, lit with two lanterns, front and back, and several glowing braziers, over which supper was cooked.

"You, Lida, fetch me up some shallots from the cellar. All right, 'hold', then."

Only a little resenting the order, Lida picked up a candle, edged past grumpy people smelling of wet cloth, and scrambled down below the decks. She crept over to the food barrels, to make a hopeful guess as to how many shallots were wanted, and how many she could carry. Back awkwardly up the ladder, to edge round the side, past piles of luggage.

Jeppa was kneeling trying to open a worn chest, and Lida waited politely to step past, not wanting to draw attention to herself.

"Madam? I think *your* boxes are over there."

Jeppa jerked, and stood up. She seemed, Lida thought, to be holding a knife, rather than the key that one would expect. But the flickering light was treacherous.

The man facing her was the Smiling Steward, not smiling.

The two grown-ups stared at each other.

Lida wondered, and didn't breathe.

Jeppa didn't correct him, or apologise, but said in a voice of deep and baffling meaning, "You know, sir, my master is the King of Marod. He can be very generous. And no one need ever know."

The man tilted his head. He looked ugly in the shifting candle-light, almost Sinister indeed. "I see. That's what you think of us all, is it?"

"I think you like money, like most people."

"How much money?"

"Where are my shallots? Lida!" the cook shouted, and Lida jumped, and hurried past and away. She almost bumped into the King, who was turning away from the brazier with a hand to his mouth.

"I think I shall lie down," he murmured to someone, and pushed past towards the cabins.

After eating, the travellers huddled in untidy circles around the heat, peering at each other in the gloom. Lida felt a little sorry for the guards posted on shore with the horses - and very envious of those with cabin space. The rain being too heavy for proper tents to be erected, the rest of them were going to have to sleep on this deck, and it wasn't dry.

King Barad had not reappeared. Prince Braidoc was

dictating in a corner to Secretary Kalla, ignoring everyone and everything else. Few others seemed inclined to talk.

"Better than riding in the rain," said Draider with determined cheerfulness. "Come on, let's have a song."

No one had a better idea, so the sweet-voiced soldier Annet began "Up and Down the Steeple", at first shyly, but then with more confidence, and people joined in. Even the Haymonese, it seemed, knew "Little Trinki", and "The Song of the Peoples."

> *Riding through the lands, riding high, riding low,*
> *What sort of lands, what sort of people,*
> *Shall we find, shall we find, as we go?*

"Marod!" called someone.

> *The woodlands of Marod are strong and are tall,*
> *The noble Queen's Thirty are honoured by all,*
> *The people are known to be loyal and brave,*
> *Fierce for truth from the cradle to grave.*
> *Riding through the lands -*

"Falli!"

> *In Falli the folk hear the voice of the sea,*
> *And it calls them to singing and fair minstrel-sy,*
> *Their lakes and their valleys, their knowledge is deep –*
> *But they never remember in whose bed to sleep.*

Laughter.

Riding through the lands -

"Ricossa!"

Ricossa's fair shores saw the gospel alight,
On a land of great plenty, and zealous for right.
The people well-mannered, both handsome and tall —
If you sneeze out of place, you will hang from the wall.
Riding through the lands -

"Haymon!"

"Let's stop there," said the deep voice of Abbot Paul, unexpectedly. He'd hardly spoken (to Lida's knowledge) all day, and looked awkward as everyone stared at him. He cleared his throat. "We'll pray now" – silent groans all round, she thought – "for better weather tomorrow. And then perhaps someone knows a story."

So he stood up, his head almost brushing the lantern, and prayed. Lida and little Fric were far enough away not to listen, and Fric snuggled against her, and said sleepily, "Are we really in Haymon, Lida?"

"Of course we are. We have been for two days."

"Why's Haymon a country without a king?"

Lida began to tingle. "Ah, there's a tale."

"Tell me! Please!"

The Abbot had sat down, and faces were turning towards them.

"The story of the Last King", said Annet, and the ship's boy cried gleefully, "A story!"

"Not that one, I suggest," began the pleasure-crushing Abbot.

But *I can do this, you silly fat man. I can make people happy.* "Please, it's what is called for," she said, and there was laughter, and someone said, "Go on, girl." Everyone was looking at her, maybe thirty people, most of them with smiling eyes. Lida took a deep breath.

"Once there were two kings," she began. "Once, and not so long ago." She paused deliberately, to tell Fric in a mock-warning tone, "This is not a story you will like – there are no dragons, no elves or magic swords or even battles. Only two kings.

"King Asatan the Dreamer ruled Jaryar a hundred years ago. He was a big man -" she gestured fatness, and blew out her cheeks for Fric - "and a great king - at least he thought so. King Garayn of Haymon wasn't quite so big or so powerful. He wasn't always sure what to do, and often had to ask for advice.

"King Asatan had a dream. Of course, no one

knows your dreams but you – and no one but the King knows what he dreamed. But he said that he'd seen an angel, who told him that his children, or his children's children's children, would rule all the west. Not only Jaryar, but Falli and Baronda and *Marod* - and Haymon, as well. And he told all the other kings and queens to bow down, and accept him as their overlord."

"The King of Marod wouldn't do that," said Fric.

"No, the King of Marod told him that the King's Thirty would drive his soldiers away if they dared to cross our border, beat them blue with bruises, and send them home. And the Queen of Falli said, 'What a dull dream. Can't you think of a better lie?' And the King of Baronda just ground his teeth, and went back to fighting with his family, as they do up there.

"But the King of Haymon was a timid little man, and he didn't know what to do. He called a great Council – a meeting," she amended tactfully, "of all the wise people in Haymon, and asked them what they thought, whether or not to surrender to the King of Jaryar, and his Dream. And they argued this way" - she gestured - "and they argued that way - but at last they decided to give in. They said they would 'accept what had to be.' Because the King of Jaryar and his soldiers were so powerful and scary."

There were chuckles around her.

"So King Garayn, and twelve lords and ladies, and his son the prince went on a long journey to Makkera, the great Green City of Jaryar. And the other king sat on his throne, tapping his fingers, waiting for him. And King Garayn walked into the throne room in the presence of all the court of Jaryar, and knelt down and gave over his lands and his people to the lordship of the Jaryari for ever, and asked in exchange that the Jaryari would please not make war on them."

Someone sniggered, but all were still. Every face in the shadowy enclosure was turned to Lida.

"And the King of Jaryar said, 'Thank you, little man. You can still call yourself a king, as long as I am a greater one. And you will pay me money every year, and I'll protect you.' He patted him on the head, like this, and sent him home.

"But on the way back, that timid king began to wonder if he'd been just a little bit cowardly and foolish. What would happen to his people now? Had he been right, or had he been wrong?" She made dithering motions with her hands. "Alas, he couldn't decide. His mind was in such a confusion, poor little king.

"So he went into his palace, and drew his sword, but not to attack the Jaryari, because he'd promised not to. He stabbed himself in the belly, like this -"

Fric and the cabin boy gasped. Everyone else knew the story.

"And so he died, and his blood ran over the palace floor. And to this day nobody in Haymon can decide whether he was right or wrong. But they thought they couldn't have a king any more, so the prince went off to be a monk, and they chose to be ruled by Consuls instead, who are two people they choose every three years, because that's as long as they trust people to rule. And they boast that this is like the Roman Republic of old, and everyone else says, 'Yes, of course.'

"So once there was a king in Haymon. But not any more."

She knew she'd told it well, and the applause confirmed it. "He was a coward," said Fric.

"There are sad stories like that for every land," said a deep voice from the shadows, which was nonsense, for no other country had a tale like *that*.

"And the Jaryari still want to conquer us all," said

Draider. He brandished his sword, and many others brandished ale-cups. Lida had made them forget the rain.

Soon after this, pallets were rolled out, and blankets unfolded, and she dutifully went to see if her prince had any last orders for her. The little building in the stern was divided into four tiny rooms, one each for the King, the Prince, and the captain; and one given over to the injured guard. "Er, a moment, please," said the deep voice and it was him, the Abbot, standing beside her master. "May it please you to listen to a word?"

Prince Braidoc looked surprised, but ushered the three of them into the cabin, where Yaif was placing hot bricks in the bed. The Prince nodded at him, and he squeezed past them, and left.

Abbot Paul looked down at Lida, and she smiled uncertainly up at him. He seemed to be chewing again. "I'm an old man," he said slowly, "and your discipline is not my concern. I - when I was a lad my master would have been most displeased if I'd insulted guests in that way."

Lida gasped. "Which guests, sir?"

"That woman – what's her name? Talinti - and her servants are our guests on this ship. Why should you humiliate them, them and their land?"

"I'm sorry, sir, my lord," she stammered. "But Fric asked, and - and it's true."

"Is it? Maybe that story is told rather differently in Vach-roysh." He waved a hand around in the air for no reason, bowed to the Prince, and walked out, bumping into the door.

Lida looked at her master, whose face was thoughtful. "It was also rather offensive to my brother-in-law," he said. "You are perhaps fortunate that he retired early." Crinkles of fear ran up and down her back. "Well. Abbot Paul thinks you deserve a thrashing."

So he thrashed her, being a devout man who respected the opinions of the church. The worst part of it was that the boat had quietened by then, and surely everyone could hear.

*

Errios sat on a folding stool outside his tent, warming himself at the brazier, and glancing up at the darkening sky. Around were more tents, and horses stamping on their lines to the right, and cheery chatter of the little groups of people sharing the evening. He could almost be back on campaign. The camp would've been tidier in 601, with fewer nobles and less laughter, but still a camp.

Antonos and his squire had gone to the local drinking-house with two youngsters from Tell. The Friendly Welcome Inn was far too dirty for them to want to stay at, but its wine and ale were apparently tolerable.

The servant pour more wine, and went back into the tent to prepare his bed. Errios closed his eyes.

Haymon in 601. He was slithering on wine-red grass by the river. Shrieks filled the stinking air. He dragged his sword from a woman's guts, and swung round in a breath's respite. Six feet away, the enemy had backed two of his soldiers against a straggly bush. The Jaryari man was already down. The dark woman was howling and stabbing forward, about to die.

Errios caught one of the attackers in the knees from behind. As he twisted to slash at the other, the woman finished off the first. He turned back to her, but she was staring at the body by her feet. Her battle companion, perhaps her lover. The scarlet ruin that had been his face and chest.

He looked round again, and saw that the battle was lost.

The Battle of the Lither, eighteen years ago.

Lifting his cup, he flexed the other stiff hand, and

stared at the space where the fingers had been.

Then he heard the laughter of Antonos and the others returning. Antonos looked the least drunk. He had to behave like a Duke's friend. "God's greetings, sir."

"And on you," said Errios.

One of his companions bowed politely, and made the other, leaning on her, sway dangerously and chuckle. Then the man slapped his own shoulders. "Shit – I've left my cloak at the inn! Why didn't you tell me?"

"You're an idiot, Berris. Weren't you feeling it cold round your neck?"

"I need my cloak. You!" He waggled a hand at a young woman passing the tent. "Run down to the inn in the village for my cloak – a blue one belonging to Berris, son of Erdris."

"I'm not your servant, sir," said the woman.

Errios was already tired. But he recognised her voice, and knew trouble was coming. "I can send -" he began.

But, "'Not my servant'? D'you know who I am?" and Berris slapped her cheek, not very hard.

"Calm down, Berris," said Antonos firmly.

"Take your hands off me," said the woman.

"Insolent bitch!" said Berris, almost laughing in his surprise. He hit her again, much harder, and she staggered against the tent.

"What is this?"

Two soldiers marched up. One of them grabbed Berris, and pulled his arms behind his back. But they had not spoken.

"What game are you playing?" demanded Berris' friend.

"No game." Duke Haras was standing just beyond the firelight. He nodded to the second soldier, and she punched Berris in the face. "Do you know who I am?"

"My lord, she's just a Lowly woman," protested the friend.

"Say that once more." It was a threat. Greedy-faced onlookers peered from shadow. "Hit him again."

The soldier struck Berris on the other cheek. Then hard in the stomach. He fell forward and vomited on the ground. She kicked him.

"Be careful, sir, how you abuse her again – or anyone in this camp," said the Duke. The woman Illi came up to him smiling. *Relieved rather than vengeful,* Errios hoped. They walked off together, followed by the soldiers.

Berris' friend led him away, helped by Antonos and his squire. Errios instructed his own woman to cover the mess, and went to bed.

Antonos returned before he was asleep. "Well, that was unfortunate. Dukes' lovers should be made to wear some kind of badge."

Errios grunted. As they lay down on their separate pallets, and the servant blew out the candle, Antonos added, "Pray that Duchess Palla doesn't find out."

*

Perhaps Antonos prayed. If so, God ignored him.

The next morning, the two of them attended the Duke's tent for breakfast, as had become customary. The fourth delegate, Archbishop Elizabeth, wasn't there. She must be at Mass; but Duchess Palla walked in with a face that could have cracked eggs. "A good morning to you, mother," said the Duke. His voice was less calm than the words.

"It's very far from being a good morning."

"You can leave us," Antonos said to the servants, and they were glad to lay the dishes on the table and leave. Errios would rather at any time face an enemy swordsman than a family quarrel, and wished he could do the same. But he had to stay, and he poured himself porridge with shaking hands.

"Well done, Haras. I have been speaking to Lady Ganola of Tell. You've just lost all their four votes."

"They'll vote for me. They're being paid to," said the Duke, also helping himself to porridge.

"It's not too late for them to throw the money back in your face. And they will."

"Give them more money."

"You don't have unlimited wealth to bribe the people you insult. How could you be so stupid?"

"Lady Ganola may consider her son's dignity and pride more important than any bribe we can offer," said Antonos more gently. "So may he. They're not poverty-stricken as it is."

The Duke lifted his chin, and took a long breath. "I was educating him in civilised behaviour."

Duchess Palla grunted a laugh. "Civilised behaviour? What do you know of that? From what I heard, the woman was deserving everything she got, and more. Disobedient, insolent -"

"She is not."

"Is she not?" A moment. "Who was that woman?"

111

And then Errios realised. Duchess Palla didn't know. Every other person at Castle Vard knew, but the Duke had managed to keep it from his stepmother. Now -

"She is -" he began awkwardly, but she laughed again.

"I see. She's the sweet creature you brought along to warm your bed at night. Because no young man is expected to endure two weeks without his carnal pleasures, even to gain a crown. That also was unforgivably stupid. Do you not know why – apart from bribes – the nobility of Jaryar are going to vote for you at Vach-roysh?"

He glowered. "Because I am -" But she marched on.

"First, because although Nerranya is the direct heir, most Jaryari don't want to be ruled by a foreigner. Secondly, because your father and sister, God rest their souls" - she crossed herself briskly - "were admired and popular, and some of that popularity descends unmerited to you. And thirdly, because unlike the Queen you are unmarried. One or two of the electors are unmarried women. And *all* the electors have unmarried daughters or sisters or cousins, who are hoping to become your queen if you become king. They'll be less hopeful if you parade your little whore around the camp."

"She's not a whore! Illi, daughter of Yenilda, is -"

"Daughter of Yenilda? You speak of her like a respectable woman."

"She is a respectable woman, and not a Lowly grade. Her mother is a – a merchant in Vard-town -"

"Where you picked her up for your pleasure, and where you will return her, when you've finished."

"That is coarse, stepmother," he dared to say. "It's not what you are implying - only carnal -"

"This becomes worse and worse," she said grimly. "What is it, then? What is this woman to you?"

"She -" Again he took a deep breath. And another. "I greatly value her company," he said.

Errios pitied him. He couldn't say the word.

"So you'll be sorry to be casting her off, when you become King, and have to marry? Or you'll not cast her off, and will expect your queen and her family to tolerate adultery? Or you do not intend to marry, and will give us another crisis like this in twenty years' time?" Her voice rose. "That your noble parents could have produced such a mewling idiot is beyond belief -"

Errios put down his bowl. He did it loudly enough

to draw attention, and pulled himself upright. "My lady," he said as firmly as he could, "you are addressing the Duke of Vard."

"I'm addressing my stepson, the greatest fool -"

"He's also our liege lord," said Antonos. "What's done is done, my lady. We can make more offers to the Lady of Tell. Agreed?" He sighed. "And my lord, please put Illi in some decent clothes, so that such a mistake is not occurring again."

Duchess Palla snorted, and walked out of the tent. The Duke also left. There would be a lot of breakfast left for the Archbishop.

"Is that how we're planning to win, young sir?" asked Errios, a little wearily. "By bribing all the electors?"

"Bribes and promises are part of it, of course. The official reasons don't cease to be true. And we have one or two other things." He sat down, and picked up a small loaf of bread. "As long as the Duke remembers which positions he's promised to which people, it should be enough."

*

By morning, she no longer hurt much, and Lida couldn't help enjoying the friendly looks she received from Draider and others. Looks of appreciation, not pity, she thought and hoped. Despite that horrid interfering Abbot Paul.

And the sun was shining.

They slid along between banks, and past villages, where people stared and waved. Lida leaned over the side, and waved back. Then she wandered across to the other side of the boat, where a man in a blue jacket, without buttons, was standing looking out at the water. The opposite bank was empty, so there was very little but trees and birds, quacking and flurrying.

She was almost next to him when she realised that it was the Smiling Steward, or whatever he was. Then she would have gone back, but he'd already noticed her. "Never hesitate," Prince Braidoc always said. "Take time, yes, but everyone notices the difference between a wise pause to think, and a foolish dither." So she finished walking up to the side, and put her hands on the rail.

"My master would have been most displeased," the Abbot had said, "if I had insulted guests in that way."

It was only a story. Everyone knows the story. And the jokes. Question: How many provinces has Jaryar? Answer: Ten, if you include Haymon. Question: What does a Haymonese do when he loses a bet? Answer: The Haymonese never lose. They merely "accept what has to be." It was only a story. "Why should you humiliate them, and their land?"

She slid a look at him, and his face was very sad. Then he saw her looking, recognised her, and made it polite. "A good morning to you."

"And to you, sir." It came out squeaky.

She wanted to apologise, but an apology would only remind him, if he needed reminding. So she floundered for something polite and humble to say.

"What are you looking at, sir?"

He turned towards her: a pale face; oddly short-cut brown hair; a very tidy look. "I was looking at the ducks."

"The ducks?"

He gestured. "Magnificent creatures, ducks, don't you think?"

"I – why do you say that?"

"May I ask your name, my lady?"

Don't call me that. "Lida, daughter of Arrada."

"Lida, if I picked you up, and took you to the top of that steeple over there, and threw you off, what would happen?"

"I would die," she said. *Are you threatening me?*

"Or if I took you to the middle of the river, and dropped you in, what would happen?"

"I would drown."

"Unless you could swim, which not many people can. But neither of those things would bother a duck at all. Ducks are happy in the air, happy on the land, happy on the water, even happy under the water. I sometimes think they control all the elements except fire." He lifted his eyebrows cheerily. "Not many of God's creatures can say the same. And they still make us all laugh with the way they waddle. Very humble. Don't you think?"

"Ye-es," she said slowly. He was smiling, so he hadn't been hurt. Surely.

So they both looked at the ducks, which were squabbling and pecking at each other in a way that was neither magnificent nor humble.

He said, "They do behave as if what they did mattered. Just like people."

Lida stared. For some reason she remembered him and Jeppa glaring at each other yesterday. Then she thought of her duty, and said, "Does your mistress really have a prophecy?"

He paused, perhaps a wise pause. "King Barad's youngest spy."

"Oh! I didn't mean -" Her face burned. To be

rebuked by someone as low as that, someone she'd almost apologised to!

Happily, she saw Mistress Fillim walking towards them, and Fillim made the tiniest "off you go" jerk of the head at her.

And the man looked sharply away, and the back of his neck was rather red.

"May God bless you, sir," she said quickly, and scurried off.

*

Brod lay, bandaged and resting, in a windowless room that was high enough for Talinti's head to be in no danger of dusting the roof, and wide enough for her to walk beside the bed if she pulled in her skirts.

The tiny place stank of sweat and blood and stale shit.

Everyone knew fresh air was dangerous to the sick. Still. Talinti grimaced, and handed him her pomander ball of dried petals to wave to and fro. "Pretend you're in church, and this is the incense." Brod looked shocked. Did he think God never smiled?

She read to him a little from her prayer book, and poured him some wine, and after a little he dozed, and she got up to leave, the floor swaying gently, pleasantly.

Outside on deck, the sweet air and the bright shining sky flooded her eyes, and she stood motionless, blinking tears.

"Madam," called an amiable voice.

When she was able to look round, she did; and there by the ship's side were the three men – the dark-clad Prince, and the big Abbot, and the merry King, his jacket unlaced to reveal the bright white linen beneath – all sitting comfortably on barrels and stools; and the King was beckoning her to a spare seat. "Join us, please. I hope your man is better?"

"A little, thank you." She didn't want to sit down with them. She wanted to find a quiet place to be alone, and understand that the day before yesterday people had tried to kill her – and Meriden, and Brod – and that those people were themselves now dead or about to be. Of course such things happen all the time. But they hadn't happened to her before, and she wanted a pause to tidy her mind – and as a guest on a busy boat she couldn't have one.

She took the offered cup. "It was most kind of you to lend your cabin," she said to the Abbot, who flapped a hand. "And you, Your Grace, are you recovered?"

"Indeed I am almost battle-fit today." He lifted his feet in gleaming leather boots onto the edge of another barrel, and leaned back against the cabin door.

The Prince said, "I must ask your forgiveness for my squire's impertinence last night."

"Oh - don't be concerned. I'm sure she meant no harm."

The Abbot said abruptly, interrupting whatever politeness the Prince had prepared, "It's possible to do great harm without meaning it." He turned his face away, and she saw his large mouth chewing at nothing.

The King reached forward for his wine, and swirled it gently. The sleeve fell back, and Talinti caught a glimpse of thin reddish lines running across the dark skin of his wrist. What kind of fighting had he been doing, she wondered idly, to get scars like that?

But then, "Ah, as we speak of harm," he said, looking up from the drink, "are the words you bring to the Council going to do me harm, Talinti, daughter of Malda?"

Suddenly she wondered how long the three of them had been sitting there, waiting for her. Where was their fourth? She glanced round for Mistress Fillim, but couldn't see her.

"It's not my wish to do harm. I hope the words will do none," she said cautiously.

"I hope not also, but they needn't be a secret, surely?"

Their faces confronted her – the King's cheerful and smooth; the Abbot's perhaps apologetic; the Prince's very still, as he sat with his elbows on his knees. She had never before seen a lay person dressed all in black.

She cleared her throat, missing her comfortable home, where almost no one challenged her. "There is a time and a place for such matters. The electors are called to vote, and to help them decide, they're to witness a debate, a, a contest -"

"A duel?"

"A game of chess?" said Prince Braidoc.

"Yes, perhaps, my prince. But a fair game. And in chess, each side starts with the same pieces. The same information. None of the electors are here, and neither are the Jaryari. They will hear the words, if the Consuls permit, and perhaps they'll understand them. I do not."

"Ah," said the King. "To tell us beforehand would be to give my Queen an extra pawn, then?"

Talinti nodded, her heart thudding.

Prince Braidoc sat back. His eyes were very dark in his long face. "For Haymon, perhaps this is a game. You come from Lithermayg? Where my kinsman Gormad the Lucky died. Did you ever meet him?"

"Yes, my lord – my prince. He and Ajuli Kingsister stayed at our house for two nights before the battle."

"A battle in which he died. He gave his life to serve his King - and protect your people."

"Yes. We remember him with honour."

"Of course. Madam, when Queen Emeli invaded your country, she was a new young monarch, wishing to win glory, and a place in the chronicles. If Duke Haras of Vard gains the throne of Jaryar, he may feel the same way. Don't you think? And he may resent the Marodi who tried to keep it from him." How could so young a man have such old eyes? "The Jaryari still believe in their Dream, of conquering Marod. I fear his arrogance; I fear war. I love my country. I think perhaps God brought us together, sent us to help you, so that you could help us in return."

The eyes bored into her.

At last she said, "I know nothing of Duke Haras. Or of your sister. But the Consuls have called the meeting, and summoned the people. I think they intended that the race should start equal."

"Hmm," said the King, staring at the sky. "Maybe I should order your fingernails pulled out one by one until you tell us. As the brutal Marodi do."

Talinti took comfort from the Abbot's expression, which was mildly disapproving but not shocked. "Have you brought the necessary equipment for torture, Your Grace? I don't believe the Marodi are as brutal as that. And you're not Marodi."

"I am not. And they are not." He shrugged. "Very well. But I still think it's a little ungrateful of you not to give me that pawn." He looked down and smiled, but it was not a comfortable smile.

"Your Grace," she said, "you didn't say that your hospitality was to be paid for. You may put us ashore if you wish. I pray every day for a result pleasing to God, and for peace." She looked down at the hands in her lap, a gesture that looked meek and was not. Waiting for his permission.

"As we all do, I'm sure. Thank you, madam." And she could go.

She'd come away from home, dragging her people with her; and now Brod was lying seriously injured in a stinking box; and Meriden was wandering the boat gaping at Fillim Queensister who had rescued them - and Kariam was laughing and chattering as if she'd been let out of prison. She must remember to thank and reward Kariam for fetching help, perhaps saving their lives.

And she herself? She was trying to grow accustomed to not being the one people leapt to obey. It was doubtless very good for her.

She had annoyed a King.

"I see blood."

*

"He stayed in our house for two nights before the battle." That memory.

"Are you saying our people aren't loyal, Malda?" cried Demis.

Everyone looked over at Talinti's mother, the lady of Lithermayg. And in the pause, the door creaked, and they all jerked. But it was only young Meriden, backing in slowly with the tray of cups and wine he'd been sent for. He turned, and stopped, everyone in the crowded hall staring at him.

Crowded, and dim. A few candles and the firelight yellowed and shadowed the faces – Malda, her husband, her brother and her children; the Kingsbrother and Kingsister;

assorted squires; Lithermayg's priest and steward; their liege lord's daughter. All gathered to consult on the eve of battle. Ajuli Kingsister was studying a map.

The Jaryari were a few days south and west. Lord Drosd, son of Ramos the Cruel, and Errios of Girifay, and their three thousand soldiers.

One glare at Meriden, and they all looked back at Malda. She lifted a hand from the sword she was oiling, and pinched the bridge of her nose, staring downward. "Loyal? Of course they're loyal, loyal to Lithermayg and Gard. They will fight. Which means that many of them will die, and they ask me why this is necessary, and I have no answer."

Someone hissed. Talinti felt her heart pounding.

"*No answer*," said Galian of Gard.

"The Queen who's already our overlady wants those of us between the Lither and the Angan to become part of Jaryar. Are we not almost that already? Ever since our King bowed to Asatan's Dream." She looked up, not at anyone in the room. "The people say this, and aren't they right to say so?"

"Malda," said her husband.

Gormad Kingsbrother said quietly, "Lady, look around you. Be sure of all the people here before you say things like that."

"I am old, Master Gormad. I don't like Queen Emeli and her demands, and I may be willing to die fighting against her tomorrow, or the day after tomorrow, killing her soldiers, who didn't ask for this war either. But to send others - my brother, my children, my friends -" She pressed her palms to her eyes for a moment, and took them away wet. "Forgive me."

"We must trust in God," said her husband Jarod, his voice whistling a little. "For victory, and for those we love, in life or death."

"The Lord protected Jerusalem from its enemies," ventured one of the boys.

"Did He? Did He, Talinti? Does all your Scripture reading tell you?"

In those days, Talinti was still shy of speaking before older people. She looked up from the arrow she was clumsily fletching, and whispered, "God protected Jerusalem in the days of the prophet Isaiah and King Hezekiah. But not in the days of the prophet Jeremiah and his king. And not against the Romans." Then she laid the arrow down on the little pile beside her, trying not to imagine its evil spike penetrating her heart, her throat. Or, somehow worst of all, her eye.

"If we lose," pursued her mother, "what will remain of us? And even if we win, what do we win?"

"We retain our freedom," said Brother Simon.

"Are the people in Marithon and Makkera slaves? Is life in Jaryar so terrible?"

"We cannot give in," said Galian. "We're all summoned to fight for Gard, for our homes."

"For Haymon," said Brother Simon.

"Haymon! Haymon is a name! You think it's worth all these people dying for a name? What is so wrong about accepting -" She paused and quoted deliberately, "*Accepting what has to be?*"

Malda's brother Demis stood up so suddenly that his bench crashed over backwards. He stepped forward. If Malda hadn't been his liege lady as well as his sister, Talinti felt sure he would have struck her.

"In this room, with these people, your words are only disgusting and cowardly," he said. "If you say them to the soldiers, they will be treason."

"I won't say them to the soldiers."

Then there was a pause. "Wine," said Gormad Kingsbrother, stretching out a hand, and Meriden scurried cautiously forward. The hero from the north took a cup, everyone's eyes on him, and he drank, and then spoke.

"May God protect us all," he said. "Yes, battle is horrible, lady. And my children are safe in Stonehill. For me, it's very simple. If my King tells me Haymon is worth dying for, then it is." He looked across at Ajuli Kingsister, his sibling in King Jendon's service. "If I die here, bury me in Lithermayg."

Talinti felt the other woman's surprise, but she only nodded, and said, "And if we get this right, fewer may die."

The next day, they rode out to war, Talinti and her mother, her brother Jasser, her squire Ros, and so many more who like them did not come back. Oddly she never remembered much of the noisy parting; only kneeling before her father, who wasn't strong enough to fight, for his final blessing. His voice croaked.

But she remembered her return.

She rode with one servant into the courtyard, the guards springing to readiness, and then relaxing. The old steward Ruma came running out of the door, and Meriden appeared from nowhere. The house seemed very quiet.

"They're gathering for battle. It will likely be tomorrow. The Jaryari have reached Eddyoy."

"Why have you come back, my lady?" asked Ruma.

"My mother ordered me home."

She said, "I am your lady, and your mother, and I command it. Or face my dying curse. Go back, live, and care for our people."

"Where's my father?"

"In the chapel. He's been praying there since you all left."

She dismounted. Meriden came up to take Brown Dancer's reins. Timidly, but determinedly, he asked, "Where's Ros?"

"He refused to come."

She looked at his thirteen-year-old face, and saw him judging her. She walked away.

*

The battle was fought the next day.

And then they started tending the wounded, and burying the dead.

The Arrival

In the middle of the morning, they arrived in Vach-roysh. The King ordered everyone not otherwise occupied to form lines at the boat's rail, "facing outwards and looking happy." Lida had no trouble looking happy, for Prince Braidoc was standing on the King's right hand, and she was beside him.

They had to pass under the Saints' Bridge, which was the land approach from the south, and Draider Queensbrother was very anxious. "One bowman, just one, on the bridge would be enough." He'd consulted Mistress Fillim, and they'd gone together to beg the King to wear armour.

"I am a son of Haymon. They love me here," he teased cheerfully, but consented to a breastplate under his jacket, and a borrowed helmet. (Or so Jeppa told Lida, as they both scolded Fric for getting in everyone's way. The King did indeed look chunkier than usual. Lida giggled.)

The bridge was twenty yards ahead of them. The King raised his hand and lowered it again. Two soldiers blew a trumpet fanfare, and from a central pole the royal standard was unfurled, floating superbly in the breeze. The three pine trees of Marod, surmounted by the chi-ro M symbol.

And from the bridge came a great answering cheer. Heads were crammed together over the balustrade, hands were waving, flowers were being thrown. "For us – for the King, and the Queen!" thought Lida. There were tears in her eyes, and she thought it was the most thrilling moment of her life.

"Watch. *Watch*," Master Draider was muttering worriedly. But they swept on into the shadow beneath the bridge, and then out again, wheeling around smartly to see more faces, and wave at them, and no one shot at the King, and they passed smoothly on to the docks.

Lida had been expecting a view like the city of Stonehill – a great wall around, and buildings rising up to an ancient castle surveying the town. That was what cities looked like. But Haymon was a flat country, and Vachroysh a flat city. In the distance, there were some large pale buildings, a spire, yes, probably a cathedral and a palace. There did seem to be stretches of defensive wall along the riverside, but they weren't complete. Yet they weren't ruins

– or at least the ruins had been tidied, and the parts she could see by the dock's entrance were covered with huge pictures. On one side the saints of Vach-roysh, Jaddi and Lumia, mother and daughter, painted twice life-size, smiling and holding out a book and a crucifix. On the other, a great boat filled with men and women on a stormy sea – the coming of the saints from Erin to the shores of Ricossa in the year 1.

The boat began to swing in towards the dock entrance. Ropes were thrown to a throng of labourers on each side. As they grunted and strained, the Queen's Messenger passed with majestic slowness between the pictures, and was guided to a docking space. The gangplank was swung over, and the King stepped to the top of it. There was silence.

Lida peered forward and a little down, and saw a tidy line of people waiting in front of the crowd. Several wore helmets and red jackets, and seemed to be soldiers of some kind, but standing before everyone else were a man and a woman in white.

The man was old. The woman was so fat that at first, looking at her, Lida could think of nothing else.

Then she noticed what they were both wearing.

She'd never seen such odd clothes. It was as if someone had taken a long white sheet and wrapped it around themselves, squintly, tucked in the edges, and then thrown a fold back over the shoulder. One of the folds had a purple stripe across it, so the white wasn't complete, but otherwise they looked like images of Death from fireside tales. Little Fric might find them frightening. Both wore silver circlets around their brows, and their hair flowed unbound, ribbons of it rising and falling in the breeze. The old man was white-haired, but tall and straight and long-nosed; the fat woman was almost equally tall, with a dignified but generously-chinned face, and several rings on her clasped fingers.

They bowed to the King. "Your Grace," said the man. "In the name of Almighty God, and the Great Council, be welcome to Vach-roysh."

The King bowed slightly back, swept off his helmet and said, "I thank you, for myself, my fellows, and my Queen. It's good to greet the noble Consuls again."

That's who they were: the Consuls. The Most Noble Jaikkad, and the Most Noble Invildi. And the garments were called "togas".

He presented the Prince, the Abbot, and the

Queensister, and there was more bowing. Then they all walked cautiously down the gangplank off the Queen's Messenger, and thankfully (Lida thought, lips twisting) no one fell off. Their horses had been brought round by the bridge, and were waiting for them. Lida mounted and rode into the city behind her Prince, several redjacketed soldiers and the Consuls leading the procession, with the rest of the Marodi, on foot or on horse, following behind.

The wide and beautiful streets were crowded with people, and again they cheered. And all the houses were white-washed, and there were boards with the Marodi pine trees hanging at corners on the left. Jaryari symbols were on the right, but they didn't need to look at them. It was beyond wonderful.

"Welcome, my lords! Welcome! Your Grace, are you joyed to be back? Blessings on the Queen!" There were many shouts, and all of them friendly, but Fillim rode on one side of the King, and Draider on the other side of the Prince, and their eyes moved constantly. The King looked about also but slowly, graciously, waving to the shouting people, his face delighted and full of laughter. They rode on, through a large square, big enough for actual trees at its corners, and past what must be the Cathedral, huge and church-shaped, but built of mixed stone. Most of it was creamy-yellow but some *green*, Lida saw in amazement. The colours seemed almost random, except above the main door, where the green stones had been placed together to form a great cross inlaid in the wall.

Lida had of course heard of the green makka stone, found in Jaryar and nowhere else – but she'd never thought it possible for an unpainted stone building to be other than grey.

They rode on. It had indeed been a palace that she'd seen from the docks – white, four storeys high, with an archway in the wall. Through into a courtyard, facing a great house with a tower at each corner. There was a wide doorway with steps, and on each side a lilac tree, trained so that the branches met with leaves and purple flowers, making an arch.

From the green land of Haymon comes cheese, and comes bread.

The flowers are fragrant, the people well-fed.
They vote for their rulers, a rare sight to see –
But they'll lick any arses if that 'has to be'.

They had arrived.

As they dismounted, and handed the horses over to

grooms, a steward in a dark blue gown and hat bustled forward to bow, and then murmur to the Consuls. The old man turned to the King. "Welcome to the Palace. All is in readiness."

"Excellent. Has the Duke's delegation arrived?"

"No, Your Grace," said the woman (Most Noble Invildi). Her voice was rolling gentleness, but clear. "We expect them tomorrow, in time for the welcome feast. The electors have been arriving from all parts of Jaryar, and we trust the Council can begin on Wednesday, as hoped."

"Ah, good. Where would you put us?"

"There are rooms prepared, Your Grace. And now, as agreed, the delegates and their people will surrender all weapons to safekeeping."

Then there was a rather tedious argument. Tedious especially to those like Lida, who desperately needed to piss.

*

"The house is on the corner of St Peter's Well Street, a little way back down towards the river," Talinti had told Meriden. "It's got a blue door, and a balcony – and sixteen years ago there were roses growing up the neighbour's wall. Falina, daughter of Shanell, widow of Madoth, glove-maker.

Hire a litter for Brod – you've enough money, haven't you? – and a child to help with the animals. And apologise to Aunt Falina. I hope her preparations haven't been extensive, but I cannot refuse the King and the Queensister's invitation to stay at the Palace. Kariam and I will call as soon as we can, to greet her properly. You have our guest-gift?"

"Yes, my lady." He patted one of the saddle-bags. "And if your letter didn't arrive, and your aunt isn't expecting us?"

"Find a room at an inn as quickly as you can, for Brod at least, and then come and tell me."

He nodded; and Talinti and Kariam turned away to ride into the city behind a King. "Our clothes are all wrong!" Kariam grumbled in delighted horror.

So now, two hours later, here was the blue door. Talinti knocked, and immediately it flapped open, and there was a man standing in the entrance. "Cousin Talinti, daughter of Malda? Come in, come in, welcome." He stood aside, and they passed out of the afternoon sun into a wood-panelled main hall. "Tormenas, son of Madoth – I'm very glad to meet you again."

Talinti took deep breaths as she entered. Her

stomach was throbbing – or was it her heart?

Tormenas was built tall and sturdy, but not aggressively so. He had a narrow good-featured face of the perfect colour of chestnuts, thick sleek black hair and tidy moustache, and bright brown eyes. Perhaps a few years younger than she. His voice was like honey, and his smile just a little crooked.

He was the handsomest man she'd seen in many years.

"Your groom's resting in here," he gestured to a door, "and your steward's gone to the livery stables to accommodate the horses – I fear we've no place for them at the house. He explained everything. You are indeed honoured! Of course I'll be delighted to host your menfolk for you – not as finely as you and your maid will be accommodated, alas. Do sit down, cousin – Jeri, wine for our guest, and take their cloaks, and wine for you also?" to Kariam.

Once Talinti was seated cup in hand, she was allowed to say, "And how is Falina?"

"Alas, my mother died eight months ago. A growth in the stomach. Your steward said you hadn't received the letter I sent to tell you? I live here alone, with my daughter and my people, and my dogs." His wave included the maid pouring wine, the steward standing by the door, and the whippet sniffing at Talinti's skirts.

"Your wife?" She'd forgotten the name.

"Dead also, in childbirth last year. Did we not advise you? She left me a darling little mischief, just three; she's upstairs at her lessons." He looked serious; then indulgent; then serious again. "Your gift is most welcome, cousin. I've rarely seen such carving, even in the best shops here."

"I thank you."

"And supper will be ready in an hour. Unless you have a royal summons to attend to instead?" His eyes twinkled at her. Talinti had no such summons, so she accepted with gratitude, and then she was finally able to see Brod.

Plainly the airy but low-ceilinged chamber was normally used for accounts and business meetings, but desks had been pushed to the white-plastered walls to make space for the pallets and luggage of the visitors, and Brod was lying raised up on a bed so that he could see out of the window and watch anyone passing by. He was fiddling with a piece of leather. "Brod, are you comfortable?"

"At least I'm off that bloody boat, begging your pardon, my lady," he said, with a grimace.

"Remember what Jeppa, daughter of Anam, said about keeping the leg still. I've arranged for a city bonesetter to visit you tomorrow." She pulled out a wooden figure with painted face and hair, and green gown, and propped it on the window ledge. "I promised Mritta her doll could see Vach-roysh even if she couldn't."

"I will guard her," Brod promised.

Meriden walked in and bowed. "The nearest stable is owned by one Kirria, two right turns from here, and looks satisfactory, my lady."

"Thank you."

Turning to Brod, he handed him a few small pieces of wood. "As you feel better, you might like to do some carving. Mritta and Yerdin and the other children back home might like some companions for -" He rolled his eyes towards the doll. A good plan, Talinti thought - Brod was going to be lying in this room for three or four days.

She said, "Her name is Princess Littialla the Mighty and Just, as I'm sure you both know. And if you're bored with that, Meriden could write out letters for you to study."

Brod looked less enthusiastic. "Yes, my lady."

"How d'you like the city?" she asked Meriden.

He thought. "There was that toy your husband made years ago – the box with the walls inside and the marble that you rolled about to find the middle." He rocked his hands in explanatory gesture.

"The labyrinth."

"Yes. In the city, we are the marbles." He cricked his neck back to stare corner to corner across the ceiling, a man unused to an outdoors blocked with so many walls. Brod nodded vigorously, and Talinti smiled.

*

The Marodi delegation had been allocated a whole wing of the Palace, with separate bedrooms for all the great people, and another room for them to sit and eat and talk together in, if they liked. Is walls were covered with huge painted flowers, purple, blue and green. "My eyes are hurting already," grumbled Mistress Fillim, still annoyed at having to surrender her sword. Although she'd not entirely lost the argument – the delegates were to go unweaponed, but Draider and the other soldiers, as guarding the King, could keep theirs.

Lida had felt rather honoured at being important enough to give up her own small blade, and found the painted flowers pretty. Also the real ones – she'd noticed flowering shrubs in pots just inside the Palace doors, and a fragrant bush in the corridor. Everywhere she went, her nose caught a whiff of sweetness. The King ran his fingers through the leaves and rubbed his hands together – and then grinned at the others' stares.

Yaif and Jeppa and one of the soldiers were sorting out luggage in one corner, Draider Queensbrother was wandering up and down planning where to place guards for night duty, Secretary Kalla was studying lists of the electors who'd already arrived, Lida was pouring wine, and everyone was a little tired, but merry, because they'd arrived at last – and before the Duke! – when Fillim said, "What?" and strode over to the window.

It was eight feet down to a courtyard – but a black head and hands were appearing over the sill, and, with a heave, there was half a woman dangling, with Fillim gripping her shoulders as if preparing to push her out again.

"Who are you?"

"Greetings, brother," the woman called cheerfully, ducking her face under Fillim's arm.

"Madi, you fool!" The King jumped up, laughing. "Let her in, Fillim." The woman came scrambling in, and he embraced her. "This is my sister, Madigam, daughter of Elda. Madi, this is Fillim Queensister, who's trying to keep me safe outside Marod. She's rightly suspicious of people who don't use doors."

The two women bowed to each other. Lady Madigam had the King's dark skin and hair, but was a little shorter than he, with a flat nose, and a gorgeous blue jacket with red stars that Lida desperately coveted. She smelt faintly of something flowery, like everything else in the Palace. "And how is our mother?"

"Unable to travel, alas, but she sends you all her blessings, and prayers for your success. Both in this little matter, and for your Queen's safe delivery. How are my nephews?"

"They thrive, praise God, and do everything expected of them. They learn a new word every day, and fight constantly, as of course we all do in Marod."

"Of course. And before we talk of your matters, *I* am going to be married."

"Ah! Who's the man? D'you like him?"

"Oh, yes. It's a secret, which is your fault. Not a *secret* secret – mother arranged it, but we can't have the betrothal until all of you are gone."

"Why not?"

Lady Madigam rocked her head from side to side. "Because the Most Noble Invildi wants everyone to see how completely fair and disinterested she is. If anyone knew your sister was marrying her son, if the Jaryari knew, they might think she would sway the electors your way. Though I don't see how she could. Anyway, as soon as all you foreigners leave, we'll be betrothed, and the wedding will be the grandest ever seen. Even bigger than yours."

"I wish you every blessing, and to him also."

Lady Madigam smiled with great satisfaction.

The Prince coughed a tiny bit, and the King asked, "So Duke Haras isn't here yet?"

"No, but the Jaryari have been arriving for days. The ones from the islands – Qasadan – came first. I hear they're complaining that the city inns don't serve fresh fish."

"The electors from Indesandu? From Exor?"

"You think I've been marking them all, early or late, like a tutor? I'm not your agent, Barad."

"But you want me – us – to win," he said.

"Perhaps." She grinned. "Like the Consuls, I'm without bias. I may think that you are my stupid big brother, and that you've risen quite high enough already without becoming King of Jaryar as well."

The King made a merry face, but some of those in the room looked shocked, as she noticed. "Oh, I apologise, *sir*. Do they really call you 'Your Grace' in Marod?"

"They do. In Marod we treat our monarchs with respect," said Prince Braidoc pleasantly. "I sympathise, my lady – my big sister is a Queen. But we would be grateful if you knew any of the names."

"I'm sorry. The Prelate has sent an emissary from Defardu to watch – Holy Secretary Mary, I believe. She's lodging with the Bishop."

"Mary - um – Mary Divendra?" asked the Abbot abruptly, and as people turned to look at him, "I've corresponded with her – she's being most helpful with information for my studies."

"Unfortunately she doesn't have a vote," murmured the King. "Anyone else?"

"There's an envoy from Ricossa – an oldish deaf woman who arrived yesterday, with a dozen servants."

"From Ricossa?"

"Yes. No idea why. Some long absurd Ricossan name."

The King and the Prince looked at each other. The Prince said, "If the name ends in b'Iri or b'Oto, she is kin to one of their Kings."

Lady Madi shrugged her ignorance. "She can't vote either, so why does it matter?"

"You are Haymonese, and the border you worry about is south. But we have an eastern enemy also."

"The Jaryari are the enemy in the south," Draider chanted unexpectedly, *"the Ricossans are the enemy in the east, treachery is the enemy within. But with God's help, Marod stands strong."*

"Amen," murmured several voices.

Lida thought Lady Madi was trying not to look amused. The Prince said, "This is helpful information, my lady. We are grateful." He turned politely away to allow brother and sister a little space, and said to everyone else, "No one knows what the Qasadani will do – they did not reply to our letters. The Duke of Indesandu is planning for all his people to vote for us. Or that is what he says. Which means that province is one that at all costs we must not offend."

Lida was a little perturbed that he seemed to be glancing at her; but then he began to speak to Kalla with her lists, and Lida could look back at the dazzling soon-to-be-married visitor.

Lady Madigam stepped up to the King, and said in a more serious tone, and quietly, "Is all well with you, Barad? Are you - happy? Mother was worried." She stretched out and gently touched the inside of his wrist, and then kissed his cheek.

"That was kind of her," he said, and his face smiled, but his voice sounded as if "kind" wasn't quite the word he meant, Lida thought. "Yes, I'm well. Ready for the contest, when the Duke finally arrives."

*

Tormenas' little daughter Bibi went to bed early, so four of them sat down to supper in the warm, rosemary-scented hall – Talinti, Kariam, Tormenas and his steward, whose name she hadn't caught. Meriden stayed in the adjoining room with Brod, but a servant carried food in to them, and the door was left open, so they could enjoy the conversation of their betters. Fire flickered in a large chimney that separated this room from the kitchen behind, and small lamps rather than candles hung from metal brackets round the walls. There was a painting that Talinti couldn't see clearly - a woodland wedding scene, it looked like - and a portrait of Falina and Madoth, Tormenas' late parents, with him and his also-late wife.

The food was excellent, and the conversation friendly, exchanging basic family gossip. It was odd how much news had failed to reach Lithermayg in the last two years. After the meal, Tormenas offered to accompany the women back to the Palace. "And do you have any plans for tomorrow?" he asked as they left. "I would be very happy to show you, and any of your people, the sights of the city."

"You're very kind. I don't wish to keep you from your business. I hope to visit the Cathedral, and the saints' shrine. We should give thanks for our preservation on the road."

"Indeed. For whatever reason, the King's warriors arrived just when needed, I hear. To protect you - and a heavenly message." Talinti perhaps looked startled, for he went on, "Oh, I was at the docks talking to a few merchant friends, and your ship's captain was eager to tell everybody that he'd been transporting a King, and a prophetess."

"He was mistaken, then," said Talinti. "Do I look like one?"

"No - but is there a prophecy?" He looked more serious, even worried. "That's a frightening word. *Prophecy* may mean death and war and judgment. Is that what's coming for us here, again?"

A moment of stillness. "I hope not. Let's talk of something else." She tried to match the charm of his smile; doubtless failed.

"I understand." He turned to Kariam. "You used to live here?" he asked. "During the war?"

"Yes. I was a little girl." She shuddered. "My parents tried to keep things from us, but my sister said the Jaryari would make us all slaves. And cursed the Consuls for painting the outer walls rather than rebuilding them."

"It was a frightening time," Tormenas agreed. He seemed to smooth worry out of his face and voice. "But now we do business with the Jaryari, and they're not cockroaches. As a trader, I'm glad to see these visitors – delegates and electors – here to serve their country, and make holiday - and serve me by buying my gloves at the same time. As I heard my Cousin Invildi say at a party last week," he said, smiling from one woman to the other, "'*We wish to be useful to our neighbours, and at the same time promote commerce and prosperity for Vach-roysh and Haymon.*'"

"Cousin Invildi" was the Consul, Talinti had learned, some connection of Tormenas' wife. She had to admit a pang of awe at his causal boast – and a ridiculous urge to cap it with, "As the King of Marod was saying to me the other day –"

Instead, "The Consul is very wise."

He nodded solemnly. "One of the most thoughtful yet innovative Consuls we've had for decades, many think, and a benefactor for the city. She and her husband are building a great house – knocking down and re-building, I should say – five miles outside town. Providing work for many people, and attracting craftsmen from all over Haymon, and *they* buy things, and need rooms to rent, and so trade, even in my poor business, is stimulated. We sell abroad, as I mentioned, but trade at home is more reliable because of the tariffs." He'd talked about the tariffs at some length during supper.

They walked back to the Palace through the pale streets, and the dusk.

When they were undressing in their own small chamber, with its real glass windows that Kariam loved to stroke, Talinti said, "I hope you're pleased to be back. And did you enjoy riding in the King's procession? Just think, Kariam, all of Vach-roysh was in the streets to welcome you home."

*

She slept well, and woke full of zest, eager to see the city. She and Kariam breakfasted in the Great Hall with the Consuls' servants and officials. The Marodi delegation had their own chamber, but on their way out through the tall corridors she saw Prince Braidoc and his squire entering the Chapel with solemn faces; and later the King listening with tilted head and serious expression to some well-dressed strangers - presumably electors from Jaryar, whose favour he was eager to win.

Meriden was waiting in the courtyard, and he was accompanied by Tormenas, who swept off his feathered hat and bowed not quite absurdly low. "Greetings this morning, cousin. You said you wished to see the Cathedral?"

*

Lida had spent an unsettled night. Possibly she'd eaten too much at supper. And her dreams were of giant white Death figures, and blood running down the walls.

But now, middle-morning, wooden sword thumped wooden sword. Lida dodged desperately backwards as Annet advanced - older than her, taller than her, and a real soldier. *Courage*. "Don't assume you'll lose, Lida," Fillim had said before the contest began. Lida gathered her resources —

not much older, not much taller, and she left herself unguarded on the left – and plunged forward shouting wordlessly. And it was Annet retreating, and then Yaif stuck out a foot and tripped the soldier over backwards, and it was a merry end to the match. Lida's forehead was cold and fizzing with glee, and her stomach squirmed. *Triumph.*

She drew in heaving happy gasps, and wiped off sweat with her sleeve. Among the ten or so Marodi, standing laughing and teasing Annet, she looked at her prince, who smiled. "Good. But you need to disguise your attack better." She nodded. "And now I must work. Yaif, fetch my parchments. I have people to meet." The King and the Abbot were already closeted with the heir to Marithon and the Bishop of South Jaryar respectively, explaining how voting for the Queen would benefit their province and diocese.

"When you've tidied yourself up, you can go into the city. Have a look round, buy me some parchment – and fruit – and bring me a report of any place you see selling jewellery. I will need some gifts, I think, to take home."

"You can go with her, Fric," said Fillim. "And we need more wine, and some ribbons, and coarse cloth – the coarsest you can find." S*omeone's moontime must have arrived* *early.*

So, following their morning of Mass for the Godly-minded, which of course meant Prince Braidoc, which of course meant Lida, and swordpractice in the back courtyard, she and Fric ran out to explore. She supposed she had to resign herself to being partnered with him.

They found their way through the white streets to the docks, and waved at the Queen's Messenger, quietly waiting to take them home again, and Fric recognised two of the crew – the fat cook dicing on the quay with a group of older women, and the pale man Asor, walking rapidly away from the dock. If it was Asor; he didn't respond to Fric's wave.

"We have purchases to make," said Lida, when she decided that Fric had played enough.

"Mistress Fillim won't worry if we don't. She never remembers small things." He kicked at a stone, cross for some reason.

"The Prince will remember. He is pernickety." Lida liked the word "pernickety" so much that she often described the Prince that way; more often, to be honest, than he deserved.

They trudged back to the central area and the

Cathedral Square to begin the choosing and haggling - and wishing she had enough money for one of the lovely lengths of twilight-blue cloth, and wondering which brooches or hairpins Prince Braidoc would think appropriate for Lady Mella, or the Queen, or even for his secret woman in Pigeon Alley. Since Fric was younger, and under her authority, he had to carry; and soon he had scrolls tucked into his belt, and a pile of stuff that he was holding in place with his chin. They paused at a junction for him to reorganise it all, and for Lida to stare at the statue of a ferocious warrior on horseback. She guessed it was King Roysh, who'd murdered his three siblings (but they tried to murder him first) to take the crown of Haymon, ages ago. She couldn't recall enough of the details to invent the rest, and Fric was disappointed.

"So, Fric?" she asked instead. "How did you come to be the Queensister's squire, so young? How did your parents know her?"

It was only a boring-adult-conversation question, but he looked down, and pulled at a loose thread in his jacket. Without looking at her, "My eldest brother sells wines in Stonehill, and he was a witness in a case she judged, and they became acquainted. When my parents and sister died last year, none of my brothers wanted me, but Haiberan said I could sleep on his floor for a few weeks, just until something could be managed." He jerked his head a little to one side. "And Mistress Fillim came into the shop one day, and heard him complaining they didn't know what to do with me. And she thought, and looked at me, and went like" – he shrugged – "and said if I could fight, she'd take me."

"How fortunate for you," said Lida awkwardly.

"Yes. And now I have to be grateful to her forever."

Lida felt unreasonably privileged, which wasn't fair. "Look, there's a tavern," she said, because she was really very kind. "I'll buy you a drink."

But as they pushed at the door of The Consul's Chair, a huge man smelling of huge-man-ness reached over and beyond them, to shout inside, "Wake up! The Duke's coming!"

Lida and Fric stared up at him. "Your pardon," he said brusquely, and then two more people, one man, one woman, barged out to join him, and distantly there was a noise.

The street had grown much busier.

King Roysh's statue was surrounded by people. The roads leading down to the Bridge, and on to the Palace, were edged two or three deep, pushing a little and chattering, and staring down the empty middle. And there was a steady thumping, growing nearer and nearer.

Fric joined several other children on the statue's plinth, trying to hold his pile steady. A tall dark girl had already joined the stone King on the horse's back. The three strange adults shoved to the front, but then the big one pulled Lida forward next to him with a grin. He was old-but-hearty-looking, with a face lined and scarred, and gaps in his teeth; worn button-less jacket and stout boots. His friends were a burly woman in grey with a thick plait hanging down from under her cap, and a man in a smart blue and green jacket. *Electors from Jaryar,* Lida guessed, if they were so keen to see the Duke. But there were a lot of Haymonese also. Just along from the plinth, she recognised Talinti with her duck-loving steward and her maid, talking to another man. The steward noticed Lida, and raised his eyebrows at her in a friendly way.

The thumping grew louder. Coming towards them, a column of people was small, then larger. Then they were life-size. In front marched two men in matching green jackets and hats, banging drums slung round their necks. Their faces were set with joyous intensity, a holy look, and their beat was flawless. Behind them came two riders, both carrying the Jaryari banner - green tower on grey background, with a cross above.

Someone somewhere hissed.

But others were cheering and clapping, especially the Jaryari next to her.

I wish we'd had drums, thought Lida.

A pair of marching soldiers, grey cloaks with a green edging, plaited hair, stern faces. And then –

"My lord Duke!"

He was younger than she'd expected, with a decently dignified bearded face, but overshadowed by his clothes. Deep purple gown and hat, with pieces of what must be actual silver sewn and sparkling on the purple. His cloak, thrown back, was patterned with purple and silver swirls and edged with white fur – how could such gorgeous things be made? He rode a magnificent black horse, and its back also was cloaked in purple.

As the Duke rode, he smiled and nodded on each side, and reached into a bag to toss coins to right and left. She jerked her head to follow the glint down. Children were scrambling, but one man dragged his son up and slapped him. "Don't touch their money!"

The Duke had passed, riding slowly, followed by presumably a servant. Then soldiers. A handsome man in red, an old priest-woman -

The whispers reached Lida before the man did.

"Errios. Errios of Girifay."

"Who?"

"Come to see the city he threatened to burn." To Lida's surprise, it was the Haymonese maid, the Chatterer's, voice. And she spat on the ground – a gesture that shocked, from one so prim and neatly-dressed.

The Jaryari woman by Lida also heard. She turned and said loudly, "But it would never have happened, would it? Your snivelling Consuls would've opened the gates, and you have no walls."

It seemed to Lida that faces went still and angry all around.

Errios of Girifay was a white-haired old man on a horse, followed by a big dark-faced woman servant. Everyone stared at him. And then a voice from behind Lida sang, "Riding through the lands, riding high, riding low," and she turned in horror.

It was Fric, singing so fast that no one could have joined in if they'd wanted to. He skipped the rest of the verse, and went on:

> *The greatness of Jaryar! Fair churches! Sweet wine!*
> *Prosperity, order, so almost divine!*
> *The people are craftsmen, in stone and in words –*
> WITH THEIR ARROGANT DREAMS, AND THEIR MURDERING SWORDS.

The people on horses stopped. There were gasps; the word "hubbub" was in Lida's fizzing head. She spun, pushed desperately and grabbed Fric's elbow, and they ran. Down the street by the tavern, and then into another.

There were running steps behind, fast and heavy. Her chest hurt.

Somebody grabbed her and jerked her towards a wall. Somebody else knocked Fric to the ground. His messages scattered.

They were in a narrow street. The three Jaryari – as they certainly were – were standing over Fric, very angry. There was no one else around. The man in the magnificent jacket kicked him in the thigh. "You impudent piece of shit. Gimme your staff, Bel. Who taught you those words? Who d'you belong to?"

He raised the stick.

"Leave him alone!" Lida squeaked, less to protect Fric than to stop him answering. However much trouble they were in now, they'd be in much more if these people learned who they were, and complained to the Prince. They might even be from Indesandu province, whose people mustn't be offended at any cost.

And then the woman Bel turned evil snake eyes to her, and Lida wondered how much trouble they were already in.

"There you are!" Another angry voice; another man striding into the alley. "Honoured sirs, madam - Shame on you both, unmannerly brats!" He dragged Fric to his knees. "Pick it all up, and get home. You're going to be very sorry very soon, I think."

"Who are you, sir?" asked the third Jaryari, the scarred one, who so far had done nothing but watch.

"I? I am my lady's steward." He managed to make "his lady" sound much grander that she actually was, Lida thought – and now she herself walked round the corner, her man friend by her side.

"Here they are. Wasting your time, and causing havoc as usual," said the steward.

"My sincere apologies for the boy's impertinence," she said smoothly. "A foolish song at the best of times, and most out of place here. My name is Talinti, and I'm a stranger in this city - like yourselves, I think?"

"These are yours, madam? Did you hear what he sang?"

"Alas, that's the version he knows. The Song of the Peoples insults us all, does it not? We Haymonese always give in, the Marodi live in squalor - Get them out of my sight," severely to the steward. He bowed and pulled Lida and Fric towards the corner. They heard Talinti say, "But this is a great day, and a fine city. Can my kinsman and I make amends by offering to drink with you?"

The voices faded, as the steward hauled them away. "Now. Run along."

"You were on the boat," said Fric, staring stupidly at him.

"I was on the boat. A piece of advice. It's not worth dying for a song. Hmm?"

He walked away. Lida's heart began to calm. They'd been *rescued*, and she felt relieved and humiliated.

"I've lost the ribbons! Jeppa will make thunder!"

"Well, we're not going back for them. Hurry along."

"Lida," he asked a little later, "what's 'squalor'?"

"'Squalor' means dirt." Lida frowned. One of her brothers had once asked why, when the Song of the Peoples was sung in every country on Ragaris, it was so rude about all of them except Marod. Now she suspected she knew the answer.

*

"Cousin, what were you thinking? Are you mad?"

Talinti had felt Tormenas' annoyance simmering throughout their tavern half hour, beneath his soothing jovial tales of his own boyhood mischief, and his awe when visiting Makkera's Glory Cathedral. They'd drunk the best wine The Consul's Chair could provide, and sampled a platter of sweetmeats and assorted cheese - "This one is green!" - in company with Bel, Jeres and Ardas. Who were not electors or great lords of course, but respectively guard and secretary to Lord Osvard of Marithon; and ship's captain to Lady Yairil of Qasadan. Ardas, the tall scarred one, was helpful in calming the others – he looked mainly amused by the incident.

Talinti had said little, confining herself to smiling, agreeing with Tormenas, and paying for the drinks and food. Avoiding any discussion of prophecies, the Battle of the Lither, and her exact connection to the troublesome children. And just as she was starting to worry about time, Bel said "I have guard-duty. And Lord Osvard will be looking for you, Jeres."

"He'll be dressing for the feast. He doesn't need me for that. However -" and they all gathered themselves together, spoke polite words, and separated at the door.

So Tormenas could release his anger at last. He pushed a hand over his forehead into springing hair, and clutched his felt hat. "Is this what you and your servants do at home – run around saving every child from a thrashing? Do you pick up birds that fall from their nest?"

Yes, when I was small, I did. I suppose our mothers gossiped about that.

"I'm most grateful -"

"That may be very well in the countryside, where you're the lady of the manor, and everyone owes duty to you. But here – Vach-roysh isn't a place to chase trouble. The Consuls' Guards don't like it. And the Jaryari are dangerous."

He was walking fast in his agitation, but spoke quietly, not looking at her. Talinti stared at the tall white walls passing by. "I'm sure you're right, cousin. But it was because I thought they might be dangerous that I interfered. That foolish boy was younger than my Araf."

Tormenas grunted; then stopped, and took a breath. "Forgive me, cousin Talinti. I was most impolite. Yes." He stood in the street, making people swerve around him – *I have still to wash and dress for a royal feast,* Talinti thought – and then he spoke slowly. "All of our lives in Vach-roysh we've heard stories of these terrible warriors. As I was saying before, I've met many who aren't terrible, of course, but these electors and their people may also be remembering our wars. It seems that this time all will be well, thanks to your generosity - but this is why," he lowered his voice further, "why talk of a 'prophecy' frightens me a little. If it's one that Duke Haras could use - or even the Marodi could. They also are not a peaceable people." His smile was thoughtful.

"Their King was born one of us," she said, looking away. "Let's hope he at least doesn't wish for war."

"Yes, young Barad of Adgor as he was." A pause, and a sigh. "Does he prosper, do you think, in the north? I suppose he's had several years to grow accustomed to the Marodi, but he certainly didn't wish to go, rumour said. I heard that he went to his father, and begged him to renounce the agreement, and call off the marriage. I don't know what reason he gave. These youngsters, who think their foolish desires count for anything in matters of state and business."

Talinti shrugged, wondering how contented Tormenas had been in his own marriage. "Everyone seemed on excellent terms on the boat."

The streets were filling up as they approached the fine buildings of the centre. Those with very short hair were doubtless servants to electors, for there were rules about hair styles in Jaryar. They had to step aside for someone actually being carried in a curtained litter, all red cloth - but the cloth looked shabby. A trio of young girls nudged past, one carrying a live goose. A man in a blue jacket whose side view somehow looked familiar to her pushed out of an alley without looking, and nearly crashed into a cake-seller's tray.

"Where are we?"

"Almost at the Palace now – the kitchen entrance is down there" – he pointed – "but I'll take you round to the front as befits the guest of King and Consuls." His smile seemed to hesitate – or calculate, Talinti thought. "I know you'll be busy at the Council tomorrow, but ordinary citizens are permitted also, and I hope to see you there."

Does he have no business to attend to? Why is he so attentive? "She's young enough to bear more children, and probably tired of sleeping alone, and Lithermayg is a fine estate."

Such suspicions were unfair, and also shockingly conceited. She said a courteous farewell, and went in, and happily Kariam had found her own way safely back.

*

Errios had to admit there were good things about Vachroysh, a city he could have taken with ease, and almost without loss, if Fate had been kind long ago. The streets were wide and clean. Marodi symbols hung on the left, and Jaryari on the right. People came out to watch and wave. Of course it was nothing to the greatness of Makkera, but it was bigger than Vard-town. The piebald green-and-white Cathedral was ridiculous however. An insult to God, almost a blasphemy.

It seemed he had some enemies among the local children. Indulgent grandfather as he was, this made him smile.

The Consuls Jaikkad and Invildi, whom they were supposed to call "Most Noble", greeted them politely at the Palace. The Marodi had arrived yesterday, and were off plotting or hiding somewhere. Errios handed over his sword with a secret growl, and was guided at last to his chamber. He was very tired.

Indeed it was a fine place to sleep, larger than his room at home. Glass in the window and a proper chimney. There was a desk to sit at, with some book on it. Very civilised. The seat even had cushions - of course he ordered them taken away. "Unless you'd like them on your pallet," he said, but his woman knew him too well for this.

And also a letter on the desk, and he knew the seal. A report from the man Asor. *I obtained work on the King's barge as ordered –*

As soon as he read it, he knew he couldn't rest yet. He set off to find the Duke.

A grovelling servant guided him to the room for the delegation to gather in. As he approached, a woman with servant was coming out. She was somewhat younger than him, with a lacy gown and a leather circlet instead of a hat to hold her shoulder-length grey hair in place. A foreigner, then.

He nearly tripped over another bloody plant in the doorway. The Duke, the Duchess and Antonos were already there.

"Ah, Errios. Did you see the Ricossan princess?

Lady Long-name b'Shen?" asked the Duke lightly. "We have an answer to our question, and the answer is Yes. A good beginning for the conquest of Marod."

Errios didn't know what the Question was. Antonos had said something about Marod and plans, but nothing about Ricossa. In any case, "My lord, I have a report." He bowed, and then had to pause to cough.

Antonos took the letter. "Yes. The Consuls have already told us about this 'prophecy' King Barad has fabricated. Let's trust we can deal with the matter quickly."

*

They arranged themselves with care. The Duchess sitting to one side next to Errios, the Duke regally in the centre with Antonos standing at his elbow, the Archbishop waiting aloof in the shadows, the servants ranged along one wall. There was a knock. The Haymonese woman and her maid walked in.

She was trim and decent-looking, and not too thin; the kind he'd always liked. If he'd been twenty years younger, Errios would have wanted to fuck her. She looked a little nervous, but not as nervous as she ought.

The two women curtsied.

Antonos named himself and his companions, and

then, "Madam," he said politely, "thank you for attending on his lordship. We're told you have a message for the Council."

"I've brought words, honoured sir," she said. *Not completely untutored.* "Which I do not understand, but perhaps under God's guidance the Council may."

"And what are these words?"

"I believe arrangements have been made for them to be delivered -"

"What you mean is," interrupted the Duke, "that the King hasn't yet told you what to say."

She was still a moment. "I don't take orders from the King of Marod. The message was spoken three weeks ago at Lithermayg, and it's for the electors."

"I am an elector," said the Duchess.

"Then your ladyship will hear the words on Friday, I believe. The delegates have no need to hear them before that day." She lifted her chin. "Or at all."

An indignant pause; then the Archbishop took a sweeping step forward, and asked sternly, "Are you a good daughter of the Church, Talinti, daughter of Malda?"

"I hope so, er, Your Reverence." She seemed to have a little difficulty remembering the correct title.

"Then you know the terrible fate reserved for those who pretend to speak for God - who produce false prophecies to mislead His people? You know what such liars will suffer in hell?" The Archbishop waited. Just as Talinti was about to open her mouth, she said, "I'm sure, as a God-fearing woman, you would welcome guidance as to whether you run any such risk with these words. Tell me, and I can help you."

"I know I will be judged by God for my actions. I do not intend to deceive anybody."

"My lady," whispered the maid. Errios could almost hear her teeth chattering. Talinti ignored her.

"I didn't ask to be given these words, and I haven't revealed them to the Consuls, or to the Marodi."

"You will reveal them to us," said the Duke. "Or, when they're proved false, I will have you whipped through the streets for your arrogance." The Duchess cleared her throat, and he stood up. He breathed in and inflated his chest. "You are a woman of Haymon, and the Consuls of Haymon acknowledge Jaryari overlordship. You owe me your obedience, and I command you to speak."

She looked down at the floor, and then up again. "King Osgar is my overlord. I don't think that gives you –

even if you are his heir – the right to command everything I do." She curtsied. Errios thought her hands were shaking on her gown. "Your Reverence, my lord, my lady, honoured sirs." And she walked out.

"Insolent bitch!" the Duke exclaimed, before the door was shut.

"Plainly an honest woman, if absurdly stubborn," said Antonos. "And it seems" - he waved Errios' letter – "that she met the King along the road, and by chance."

"I don't believe in such chances."

"It doesn't matter," said the Duchess. "With all respect to Her Reverence, I've never heard a supposed prophecy that couldn't be interpreted many ways. Put your heart back in its box, Haras. You are going to win. And very soon we have a feast to attend."

*

The Great Hall was almost dazzling with surely scores of candles, and brilliantly polished silverware. There were long tables for the visiting electors, gathered from every corner of Jaryar and looking in holiday mood, but Errios was guided to the dais itself, and the High Table. For the first time in his life.

Normally a High Table would have had seats on

one side only. The king or lady or abbot would stare down at his or her people, and be gazed at in return. But this one had been arranged so that the Consuls and the two sets of delegates faced each other. Errios scowled. Duke Haras should have been the centre of the electors' attention, on this first night, with his cousin-rival far away in her northern fortress. Instead the Duke was sitting next to the Consul Invildi, with her absurd toga-cloak, awesome girth, and irritating gentle voice.

Errios was opposite. The Vard delegates were to Invildi's right; next to her on the left was the old Consul Jaikkad - and then the Marodi.

The King, who looked silly, and so talkative he was probably already half-drunk. The Prince, quiet, and dressed in arrogantly-holy black. A handsome young woman, the Queensister, facing them on Errios' side. And next to him, a large awkward-looking monk, perhaps nearly his own age. But this one had worn better.

There was no sign of the Ricossan princess. So it was just the Consuls and the delegates. Even Duchess Palla had been pushed off to the side of the Hall somewhere.

Before each guest was a bowl of warm water to cleanse fingers, a cloth, and a pretty object carved like a rose. Doubtless one of the famous Haymonese candied sweets. There was a little sword-shape in pastry across the top of his – doubtless a stupid compliment to his years of warfare. The Marodi monk's was decorated with a cross.

Errios was already starting to feel sick. Each of the people at the table had their own servant or squire to wait on them of course, carrying food over from large trestles on the right. His woman leaned over his left shoulder correctly to say, "There are less strongly-flavoured dishes if you wish, sir. Roast goose, fried breads, pigeon pie, cabbage and dried fruit in vinegar."

This was a relief. Haymonese meals, he'd heard, started with fiery spice, continued with heavy breads and doughs with meat, and ended with cloying sweetness. Someone must have told the cooks that not everyone liked this. He had only to endure the smell of the spice on other people's platters, and on their breath. And the wine was good, as far as he could judge, earning praise even from the fastidious Archbishop.

In Jaryar, there would have been entertainment. But the music played by two lute-players behind the table was quiet and dull, and no one sang. And perhaps this was planned, and the feast was part of the debate. For many of the electors at the tables this end were also quiet, listening to them. King Barad looked down the Hall, and smiled. "We should put on a performance of some kind after supper," he said. "Your Reverence, do you dance?"

One of the serving girls giggled, and Prince Braidoc frowned at her.

"It would not be seemly," Archbishop Elizabeth replied, after a disconcerted pause.

"Not without more musicians, and those we neglected to bring," commented Antonos. "Unless one of your people has a lute or a set of pipes concealed in a pouch?"

Duke Haras made polite enquiries about the Marodi royal children, and was told smugly that they were thriving. The older Consul made a rambling speech praising the Archbishop's noble campaign against eccelesistical corruption. Errios grew bored, and watched Antonos' squire trying to catch the eye of that girl behind the Prince. She was indeed a pretty child, reminding him of his first wife, mischievous Dellevin. How many long-ago feasts he'd slipped away from to kiss her behind the door!

The girl didn't seem to have noticed young Justar – until suddenly she flashed round to him with such a grotesque expression that he spluttered, and the conversation almost stopped. The girl's face was innocently smooth at once, and Errios secretly smiled.

"May I – may I enquire as to the health of King Osgar?" asked the old monk suddenly. Errios thought the Prince had given him a nudging stare.

Probably they'd discussed it beforehand, and chosen the holy man to ask the question. From anyone else its greedy eagerness would have been too obvious. *Our King isn't dead yet*.

"He is as well -" began the Archbishop, but the Duke spoke louder.

"Our King is much improved, praise God. My stepmother visited him in Makkera two months ago, spoke with him of many things, and received his blessing for our mission here. She reported that his mind and body are growing stronger all the time."

An exaggeration, doubtless, but justified in the circumstances.

The Archbishop was the only one who lived in Makkera. She added, "'But of course we all pray for him daily. As you do, I'm sure?" to the monk.

Who gulped, and said, "Er, yes, I pray for the sick,

we all do. I fear I've not prayed for foreign kings." He looked downwards.

Well, thought Errios, *so I'm not the greatest fool at this table.*

But he had words to say, and should be listening for his chance. The Consuls were explaining what everyone knew, that the debates starting tomorrow would take place in the adjoining Theatre, part of the Palace complex, where the elections for Consul were held every three years, and the Assembly met to argue and pass laws the rest of the time. *The great people of Haymon having nothing better to do.* The first two days of the Council were for speeches by the delegates; the third for the electors to debate among themselves. This had been decided by letter during months of tortuous negotiations.

But "There is one other person to speak, by your leave," said the King. "I think it's been arranged for us to hear from a woman, of good birth and property, worthy of respect, who claims she has a prophecy to relate to the Council."

"So we've been told," said Antonos dryly.

The Archbishop's expression was as sweet as the candied flower before her. "Ah, yes. We know from

Scripture that so-called prophecies can be true or false. Is it authenticated?"

"I confess I don't know how to authenticate a prophecy, other than by waiting to see if it comes true," said the King, false charm oozing. "The words were spoken by a woman called Upali, who died at Lithermayg, on this Talinti's lands."

Upali. The name was familiar from somewhere.

There was a silence. Then Antonos said, "Upali – she was the madwoman banished from Marithon province, was she not?"

"I believe so," said the Archbishop.

"Then we need hardly listen to what she had to say," said the Duke.

But Antonos said slowly, "She spoke other words that came true." *Abbos and Rosior.* "Forgive me, Your Grace," softly to the King, "it is being hard to believe that you don't know these words already. And if they hadn't been favourable to you, you could have sent her home."

"Plain speaking, sir," said the King calmly. "I understand your doubts, and if the positions were reversed, I might have shared them. But I don't command her, or anyone in Haymon. You have my word, and that of those with me, that we do not know. In this place – don't you agree? – we are opponents, but we're not enemies. I know no reason to doubt the honour of any of your delegation, and I think we've given you no reason to doubt ours." He grinned. "To be frank, I asked her, and she wouldn't tell me. I was greatly annoyed."

Antonos smiled, and said, "I have no reason to doubt your word, Your Grace." He looked, as if for agreement, at the Duke.

But Duke Haras said curtly, "I know of no such reason, but then I know little of any of you at all. I have not concerned myself with the barbarian north."

"If you become King of Jaryar, you'll have time to remedy that," said the King cheerfully, raising his voice a little. "You will I'm sure be advised about all of us northerners, with whom you and your countrymen trade, especially those in An, Marithon and Qasadan provinces."

The hall was becoming less noisy. The electors were listening. Errios was beginning to sympathise with Duchess Palla.

"Talinti of where, did you say? Lithermayg?" asked one of the Consuls.

Where we fought the battle, thought Errios, and

doubtless many others. A battle, a war, that few in Jaryar were proud of. Bad memories stirred in his fingers. But Antonos turned the conversation by saying, "Where Gormad the Lucky is buried, I believe. The legend. True greatness knows no borders."

And suddenly everyone was smiling. Antonos continued, "Did any of you know him?"

The old Abbot said, "When I was a boy, our masters were in the same Six." *Whatever that meant.* "He found me very dull, I fear. Gormad had enough mischief for half a dozen boys. I didn't see him after we grew up, but they say he never changed – always kind, and daring, and rarely thinking before he spoke. Some heroes are over-praised, but I believe his fame was deserved." He stretched out a hand, and knocked over his cup.

"He was kin of mine," said the Duke.

"Of course -"

"Yes, he was descended from King Jendon, that is, er -"

"Queen Darisha," muttered Antonos and Errios simultaneously.

"Queen Darisha, my ancestor. That is, if one recognises such - he was a prince's bastard, I believe -"

"So, my lord," said Prince Braidoc quietly, "do you wish to claim kinship to Gormad Kingsbrother, or not? I am certainly proud to do so. My sister the Queen and I remember him playing with us, when we were children. But then I'm honoured to be connected to all my sister's siblings in the Thirty." He nodded courteously to the Queensister woman sitting opposite him.

The Duke's face hardened, and his voice rose. "Of course. Mistress Fillim, is that not the correct address?" She nodded. He continued, "The fabled Queen's Thirty. 'Branded for the Queen', yes? That is Marod. A land where if the Queen is wishing to honour someone, she burns them with hot iron. Somewhat barbaric, I think. I wonder what she does to her enemies?"

All the Marodi stiffened.

"In Jaryar, of course," said the King, "wouldn't Jeppa here be whipped for letting her hair grow below her shoulders?" He gestured to the servant standing behind him. "Some would call that barbaric. But each country has its own ways."

Errios wondered if calling his servant by her name meant that the King was sleeping with her. It probably would have done in Jaryar.

King Barad went on, "At meetings like this we can learn about our differences. Perhaps none of us is more barbaric than another." He picked up the crystallised rose in front of him, sniffed it, grimaced, and tossed it to the other hand.

Now was as good a time as any.

"Perhaps," said Errios, and cleared his throat. He didn't like public speaking, and he'd had to learn it by heart. "I believe, Your Grace, that your Queen's Thirty have a famous rule, 'We do not kill children'?"

"'We do not kill children, we do not commit rape, we do not take pleasure in torment'. Yes. Not the Thirty alone. All of Marod believe this."

So much the better. "A very good rule," said Antonos.

"We can all agree on that. I have heard of a village in Marod called Roddog," said Errios, "where this rule was - kept." He pushed himself to his feet, and reached up to touch his holy phial for luck. "Where the villagers had done something to offend the Queen, committed some crime perhaps, and she sent soldiers, members of her Thirty, to hang the ringleaders. That might well be just."

Was the whole hall listening? He raised his voice. "Then they burned the town, and herded all the people, young and old, innocent and guilty, into the square. And someone said, 'We do not kill children.'" He paused and coughed. "So they divided the villagers, those older than fifteen, and those younger, and made the children watch as their parents and elders were slaughtered, one by one. And then rode away, and left them to live or die."

That's what you Marodi are like, he thought. And many of the electors knew him and trusted him, and would remember.

"This cannot be," the King murmured, in real or pretended horror.

"My great-grandfather was one of those children. They fled the Queen's wrath through the snow, and those who survived were given shelter in Jaryar. Was that not barbaric?"

A pause. "Yes, it was," said Fillim Queensister. "But, sir, if I may, your great-grandfather's time was long ago. In the days of Queen Arrabetta, many terrible things were done by her order. That's why she was deposed, by the Thirty and her people."

"Um, er, Croddog, that was the village. The tale is in our archives," said the monk.

Prince Braidoc nodded. "We try not to deny or

forget the faults of our past. No one, sir, would deny that such an act was monstrous, and hateful to God."

Errios hoped that this flummery wouldn't distract anyone from the truth he'd told. But for now he could only sit down again, and to his further fury he felt his old eyes pricking. He looked down at his plate, and his hands, blinking.

"Your Grace, my lords and ladies, I think we can all agree a need for better understanding," the Consul Jaikkad mewed. "That is part of the reason why your Council is taking place here, on neutral ground, so to speak."

It's here because the Queen and King of Marod don't dare set foot in Jaryar, although they wish to rule it. He was so tired.

At last the meal was coming to an end. Those with strong teeth and a liking for exceeding sweetness began to nibble and crunch at their little flowers. Others wrapped them in cloths and stored them in pouches.

"Until tomorrow," said Invildi. She rose, her toga draping itself gracefully despite her bulk, so she looked as imposing as a statue. "There will be Mass in the Cathedral, and then the oath-swearing in the Theatre."

It was over. Errios' servant helped him up, and he exchanged a look with Antonos. The Duke hadn't shone brightly tonight, there could be no doubt. Then, as he turned away, he heard a thump, and a gasping noise.

Everyone was staring at the other side of the table, where one of the servants was suddenly on the floor, writhing in apparent pain. It wasn't the young one he'd noticed.

"Jeppa? Someone, help her!" the King exclaimed. A horrible noise came from her mouth. Her face bulged and reddened. Her back arched. The poor woman was plainly very sick, and her master and a young priest who'd been serving were kneeling next to her. Then her whole body shuddered, and she lay still.

"Oh God," said King Barad, shaking her shoulder.

The Queensister bent over the woman to listen for breath, and then closed her eyes. "She's dead, Your Grace." She lifted from the floor a little rose shape, fallen from the still hand.

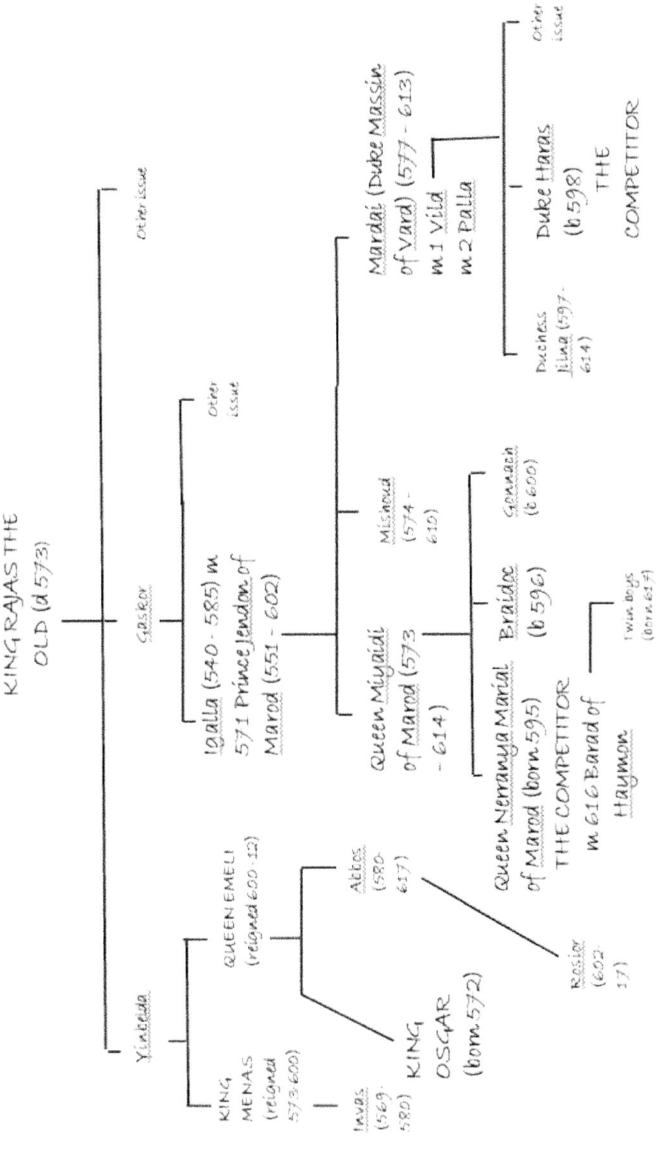
KING RAJAS THE OLD (d 573)
Yinbedda
Gaskor
Other issue
KING MENAS (reigned 573-600)
QUEEN EMELI (reigned 600-12)
Igalla (540 - 585) m 571 Prince Jendon of Marod (551 - 602)
Other issue
Invas (569-580)
KING OSCAR (born 572)
Attos (580-617)
Rosior (602-17)
Queen Miyaidi of Marod (573 - 614)
Mishoud (574-610)
Mardai (Duke Massin of Vard) (577 - 613) m 1 Vila m 2 Palla
Queen Nerranya Marial of Marod (born 595) THE COMPETITOR m 616 Barad of Haymon
Braidoc (b 596)
Gonnach (b 600)
Twin Boys (born 617)
Duchess Ilina (597-614)
Duke Haras (b 598) THE COMPETITOR
Other issue

The Beginning of the Council

"What the fucking hell is happening?" demanded the Duke, thumping the table, and making goblets bounce. Errios was thankful that he'd restrained himself as long as he had, until they'd all reached his private chamber. No, two chambers. The woman Illi had scurried into the inner room as they entered.

"Who can tell?" Antonos replied. "It wasn't a pretence. She did seem to be dead, the Lowly woman. Perhaps Cursing Upali prophesied it," he added bitterly.

"God rest her soul," said the Archbishop, sinking onto a chair, and fanning herself with her hand. "Of course the food wasn't well prepared – perhaps something affected her, or she might be subject to seizures. That's the most probable cause."

Can she really think so?

The door burst open. Duchess Palla marched in, skirts whipping around her. "One, two, three, four," she said, looking round. "All *here*. Have none of you a grain of sense? They're talking of murder! Murder! Who d'you think the Marodi are going to blame? The Consuls are examining the body, with physicians, and interrogating the kitchen staff. Do we have a physician?" Without waiting for a reply, she went on, "And neither do the Marodi, but their Mistress Fillim is nosing about. We need to be in that room! One of you must be there, expressing our shock, finding out what's going on!"

"The lady is right. I'll go," said Antonos. He snapped his fingers for his servant and squire to follow, and strode out.

"What d'you mean, 'blamed'?" Duke Haras was staring at his stepmother.

She sighed loudly. "The King's servant is dead, and no one would waste poison on such as that. So it will be said to have been aimed at him. By us, most probably. Have any of you or your servants been in the kitchens today? Stop!" she cried, as the Archbishop began to protest. "Stop. I don't want to know." She wasn't tall, but her gaze held them motionless. "I do not want to know what you – any of you – may have done."

"What I have done?"

"I do not want to know." She turned, and went out.

Oh.

*

It was Lida's task to keep everyone supplied with wine, but as she wandered around the room from one trembling person to another, her hands shook so much that drops kept splashing, like red tears, to the floor. The King sat leaning forward in a chair, elbows on thighs, face in hands. The Prince was also sitting, still and intent, his fingers laced together; only his eyes moved from face to face. The Abbot and his attendant monk Brother Jude stood by the King, heads bowed and lips moving, presumably in prayer. Master Draider waited by the door, sword drawn. The Prince's servant Yaif (who'd been waiting on Fillim at the feast because Fric was too young) sat cross-legged in a corner, bringing his palms together and away, together and away, like confused slow applause.

They were all accustomed to listening to the King talk, and he said nothing.

Mistress Fillim was not there. She'd gone with one of the soldiers and Secretary Kalla to attend the Consuls in tests they were doing. Tests on the candied rose, and on Jeppa's body.

Jeppa's body.

She served the last person (Brother Jude) and sat

down on the floor next to Yaif. Solidness at her back and under her. Cold in her stomach. She glanced sideways. "Terrible," Yaif whispered, and continued to bring his hands together and away, as if he couldn't stop. "Terrible."

Lida kept remembering the Hall, a frozen scene from a pageant – Fillim's face blank as she lifted the sweet, the King's mouth open, the Prince looking sick, the old Consul having to sit down trembling, the Jaryari Duke rather disgusted -

At last, the Abbot's deep voice. "She was a good woman," he said. Lida wondered if he'd been all this time praying for Jeppa's soul. He started to speak again, but was caught by a spluttering cough. Everyone waited for him to finish. Then, "We - we cannot know, Your Grace, until Mistress Fillim returns, but unless she had some strange illness -"

"Of course it was foul play," said Prince Braidoc quietly. "She was in good health. It looked like empodene poisoning, very sudden. But is that not usually given in a liquid?" He looked round as if for someone more informed about poisons.

"She had nothing to drink. She was busy serving," said Draider diffidently from the door.

The King raised his eyes. "She drank nothing. She ate nothing, until I passed her that, that thing. She likes sweetmeats. I don't."

The Prince stood up. "And you don't. That was what saved your life."

"My life?"

"Don't be a fool, Barad!" Lida had never before heard her master raise his voice. "If it was poison, it was meant for you. Jeppa died by mistake."

Some looked up surprised, but not all. Lida felt as if she'd been dropped into a fathomless river, as someone had suggested to her in jest. She wished wildly for a person her own age, someone to share the unbelievableness.

There was a knock, and the door began to open. Draider blocked it, but a woman called through, "Brother? Are you there?"

"Madi?"

Lady Madigam pushed in, and ran over to the King. They held each other tightly. "Are you – what's happened?"

"I'm well. It was my servant who died."

"God rest her soul. They're talking of poison downstairs. Was it intended for you?"

"My lady," said the Prince, "and my King, what is

the custom here, with these sweets? Are they usual?"

"Yes, at most great feasts."

The Prince said thoughtfully, "I tasted mine, and I am still here."

"I tasted the Abbot's," said Brother Jude shyly.

The King said, "Mm. Not everyone eats them, or likes them. They're often taken home for children, or to eat later."

"Which would have made it less obvious. A healthy man like you suddenly dying - Such things would be prepared in advance, of course, and these were individually decorated. Yours had a crown; mine had a tree. Lady, your brother doesn't like such things. Would anyone here have known that?"

He turned to Lady Madigam, who'd released her brother, but still stood very close to him. She swallowed, and looked straight at the King; they were almost the same height. "The Consul Invildi asked me last week how they should welcome you – what you and your people would like. I remember I told her I didn't know about anyone you were bringing, but that you didn't like over-spicy food."

"Not a true Haymonese," he murmured, a small smile returning.

"No - but I don't think I mentioned sweets." She grimaced. "I said you'd want people to talk to."

"Or talk at, you used to say."

Another knock. "Who is it?" Draider demanded.

"Fillim and Kalla."

There was a knife-slash in Fillim's jacket sleeve. None of the rest of them had thought of that yet. She looked suspiciously at Lady Madigam, bowed to the King, and said, "Poison, Your Grace. Parts of the rose were fed to a rat, and a dog – both died almost instantly. The Consul's physicians did tests on it. It appears that empodene had been smeared all over." She swallowed. "I suppose this has already been said, but it seems to me that this was an attack on you, Your Grace."

"It has been said."

"And Draider has only five soldiers, and they cannot stay awake all night. The Consuls have offered to lend us some of theirs – to us and to the Vard delegation also. Does Your Grace trust the Consuls?"

"I have no reason not to," he said. "But I had no reason to believe anything like this - Oh God."

Fillim was pacing up and down, finger-tips rummaging at her temples. "One of the Consuls' guards at the end of the passage, one of our soldiers outside your door as before, and one outside the window. I will sleep in your chamber, if you permit -"

"Fillim." Master Draider took an awkward step forward. "Forgive me, sister, but you're a delegate. You were sent to think and speak for the Queen. I was sent to lead the soldiers."

Fillim frowned. Lida wondered if there would be a fight.

"I will watch the King," he said. "That means the other three soldiers can sleep half the night, and then relieve us. Yaif will sleep in your room, my prince. We also have Kalla and the others. They're loyal, and will sleep in the passage. A killer would be unlikely to get past them all. But you should rest, sister. And tomorrow find out who did this. You have the mind for that. I have not."

Fillim turned first to the King, then to the Prince. Both nodded. "Brother," she said to Draider, and they embraced briefly.

"What are the Consuls doing?" the Prince asked.

"Questioning the kitchen staff."

"You should join them. But Draider's right. You must also sleep," said the King.

"And in case we had forgotten," added the Prince, "the Council still begins tomorrow. We must be ready for the debate, including what we talked of yesterday."

What was that? Lida wondered.

"Forgive me, Your Grace," said Abbot Paul suddenly. His lips were chewing, and he was fiddling with his fingers. "If we think - it certainly seems like murder. But who would do such a thing?"

"The Jaryari," said Draider at once.

The Prince said more calmly, "We do not know much of Duke Haras, but we think he would do anything to gain the throne. We believe he has bribed most of the electors."

"Br-bribery isn't murder. And – in any case – how would killing the King help him to win? The claim is Queen Nerranya's, not yours, Your Grace."

"True." The King shrugged.

"Yes. We know nothing, except that Jeppa is dead." The Prince's voice was grim. "But we already suspected that we have come to a nest of snakes, and that Haras is a viper. Barad, you must be careful. Eat nothing that someone else has not also tasted. You must never be alone."

"I never am alone."

"Do not be." To Lida's surprise, he added softly, "I don't want to have to save your life again. Be careful."

"This applies to you also, Braidoc."

"I suppose we don't think Jeppa had any enemies?" asked Fillim suddenly.

The King said, "I see no reason to think she would. She wasn't universally loved, but - She was very loyal." His voice changed. "Fillim."

"Your Grace."

"Draider is right. This is your task. You will find this murderer.

"And then we'll have vengeance."

*

After the Consuls' red-jacketed Guards had questioned every table about anything suspicious they had seen, heard, or *tasted,* Talinti and Kariam were allowed to retire. Talinti's heart and stomach were sick, and Kariam didn't wish to be alone, so they went together to the Palace Chapel.

The Cathedral they'd visited that morning with Tormenas had been enormous and awesome, and the Chapel couldn't compete. The walls were whiteplaster, not cream and green stone, there were no statues, and the carved figure of Christ on the cross above the altar was shining black, not gold. Along the left wall were a few recesses where people could kneel to whisper their sins through latticed windows to a priest behind. No one was confessing this evening. A few clerics in black, and one or two of the Marodi from the boat, were standing or kneeling to pray. The Abbot, the secretary, one of the soldiers.

The wall paintings of holy lives seemed to be the same saints and style as in the Cathedral, perhaps even the same artists. Kariam wandered over to look at them.

Talinti stood before the altar, bowed her head, and put her hands over her eyes.

It had started out as such a good day – the Cathedral and the saints' tombs and the First Translation a sight to remember all her life – but then more and more alarming and demanding events. *"I will have you whipped through the streets."* And now this. When everyone was already tired.

That's a selfish way to think. Jeppa was her name. God rest her soul. Murder. "I feel fear, I see blood."

This may be only the beginning.

She prayed and worried, and tried to gather herself together. How long this took she didn't know, but at last, yawning, she crossed herself and turned away. Prince Braidoc of Marod was rising from his knees at her side, so that they almost collided, and both had to apologise with silent grimaces.

They walked together out of the Chapel, Kariam falling into place behind. "May I offer my sorrow to you and the King?" Talinti asked shyly.

"I thank you. A terrible evening." His eyes glittered, and he said less gently, "Were you expecting this, by chance? Your – message - did not mention murder at a feast?"

Dear God.

"No. No." *"I see blood." But not poison, which this must be.*

"Forgive me. Of course not. I will pass on your condolence, madam. My friend the Abbot says we should not jump to hasty conclusions. But if you or any of your people hear or see anything of interest, you will assist us in finding the truth?"

"Of course, my prince."

"Jeppa was a good woman, who will be in heaven now, and we will find the murderer, and send him or her to hell, and that will be some comfort. But still this is not news

I would have wanted to bring home to my sister."

"No."

"Nor you, I suppose, to whoever you left at home."

"My children."

They'd reached her chamber. She put a hand on the door, and turned to look at him.

"We all need comfort," he said again. Quietly, "You seem distressed, madam. Talinti. You do not have to remain so." He leant a little closer, and laid a hand on her arm. Even more quietly, "I think perhaps you have been a long time alone. What would you like to remember about your visit to Vach-roysh?"

She wondered if she were dreaming. *His eyes.* "I think sleep will be the best help; I thank you. I wish you good night, my prince."

"Good night to you," said the young man, stepping away. Perhaps she'd imagined it. "Ah me, where am I? I need to be in the north wing – can you guide me, I wonder?"

This was to Kariam, who was caught mid-yawn, but said quickly, "Oh, yes, my prince" – and they'd disappeared round the corner before Talinti could speak. So she went in, lit a candle, and got into bed alone, and it seemed a long while before Kariam came back, giggling.

All lights were put out. There was a little uneasy sleep.

And then she was awake in the dark, not knowing why. There came a second sharp knock, and Kariam squealed.

"Who is it?" asked Talinti, stumbling to the door.

"Fillim Queensister." She entered briskly. One of the Guards stood behind her. "Forgive my waking you, but I'm asking questions about the death tonight. Can you both come with me?"

Talinti gripped the solid door-frame. Dragging herself to alertness, she said, "I trust we may dress first?" and the intruders withdrew to allow this.

"What's happening?" Kariam's hands and voice trembled.

Talinti bundled her quickly-plaited hair under her cap, and sat on the only stool to lace her shoes. "Courage, Kariam. We've done nothing wrong."

Kariam nodded, but she didn't stop shaking.

They were escorted down very quiet passages, and through very empty chambers, their footsteps and rustling skirts the only sound. Lights burned in occasional cressets.

Talinti thought of Meriden's marble-in-a-box – but this box had a lid.

"Wait here, please," Fillim told Kariam in a shadowy antechamber. Talinti she ushered into a smaller room. One of the Guards stood by the door. An unfamiliar woman in a black gown and a red peaked hat was sitting at a table with parchment.

"This is Lady Rudulla, the Consuls' Questioner. She and I are looking into this matter."

"I see." Talinti sat down as indicated.

"My friend Jeppa was poisoned with empodene. The poison was smeared on a sweetmeat intended for my King."

She moistened her lips. "I know nothing of this."

"And I've been reminded that the King was ill one night on the boat. The second night after you and your people joined us. The night it rained."

"I don't remember."

"So you understand that I'm interested in your party, madam." The other woman was writing rapidly.

"The King invited us aboard."

"Yes, of his generosity. Because you seemed to be in trouble."

So the questions began – what were they doing there, why that route, how had they been attacked, what physic had they brought with them (she didn't know), what she thought of the Marodi and their royal family, how long Meriden, Kariam and Brod had been in her service, what she'd been doing that afternoon, and what had she seen?

Talinti answered as well as she could. She described the attack by the river, shivering a little. She mentioned passing the street Tormenas said led to the kitchens, and the various people she'd seen there.

And she said, "If I'd wanted to murder your King, which I did not, I wouldn't have involved my servants in such a crime."

Lady Rudulla laughed a little. "A visiting lady sneaking round near the kitchens would look suspicious. A servant less so."

She answered, and answered, and Lady Rudulla wrote. After a while, there were two knocks on the door, but Fillim paid them no attention.

At last, she sat back and said, "Very well. And the words of this 'prophecy' of yours?"

"It didn't mention poison or murder, and it has no relevance."

A long pause. Then the young woman stood up, and slowly drew out her knife, long and sharp. They both looked down at it. "If I thought these words were useful, I would make you tell me. I would, and I think I could, quite easily. But I don't think that God would choose to speak to us through *you*, or through this dead woman from Marithon province. Thank you, madam." All three women stood, and Fillim opened the door.

There was a Guard there, a man, with Meriden. He was tidily-dressed as ever, but he still looked like someone who'd been dragged from his bed in the middle of the night, and not told why.

"This is my steward. He knows nothing of murder." She saw him blink.

The man opened a different door. There was another Guard inside, and Kariam sitting on a bench, hugging her drawn-up knees. Lady Rudulla walked in, and Meriden was nudged through also.

"If you're going to question my servants, I wish to be present."

"That's not possible, madam. You can go back to bed now, or wait here if you prefer. Please do not leave the Palace," said Fillim.

"Meriden," said Talinti, "I've no doubt that you and Kariam will answer honestly. We have nothing to fear from truth." He nodded, and went in, and she was alone.

There were chairs in the antechamber, and she sat down, only now realising how much she was shaking.

"I would make you tell me. I would, and I think I could, quite easily."

She was a lady, and her interrogation had been polite. Few people thought it necessary to be polite to servants.

Many good things were said about the Queen's Thirty, but they weren't usually described as gentle. Many less than good things were said about the Consuls' Guards.

There were laws in Haymon against torture. Exactly what that meant she didn't know.

She heard the murmur of voices, but not the words. Once someone laughed. Once she thought Kariam squealed. There were a few sharp sounds that might have been slaps.

That man in blue coming out of the kitchen alley yesterday. Had I seen him before, or am I imagining it?

Very slowly the light grew.

At last the door opened. "Are you still here, madam?" Lady Rudulla came out, and Fillim, and the Guards.

So Talinti walked up to them, and said politely, "It is full morning. Can we have something to eat?"

"I'll have food sent," said Fillim, standing aside. There were web-lines by her eyes, and Talinti realised she hadn't been to bed. "You can go in, if you wish."

Kariam was sitting leaning against the wall with her eyes shut. Meriden was just sitting, on the other side of the room. There was one lamp hanging from the wall, and one candle on the table. There were no windows.

A room without windows is a store-cupboard, if it's small. If it's large, it's a prison.

"Have they hurt you?"

"Nothing to distress ourselves over," said Meriden. His pale face was bruised beneath the eye. But they both seemed to have the right number of fingernails and teeth, and there was no blood.

"Why did we come here, my lady?" Kariam wailed. "Why do they think we've done anything?"

Talinti put her arms round her, as she might have done for her daughter. "I hope we've now convinced Mistress Fillim that we're all probably innocent, rather than probably guilty, of trying to harm their King. Or this poor woman Jeppa. I barely spoke to her. You talked to her, I think, didn't you, as maids together, but I can't believe you discussed anything sinister."

"No, indeed!" said Kariam, snuffling indignantly.

"What about Brod?"

"They left one Guard to question him. And to look through our luggage, I suppose," said Meriden, scowling. "To see if I brought empodene."

"Did you?" It might have been legitimate; in very small quantities, it was used for pain relief.

"No, my lady."

Breakfast was indeed brought – bread and ale and a dish of pickled apple. Kariam had recovered enough to eat, but she whispered, "I can't believe that this morning we were all so happy."

"Yesterday morning, now," Meriden corrected, and she glared at him.

"It isn't possible! I can't believe this is happening to us!"

"Mm. To ordinary people like us, begging your pardon, my lady. It's like something in a tale. If this were a tale - I suppose the King's servant would have been killed by mistake for him. That would mean the Jaryari were responsible."

"That's what Mistress Fillim thinks, I'm sure," said Talinti, "and she wonders if we are agents of theirs." She swished away down the little room, a slice of bread dangling from her hand. "But it may not be so. That Duke would have to be very stupid to try such a thing."

"What else could it be? Some strange accident?"

"Empodene doesn't get on to one sweet among ten by accident."

She saw Meriden looking at her curiously. In the silence she remembered his arms around her that night, those two nights, long ago after her husband died.

Waving a hand as if to dismiss the matter, she said, "Pay me no heed. I'm very tired. Perhaps we should try to sleep." The bread in her fingers slowly tore, and half the slice fell to the ground. "By the by, Meriden, thank you for your help yesterday. With those Marodi children. I was causing trouble, as usual."

Meriden smiled wryly. "But you didn't cause this trouble, my lady."

They ate, and sat down, and were silent for a little. Then Kariam suddenly said, "Could Tormenas help us, my lady? He's your kinsman, and he seems to know many high people."

It was true that he'd been boasting about his connections - in Vach-roysh, and even in Makkera. He was related to the Consul Invildi; he'd done business with Duchess Palla. But he'd never been to Marod.

"And he admires you so much," Kariam went on.

Talinti looked up at the ceiling.

They continued to wait.

*

When they gathered for breakfast in the flowery room the next morning, Lida saw tiredness on every face, and felt it on her own, stretching her eyes. It had been a night in a corridor stuffed with extra bodies. Who were there to stop assassins getting in, because the Duke of Vard had tried to murder the King. Fric kept close to her, as if any adult might suddenly die or turn into someone else without warning. "She can't be dead! She can't!" he'd wailed over and over as she tried to explain last night, until at last her patience tore apart, and she boxed his ears.

As yesterday, there was strange Haymonese food, but also good plain porridge and bread, which was tasted grimly by Yaif and another soldier before the King or

Prince took any. So that was safe, and the others could fill bowls. Lida saw Secretary Kalla casting longing glances at the smoking dishes of some red paste stuck with cloves; and it was the Prince who took pity, and moved to take some, so that Yaif hastily tried it, and then Kalla could dare. The Prince smiled, and yawned, and Lida wondered how much sleep he'd had. And then Mistress Fillim came in, marching and bowing smartly, but shutting the door with more of a jerk than usual.

"What news?" asked the King.

"The Consuls' Lady Rudulla let Antonos stay while we questioned the kitchen staff. He expressed the Jaryari concern – for their own lives as well as ours, if there's a killer in the Palace." (Draider muttered, "Their lives!")

"And his eagerness to help in our enquiries."

"Which are also the Consuls' enquiries."

"Yes." Fillim picked up a cup, and held it out. She had to shake it, and Lida had to elbow Fric, before he remembered his duty, and scurried forward with wine for her. "Your Grace, the Prince had a thought during the night, about the journey, and came to me with it."

Everyone looked at Prince Braidoc. "I was praying in the Chapel, like many others," he said quietly, "and I suddenly remembered – whether or not by God's inspiration I do not know – that you were unwell one night on the boat, brother."

"I suppose I was."

"What was wrong?"

"Only a headache, and I felt sick. I vomited a little." (Lida looked at the floor, embarrassed at a king talking of such things.) "I was well by morning." He stared at his brother-in-law, and his hand clenched on the white tablecover. "You think this was a second attempt?"

"It's possible," said Fillim, "that you were poisoned on the boat, either to kill, or to prepare people's minds that you were in poor health, and make your death less of a surprise. And in that case, anyone on the boat may be guilty. Any of the crew – or that Talinti and her servants. I've been questioning them, with Rudulla and the Guards."

The man who liked ducks! thought Lida. *Who saved us from a beating yesterday.*

"They seemed harmless."

"Harmless, and indeed godly," the Prince agreed. "But the devil can disguise himself as an angel of light. Is there more?"

"Yes. In our questioning, Talinti's maid said that

Jeppa was annoyed by one of the crew and his inquisitiveness."

"Inquisitive about what?"

"About you, Your Grace, and our party, and whether we were all friends. Things that Duke Haras might have wanted to know."

"Ah, yes," said the King, the tone less happy than the words. "Braidoc, she did complain of such a one. You were there."

"You are right. He had asked her if we differed about religion, and if Fillim had a lover anywhere. You said, it would be intelligent of the Jaryari to place a spy among us."

"I remember," agreed the Abbot. "A spy needn't be a murderer."

"No, but he needs to be found and questioned. Do we know his name?"

"I asked Jeppa to find out. The small pale man – is this the one you mean, Fillim?"

"Yes, that matches what this Kariam said. She didn't know -"

"His name is Asor," said Draider from the door he was guarding. "I learned all the names. He was hired in

Graijin – at the border."

The King said briskly, "Annet, take two soldiers, speak to Captain Goff and bring this man. And Fillim, go to bed. I think you've been up all night."

"I have Mass to attend in an hour."

"God will pardon you." If Fillim had been looking (Lida thought, but she wasn't) she would have seen both the Prince and the Abbot nod.

"And then we have a Council to attend, and a vote to win," said the Prince. "Jeppa wanted us to win. She would have liked to be the servant of the King of Jaryar." His face quivered, and tears pricked behind Lida's eyes.

Fillim bowed and went out.

"Antonos of Tayn," said the King thoughtfully. "He's said to be clever, cleverer than the Duke."

"Not difficult, I believe. And there are the old warrior, and the Archbishop – forgive me, Brother, but priests have been known to murder – and the Duchess. Any or all of them could have ordered it."

The Abbot coughed. *He was going to say again that they didn't know,* Lida thought correctly. "Er - Your Grace, it might be wise not to be openly suspicious until – and unless – we're sure."

"Until, I think. But yes. They will commiserate with me, and I will thank them with a smile." His voice was grim.

The Prince added, "We will be very civilised and pleasant. We were planning in any case to send our cousin a gift, were we not? Let us invite the delegates to meet with us this evening before supper. Then we can discuss the progress of the investigation, in which they seem, understandably, to be so interested." Lida had recently learned the word "sarcasm".

The King nodded. "Kalla, please prepare invitations this morning." Kalla jumped and nodded, drawn to everyone's notice in the act of licking a sticky finger.

"Now we have Mass to attend. And then it begins."

*

"If Mistress Fillim needs any errands run, or other help, I will tell her she can make use of you," the Prince murmured to Lida, on their way to the Cathedral. "I fear she may think you are most useful keeping Fric out of mischief." Lida dared to pout, and he smiled gently. "But also this abominable thing that has happened makes it more important than ever to learn all we can. Observe the Jaryari – the delegates, their servants, but also the electors – try to listen to their gossip. Report to me with what you learn."

"Yes, my prince." So, after she'd counted all the wonderful statues in the Cathedral, she had permission to spend most of the Mass studying gorgeous gowns, patterned sleeves and embroidered caps for clues, and working out who was connected to whom.

The electors stood in little clumps. She realised that most of them wouldn't know each other, and so it was likely that they were grouping themselves by province. (That was quite a clever thing to have worked out.) A few were huddling cloaks firmly around their bodies, as if cold. Once she'd noticed this, and deduced that they came from the southern provinces, Tell and Exor and Indesandu, she identified southern fashions as including pointed moustaches and a lot more golden jewellery – necklaces (and lower necklines) for women; arm rings for men. Not many of the Jaryari were bearded, but two who were stood together and wore hose and jacket, not gown, and one of them was the big man she recognised from the terror of the day before. She took a step backwards.

This wasn't really the information Prince Braidoc was looking for.

During the psalm being sung by a group of child

choristers, very beautifully Lida supposed, she studied the sinister delegates themselves. The Duke had changed from purple to equally magnificent midnight-blue, gold stars on his sleeves, and on the hose below his knee-length gown. He tapped his fingers boredly on the arm of a stone saint. The old man with the plait – which meant he was, or had been, a soldier, she knew that much – seemed very holy, and was continually crossing himself, and muttering the responses with closed eyes. The younger man, Antonos, with a pale inquisitive-looking face and thick dark eyebrows and hair, had a gown of blue with silver stripes down the sides. He was looking around, she thought, not too obviously; and once his eyes met hers, and he smiled, and she looked hastily away. His squire (not much older than her; dark-skinned; big nose; buttons of course) seemed to be looking around in much the same way she was, and she remembered making him choke last night. It seemed an age ago. He gave her a cold look, and she smiled pleasantly back.

Standing with the delegates in their front place of honour, was a small woman in simple green, duller than some of the others, and a hat with a plain veil down the back. Lida wondered who she was, and then her studies on the boat came back to her, and she remembered Duchess Palla, only ten years older than her stepson, said to be an insignificant figure.

It was time to go forward and kneel before the priests, and she must make herself holy. She fixed a devout expression on her face, clasped her hands, and chanted "Lord-have-mercy-Christ-have-mercy-Lord-have-mercy" in her head in time with her footsteps joining the queue. And suddenly she thought that if the Duke or any of his people had murdered Jeppa, they were taking the sacrament in a state of *unconfessed mortal sin*, which must be as sure a route to hell as it was possible to get. *Unless* they'd slipped out to chapel or Cathedral to confess and do penance and be absolved already, as a sensible murderer would do. Maybe she should try to find out.

She whispered her idea to the Prince as they left the Cathedral, and he said, "That is a good thought," and her soul basked.

"I saw the Duke's secretary in the chapel last night when I was praying – I was not confessing – and a young woman with short hair, and our friend Talinti, but I do not remember any of the others. In any case, Lida," and his face grew sombre, "you are assuming that whoever did this fears

God."

*

Today was the day they were called for, Errios knew; the time when everything had to be divinely blessed, and right. He almost forgot last night's events, and his distaste for the spotted stone, the cloying perfume and flowers everywhere. He concentrated hard, said the words and listened to the prayers, and tasted the Saviour's goodness, as he was supposed to do.

Peace lasted only as long as the Mass, for as they came out, they were ushered to hastily-arranged benches in the Cathedral Square. Fortunately it wasn't raining. The Marodi delegates nodded stiffly in their direction, and the Duke and his companions nodded stiffly back. It was then that he noticed that all the Marodi, from the King down, had a jagged gash in the right sleeve of their colourful jackets or gowns, so that the white shirts showed through. "What's that for?" muttered the Duke. Antonos shrugged, but their secretary leaned forward to murmur, "It's a mourning ritual, to tear the clothes after a death. They'll be mended after the funeral."

"Oh."

Errios wondered again just how much the woman –

Jeppa? – had meant to King Barad, and if there were a minor scandal here that they could make use of.

But the old Consul Jaikkad was hobbling up to the King and the Duke, accompanied by a few others. "May I present His Reverence Prelate Peter's emissary to Vachroysh, Holy Secretary Mary Divendra of Defardu?"

Bowings. A pale-faced but otherwise non-descript skinny woman.

"And a noble visitor also from City Qayn. The Lady Jiriet Ban Li b'Shen."

"Eh?" said Lady Jiriet, putting a hand to her ear.

The Consul had to shout. "My lady, His Grace the King of Marod, and the Duke of Vard."

"I am most pleased to make acquaintance with you both," she said. Neither she nor the Duke indicated that they'd met yesterday. For whatever the secret "answer" had been.

"I'm delighted," said King Barad – very loud, very polite, very cool. "Had I known Your Ladyship would be here, I could have brought letters with me, and saved our messengers a journey. You're aware of our debates over February's incidents at Makaim?"

Everyone was looking puzzled, which gave him the

chance to say, "When three of our youths dined with their cousins just over the border in Ricossa, and offended some religious rule - and one of your lords then sent soldiers back to Marod in disguise to kidnap and mutilate them?"

"Mutilate" means "castrate", of course. The Ricossans have some vile customs.

"I had not been advised of this allegation," said the lady stiffly.

"No, but then there are always these border incidents, aren't there? Those houses set on fire just after Christmas, I believe, and our own people aren't always blameless. We all need to talk to each other. But let's leave this to my wife, and your King Aigith."

As they turned to leave, "I wasn't aware Queen Nerranya had trouble with our Ricossan neighbours," said Duke Haras, with a satisfied smile. "We have none. Ricossa is a valued partner in trade."

Too late Errios saw the trap.

"Ah, indeed, and we trade also. But - Vard doesn't have a border with Ricossa or Defardu, but perhaps some of your countrymen in, for example, Lefayr, know the kind of minor difficulties there can be, even between friends." The King glanced over heads, doubtless looking for Lefayri delegates. Errios was infuriated to hear an agreeing murmur.

Prince Braidoc said pleasantly, "You were saying last night, my lord, how little you knew of the barbarian north. How much do you know of the east?"

One day they will pay for that, Errios thought. Foolishly, he knew. The parties paraded off through the streets, and a few Haymonese idiots cheered.

Back to the Palace at last. *And now it begins.*

∗

Into the Theatre. A rectangular hall, long enough for three hearths each side, ridiculous extravagance. At one end was a dais much wider than normal. It was a stage for orators to strut on, with three steps at the front, ten chairs and a table. Before it, numerous benches, and an aisle down the middle. Grey light poured in from high windows. The walls were brilliantly white.

At the back of the stage hung a large Jaryari banner. Errios was pleased to see this. The Marodi were not. "It's the custom in Haymonese halls to display the liege lord's banner on ceremonial occasions," he heard the Consul Invildi explaining apologetically. "King Osgar is still our lord." Mistress Fillim made a babyish pout, but said nothing.

The eight delegates took their places on the stage. Electors – all fifty of them – filed to their benches. Errios supposed he ought to know many of the older faces, but he was too short-sighted to be sure. Then everyone stood while a jewelled casket was carried in by two priests and laid on the table. A very ancient book was lifted out with reverence. This must be the translation of the Scriptures out of their original Latin, begun by St Jaddi of Vach-roysh over four hundred years ago, and continued by her daughter. Errios didn't greatly value books, but he couldn't deny some awe. He bowed his head with everyone else.

"We are gathered for the Council to determine a lawful heir for our gracious King Osgar, son of Jonostar, long may he reign," said Jaikkad. He named all the important people, including the visitors from Ricossa and Defardu, for the benefit of those who didn't know them, and then said, "We will read the Proclamation, and then there is a preliminary matter for the Marodi."

So the Proclamation was read. And perhaps Antonos had nudged the Duke, for he stepped over to King Barad and recited courteously, "We've heard about the sad death of your servant last night. On behalf of myself, my stepmother the Duchess, and my delegation, I offer you condolences and sincere assistance in finding the killer."

For that must be the "preliminary matter".

"You are most good, my lord," said the King.

But it was Fillim Queensister who stepped to the middle of the stage, bowed to Vard, to the Consuls, to her King, and to the hall full of people, and said, "Before the oath is taken - we haven't yet agreed the procedure for the final vote." *What?* "Should the electors stand up and each declare their decision, or should the votes be written down unsigned, and counted by the Consuls? That way no one would know which way any one individual voted."

"Preposterous!" cried the Duke.

Antonos stood up and said, "A great deal of trouble to go to, surely? What reason can there be for this?"

"Why, to put the result beyond attack in the future. Suppose some mischief-maker claimed that a delegate had been threatened, for example, or even bribed, and therefore the result was invalid? I don't wish to alarm, and of course neither side has done so. But even the suggestion might lead to confusion at a time when we would all wish for unity and peace. If the vote's secret, bribery and threats are useless. And so, when the result is declared, everyone can trust it absolutely, here, and back in the cities and villages of Jaryar."

There was anger in the hall. There was shock. But there was also amusement. "An excellent notion," called someone. Errios thought it might be Lady Ganola of Tell.

Murmurings, and, "Surely there's been no such attempt, and therefore there is no need," began Antonos.

"Of course all the noble delegates will vote according to their conscience, in the sight of God," said Fillim. She was enjoying herself, Errios realised with disgust. "But even without such allegations, consider. If the electors before us choose Queen Nerranya, she doesn't wish to know which of them voted for her cousin. She would prefer to start unprejudiced. I'm sure, my lord, that you feel the same."

"I would want to know who is loyal to me!" said the Duke.

Fillim's expression was eloquent. Before she could speak, Invildi said, "My lord Duke, after the sacred oath that all are about to take, you're not thinking that any here will be disloyal to their future King? Or Queen?"

The Duke was silent. Antonos exchanged looks

with the Archbishop, and the Duchess, rose, and whispered in his friend's ear.

"Very well. As you say, nobody here has anything to fear from secrecy."

How much money has the Duke paid, to people who can now ignore their promises, and vote for the enemy?

Then the pious folderol began in earnest. The Holy Secretary, sent by the Prelate in Defardu to pretend that this was something to do with him, was beckoned onto the stage. She said a long prayer. A trumpet was blown, and the Consul Jaikkad called for the province of An. Its four electors stamped up, and swore solemn oaths that they were who they were, and explained how they'd been selected. Then each placed one hand on the Book and swore before God to consider and vote honestly, to abide by the result in all time to come – they, their families, and their people – and to punish any who did not. Holy Secretary Mary nodded solemnly.

The same process was repeated for each of the other eight provinces. Exor, Indesandu, Lefayr, Marithon, Qasadan, Tell, Vard, Vendor. Then the priests, abbots and abbesses. Including the Archbishop, who was an elector as well as a delegate, the only person who was.

And then the assembly dispersed for food and rest.

"The barbarians are cheating us at every turn!" grumbled the Duke as they walked to the Great Hall.

"You're still a native-born Jaryari, and that matters, my lord. But, if I may, don't talk of them as 'barbarians' so often."

"Why should I not?"

Antonos sighed. "Because, my lord, the Marodi here today don't look like barbarians. And also because many of the electors have some Marodi blood. As you do."

*

A secret vote, hee hee. Lida had sensed her Prince's satisfaction, and also Fillim's and the King's, but it had taken her a little while to work out the reason for it. Now she could hardly restrain herself from skipping with glee.

But Fric sidled alongside her as they entered the Palace. "Lida," he said irritatingly. "Lida, please -"

"Not now." She wanted to plan how to describe the city to her friends at home.

Fric turned and shuffled a few steps along, head low. "Master Draider -" Lida's conscience nudged her. It must be important if he was willing to bother a Queensbrother.

"All right, then. What is it?" She pulled him away, over by the wall.

"Lida -" The little boy glanced away and back. "In the Mass the, the priest was talking about hell. Hell is fire, isn't it?"

"Yes, I suppose." She remembered pictures. "Fire, and there's worms, and monsters devouring you forever. Why?"

"D'you go to hell for wishing someone was dead?"

Oh. "Who did you wish dead?"

"Jeppa," he whispered.

"Why?"

"She - everyone's saying she was so good, but she was always hard to me." (*Jeppa was hard to everyone except the King,* Lida thought.) "You remember we bought the ribbons yesterday, and lost them. She was so angry. She boxed my ears, and said I was a bloody useless little runt."

Lida almost smiled, but "runt" wasn't very pleasant. And suddenly she thought that it might be particularly unpleasant for Fric, whose parents were dead, and whose brothers hadn't wanted him. Jeppa probably hadn't known that.

"We were at the feast, and I was hating her, and

wishing she would die – and then she did." He looked up at Lida, and she saw his eyes glistening with fear. "Am I going to hell?"

Her heart swelled with kindness. Really, had no one taught this lad any doctrine?

"It's a bad sin, but you don't have to, no. You go to the Chapel – or a church – you know about going to confession? Your parents went?" He nodded. "There's always priests around a chapel. You confess, and you'll be given your penance, and then you're absolved and clean. Whenever you do a bad thing, that sorts it out." Prince Braidoc went cheerfully to confession after each night in Pigeon Alley, so she knew. "You'll get prayers to recite, or they might make you fast for a day, or something. And rich people sometimes have to build churches, but you won't have to do that. It works for everything. It's something to do with the Redeemer."

He thought. "Suppose I die before I confess?"

"Well, that's not likely. Not if you go soon."

"Can I go now?" He cast a quick look at Fillim, who was talking to someone from Jaryar.

"Yes. If she asks, I'll say you were feeling sick." He nodded, and scampered off.

How lovely it was to be learned, and teach people about God.

She wandered towards the courtyard, where most of the electors were standing gossiping and eating whatever their servants had thought to bring for them, wondering how much she would be able to overhear, when a voice said timidly, "Errm," and she turned.

"That is the Jaryari tower, is it not?" It was a faintly-familiar man, one of the Palace servants.

"Yes, the Jaryari delegation have rooms up there." *You should know that.* Even to Lida's eyes, the man looked nervous. "Is something wrong?"

"No, no. I have an errand to deliver." He opened his arm so that Lida could see the items he was holding: mostly documents, in Kalla's hand, and also a bottle.

"Our invitation letter," said Lida.

"Of course, you're with the King of Marod, aren't you? You know his servant was murdered?" The man glanced at the door to the tower as if it might bite him. "The Duke is a fearsome man."

("Learn all we can," the Prince had said.)

"I could deliver these for you."

"They are very important - "

"I promise I will deliver them," said Lida. "On the honour of Dendarry."

"Oh, madam -" And indeed he was grateful. She was a little taken aback by the detailed instructions about who was to receive what, and where, but in a few minutes she left him, arms full of objects, and walked to the entrance to the North Tower.

She might even meet that squire again, and he would see that she was really quite a significant person, a useful member of the King's party.

At the first turn of the spiral stair, there was a guard, sword drawn. "What are you doing?"

"I'm delivering letters for the delegates, if it please you, sir. From the Marodi delegation. I'm Prince Braidoc's squire."

"This isn't a letter," he said, taking the bottle from her. "Poisoned, perhaps?"

"It's not poisoned!" She indicated the label round the neck. (*"There is no need for us to be enemies. Barad and Braidoc, on behalf of the Queen."*) "And it's sealed. I haven't tampered with it. Sir, if you wish to keep back the wine, at least let me take the letters."

"Keep back the wine? What are you accusing me

of?" He let her pass, obviously deciding at the last minute not to cuff a foreign squire. *Jaryari oaf.*

Errios of Girifay, on the first level. Duke Haras on the second. There were no further guards. Errios of Girifay didn't answer when she knocked softly at his door, so she crept in, and found a room similar to her Prince's. There was no servant, but the old delegate was snoozing in a chair. She grinned, laid out the two letters for him as she'd been told, and went quietly out.

There was no one at all in Duke Haras' double set of rooms, but there was a stain on the floor smelling strongly of wine. Would her Prince want her to look around? *"King Barad's youngest spy."* Heart thudding, she tried to open a small chest on the table. It was locked. The larger chest contained clothes of course, neatly folded, and a small paper packet. She opened it, noticing a faint smell, not quite like lemon. The paper contained chopped-small pieces of greenery. *Could this be empodene, or the plant or whatever that empodene's made from?* Her toes tingled.

There was nothing else. She arranged his one letter and bottle, and left. Her legs were beginning to ache.

Archbishop Elizabeth was also out – her servant nun was tidying something, and merely nodded at Lida's explanation.

And up again. The invitation for Antonos of Tayn. Beside the bed was a little box, and in it some more of the green lemony stuff. *Curious.* Antonos or his squire didn't keep his clothes as tidy as the Duke's.

Finished, and frankly she hadn't learned or achieved much.

There were footsteps coming towards the door!

Of course she had a perfectly genuine reason to be here, but the guilt of the spy was on her, and before she'd thought she'd dived under the bed, its long hangings shielding her from view. So often she and her brothers had hidden under beds, from their parents or their tutor.

"Not a good morning," said a woman's voice. There were two people. "Where's your man?"

"Don't worry, he's eating and dicing downstairs, and I sent Justar to smile at any female delegates he could find. No, not good at all. So much money thrown away. Perhaps thrown away."

There was a pause then. Peeping under the fringe, Lida could see feet, standing close together. Then,

"Palla. Haras told me you said you didn't want to know."

"I don't."

Harshly.

"Know this. I didn't do it, and I don't know who did. Believe me."

"I may believe you. I haven't yet forgiven you for keeping quiet about his little whore."

"She really isn't a whore. I don't like it either, and I tried to persuade him to leave her behind, but he can be very stubborn. He likes her."

"Likes! Why cannot he be content to tumble the maids, like -"

"Haras is too decent for that."

"You call it decency?" The woman gave a very delicate snort, reminding Lida so much of her mother that she wanted to giggle.

"It is decency. If a duke invites a servant to bed, no matter how sweetly, it's a very brave servant who'll risk their place by saying No. It is more decent to look elsewhere. And I don't see that Illi is doing him any harm."

"She is doing great harm if she makes him unwilling to marry!" The woman paused; then sighed. "Why did God make him such an idiot? How can you endure him? It's my duty to do so, but you -"

The man laughed. "He's been a good friend to me. Apart from introducing me to you. He has good qualities. He's loyal, to Illi and others, for one thing." His voice became warm. "It's a shame that the qualities I admire in him are the ones that drive you mad. Because you are so wise. Wise, sensible, ferocious woman. Come here."

They sat down on the bed. And Lida realised, belatedly and with horror, why the man and the woman were in the room together alone. And what her fate might be if she were caught.

*

Prince Braidoc didn't smile, but his voice and eyes told her that he was very amused indeed. "You are telling me, Lida, that Duchess Palla and Antonos of Tayn committed fornication while you were hiding underneath the bed?"

"No, sir, not actual fornication. They only kissed, and talked, I think. He said, 'Let me just -' and she said, 'Later.'"

Her heart was still thudding.

He shook his head, and now he was smiling. "Well done, Lida. We can give thanks to God for this, and make use of it, I think. And you should draw a lesson. How foolish to send people on a diplomatic errand of great importance if they have secrets to hide."

"But perhaps the Duke doesn't know."

"Perhaps he does not, indeed. Come. I am due back in the Theatre."

*

The prisoners were roused by the scrape of the door, and there stood Fillim, and the Consuls' woman, and a little man of Meriden's colour, with the look of a defiant youth caught in mischief.

"Is this the man you mentioned?" Fillim asked Kariam.

"Yes. Yes, it is."

The three vanished, but only a little later, Fillim re-entered, to say, "Madam, I see no reason to keep any of you further. You may all go, but I need your oaths to remain in the city, sleeping at your current lodging, here or elsewhere, until the end of the Council."

Free to go.

She escorted them to the courtyard. They were out in the street. Talinti took a deep smiling breath, and said, "Well."

Kariam said, "Your pardon, my lady," and stumbled over to lean against a wall. She put her hands over her face, and began to shake. Talinti exchanged a quick look with Meriden.

"I hope Brod and your kinsman haven't been too worried. We've been troublesome guests," he said. Reading her thoughts, "If I may, my lady, a gift might be appreciated?"

"Indeed. I will go on, and reassure them, and you two may decide together how much of my money to spend."

So Meriden and Kariam walked off towards Cheesemongers' Row, there probably to spend half an hour weighing up the merits of crumbly moon-cheese, medium strength Finmayg with prunes (Meriden's favourite), green-veined Gimertoq, and others, until Kariam was herself again.

For two Haymonese, if they agree about everything else, will always argue about cheese.

But Talinti had something different to think about.

*

"Talinti, my friend! Is all well?" Tormenas grasped her hands almost as soon as she entered the house – and her backbone shivered at his touch. "We've been so worried."

"I'm very sorry to have been the cause," she said

sincerely. "I know a visit from the Guards is not pleasant." *Or good for business.*

"They came and they went. But was there truly a murder? Has the criminal been caught?"

"Not yet, I think. We were all three questioned, and all three freed. Meriden and Kariam will be back here soon."

"I'm relieved. But murder, in the Palace!" He was still holding her hands. Bending his head forward, and speaking low, "Was this predicted? Is worse coming? There are rumours. People in the city are afraid."

Talinti hadn't noticed much fear, walking back, except her own. "No. It's a shock to me, as to everyone."

"But it may be the start of a judgment? Is that what it says? Will we all be falling down dead after supper, if we don't repent of our sins in sackcloth and ashes?" He smiled a little, pressing his lips together.

"I didn't bring any sackcloth with me. If you have sinned, cousin, by all means repent. I hope Brod wasn't hurt?" She turned her head so plainly towards the closed door that Tormenas had to release her and allow her to enter. He followed her in; after all, it was his house. "Brod?"

"No damage done, my lady. But the bastards went through everything." He gestured to the various items that had plainly been pulled out of their satchels and box, strewn around, and then shoved into piles by the maid. Brod himself was fiddling with a knife and a small branch, trimming it to the vague shape of a figure with splayed-out hands. A tray was sitting on his lap to hold the shavings. "It's for the Marodi boy from the boat, that Fric," he said, answering her look.

"You're making friends better than the rest of us." She had to go back to the hall, and sit down, and accept a cup of some strange drink that was hot as well as wet.

"The Guards don't think there's a connection with the words you brought, then?"

"The Guards and the Marodi were more interested in where I was yesterday afternoon - with you, of course. I'm sure we're not the only people they're questioning."

"No, the Palace servants, and those who supplied food for the banquet, I suppose." Tormenas sighed. "I hope the foreign visitors do not take fright of all our spices and taverns."

"They may decide the taverns are safer than the Palace. They can hardly leave, before the Council is finished. What's your experience of them as customers? What styles do they like in Jaryar?"

So he was distracted, and she let him rumble on, using the courtesy her parents and tutor had slapped into her long ago. Below his almost-monologue, she made her decision.

*

The presentations themselves were to begin at last. Errios had refreshed himself with nap, drink and bite. The Haymonese saved the main meal of the day for the evening, when nobody needed it, it seemed. Now he took his place again on the stage, and saw that Marodi servants were setting up a large frame against the wall, covered by a cloth. When everyone was seated, Fillim Queensister pulled the cloth away, revealing the picture of a youngish woman. He couldn't see the features clearly.

"Our Queen, who cannot be here in person," she said, bowing to the Jaryari. "It's a true likeness, painted last year by your Mafas of An."

"So she chose Mafas, did she, your Queen?" said Duke Haras. "There were no adequately skilled painters in Marod?"

Fillim smiled easily. "I think most would agree that

Mafas is the most renowned painter of this generation. Just as Marodi wool is the best wool, and the wines of Tell and Exor are the best wines, and we may even admit that the Ricossans make the best lace. Queen Nerranya values excellence wherever she sees it. As I believe we all do here.

"But it's not my turn to speak. By your leave." She bowed to the Consuls, and sat down.

The Consul Jaikkad stood up, and bowed in his turn to the Duke. "The Council will now begin. Your first delegate may speak."

"I speak first," said the Duke, heading for the centre. "And I bring a letter from King Osgar himself, our gracious lord, God's anointed sovereign."

This was how they had planned to include five speeches instead of four.

The Duke began to read from his parchment.

Osgar, by God's grace King of Jaryar, Overlord of Haymon and the Isles, and of <u>all the West</u>, to the most loyal electors gathered in Vach-roysh, greeting. You have a vital task to perform. It is my wish that you perform it with prayer and wisdom, and that God may lead you to choose my cousin, your friend and countryman Haras, son of Massin, Duke of Vard, third of that title. He is well deserving. He is of your own blood and people. He knows the land and the laws. You *must choose freely, but consider that Vard is at the heart of Jaryar. The Duke of Vard knows you…*

It was rambling and repetitive, but at least it was from the King. Duke Haras folded the parchment, and laid it down.

"When my honoured father was ten years old, his father, King Jendon of Marod, sent him south for fostering, and his cousin, then King Menas of Jaryar, created him first Duke of Vard. That showed a clear intention by both kingdoms that any connection between Queen Igalla and her homeland should run through him.

"Many of you remember my father, Duke Massin, respected and valued throughout our land. You may also remember my sister, Duchess Jilna, who held Vard for less than a year, and whom I still mourn. I am less than they were, but if you approve, I swear to you that I will be the greatest king God can make of me.

"I say nothing against Queen Nerranya, my kinswoman, or against any of her delegates. She is God's anointed of Marod. But however noble and great she may be, she is not ours. She does not know Jaryar, she does not feel Jaryar, it's not her home."

He went on a little longer. He'd learned his speech

thoroughly, and he spoke it well, Errios thought. There were nods and agreeing murmurs as he spoke, and applause as he sat down.

"The first delegate from Marod."

King Barad stood in his turn.

"Thank you, my lord. As it happens, I also have a letter to read. But first –" Abruptly, he turned to the Duke, and said, "By the by, my lord, did you know that it was once suggested that you should marry my wife?" Errios couldn't quite see, but from the stir in the hall, he thought the Duke was taken aback. "Oh, yes. I understand that years ago, your father, her mother, and King Osgar discussed that possibility. They didn't think then to cut off all links between the two lines. I don't know why the marriage didn't proceed. You certainly cannot have her now."

He smiled, and there was some laughter. Errios remembered Asor's report, and ground his teeth.

The King faced the front. "I have little to say, which is unusual for me, but I would say this. If you vote for the Duke, as is your right, he may well prove an excellent king. He will doubtless marry, and father heirs for the kingdom."

A hint that Nerranya already has heirs.

"And then, when he's old and grey, perhaps, his youngest child may say, 'I should be king after you, not my elder sibling. I am the more suitable, the more loved. Wasn't that your argument, Father, at Vach-roysh all those years ago?'"

Murmurs.

"Duke Haras is asking you to set aside the simple rules that everyone in Ragaris understands – the eldest takes precedence. Think of what that could mean to any family blessed with more than one child. For all the years to come. Do you wish such disorder? Do you want to see Cain and Abel fighting each other all over Jaryar?"

He paused. "My letter."

Nerranya Marial, daughter of Miyaidi Saranal, of the Marodi, to the loyal and worthy electors of Jaryar, greeting.

I regret that I cannot be with you today. But I believe you would think less of me if I neglected my God-given responsibilities where I am, to travel on this errand, important though it is, and risked the health of the unborn. Nonetheless my thoughts are with you, and I have sent those whom I trust, and who are dear to me.

You believe that I am a stranger to you, and always will be. This argument will rightly have weight. But I am not so great a stranger as you may think.

My grandmother Igalla died before I was born, but my mother and grandfather often spoke of her. They spoke with admiration of her courage in coming north, of how she came to love Marod and the strangers there, of the customs that seemed odd that she grew to appreciate - and of the changes for the better that she introduced.

Nor did she or they forget her Jaryari heritage. At my christening I was given the Jaryari name Marial in addition to the Marodi one Nerranya, and I was assigned to the protection of a guardian saint, St Ansha, as is the Jaryari way. My husband and I have followed this custom with our own children.

I do not know, and have never seen, the provinces of An or Vard, but in years past I visited Marithon and Indesandu. When I was a little girl, I worshipped at your great Cathedral in Makkera. I have hunted in the forests of Gizayn, and was privileged to hear your poet Janioli of Lefayr play and sing in the sun-favoured city of Aid.

One more thing I would say. I hate war, as all Christian people do. A single monarch ruling over Jaryar and Marod is unlikely ever to make war on herself.

I remain your true friend, Nerranya.

So, Errios thought, *we've been preparing for this encounter for months. That bitch has been preparing for years.*

*

"Some say Fillim's line is more noble even than the Queen's. Oh, yes, she's one of the highest-born ladies in Marod. Many great lords are seeking her hand." Kariam's words, as she entered with Meriden and two portions of cheese wrapped in linen, sounded as if she'd fully recovered her spirits, and her malice. Meriden would be quite aware of the impossible gap between him and the Queensister's attention.

"I need you to write something for me," said Talinti.

"My lady." He pulled off his cloak, and followed her into the side room, where Brod, still carving, looked up at them.

Talinti took out the parchment and handed it to him. "Upali's words. I need three copies made, and there will be three letters."

He flicked a look that seemed to say *Three copies. Is this a punishment?*

The door opened, and Tormenas stood there, gesturing with the cheese-parcels in his hand. "This is most thoughtful, cousin -" And then he paused.

Talinti said, "I think I've been wrong. The delegates of both sides heard that we may have a – message." She swallowed. "And of course they wanted to hear it as soon as possible, before the electors do. To be able to think beforehand about what it means, which they're more likely to know than I. As long as neither takes precedence over the other, it's unreasonable not to let them. What do you think?"

"You're right, my lady," said Meriden; and "A very wise and godly thought," said Tormenas, almost at the same moment. Talinti blinked, wondering which of them – if either – she'd actually been speaking to. "The Consuls will wish to see them also, and all simultaneously. Three copies, therefore."

"Dear Talinti. Of course you're right, but your steward is weary. Can I not assist? I would be delighted to write for you. I may not have a hand quite fine enough for the eyes of a King, but do any of us?"

"Meriden does, if anyone. Thank you for your offer, but he'll find it no trouble, I am sure. What were you saying about the plans for your cousin's new manor-house? About the shapes of the windows?" She shut the door behind them, and walked him firmly back to the hall table, where they sat down, and Kariam assisted her in encouraging his talk.

A little later, when the other two were comparing memories of the Bloody Elections of '09, she poured out a cup and took it through to the visitors' room. Meriden had finished two copies, and was half-way through the third, and his writing was indeed just adequate, she thought, for a king.

"They call this morbah. What do you think?"

"Good wine spoiled, my lady," he said cheerfully, after tasting it.

She waited until he'd finished, and then dictated brief letters. ("*Talinti, daughter of Malda, of Lithermayg, to Barad, by God's grace King of the Marodi, and the Queen's other noble delegates, greeting.* I don't think I need to name them all?"

"*No*, my lady.")

As if casually, she murmured, "How many people have asked you for the words we're bringing?"

He considered. "Five."

"Offering money, perhaps?"

"Fillim Queensister didn't offer money." He looked down at the parchment.

Talinti stifled the urge to ask for more details about Fillim, and said, "But the others did. Who?"

"The Prince's servant, on the boat, I don't know his name, and the King's servant, the one who was killed. And one of the crew – Kariam told them this morning he seemed very inquisitive. And -" He gave her a look that was perhaps hesitant, and jerked his head towards the hall door. "While you were looking at the tombs and the Book in the Cathedral yesterday."

Tormenas. So she'd been right. She'd seen them standing close together when she came back to the nave; had also seen Tormenas' face.

"I fear I offended him, my lady."

"Mmm. How much did he offer?"

"Not enough."

*

When the Council broke up for the evening, Errios was the last to leave the platform. He walked slowly up to the portrait, which he hadn't been able to examine before. It showed a real face, a face that looked like someone the painter had met and studied. This was Mafas' style. Much admired, so Errios had heard. And yes, more interesting than the traditional pictures, where men were merely bearded, or not; and women were distinguished only by the shape of their head-dresses.

Mafas had earned his gold, the disloyal money-grubber. The Queen sat looking outwards, but slightly to the viewer's left. One hand rested on a book, probably the Bible; the other stroked the Marodi banner draped over a table beside her. Showing in the language of art that she was devout, that she loved her country, and that Marod exported cloth. She was dressed in blue and gold with a cross on a chain around her neck. Black hair showed beneath a cap studded with pearls, the other Marodi export. She was smiling, but with a firmness in the smile.

Errios had feared that she would look like Igalla. Or like his very hazy memories of Igalla.

She did not. She looked like her cousin. The high cheek-bones, the slender brown face, and even the small ears, reminded him, would remind everyone, of Duke Haras. The looks they had doubtless both inherited from their Marodi grandfather.

*

Before they ate or rested, the Jaryari delegation had to go to King Barad's ridiculous gathering. No one dared to stop the Duchess from joining them, although the invitations hadn't mentioned her. They filed into a large room with their personal servants and two guards. The walls were covered with huge pictures of flowers. Errios' youngest grandchild could have painted better. They were greeted by the King, the Prince, the Abbot and a few of their hangers-on. The Queensister wasn't there. Nosing about somewhere, doubtless. But there was another woman, squat and dark and grey-haired, wearing a red hat. The Consuls' investigator, Lady Rudulla.

The Marodi sat on one side of the table, and the Jaryari on the other, and the Lady at the end.

"Before we begin," said King Barad, in the honey voice Errios already detested, "my brother and I ordered wine delivered to your rooms today, as a gift between cousins by marriage. It occurred to me afterwards that you might have found this a sinister gesture."

"Not at all," said the Duke, almost as sweetly. "In fact, I brought the bottle with me, still unopened. You'll take some?"

The girl Errios had seen at the feast poured ten cups, spilling a little. One of the Marodi guards said, "By your leave," and took the tenth and drained it, and Antonos drank second. Then the rest, including Lady Rudulla, could twist smiles at each other, and drink, and apparently nobody was poisoned.

"My lady," said the King then, gesturing towards the red hat, "we're all eager to hear what's been learned about this murder - assuming, ah, that it was murder."

"It was murder." But this seemed to be all the woman had managed to learn. Although it took her some time to say it. At last, "To sum up, the sweetmeats were individually designed for their recipients, as you saw. The King's would have been easily identifiable by the crown decoration. They were made up in the kitchen, and then set on a tray in the passage. The kitchen door was open, as was the separate pantry door, and no one can swear that a stranger might not have slipped in. There might even have been a moment for someone to do so while you were all approaching the table to sit down.

"Your Grace, my lord Duke, we have questioned the kitchen people, and find nothing suspicious so far in their answers. But we continue to investigate them and their backgrounds."

"Thank you," said the King. Antonos and the Archbishop murmured in agreement.

There was a silence. Prince Braidoc broke it by

saying, "I could not help observing last night that the name Upali was not unknown to you, but I confess it was to me. We do not yet have her words, but can you tell us anything of her, my lord?"

"Upali, daughter of Galian, was a trouble-maker in Makkera. 'Cursing Upali', she is sometimes called." Archbishop Elizabeth fingered the rosary at her belt, and shook her head solemnly. She reminded Errios of his children's tutor reporting naughtiness. "King Osgar's heir until a few years ago, as you will know, was his younger brother Abbos, and Abbos had a son, a boy of great promise.

"Upali was the younger daughter of one of the larger landowners in Marithon province, and she was engaged in a love affair of which her parents, for various reasons, didn't approve. And as a favour to them, Prince Abbos spoke to the lover's family, and matters were broken off, and Upali spoke rash and vindictive words against the Prince."

"She cursed him, and his son," said the Duke.

"So it was said afterwards. She said, 'You will die soon. Your child also. And I will not weep'. Or something similar. And seven months later, the Prince and his son were travelling to visit the island of Qasadan, and a squall came up, and all on board were lost.

"Upali claimed only to have said, 'It *may* be that you will die soon'. Still, she narrowly escaped accusations of witchcraft. The Bishop of Marithon offered her the chance to prove penitence by publicly praying for their souls, and she refused. So she was banished from Marithon. That was - it would have been in '17."

"I believe I heard a rumour that she was telling fortunes in An province," said Antonos. "But I cannot swear to its truth. Perhaps someone should've sent her off on pilgrimage to Defardu in the old way, for her to work out her guilt."

"Ah," said the King. "Prelate Peter could have allotted her a year's hard labour, and a thousand prayers, as they used to do."

Duchess Palla surprised Errios by saying, "Some lords, my uncle in eastern Indesandu for example, still make such orders. And it's often done in Ricossa. When a death has been caused accidentally, or after grave provocation, to turn aside any bloodfeud. That was hardly the case here."

"No, and from what you say, she would have spit in the face of such a suggestion."

That seemed to be all about Cursing Upali. Errios was weary of this pointless meeting, and loathing these polite people.

Perhaps the Duke felt the same. As he rose to leave he said, "Your remarks were interesting this morning, Your Grace - about following the rules of succession. What was it you mentioned afterwards, Errios?"

He wished he'd had warning to prepare. "Er, yes. You assserted that your Queen is the eldest child of the eldest child, and therefore the heir." King Barad looked politely interested. "But I've studied, I've been privileged to study the genealogy of Marod, and, errm, if we go back not so very far - there was your Queen Arrabetta, was there not, and she had a younger brother called Lukor? And your Queen is descended from him." He had to shut his eyes to get this right. "But of course the eldest child of the eldest child and so on of *Arrabetta*, who would that be? Would it not be your Mistress Fillim? By your argument, should she not be the Queen of Marod?"

"Did her grandfather not have some such notion?" asked Antonos, "and wasn't he killed – executed, forced to commit suicide, or whatever – for thinking so? What happened to following the strict law of succession then?"

A pause, *ha*, before Prince Braidoc said calmly, "It would be Fillim's older brother in fact. But the history of Arrabetta's deposition is well known to us all. It was long ago."

"Indeed," said Antonos. "We can all hope that Mistress Fillim agrees with you, and doesn't harbour any unnecessary ambition, for herself or her family." He got up, smiling smoothly. "Our thanks for your hospitality. And our prayers that she - and Lady Rudulla - will soon find the killer." They left on that sweet note.

As they were heading back along a corridor, two people approached them deferentially, one a guard. The other curtsied, the Haymonese woman. "My apologies for intruding, my lords, Your Reverence, honoured sir. I have a message for the delegation."

"Thank you." Antonos took the parchment, and the woman stepped aside.

When they reached their own meeting-chamber, Antonos read the letter and its enclosure aloud. And the Duke smiled.

*

"To the hall with six flames
Call the great of the nine

For an heir to the King;
They will seek for a sign.
From the north see a wife,
From the south see a son;
And the second will rule
When the counting is done.
There is hate, there is death,
I feel fear, I see blood,
But one has stooped low,
Raised a bloom from the mud.
Bowing down to be raised
For the Dream, and God's law.
But the sheep, they all wait
For mild peace or grim war."

"This is a prophecy from God?" King Barad had shaken himself, almost like a wet dog, when the Jaryari had left. Then the woman Talinti had come. He'd spread the parchments on the table after reading them aloud, and the Prince and the Abbot bent over them.

"It might be so," the Abbot said thoughtfully.

Lida had been waiting for the words "Thus says the Lord", that prophecies always began with in the Bible, and she was confused.

"The *second*. I suppose there's been blood, if you include any unnatural death." The King frowned.

"Jeppa didn't bleed."

Secretary Kalla said timidly, "It says six flames. There are six hearths in the Theatre. Three each side."

So there are!

"Hmm."

There was a knock, and Fillim entered. She looked tired but pleased, Lida thought. The King waved the document at her. "Ah, sister. Talinti has seen fit to let us – and the Jaryari – have a copy of her mysterious message."

Fillim read it and arched her brows. "It seems, Your Grace, like those words of God that can only be interpreted correctly hundreds of years later."

Lida thought that the Abbot didn't entirely like that. And, "Must a prophecy be from God?" she found herself asking suddenly. "Does it have to be?"

Everyone was looking at her, none of them pleased. Children should be silent. Burning, she wished she could sink and hide in the patterns on the carpet. The Abbot coughed, and then took unfair advantage of the silence to speak, wagging a hand around. "Prophecy of the future cannot come from natural knowledge, child. It must therefore – that is, it's traditionally believed – it must be *un*natural, supernatural. And so it must be from God – or from the devil – or it is merely some person's foolish imagining, that means nothing." With the small amount of attention to spare from her embarrassment, Lida thought he was looking worried.

"Which this may be," said the Prince. "We should all consider. Welcome, Fillim. Shall we come back, friends, to the crime we are investigating?" As people looked at him, "My squire has made some interesting discoveries in the Vard tower, where she went to deliver our letters."

The King sat down, twisting his head to smile at Lida. She felt better.

"First," the Prince said, "it seems that the Dowager Duchess is not living a chaste life in widowhood, and our friend Antonos is her lover."

"Ah. That's more gossip than useful information, is it not? Do we care? I suppose it proves that Antonos and the Duke aren't lovers." Lida blinked. "That's what we wanted – the reason why Haras remains unmarried."

"Hmm, yes. Lida also heard the Duchess complaining bitterly about her stepson's stupidity. It seems he brought his own lover with him to Vach-roysh, a very low-born woman called Illi. Is that right, Lida? The Duchess has only just found out about her, and was very angry."

"Yes, my prince."

Draider chuckled.

"They lead complicated lives in Vard," said the King.

"Your Grace, I see no connection to Jeppa here. We don't want to cast the first stone." Abbot Paul, of course.

The King looked faintly annoyed. "Brother, we need to win. I'm duty-bound to bring forward any arguments to show that Haras would be a less worthy monarch than my wife. Am I not? If there's doubt that he'll marry, as kings should do, the electors ought to be concerned. I know you don't wish to dip your hands in pitch; none of us do; but these are the bastards who want to conquer all the north. And may have murdered Jeppa."

"By mistake for you," the Prince agreed. "Thank you, Lida. Have I left anything out?"

"Oh, yes, my prince, there was something I forgot. Your Grace, both Antonos and the Duke had little packages or boxes of green stuff, stems of some plant, I think, cut up. I think it smelt -"

"Like lemon."

"Yes!"

And then she noticed the way almost everyone in the room was smiling, a smile no one likes to see aimed at them.

"Lida," said the King, "hmmm." He lifted his eyes to the ceiling. "How should I say this?" Somebody laughed. "In a few years' time, an amiable young man may take your hand, smile sweetly, and whisper to you, 'Do you know where the herbs grow?'" (And now she longed to say, *yes, I understand, please stop and don't embarrass me any more*, but of course she couldn't.) "And what he means by this is that he's inviting you to his bed, but he doesn't wish to make any little bastards, sons of Adam or daughters of Eve, and he hopes that the use of these herbs will discourage conception. I think these are what you saw."

Everyone except the Abbot was still smirking, and she wished she were dead.

The Prince came at last to her rescue (but he'd been amused too) by saying, "It confirms what you heard about both Antonos and the Duke, that they needed them, which is useful. And of course, Lida, you should remember that there are other reasons not to commit fornication than avoiding pregnancy, and the herbs do not always work anyway.

"In the meantime, Fillim, have you anything more?"

"Yes, my prince, my king," said Fillim, and her voice made everyone look at her. "We've found the man Jeppa thought too inquisitive. He's admitted that he obtained work on the Queen's Messenger in order to spy on us for Vard, and he's told us who hired him."

The Second Day of the Council

There was pleasure in the air as the Vard delegation met for breakfast the next morning.

"I wonder if any more of the barbarians have died in the night?" Duke Haras, helping himself to pickled pear. The Duchess frowned, but only a little.

Antonos said, "We're agreed, then? Let's say nothing openly, but if anyone -" he nodded courteously at the Archbishop - "is speaking to clerics in particular, we imply we're humbly hopeful of God's approval."

"Keep an eye on the Lithermayg woman. She still has time to change her words." Errios was going to have to make an important speech to sixty people very shortly. He was less at ease than the rest.

"She has no reason to change them now – unless the Marodi threaten or bribe her to do so. They'll also have read them. So we should certainly watch to see if any of them talk to her, and overhear such conversation, if we can. I'll ask Justar to manage it. Talinti can walk where she pleases, and unlike the four of us doesn't have to spend all day at the Council." Antonos caught his squire's eye.

"Yes, sir."

"Not all day. The Marodi will be attending that poor woman's funeral, so our business will be delayed this afternoon," said Archbishop Elizabeth, patting her lip. "Their Abbot Paul will preside. I'll attend, out of courtesy to him, and so will the Holy Secretary."

The Duke rolled his eyes.

"I've given my servant leave to go," said Errios, "and, my lord, she said your man also wished to." The Duke's plump elderly manservant, standing behind his chair, nodded nervously.

"What generous fellow-feeling among the Lowly," said Antonos, smiling pleasantly at the two servants.

"Did you ever speak to the woman? You can go and pray for her soul, if you wish," said the Duke. Surprised but amicable.

The Duchess said, "Be careful if any of you happen to be standing near the body. There are those old beliefs, about murderers and their victims' corpses. Do not be fainting or shrinking away or anything of the kind. We're innocent, and no one must doubt it."

"Indeed," said the Archbishop, making a scornful

triangle at the corner of her mouth. The Church frowned on such ideas.

Errios, in any case, had no intention of standing through a religious service twice in two days. "You'll come and find me when it's over," he told his woman, and she bowed and took his empty bowl. It was time to leave. They crossed the courtyard under watery sunshine, smiling and nodding to the bunches of electors. And abruptly the Duke said, "But what is this?"

He bent down and picked up a many-petalled white flower from the ground. "The Haymonese blossoms are very beautiful. It would be a shame to trample on it," he said, more loudly than he needed. He unfastened a button on his gown, and poked the flower through.

One has stooped low, Raised a bloom from the mud, Errios remembered from the gibberish last night. He wondered who'd thought up that little show. The Duchess was smiling patiently. They went into the Theatre.

The bloody portrait was still there.

It took an age for everyone to arrive, sit down, and stop chattering. Perhaps he should have brought written notes, but what a fool he would've looked fumbling through them, losing his place, perhaps dropping a page.

He scowled, and touched his lucky phial again.

At last there was a smarmy speech from Invildi, repeating what had happened yesterday for the benefit of those who hadn't bothered listening, and indicating what was planned for today, including a break in the middle for the funeral.

And then it was his turn.

✳

"And now we will hear the next speaker from Vard." Lida, leaning against the wall and twiddling her toes, looked up with a sigh. It was the old man, Errios. He straightened slowly, but his gaze as he stared over the hall was direct, and a little frightening.

"I am here with this delegation, my lords, my ladies, as one who has experience of Marod. I'm not here to speak any evil of Queen Nerranya, nor do I know any. She may indeed be the pinnacle of perfection that her people claim.

"But I know evil of Marod. And so do you, my friends. They put on handsome faces here, but what lies behind?" (Lida put a hand up to touch her own cheek.) "A violent people, rebellious, and arrogant. A nation that despite its blood-soaked history prides itself on its holiness. What's their famous saying? *We do not kill children, we do not commit rape, we do not take pleasure in torment.* Such an excellent rule. No other country has one like it.

"No other country needs one.

"And they still break it! The Ferrodach massacre happened within the lifetime of many of us here. I'm biased, of course. This is what the Marodi did to me." He lifted his left hand, and everyone could see that two fingers were missing.

"I don't need to recite the chronicle of murder and torture that is the history of Marod."

But he did – or at least reminded everyone of the horrors of the Marodi War of the Three Kingdoms two hundred and fifty years past, the tyrannies of Queen Arrabetta one hundred years past, and the nasty story he'd told at dinner two nights ago. Lida kept her back straight and her head still. She must shame Fric, who was crying, shame him into ignoring the insults, and copying King Barad's calm smile. He was just an odious hate-filled old man.

"And my own story. I fought, like many here, in the Battle of the Lither, eighteen years ago. There were heroes on both sides, as there always are. I'm not going to cast shame on Gormad the Lucky. But there was also barbarity.

"I was ordered by my commander to surrender, and I was taken for ransom, which my wife paid in due course. Nothing untoward about that. I was kept in what might have been a sheep-pen, for two days and nights, with a dozen others, in the keeping of a Marodi nobleman, a youngster now dead, whose name, I learned, was Addin. He 'took pleasure in torment.'

"I don't know the truth of all the stories the prisoners told about Addin. I know that his men dragged some of the women away, and they came back weeping. I stopped him from doing that. He couldn't kill or silence me, I was too valuable, but his brutes dragged me out, and brought me to a fireside. 'Take a message for your Queen Emeli,' Addin said. I won't repeat the foul way he spoke of her. Then he said, 'Tell her that Haymon is not hers. Jaryar has nine provinces, not ten. Only nine.' And his soldiers held my arm down, so that he could hack off one of my fingers. 'Only nine,' he said again. But his butchery was so clumsy that I lost another as well.

"That's how I remember the Marodi.

"And one thing more I would say. You are here to choose an heir for King Osgar, when, God preserve him, he dies. But he's not dead yet. If you choose a foreigner to succeed him, how long will she be willing to wait? How safe will our King's life be?"

Lida gaped. Everyone on the platform tensed, even the Duke. Mistress Fillim jumped up. "How dare you?"

The old man turned and bowed to her, and her companions. Then he sat slowly down, very pleased with himself.

"I hate him, I'm going to kill him," muttered Fric.

*

The next speech was Prince Braidoc's, and he didn't refer or reply to Errios in any way. He was there to praise his sister, her every virtue, and he did this smoothly. Lida's heart began to calm. But she still wished someone would beat that old man to a bloody mess.

The Prince was followed by the Abbot and the Archbishop, mainly listing the different ways people were appointed to high office in Scripture, and by the time they'd finished, the noon bells had rung. Old Jaikkad told everyone to go away for an hour - *food at last,* thought Lida - and just as they were all stretching arms and legs, Master Draider and several other people walked up the aisle, and onto the stage. They beckoned to Mistress Fillim, and spoke to her and to the Consuls. Then they turned to meet the eyes of the Vard delegates.

"Errios, son of Broxos? Will you come with us, please? There are questions we have to ask you."

"Questions can wait, surely," said the Duke.

But the head of the Consul's Guard said respectfully, "My lord, this is an investigation into murder."

And to her fierce joy, Lida saw him lead Errios away. Fillim followed the group out, a satisfied look on her face.

*

Errios was taken to a small room, and left there to sit and curse for a while, and then Invildi came in, with a secretary of some kind - and Fillim Queensister.

He was so angry he could hardly see.

"What do you want, bitch?" he said.

There was a table. The other two sat at it, facing him. Fillim stayed on her feet. "You hired a man to spy on us, and to kill the King."

"*Lying* bitch."

"Let's start at the beginning, then. You hired a man called Asor, son of Nassayn, to spy on us."

"That's a load of crap."

The Consul nodded to the guard at the door. She

opened it, and pulled in a pale shabby man. There was a cut on his cheek, and he moved with reluctance.

"I've never seen him before," said Errios.

"You didn't have to see him to hire him."

Fillim snapped her fingers at the man, who muttered, "Yes, this is him. I've worked for him before. A man brought me a letter with his seal, and paid me to join the boat."

"Describe this person."

"He was about fifty, clean-shaven. A cleft in his chin, your colour, lady. His hair was grey. He said he worked for Errios."

"My servant is a woman," said Errios.

"You're a wealthy man in the Duke's employ," said Fillim. "The servant you brought to Vach-roysh is a woman. You doubtless have others. Do you employ such a man as described?"

"There are many such men. I know nothing of this."

"I think you're lying, sir. You paid this man to get work on the King's ship, and to spy on us. He's confessed it."

"After you broke his face."

Fillim leaned forward, and spoke softly. "I suspect him of trying to murder my King. How gentle would you have been with such a one?"

Errios shrugged. "Very well. Yes, I hired him to find out what he could."

"You did." The secretary was scribbling. Fillim went on, "And to report to you."

"Of course to report to me. Are you a fucking idiot?"

"And to poison the King."

"No. Why the hell would I want to poison your King?"

The Consul gestured, and the man was taken away.

"This spy of yours got a place on our boat. What were his instructions?"

"What d'you think? To find out anything we could use. He didn't find much. Only that your King and Queen aren't quite as devoted to each other as you all like to pretend. If I were Nerranya, I'd want a husband who shared my bed more than once a month. Or is it she who can't endure him?"

He was pleased to see that he'd annoyed her, but she said, "You're right. This gutter stuff isn't worth paying for. You paid him for murder. The King was sick on the boat. His servant was killed when he arrived. On your orders."

"That," said Errios, "is a fucking lie."

"We have the evidence." She pushed a piece of parchment across to him. "Read it out."

Errios held it close to his face, exaggerating his short-sightedness to irritate her more. He read,

Asor to the noble Errios, son of Broxos, greeting.

I have been to the kitchens, and it is done. A few hours more, and he will be out of the way. A.

"What nonsense is this?"

"You've seen this before, I think?"

"No, I haven't."

The Consul spoke for the first time. "It was found in your chamber."

"Found by her."

"No. Found by one of my officers, searching this morning, after Asor named you."

"Put there by her, then."

"Sir," said Mistress Fillim, "someone tried to kill my King, and I need to find out who it was before they try again. Why would I want to plant false evidence on you,

270

while the real criminal goes free? I think you're the idiot. Or you think I am."

"I haven't seen this letter before, and I didn't order any murder. Why should I? It makes no sense. How is your King Barad 'in the way'?"

Fillim's look was hard. "Isn't it obvious?"

*

"You must admit the arrest made a curious end to the morning," Talinti said to Meriden, as they sat in The Consul's Chair, trying to eat beef pasties with dignity, and licking their fingers when they failed.

"Oh, yes. I was thinking of making a show for Christmas out of the Council. If you approve?"

Talinti smiled. "As long as there's a part for Mritta."

"Mritta can play the Queensister, with a wooden sword. And I can be the villainous Errios, if Brod isn't well enough. A pity Kariam missed it," he added. "She would've enjoyed a moment of vengeance." Kariam had asked leave to spend the morning visiting dear friends and old haunts. "As long as you're back in time for the funeral." "Of course, my lady," and she'd disappeared with a happy swirl of skirt.

"But I cannot see the reason -" Talinti was

beginning, when -

"Well met, kinswoman! You remember our friend Ardas, son of Gaskor, d'you not?" The tavern was abruptly full of people. Tormenas, the Jaryari captain from two days before, a grandly-dressed woman and a short-haired female servant. "My lady, may I present my cousin Talinti of Lithermayg? Lady Yairil of Qasadan," he said, allowing awe to edge his voice; and he bowed, and Talinti rose and curtsied, and they all sat down.

Talinti was conscious of gravy growing sticky on her hands. She couldn't know if there was any on her face.

Lady Yairil was a thin slow-moving woman with a highly-jewelled hat, and many rings. Ardas said to her, "These are the local citizens who stopped my comrades thrashing a boy in the street."

"We're not quite local," said Talinti. She'd had more than enough questioning about Upali's words, so she went on, "I'm visiting my kinsman, and finding the Council very interesting. This is my steward, Meriden, son of Andor." She emphasised the last three words slightly. People said that in Jaryar servants only had one name, or none.

Ardas ignored this, but leant forward to say quietly, "There's a young man over there staring at you, madam."

Talinti couldn't see beyond his bulk, but Meriden said, "The lad with the feathered hat? He's one of the attendants to the Vard delegation."

Watching me? thought Talinti, trying for an indifferent shrug. She was irritated by more signs of petty intrigue.

For no reason, she thought *I did know that man in blue in the alley from somewhere. Whoever he was, he may have had a perfectly good reason for being near the kitchens. Near the kitchens just before a murder.*

Tormenas returned from placing an order with the host. All were silent, waiting for the Lady of Qasadan to speak, or not, as she chose.

"You have a fine city," she said at last, inclining her head, and blinking at a space between Tormenas and Talinti.

"Nothing to be named in the same breath as Makkera, or your own city of Adjef, but I hope your ladyship is finding your historic errand profitable and pleasant as well as, uh, worthy." Tormenas had failed to find another word beginning with "p". "Vach-roysh is happy to welcome all of the electors."

Ardas said lazily, "And so, my friend, you said

something about special prices for the high-born visitors, did you not? Your shop is on St Peter's Well Street?"

"I do business from my home there, certainly, but I also have a booth on the edge of the market."

Tormenas is making good use of his opportunities, Talinti thought.

Ardas said to her, "I think I saw you standing at the back, madam? What did you think of this morning?"

"Do you believe this man Errios is a killer?" she asked warily.

Lady Yairil said, "You foreigners think all Jaryari are killers. That's our name here, we know. *'Arrogant dreams, and murdering swords.'* Forgetting the gratitude you owe us for protecting the west from Ricossan tyranny."

Talinti saw the graves after the Battle of the Lither, and she thought even Meriden, even *Tormenas*, stiffened. *Your soldiers burned our villages to protect us, did they?* She said nothing.

Ardas tapped his fingers on the table, and said abruptly, "Aye, to a Haymonese I wager this Errios is a monster, and murder is no surprise. But to us - I've known men and women who fought with him, and they spoke him reasonable fair. He must have grown addled with hate in his age."

"If he did it alone," said his lady. The tavern lad leant in to place jug, cups and plates of cheese on the table. She ignored him, and went on, "Young Duke Haras has no name for good sense. I doubt a loyal man like Errios would commit murder without orders from above."

"He was pouring out enough hate this morning," said Ardas.

"If it was all true," said Talinti. Some parts she badly wanted not to be true. She and her father had had no control over the treatment of Jaryari prisoners in their pens, but the thought of rape and torture on or near Lithermayg made her sick.

Ardas shrugged. "Someone cut off his fingers. But as for all those tales of horror from the past -"

"Every country has its dark tales," said Tormenas.

"Of course they have. So some children were burnt alive in Marod two hundred years ago. On Qasadan we were still eating each other back then." He shrugged. "What these high folk from Vard and Makkera don't understand is, why should we on Qasadan hate Marod? They do us no harm. Maybe they raid into Marithon and An, maybe over your border too. But our quarrels are with the ships from

Baronda. We've no problems with Queen Nerranya and her Thirty. Am I speaking too free, my lady? This is what I've heard in your hall."

"I have no hatred for the Queen. But that doesn't mean that anyone will vote for her," said Lady Yairil. "Even after tomorrow's revelations."

"Aye," Ardas explained to Tormenas and Talinti, "the gossip is that it will all be made clear tomorrow. Some wild-eyed prophetess is here, and she'll proclaim God's word, tell us whether Errios is guilty or not, which side are the devil's spawn, and which the angels of light. Perhaps."

"Or perhaps not," said Talinti uncomfortably.

"Aye. Maybe it'll be all -" He waggled his fingers as if imitating smoke, and lowered his voice. "*Marod is a half-eaten bowl of cherries, and Vard is a belt without a buckle, and the goat will leap to the stars. Make sense of that.* My apologies, my lady, madam. I didn't mean to offend." He grinned.

Talinti was neither offended nor amused, but she was a little hurt. *Which is absurd.*

Lady Yairil gave a deep chuckle. "You will tell me all about it afterwards. I think I've been persuaded to spend tomorrow morning at this gentleman's shop, among others." She nodded at Tormenas, who tried to conceal triumph.

Ardas caught Talinti's eye, and said, "I stand with all you interested townsfolk and visitors by the wall, and listen and report back to my lady. Sometimes a dull task, but my duty. There's no need for her to attend herself, until the vote in the afternoon."

"Since Prince Abbos drowned, merchants have been cowardly about crossing the sea to Qasadan," Lady Yairil deigned to explain. "My children and I need decent cloth, and I require well-fitting gloves especially, and I want to find someone to paint a family portrait. Such things need to be selected personally. And, thanks to the Duke, there is money to spend."

Money to spend. Bribes to spend.

"So your decision is made, then?" said Talinti before she could stop herself. Her head still buzzing with anger, she jerked her head towards Lady Yairil's maid, who'd been standing silently beside the table all the time. "What are your views in this matter, madam? Do you agree with your lady? Does the Duke deserve to win?"

She saw Tormenas' shock. The woman stared. So did everyone.

"After all," said Talinti, "whoever rules Jaryar will

be your monarch also."

Once again, it was for Lady Yairil to fill the tingling silence, and no one else. "In Haymon," she said, "do you allow maids and peasantry to choose your Consuls?"

"No," Talinti admitted. "But they might have an opinion. Do you have one?" she asked Meriden. "You've heard the speeches."

"I do not, my lady," he said, to her annoyance. "But I'm flattered to be asked."

"Well, girl? Answer." The lady glared at her woman – not much younger than Talinti – who twisted her fingers together, and murmured, "I don't know - I don't -"

"Why, cousin," asked Tormenas, "is it worth lowly folk wasting their time on these high matters? Your steward is right. No matter how wise their thoughts, no one would take notice. This is true in any country. And while they pondered, the floors would go unswept and the children uncared-for."

"Alas, we're all against you," said Ardas, with a smile. He lifted his cup. "I'll have another of these, I think. And you?"

"I thank you, no. We have a funeral to attend."

"So the grand show is to be decided by bribes

behind the curtain," said Meriden as they walked back to the Palace. He sounded quite matter-of-fact about it, but Talinti was angry. Izzan would have said, *What did you expect?*

So she turned her mind to the funeral to come. She had been to too many funerals, but since Izzan's she was conscientious about them, which was why Kariam was under strict instructions to return by the second hour. Her maid was indeed waiting for them in the chamber – sometime storeroom, sometime office, currently guest room, crammed with the bed and the maid's pallet, and a desk and a chair and a crucifix on the wall. And a grate with enough ash, from yesterday's evening fire. Kariam protested inevitably, "But we barely knew her, my lady!"

"The people who knew and loved her are far away. The Marodi were kind to us on the boat."

So the three removed their hats and smeared ash in their hair as was the Haymonese way if not the Marodi, and went down to the Chapel.

*

The King left a guard in their rooms, in case the Jaryari tried any mischief, but the other sixteen Marodi grouped themselves formally together, looking sombre and with their sleeves cut, and Fillim led them in silent procession down the stairs, and into the Chapel. Lida noticed that other people fell silent as they passed, and she wondered if Jeppa would have been pleased.

That was the last time she thought of Jeppa, as a person, for some while.

The Abbot was conducting the Mass, assisted by two of the Palace priests, and the Archbishop of Makkera and the Holy Secretary sat in formal carved chairs at the side, as visiting dignitaries, and watched. This seemed to make Abbot Paul nervous, and it was a few prayers before he was properly audible to those standing before him. In the space between lay Jeppa, wrapped in white except for her face; not in a coffin, but on a bier, because she was to be burned afterwards. The pyre had been constructed in the courtyard during the morning's session, and Lida had gathered from the gapes and pointings that this was regarded in Haymon and Jaryar as odd.

She positioned herself to the side, and peeped around. The Duke and his friends hadn't come. (Errios was in prison, of course, *ha*.) But Lady Madigam walked in with a maid just before they started, and took her brother's arm. He looked at her fondly. There were the Lithermayg people, with bare and greyed heads. The Consuls and their bodyguards. And at the back stood half a dozen uncertain-looking folk in plain dress, some familiar. Servants from the Palace – and a few, short-haired, perhaps from Jaryar.

Fric stood next to her, staring at the ground, and twisting his fingers together, but no longer seeming afraid. He must have found a priest yesterday.

"Let us call our sins to mind, and seek God's forgiveness," intoned the Abbot, and all knelt to pray.

Lida had nothing in particular to repent of at present.

*

Six weeks after Izzan's death, Talinti had said, "Meriden, I need to talk to you," and had led the way briskly into her room. They sat down either side of the empty hearth, she facing the door, in the carved chair that came from her grandfather's house; he on the bench opposite. Neither of them looked towards the bed.

Probably he knew what she was going to say. It was hard to say it. *"I was lonely, I missed him so much, I couldn't bear to be alone."*

Four days on, they sat in dull Saturday afternoon sunlight, waiting, until she had the strength to say,

"Meriden. I'm going to confession this evening. I will confess what we – I - have done, and Sister Salome will assign me some penance, and make me promise not to do it again."

Meriden said nothing.

"I've treated you very badly."

"No, my lady."

"I have. I'm sorry."

She was looking straight across the small table, at the lacings on his brown jacket. The plainest jacket, because this morning he'd been inspecting fishpond repairs, and there would have been mud. Contrary to what they say in tales, it's not easy to read a face. What would she see if she looked up at him? Anger, confusion, hurt?

"Such things happen," said Meriden. Which they both knew was true.

"They should not." Also true.

She looked up.

And what she saw was dislike. She heard it, too – dislike edged with cruelty – as he said, "I suppose you don't want me to tell anyone."

That had not occurred to her. In her guilt and shame, she hadn't considered the things he could now say about her, laughing, to an eager audience, next week, next month, next year, in the taverns or the market places. What he could say about her to her children.

Unless she took measures, made threats, to ensure that he would not.

There was a silence. "I will not, of course." He stood up, and surprised her with, "He was a good man." That was generous. Izzan hadn't been popular with the servants. "I am sorry for your loss."

"Yes," she whispered.

He leaned across and kissed her briefly on the lips, and walked out.

A kiss she had not authorised; one he had taken. That she could have dismissed him for.

She went to confession, not mentioning names, and learned to sleep alone; and over time wept less often for Izzan. Meriden, so far as she knew, told nobody; and years passed. But she couldn't quite forget what they had done, silently, sinfully, in the dark.

It was as well he disliked her, she thought. Otherwise she would have been tempted to do it again.

*

"We have been told," Abbot Paul concluded, "that Jeppa,

daughter of Anam, was a loyal and valuable servant to her King and her country, and so she was. But she is gone now where such words do not matter. She is where all the redeemed are alike servants of God, and all alike ladies and lords in glory. A place where every secret is revealed, and the humblest good deed is remembered. Amen."

"Amen." They all crossed themselves, and the holy bit was over. Four Marodi soldiers and servants, including Yaif, lifted the bier and carried it out, and everyone followed. To Lida's deep amusement, Kalla had to rouse Mistress Fillim, who'd fallen asleep leaning against a pillar. She nudged Fric, and he giggled.

There were many more people gathered in the courtyard to watch. Lida saw the evil Duke himself, standing at an upper window with his stepmother. Jeppa's wrapped body was laid on the box-shaped pile of logs. A Palace guard passed the King a lighted brand, and the Abbot prayed, "In the name of the Father -"

"Don't they bury people in Marod?" the Haymonese maid, the Chatterer, whispered.

Draider overheard. "When people die at home, we bury them. When they die in a foreign land, we burn them, and take the ashes back. The Marodi rest in Marod."

"Except Gormad the Lucky," said the steward unexpectedly.

Draider glared at the contradiction, but had to agree, "Except him."

The fire had been set, and all along their side orange snapped and danced upwards.

Like the fires of hell. She had saved Fric from them. She slipped round to her Prince, who was standing with the King - and with the Abbot and the Archbishop, the holy people. Almost (not quite) she felt she belonged here.

And to her enormous secret glee, she arrived in time to hear the Archbishop say, "I cannot think your words were well-chosen, Brother. What made you speak so, about all the redeemed in heaven?"

"Was the Abbot teaching bad doctrine?" asked the Prince with quiet interest.

"Not bad, but unwise, considering those listening today. Some were very low people. It is not helpful or kind to encourage them to think themselves higher than their place."

The Abbot looked suitably abashed. (*Good word. Bash him.*) But King Barad shook his dark head all too solemnly, and said, "Ah, Your Reverence, you speak truly.

Brother Paul's words reminded me very strongly of my dear Aunt Sakirra. Weren't you reminded, Madi?"

"Aunt Sakirra would not have approved."

"No," he said, and there was definite mischief in his voice. The Archbishop tilted her head a little suspiciously. "There was a supper at my aunt's home, when I was about fifteen, and the local priest was invited. She didn't like him; he was always warning her, and all her guests, about hellfire and damnation, and on this occasion he mentioned the burning flames again, and she said, 'It's fortunate that my maid knows how to use a fan, and will be able to cool me down.'" The King flapped his hand near his face expressively. "The priest was a brave man, and he dared to suggest that her maid, unlike her, might be in heaven, and she raised one eyebrow - I can't do it so well - and said, 'Then I shall send for her.'"

He smiled at the Archbishop, and Lady Madigam laughed. No one seemed to know what to say, until the Archbishop's secretary said timidly, "I think, Your Reverence, we're wanted back in the Theatre."

Four soldiers (two Marodi, two Haymonese) were being left to guard the fire, now burning hot and fiercely. Sparks tumbled upwards. As Lida followed her King and

Prince past the servants and Palace hangers-on, a group that had grown from those in the Chapel, she heard a low murmur, and realised that it was a song.

That song. The poor people at Dendarry sometimes sang it on the road walking away from a funeral. It was in the Old Tongue, no longer respectable, the language of riff-raff. She caught as usual "dlee", the only word she knew, which meant "death", and she looked at the faces of the singers, staring at the ground, and wondered why they were singing for Jeppa.

The Archbishop scowled.

The Lithermayg woman was looking very shocked about something. Perhaps she was unused to burnings.

Their group came level with Fillim Queensister, waiting to join them.

"I'll see you later, brother," said Lady Madigam. She hesitated, and then said, "Take care of yourself."

"We've caught the murderer, Madi."

"I hope so. Why – why in any madness would anyone want to kill you?"

King Barad shrugged. Then he looked up at his adopted people, and said, "So. We've mourned the dead, and are ready to avenge her. Then all that remains will be to win the vote."

"And by God's grace we will," said the Prince.

*

The Duke and his friends (not Errios) were in the Theatre before them, looking politely impatient. Electors were winding their way to their benches, and Lida and others pushed slowly to the back.

The Consul Invildi rose. "I am permitted by delegates of both sides to inform you all that, following Monday night's murder, the chamber of Errios, son of Broxos, was searched, and a letter was found, seemingly confirming orders from him to kill the King of Marod. He and his servant and another man are still being questioned. No one is suggesting any guilt on the part of the rest of the delegation."

Merely a statement of what everyone had already heard. But Antonos stood up and asked, "Do the investigators have any idea why Errios would wish to do such a thing?"

"King Barad is described in the letter as to be put 'out of the way'," said Fillim. "I think a simple reason could be found. If my King were to die, Queen Nerranya could in theory marry again. She could marry Duke Haras, and unite their two claims."

"You think I'd want to marry her?"

"Others might wish it for you, my lord," said Fillim, smiling tightly.

"She's my first cousin!"

"You've already heard that your father considered such a marriage, long ago. Errios may have thought it a possibility."

"Errios and perhaps others," said Prince Braidoc.

Everyone in the Theatre, Lida thought, was fascinated by the exchange.

Antonos didn't sit down. He turned to the rows of electors, and said, "We must continue with the Council. But let me say this, to make it quite clear. My colleague, my friend, Errios, may be accused, but he hasn't been found guilty. This evidence hasn't been examined closely, or tested. He insists that it's false.

"If it is not false, then I deeply regret and repudiate his actions. We all do. No such violence was ever authorised by any of the rest of us." He spread out his hands. "If Errios did this, and you all heard this morning how he hates the Marodi, then he acted out of some crazed fury, a madman, alone."

"If he did it, but I dare say it's all lies!" cried the Duke, jumping up. He took two steps towards the King, who met his gaze courteously. "There was no murder plot at all, is my guess! Errios warned us to beware of the Marodi. It occurs to *me*, sir, that the person who is dead is this Jeppa. Poisoned with a sweet that she took from the table – from your place? What easier than to poison it, hand it to her, and then exclaim that someone is trying to kill you? No risk to you, only an excellent chance to accuse us!"

The silence was complete, except for the Duke's pants. Then the King said quietly, "You are accusing me of this murder, my lord?"

"No," Antonos was murmuring, but the Duke lifted his chin, and said,

"That seems to me the obvious explanation."

The King stood up. He walked forward without haste until they stood very close to each other, and every eye in the room was on him.

"Jeppa, daughter of Anam, had been in my service since I married the Queen," he said - not loudly, but everyone could hear. "She had a husband and two children in Stonehill, who don't yet know they are widowed and motherless. You suggest I deliberately killed this faithful woman, for no reason but to make false accusations and have your friend hanged? When I arrived here, I gave up my sword, but when I leave, I'll take it again. Withdraw that allegation, or meet me wherever you please after this debate is over, and I will kill you."

He was in fact slightly the shorter of the two, but Lida had no doubt whatever that he would kill him.

Duke Haras licked his lips. "It's a possibility," he said.

"The investigation is considering all possibilities. Withdraw your accusation, or I will kill you."

"Very well," he muttered. "I withdraw it."

The King bowed, and turned away. Over his shoulder, he said, "By the bye, my lord, I suppose you're aware that your good friend Antonos is fucking your stepmother?"

There seemed to be a single gasp from the hall. The Duke spluttered. "What –"

"One insult for another," said the King. "But unlike yours, mine is true."

"That is a lie!" cried Antonos.

"She wasn't alone with you in your bedchamber yesterday afternoon? You were both somewhere else?"

He sat down. Lida's heart swelled. She saw – everyone saw – Duke Haras stare at Antonos, and Antonos look back, and then away.

There were the final two speeches of the day. On behalf of the Queen, Fillim made promises to respect Jaryari traditions and laws; and Antonos spoke of something or other, the ancient ties between the nine provinces that did not include Marod. And then old Jaikkad announced that tomorrow they would hear the Prophecy (excitement murmured around the room) and the electors would ask questions and debate, and then a vote would be taken, in writing, in secret. And then it was over.

Lida scurried up to her prince as the session finished, Fric at her heels. Several electors were gathered round him. "Praise God for keeping you safe, Your Grace, and sparing your Queen and people such a terrible bereavement. The man must have been mad." She thought it was the Duke of Indesandu.

"Thank you for your kind words."

As the party moved off, the King still talking to Duke Voros, Lida picked out more murmurs.

"This Antonos is a married man. He doesn't live with his wife, but still."

"Aye. Two adulterers and a murderer! That's who the Duke brought to persuade us he was God's choice for Jaryar!"

"Queen Nerranya may be a foreigner, but she seems to live clean."

"And she'll know there's more to Jaryar than just Marithon and An and Vard. She's travelled to Lefayr."

"He's never been off his grand estate, I wager."

It was all so good.

Fric ran up to his mistress. "Will they hang him soon?" he asked.

"What?"

"The murderer – will they hang him?"

"All murderers deserve death."

"And this one especially," Draider added.

Fillim breathed in, looking down, and narrowing her nose. "Fric, run along, and play, or something, before we dine."

"Yes, madam." He grinned, and ran off.

There was something wrong with Fillim's face. It was pale, it was shocked, it was - doomed, Lida thought. She was watching Fric go, and then she turned to stare after Duke Voros. Lida thought she murmured, 'No. Not possible." Which was strange.

The delegation, with Lida, Yaif, Secretary Kalla and Brother Jude, crossed the hall to the South Tower, leading to their rooms. The Abbot came flapping up to the front. "Here is my lecture," muttered the King. To Brother Paul, "I know what you would say. It was undisciplined and unseemly."

The Abbot panted. "And if I may, Your Grace, it was unkind. The Duke had insulted you, but Antonos hadn't, nor had the Duchess. None of us would like our secrets thrown to the world."

The King gave him a quick startled look. *But surely kings don't have bad secrets*, Lida thought. Any more than she did.

She helpfully jumped forward to open the door for everybody.

"So, Fillim," said King Barad, "let's hear the evidence properly."

*

"That scene will be in my play," said Meriden, as people began to shift towards the doors. "When the Duke threatened – no, when the *King* threatened to kill the *Duke*. Unless you don't wish it. Are you ill, my lady?"

"No – I – no." Talinti tried to smile. Her head was twisting inside.

Ever since the funeral, when she had seen – and recognised – that man. It was certainly him. And so - He might have had a good reason for being there. He might. If not -

"Where are the Marodi?"

"They've gone to their rooms, I suppose." Meriden sounded puzzled.

They were at the door. "I will go back with you to Tormenas', and then I need you to write to her. To Mistress Fillim," she added.

"Again? My lady -" Meriden stopped, staring ahead. He glanced around the courtyard to see if anyone was close by. Then, "My lady, some people think – some people are saying that we're putting ourselves forward too much, and intruding on the Council's business -"

"Some people! I don't care what 'some people' say!" It was a relief to be angry.

"No, my lady. Mistress Fillim may not be pleased, either."

She may not, indeed. Lady Yairil's words came back to her: *"I doubt a loyal man like Errios would commit murder without orders from above."*

So are they all in it, all the Marodi? All their exclaiming just a pretence?

They walked along a broad pleasant street; shadows were darkening, but the house-walls were still fresh white. Like the whited sepulchres in the Bible. And high. Somewhere church bells began to toll the hour.

"Meriden," she said suddenly, "would a servant – or a squire – commit murder without orders? What do you think?"

She watched his surprise, and then his thought. "If it were a private murder. I have sometimes been tempted to murder Kariam. I wouldn't kill any of your enemies without your leave." A serious smile.

"No." Talinti was remembering the horrible hours the day before. "A Queensister, just for example, is a great person in Marod. Any servant would obey her, and *she* would obey her lords. When she questioned you and Kariam yesterday, what d'you think? Was she truly searching for answers? Or merely seeking a confession, a scapegoat?" She stared at her hands before her.

"If she'd only wanted a confession, and didn't care whether it were true, she would've been more violent, I think."

And besides, she thought, *Errios was a more convenient scapegoat. Very much more.*

They were silent until they arrived back at the house, and walked in to find food-preparation bustle, and Tormenas bouncing his little daughter in his arms. The look he turned on Talinti was wary – part annoyance, part apprehension. She was familiar with such expressions from home.

"I am sorry, cousin, for upsetting your friends at noon," she said, not quite gritting her teeth.

"Don't worry. I think the lady will still want her reduced-price gloves tomorrow. But a word, if I may." He thrust the child into Kariam's surprised arms, turned an obvious shoulder to Meriden, and led Talinti through the back kitchen, and out to the yard.

They stood between the privy and the hen-house. "I don't know what your man told you about our conversation, but I think you're angry with me."

"He told me nothing I'd not already guessed. You offered him money to betray my trust. Is the message I bring worth so much to you?" Her head was aching, but she had to be polite. She had a question for him in return.

He sighed. "Talinti, I'm a merchant. I need to turn strangers into customers, and I do this by making them *friends*. Everyone knows that in Vard-town the Duchess is everything. If when I'm next there, she remembered me as the man who brought her good news – news that she had before her enemies - that would be useful for me, yes. That's how we work. D'you think the Marodi aren't looking for advantages, too?"

Fillim had asked, and the Prince's servant, and Jeppa. "No."

"So, yes, that's why I pestered you about the prophecy. Can we still be friends?" He put a charming smile on his face, and she dragged up one to match.

"Of course. Tormenas, do you remember, the first afternoon, after the Duke rode in, you and I walked back to the Palace, and a man came out of an alley, and you said the Palace kitchens were down there? He nearly knocked into a woman selling cakes."

"I remember mentioning the kitchens, but I don't remember a particular person."

"I'm sure there was a man. He was rubbing his fingers on a cloth, and he looked nervous. A big man, in a blue jacket. I thought at the time I'd seen him before, and now I know. He was at the funeral. He is one of the Marodi."

Tormenas was pushing open the door. "You're suggesting," he said slowly, "that he might have had something to do with the murder. A spy for Errios."

"He wasn't the little one they brought in for us to identify. I should tell Mistress Fillim."

"You wanted to write," said Meriden. He was standing waiting for her, with parchment and pen.

Tormenas scowled at him. "It's supper-time, sir. Cousin, is this not over-scrupulous? She asked you all her questions yesterday, and you told her everything."

"Everything I knew or remembered then. This is something new."

But now they were in the hall, plates and silverware and peppered cabbage, with pork and bread, on the table, and he waved her firmly to a place, and cleared his throat, in preparation for giving thanks to God. In courtesy, she had to nod Meriden to his and Brod's backroom, and sit down.

After a few mouthfuls, Tormenas set down his knife, put one elbow on the table, and twisted to look at her. "There was a man in the street. It means nothing. It will of certainty mean nothing to Mistress Fillim, and will only irritate her. Errios of Girifay is an enemy of us all. He hired a spy – this we know" – he jerked his head at the nodding Kariam – "and he arranged this murder. There's no reason to believe otherwise."

"Have you ever watched a hanging, Tormenas?" Talinti asked.

"Of course."

"So have I. I have ordered them. I think he's innocent."

His face struggled to cover anger with politeness.

"I know," said Talinti. "I do this all the time at home; cause trouble. So my uncle says."

*

Errios was fed, and then left to rot with one of the Consul's Guards at the door. He demanded his servant, and was told that she was being detained and questioned elsewhere, but was unharmed. Possibly a lie.

"If you hurt her, you will regret it for a long time."

He was surrounded by lies. *I'm not fitted for this work.* Had he completely failed, or was it just a mess created by someone else, into which he'd been dragged? Who had betrayed him?

He was very angry.

It was a small, dimly-lit room, but it was a room, not a cell. He wanted to sit still and dignified, like a great warrior of old, but he couldn't. Instead, he got up and walked around the table as briskly as he could, which wasn't very brisk, under the eyes of the pig-faced Guard. His joints nipped at him and he stumbled, so he moved to stand by the shuttered window, staring at wood-grain to hide his humiliation. He was a soldier. But he'd handed in his sword.

When he was tired, too soon, he sat down to clench his fists and think curses. He cursed the Marodi: the whole country; the individual delegates; and the Queen; he cursed the Consuls and their investigators; he cursed Asor; and he cursed himself for having hired someone who was incompetent at best, a double-dealer at worst.

Antonos' instructions, that day in the Duchess' room. "Get us a spy. We need to know their secrets, and how happily or unhappily they all live together. We may be able to prise them apart." That was what he'd done.

Could someone else have given Asor different instructions, pretending they were from him? Or had the fool thought of this for himself? That letter – if it wasn't from Asor – if Fillim Queensbitch was telling the truth -

then a killer was protecting themselves with false evidence. One of his delegation? Was it his duty to take on their guilt, even confess to and die for it? He'd always thought himself loyal, but at that his soul revolted. The Duke - a generous and rather quiet child he'd been, between tantrums. Antonos, so smooth and pleasant. The Archbishop, with her aloof stare. The Duchess, whom he knew to be ruthless and clever. Had they arranged for him to be the scapegoat, if one were needed? Was that why he'd been chosen to come?

Or had Asor acted alone?

Or could the murderer be some spurned lover of this woman's – or of the King's? Someone from his Haymonese youth who had reason to hate him, nothing to do with the Council?

Light faded, and the single candle burned low. More guards came and escorted him to his own chamber, so they couldn't be accused of leaving a delegate without a bed, but he was plainly still a prisoner.

The shadows grew tall, as he sat in his chair. He reflected that trying to kill a king is a very serious crime. Were such people merely hanged in Haymon, or were they burnt, or cut to pieces while still alive, as they would have been in Jaryar? Did it make a difference that it wasn't a Haymonese king?

People would call him a murderer. If Vard lost the vote, they would blame him. What would the Duke be willing to do for such a one, or for his family?

He thought of never seeing his grandchildren again, and suddenly he was shaking unstoppably, and his eyes were filled with tears.

*

There were torches at street corners, but in between was dark. The bells were tolling again, jangling Talinti's nervous shoulders as she and Meriden walked the now-familiar path to the Palace. As soon as one set finished, another began, and it seemed a while before there was quiet. Then she could say, "Don't come to the Marodi with me. Please wait in the Outer Hall."

He glanced at her. "You shouldn't go there alone, my lady."

Perhaps he shared her unease. *The King, who spoke so easily of killing. The Prince, with his black clothes, and his glittering eyes. Mistress Fillim, sworn to kill for them, who left corpses behind her at the river. The Abbot - she knew no ill of him, but only the very simple think every monk is a saint.*

They might all be in it.

She'd brought three innocent people to this city; and there were Tormenas and his household to consider also.

So, "I will go in alone, if the guards allow, and you will wait. You have the second copy. If I don't return to send you home in, let's say an hour, take it to whichever of the Consuls you can find. And ask them for protection for you and the others." Her heart thumped, as she spoke her fear aloud. She smiled. "But I'm sure such precautions aren't necessary."

"This is why you left Kariam back at the house," he said thoughtfully.

They walked on, past a large building so brightly lit and flower-festooned that it was plainly a whorehouse, and a couple of Consuls' Guards in their red jackets patrolling in case of trouble. The female gave Talinti a hard look, but evidently decided they weren't sufficiently suspicious to be stopped.

Round a corner. With an effort, "Despite all this, it's a beautiful city. Do you not think?"

"I don't care for the city," he said, after a pause.

"You'd prefer to spend all your life at home with

the chickens? You have no interest in anywhere or anything else? In the vote?" He was maddening her, as so often.

"No. I am interested in my duty," he said, flat and dull, and she felt such a mixture of fear and exasperation that she nearly hit him, and had to turn away, clutching her hands together.

Give me something, she thought.

And then he did.

"At home, in the country," said Meriden, staring forward at the cobbles, "we could be anyone. Here, I'm reminded -"

"Reminded?"

"Of who we are."

"Who we are? Haymonese?"

He shrugged.

Haymonese. *"The country of flowers and cowards."*

Talinti felt very curious, but reminded herself that she was entitled to her servants' obedience, not their secret thoughts. "I don't mean to pry. There's nothing here then?"

"Nothing." Perhaps feeling he was being rude, which he was, he said, "I think tomorrow I'll try to visit the Garden Kariam mentioned. Where King Garayn is buried."

He did have a strange affinity for graves.

They walked on in silence, but she was glad that he was there.

*

Years before, Lida had heard her uncle ask her mother, "Is she really as shallow as she appears?" She knew they were talking about her, but she was distracted by the lovely word "shallow" (water twisting itself in knots on the surface of streams; sunlight dancing on ripples) and she didn't hear the answer. It was some time before she understood that "shallow" wasn't supposed to be a good thing for a person to be.

Now she wished she were truly shallow. She stood at the High Table in the Great Hall, waiting on her master, and her bowels were heavy and sick and cold, and her back coated with shiver, and she could barely swallow. A shallow person perhaps could throw it off, and move her mind on to the next exciting day, and again and again she tried to do this, but she could not.

She was guilty. If she didn't get rid of this thing, of what she had done, or rather had failed to do, she would bear it for ever. And maybe go to hell. ("What if I die before I confess?" Fric had asked. So blithely she'd said, "That's not likely." But it was possible.)

She had to get to confession *now*, and the feast was going on forever.

There was chatter among the electors in the Hall – little twiddles of talk beneath the acres of smoky air, and the arched ceiling fading into gloom. And there was delicate music, songs from minstrels walking up and down between rows with their lutes.

A dark-faced man with a bushy beard brought his song to an abrupt end just below the dais, and strummed a loud discord. Lida jumped; her hands trembled, and a dish slipped. She grabbed at it, but not before some of the baked onion sauce splattered on the table, narrowly missing Prince Braidoc's black sleeve, and everyone – well, the Prince, and Brother Jude, and the old Consul and the handsome Vard squire – looked at her. "Your pardon, my prince," she stammered.

The High Table was heavy with the absence of Errios from the Vard end. Lida couldn't bear to look at his empty place. Only the King and Invildi seemed able to talk, and they discussed news from Haymon – mostly new building projects since the King had left three years before. The Consul's smooth voice should have calmed anyone, like snow on a garden, covering all blemishes. But Lida couldn't listen. Again and again her mind watched the moments upstairs when she could have spoken – should have spoken – a mere "But" would have stopped them – and she hadn't. And so she was guilty. *Thou shalt not bear false witness:* she hadn't exactly done that, but nearly.

("He confessed to part of it, to hiring the spy, but not the rest," Fillim had said. "There'll have to be a trial, even perhaps an appeal; all that will take time. But the Vard people may not admit his guilt, and want to delay -"

And so they'd gone on and on, and Lida hadn't said, "But.")

The dinner was over at last, and there were no sweetmeats. "You were clumsy tonight. Make sure you sleep well, to be fresh for tomorrow. Tomorrow the electors argue," Prince Braidoc told her curtly. "I do not need you – I am going to pray in my chamber. We need much prayer." He turned away to speak to Yaif.

Prayer. Yes. At last.

Lida bowed, dodged away from Fric, and slid towards the door. Out. She wound her way past all the bunches of people chattering, and the guards, and the occasional single figures walking from task to task, and found her way to the Chapel.

Without the funeral crowds, it was a big and empty room. Kings and queens had worshipped here once. On either side of the altar were containers like jugs, full of tall fresh flowers. The wooden floor echoed. There were two candles on the altar, but no other light. And there were no people, except one woman kneeling at the rail.

Lida waited, itching in the cold, until this person rose, and then approached her. She was in black, so she would do. *Now.*

"Your pardon, sister, but may I – may I make confession?"

"Oh, you startled me! You cannot confess to me, child. I'm only a novice." She looked down her long nose at Lida.

She must do it. Even though the thought scared her.

"Please! It's very urgent."

"It may be - wait here." So the woman went away through a side door, and Lida twisted her fingers, and stared up at a painting of Moses holding the Ten Commandments and looking very stern, and tried to plan what to say.

"One of the visiting priests can hear you. Over

there."

"I thank you, Sister." At the side of the chapel was a series of niches set in the wall. Each had a cushion to kneel on; each had a shutter through to where the priest waited.

Lida knelt down, crossed herself, drew a curtain across hiding her from anyone else in the chapel, and, with her heart beating and her stomach crawling, knocked on the shutter.

It slid open, but in the darkness she couldn't expect to see anyone. "Speak," said a deep voice.

Priests ceased to be Brother or Sister in the confessional. "Bless-me-Father-for-I-have-sinned," she'd gabbled, before she realised that she knew the voice. *Oh, please God, not him. Not him!*

There was a pause, and he had to prompt her. "How long has it been?"

"It's been eight days since my last confession."

"What have you to confess?" asked Abbot Paul.

"I - I told a story that insulted our guests" (because he would remember) "but I was punished for that – and -"

"And," he said.

Deep breath. "There's a man accused of murder, and they were saying what the evidence was, and I knew part of it was wrong, and I should have told them, but I didn't."

This time he paused. "What evidence was wrong?"

"Mistress Fillim said a letter was found in his chamber, that proved his guilt, but he didn't put it there, I did. When I was delivering the King's invitations. It was with all the rest of them, and the wine for the Duke."

More pause. "Why did you put the letter there?"

"I was given – I offered to deliver them all. The Palace servant didn't seem to want to go. I didn't know it was anything different from the rest." *Please*.

"We're talking about the accusations against Errios of what-is-it? Of Girifay. Why didn't you speak up?"

This was the important question, the one about motive. Lida screwed up her face, and twisted her fingers, and tried to be honest. Because God knows all. "I thought I couldn't interfere. Mistress Fillim knows everything, or seemed to. And everyone laughed at me yesterday." Her voice grew quieter. "And a little because he was so hateful."

"Do you have anything more, daughter?"

"No, Father."

So she waited, still a little nervous, but mostly relieved, for her penance. It was said, and off her shoulders, and even hours of prayers would be worth it.

"Your penance will be to say the Our Father."

"How many times?"

"Once. And to put right what you've done wrong."

What could he mean? The surprised relief at the "once" turned to horror. "I can't put it right."

"You must. Or you must try. Or you will not be absolved."

"But I've got to be forgiven! I've got to be! When you sin, you confess, and it's gone! It's just gone! That's what you do, give penance, and forgive!" She couldn't stop the complaint bursting out. "I'll do any number of prayers."

"God is not a shopkeeper." A cruel horrible pause. "Do you think you can buy forgiveness with your many words, like the heathen?"

But my master does.

"Our Lord died so that any who repent and trust are forgiven, whatever they have done. We cannot pay for forgiveness – it's all His grace and mercy. Penance merely proves the repentance is real.

"I see no repentance, if you leave these people suspected of murder, and you know the accusation is false. Show your sorrow by amending your life." Lida squeaked.

"If they're hanged, their deaths will be on your soul. You don't want that, at thirteen."

I'm fourteen! Lida thought, a shallow complaint on top of her despair.

"You will do your best to put it right, by explaining to the necessary people."

The necessary people. The King, the Prince, the Consuls, Mistress Fillim. I can't. "How - how can I?" *How could she drag them back to what was settled, how could she make them listen to a mere squire, would they even believe her?*

"That's what we can talk about. Stand up."

He closed his shutter, and Lida clambered off her knees, wiping her damp face with the back of one hand.

The Abbot came through the door, moving briskly. "Come over here, child. Now. Why did you deliver these things?"

Lida explained about the man who hadn't liked the look of the Vard tower. She described him as best she could.

"What exactly did you deliver?"

"There was an invitation for each of them, Secretary Kalla had written them. So the Duke had an invitation and a letter, sealed, and a bottle of wine, and the Archbishop had an invitation and another letter, sealed with the Abbot's seal – your seal."

"Yes, I sent a courtesy letter to my Archbishop. And the others?"

"There was nothing but the invitation for Antonos, but Errios had that and also the other letter as well. The one Mistress Fillim read to us."

She glanced up at his face. He was pushing out his lips thoughtfully. "Well. Errios' sight is poor. Did you put it together with the invitation?"

"No. I was told by the man – the invitation in the centre of the desk, the other one in a corner, underneath a book. He was very fussy about it."

"Underneath a book. Not many people move books. Did you read this letter? How can you be sure it was the same one?"

"It was folded, and there was a plain seal. But the parchment was torn around it, so the letter was already open. I thought that was odd." He nodded. "I'm sure it was the one Mistress Fillim showed us – there was a little mark at the edge."

"You may have to swear that this is true, Lida."

"It is true!"

"Lord, have mercy." The Abbot put his hands over his face. His fingers seemed to shake. Then he took them away. "Well."

She jumped at the sound of footsteps; it was Brother Jude. "Thank you for coming, Brother." The Abbot swallowed, and went on more strongly, but waggling his hands. "I need you to identify and find one of the Palace servants – an elderly man with not much hair, and what there is greying, pale, a small beard, and with three or four black spots on his cheek. Ask him to come with you to – to the King's chamber as soon as possible. If he won't come, send a message to me there. When you've found him, do not leave him."

"No, Brother Abbot." The monk bowed, and scurried away.

"I don't understand," said Lida nervously.

"It's not merely a question of your soul. Who gave him the letter? False evidence in a murder investigation. There is great danger here until we can find the truth. Come."

He led her towards the door, robes flapping. But then he stopped abruptly and turned. "You told me these things under the secrecy of confession. You can tell the

King and the others, or I can, but only with your leave. You may choose which."

Lida nodded. They marched on through the Palace, which was quietening down now, corridors shadowy. Abbot Paul moved briskly for his age and bulk, and when she glanced at his face, it was grim. This wasn't reassuring, but somehow he was. A solid man. She remembered him swinging his staff over the heads of the robbers by the river.

Master Draider and another guard were at the passage door. "Greetings." The Abbot took a deep breath. "I need you, if you would, to request all the delegation to assemble at the King's chamber immediately. And we'll need, oh," he screwed up his face, "the secretary - Kalla - and Yaif as well. And yourself." Draider looked curious, unused to even polite orders from the Abbot. Who coughed, but went on, "Jude is on an errand, but please let him through when he comes."

In the midst of her confusion and fear, Lida felt excitement. Something was happening. She and Brother Paul were making something happen.

They knocked. The King was sitting writing, with Kalla beside him. "My apologies, Your Grace." The Abbot bowed awkwardly. "I've presumed to summon all the delegation here. We have something to discuss."

"This is proving a long day," said the King, but he gestured a welcome. Prince Braidoc entered, and raised his eyebrows questioningly at Lida. She gave him an apologetic look. It had occurred to her that perhaps she should have gone to him first. Kalla got up, so that he could sit down.

Draider Queensbrother. Fillim Queensister. "What's wrong?"

"My apologies to you all. Lida was too shy earlier in this room to tell what she knew -"

Yaif came in, bowed, and sat down cross-legged by the wall as usual.

"What she knew?"

Running footsteps. Brother Jude ran in. "Your pardon, Your Grace, my prince," he said, gasping for breath. "The man you sent me for, Brother, is dead."

The Long Night

Everyone stared at him in bewilderment.

The King's chamber was large, and hung with tapestries. Pointed windows, glazed with small square panes, hadn't yet been shuttered for the night, but all outside was dark. There was a large bed with white and gold hangings, a fire in one wall, two chairs and a desk, carved in honey-coloured wood - and now nine people. The air was full of breathing, and confused looks.

"What man is this? Who is dead?" asked the King.

The monk glanced pleadingly at the Abbot, who helped him. "I – it's the man who would've delivered our letters to the Vard delegation, if Lida hadn't done so, as we heard yesterday. I thought we needed to speak to him." The Abbot had raised one hand to his forehead, and seemed unable to take it away.

Dead, Lida thought numbly.

"His name was Gardis. I went to the servants' dormitory, and he was lying on his bed. I called the steward and the Consuls' investigator – they're there now. He - he was just lying dead – no sign of violence." Brother Jude started to shake.

"Or poison?" The Abbot's voice scraped.

"He didn't look - discoloured, or, or anything. I don't know."

"I should go," said Fillim, crossing towards the door, but the Abbot dragged his hand away from his face to wave vaguely at her. "First, Mistress, may I tell you why we are here? I think you – you said earlier that the man Asor admitted spying on us, that he said the Duke's guards had orders to let him through to leave a message for Errios, but, *but,*" he shook his head confusedly, and people stared, "he'd only done this once, on the day the Duke arrived?"

"Yes. He hasn't yet admitted to the second letter, about the murder." She was flicking her fingers impatiently, looking at the door where Draider stood.

"That's what I thought. Lida here came to confession tonight."

And suddenly the familiar eagerness to *tell her story* came pouring back to Lida, despite the circumstances. "The letter you found and read, about the kitchens, Mistress Fillim, was with the papers I took from that man, who's dead. I put it in Errios' room." Then she breathed, heart pounding.

"Why didn't you say so earlier?" demanded Fillim furiously.

Lida shrank.

"She was nervous of a murder investigation, and of speaking before adults. As she has confessed. And so I wanted to ask this man who gave him that letter. But now we cannot ask him, because he's dead."

"You think, killed?" said the King.

Fillim turned away, and began to pace a small path between the Abbot and the corner. "So," she said, "you're suggesting that the letter wasn't put there by Asor. But it might still have come from him. If he was in a hurry, he might give it to a servant to pass on."

"Would you do that, with a letter boasting of murder?"

"In a foreign land?" asked Draider, unexpectedly.

Lida saw the King and the Prince exchange a look. The King rolled his eyes upwards.

"Brother Paul," said Prince Braidoc, bending towards him and speaking with heavy gentleness, "it is late. This is a little unnecessary, is it not? Why should this man's death not have been natural? Leave the matter to his employers. We have work to do tomorrow."

"Much as we respect you, your perpetual moral scruples are growing a little tiresome," said the King, less heavily, less gently.

The Abbot wavered on his feet. "I don't wish to cause trouble, Your Grace." He opened his mouth and shut it again. And again. The King turned back to Kalla.

Lida felt everyone thinking, *Should we leave?* Draider put a hand on the door handle.

"But -" she whispered.

"When I was," said the Abbot, and his voice was hoarse, "when I was thirteen years old, I helped to commit a murder."

The room stopped. Mouths hung open.

"That's not a fate I wish on you, Your Grace, or on this child, or on anyone here."

"Who are we murdering?" asked the King, coldly.

"Errios, perhaps, and his servants. A letter was found in his room. If he didn't know it was there, he could have missed it. But if he did know, why didn't he destroy it? Especially -"

"Especially after Jeppa died, and we started to investigate," said Fillim, slowly. "If the man Asor didn't - someone else gave it to this Gardis, who gave it to Lida.

Asor is a spy, but it may be we need to look elsewhere for the poisoner."

The Abbot took a step back, towards the bed. No one could look anywhere but at the King. After a moment, "It did come to my mind," he admitted, "that the letter was very frank for a murderer to write. Almost too recklessly so."

"Someone created false evidence against Errios," whispered Fillim. "The real killer." Her face seemed a different colour from usual; paler. *Not possible,* she'd said earlier, about something. She looked round at the eight other faces. "And therefore not from Vard. Why would they accuse their own?"

"Not Vard!" exclaimed Kalla softly. "Do – do you mean the Consuls?"

The King said, "Kalla, what did you give to this man – wait, was it the same man?"

"I didn't know his name. I had the invitations I'd written, oh," she swallowed, and flapped her hands about helplessly, "and, Your Grace, you gave me a letter and a bottle for the Duke, and there was one – a letter – from you, Brother. There was only the invitation for Errios. I went to the hall and asked the steward if someone could deliver them, as I was instructed. And he called a pale old man, not much hair, with a grey beard -"

"That's the man," said Jude, and Lida nodded so hard she felt dizzy.

"So either this man Gardis happened by evil chance to be working for a murderer," said Fillim, "or someone came up to him, and said, 'Oh, and just add this one for Errios.'"

"Or Kalla is mistaken, which seems unlikely," said Draider.

"Don't worry, Kalla, we believe you," said the King. But Lida caught a sharp look from the Prince. *Could Kalla possibly be lying? But why?*

"If I were such a man," said Fillim slowly, "and it was the morning after a murder, I might not agree to add extra letters. Unless the person giving it to me -" There was a pause. "Belonged to the Marodi delegation. And who else would know that any letters existed?"

The room seemed to grow cold.

"Lord have mercy." Brother Jude crossed himself.

"Amen," said the Abbot, and then, "It seems to me possible that one of our people is involved in this murder — perhaps two murders."

"Stop," said the Prince. He had been silent, sitting with finger-tips pressed together, eyes moving steadily from speaker to speaker. "If this man, who? Gardis? was killed to stop his mouth, how, why would anyone from Marod have killed him? We have only just heard about this puzzle, this suspicion. But he was dead before any of us entered this room. Except Brother Jude, whom I'm sure none of us doubt." Brother Jude looked startled. "I agree there is a mystery here, if Lida is telling the truth, and her memory is accurate."

Lida squeaked.

"She's your squire. Have you known her dishonest or careless?" asked Fillim.

The Prince looked a little sadly at Lida. "Dishonest, no. But I have observed that she does like to be the one looked at and listened to – the one with sensational news."

I thought he liked me! Lida thought, and her eyes filled with tears.

"My prince, er, Lida didn't call this meeting. I did," said Abbot Paul. "She came to confess in her guilt before God, because she hadn't spoken earlier. This gathering was not her idea."

Someone knocked on the door, making Lida jump.

Draider drew his sword before half-opening it.

"What do you want?"

On the threshold, the woman Talinti looked in surprise at the crowd of eyes. "I beg your pardon, sir. Your Grace. I have information for Fillim Queensister, and I was told she was here."

"Information?" Fillim strode over and took a parchment from her. She unrolled it, and moved to the desk to read it by candle-light. Draider kept his sword pointed at the woman, who met his eyes steadily.

"Thank you," Fillim said, looking up. "You can go."

She seemed relieved to do so. Draider shut the door.

"Is the message of any assistance?" asked the Prince.

"I - am not certain. Please, allow me a moment." She stood, looking downwards; she paced across the room under everybody's eyes; then turned to the King. Her face looked hard. "Your Grace, I know you will say you trust everyone here, but *do* you trust Draider?"

"What -" exclaimed Draider, but the King said seriously,

"With my life."

"Good." Fillim stepped across to Draider, and whispered to him, face turned away from everybody else. He looked puzzled; then nodded, bowed, and went out. Fillim took his place by the door. "Your pardon, Your Grace, there's an enquiry I asked him to make. It'll probably mean nothing."

The King stood up. He said sternly, "Fillim, is there a suggestion that someone – someone *here* – committed these crimes?"

"I think we must accept that there may have been Marodi involvement."

"I did nothing, nothing, I only gave him what I was told! There was no other letter for Errios!"

"Peace, Kalla."

Fillim stood facing the King. Everyone else watched. "When we learned there might be a spy, Prince Braidoc pointed out that you had been ill on the boat. Perhaps poisoned. How would this have been done? What did you eat and drink?"

"I can't remember. It was days ago," he said, frowning. "It would've had to be at midday – I began to feel bad during the afternoon. I think I'd eaten what everyone else ate – pottage seasoned with garifa, and was there cabbage that day? We were all served from the same pot. I – somebody brought me a drink when I asked. One of the servants, or maybe it was a soldier. I don't think one of the crew."

"Not Asor, then. How ill were you?"

"I vomited once, not much. I felt very queasy, as some people do on water, but I normally do not."

"You also said," said Fillim, "that Jeppa complained that one of the crew was too inquisitive. We now know that she was right, and it was Asor. When did she complain, and who knew about it?"

"I knew," said the Abbot.

"Yes. It was – she came to me when we'd finished loading the Lithermayg people and their possessions, and said he was distracting her with questions. The Abbot and Brother Jude and Braidoc were with me. And I suppose she might have mentioned it to anyone else."

"And you were ill next day?"

"Yes."

Fillim shut her eyes, pressing fingers to her bent forehead.

"Well, we can tell the Consuls to release Errios and his people," said the King. "You were right, Brother." His face was weary. "The Duke will demand an explanation, and make it all an accusation against us."

"Against you. We are running too fast," the Prince began.

But then the door opened, and Draider came back in. He spoke quietly to Fillim, and passed her something small. "God help us," she said.

"Fillim," said the King, with some annoyance, "do you wish anyone to leave, before you explain your thoughts? Which you are *about to do*, I think."

She bowed. "Yes, Your Grace. No one should leave. This is Talinti's message." She read from the parchment. "*Please allow me to add to your information that about an hour before the feast began on Tuesday night, I was walking along Springrose Street with a friend. We passed a small alley that leads to the Palace kitchens. I saw a man come out. He was rubbing his fingers on a piece of cloth, as if they were sticky. He was a broad-shouldered man with brown skin, and curly black hair, wearing a blue jacket. I thought I had seen him before somewhere, but I did not remember where until today. He is one of the servants or soldiers of your delegation, although I do not know his name. He was at the funeral, helping to carry the bier.*"

Fillim turned to Yaif, silent in the corner. His jacket

today was red. "Yaif, what did you do today after dinner, before you came here?"

"Today? I – I was in the Palace."

"Where in the Palace?"

"In the Chapel."

"All the time?"

"Y – yes."

"I didn't see you there," said the Abbot. He looked at Lida, and she shook her head.

"One moment." Fillim walked to the little table, where there were a bottle and two goblets of wine. She picked one up, threw the dregs into the spitting fire, and re-filled it. The Prince, Draider and the Abbot were staring at Yaif; everyone else at Fillim. She lifted a little packet made of folded parchment, poured some of the contents, a powder, into the cup, and swirled it around.

Then she took a slow, deep breath. Her lips moved.

"My prince," she said, "Draider found this in your chamber. What will happen to me if I drink it?"

No one breathed.

"I have no idea," said Prince Braidoc. "I have not seen this, whatever it is, before."

"Why was it in your room? Why was your servant

outside the kitchens just before the feast?"

"I was not!" said Yaif, and he stood up slowly.

"Where were you?" asked Draider.

"I think," said Fillim after a moment, "that Duke Haras was right. Nobody tried to kill you, Your Grace. It would have been a terrible crime, for very vague gain. But someone wanted to accuse Errios." She turned her eyes on the Prince. "Several people on the boat had reason to suspect there was a spy from Vard, as there was, and as soon as this suspicion was known, the King was slightly poisoned, not to kill, just enough to prepare the way for further poison at the feast. You – most of us, but certainly you – knew that the King wouldn't eat such a thing as that rose, but that Jeppa would. You ordered your servant to give the letter to the man Gardis. Who is now dead."

No, no, no.

"This is nonsense," said the Prince, looking up at her calmly. "There are many men in the city resembling Yaif. And why would he or I want to silence this Gardis before we even knew of Abbot Paul's summons tonight? As I pointed out before."

"You expected the letters to be delivered by a servant. But then Lida told you – told all of us, yesterday –

that she delivered them. You would've known then that her memory might be dangerous to you. You surely noticed that she was very distressed and nervous during dinner, just after we'd been discussing the evidence against Errios. I certainly did."

Her voice had been careful and steady. Now she spun abruptly towards Yaif. "You weren't in the Chapel tonight. Where were you?"

"And he has a blue jacket," Brother Jude exclaimed. "He has a blue jacket."

She's like me; she enjoys an audience, Lida thought wildly. She couldn't bear how fast things were happening.

"This is nonsense," repeated the Prince. "Everything you say is '*suppose*'."

"There is this." She lifted the little packet. "Do you doubt Draider's word?"

"Anyone could have placed it in my room. This Talinti could have done, and be lying now. She may have been paid by Vard. Her so-called prophecy looks favourable to them."

"But why would she? Why would anyone plant false evidence on you, *and* on Errios?"

The King said, "We agreed that Yaif and Brother

Jude were to attend me, in place of Jeppa. I did wonder where Yaif disappeared to this evening, when I might have needed him." He looked down at the only person still sitting. "But Fillim, this is my brother."

"Before we left Stonehill," said Fillim, "the Queen called me to the Willow Chamber. She said, 'My letter to the Council says I am sending those I love and trust. I trust you, Fillim, and the Abbot. I love and trust my husband. Braidoc I love. And he wants us to win. Almost too much.' She said, 'Be careful.'"

Somebody let out a slow gasping breath.

"We could -" said Lida suddenly. Everyone looked at her. "We could ask the kitchen workers if they recognised Yaif."

"Or his jacket," said Brother Jude.

"Talinti sleeps in the Palace. We can call her back," said Draider.

Yaif opened his mouth, and made a noise. Not a word, not a gasp, just a sound.

The Prince stood up at last. "Barad. Can I speak to you alone?"

"No," said several voices.

"No," said the King.

The Prince took a step towards him. He reached out a hand, and gently turned his brother-in-law's wrist, flicking back the cuff. "You owe me a debt," he said.

The King looked down at the red spider-lines that Lida had never noticed before. "I haven't forgotten that you saved my life," he said. "Speak."

Lida glanced round to see if anyone else was as puzzled as she was; and most of them seemed to be. Looking back, she found the two men staring at each other - and the rest of them, she thought, were not even an audience. They were more like eavesdroppers.

The Prince spoke quietly. "I saved you for this hour. Barad – my King – we are playing here for a great prize. Hear me out. Nothing like this has happened for a hundred years. We are playing for your wife, my sister, to become Queen of Jaryar. Queen of all the West, from north to south, from the Bay of Marod to the Long Bay, overlady of Haymon, the greatest ruler on Ragaris. Think what that means for Marod. Think what she could do. She is, she would be a magnificent Queen, you know this. And consider Duke Haras. He insults everyone around him; he thinks a crown is something to buy at a market. A fool, and a brute. Even the Jaryari deserve better than him; and if he becomes King, what will that mean for all of us? Queen Emeli, but stupider, and worse. Jaryar deserves Nerranya."

"Queen of the West!" someone murmured. Lida hadn't realised it before.

"Tcha!" muttered the Abbot.

"Abbot Paul is unworldly, but you and I have a duty to our people. Haras will make war on Marod – he is doubtless already planning this – it seems likely, does it not? Think of the prophecy – *Asatan's Dream,* and *Death.* Whether or not we believe it, the electors will. If Haras wins, thousands will die. And whatever he is planning, Errios is part of it. He is not an innocent; he is our enemy. Think of our people slaughtered; our freedom."

The King nodded. "So you think that -"

"God sent us, sent you, for this hour. To save Marod. Sometimes this means doing things that are sad, regrettable -"

"Killing Jeppa was 'regrettable'?"

"A few people are sacrificed for victory, yes. In war, all the time. Sometimes in peace. Do you think I did this lightly? It was the hardest, most terrible decision - but we have to win. Jeppa would have been willing to die for you and for Marod, you know she would. She deserved all the praise the Abbot gave her, and she is in heaven now. Honour that. Put up a statue; endow a church. But we have to win."

"If we build a church in her name, will that satisfy her husband and children?"

"No," said the Prince, very sadly. "No, it won't. But it will atone, in God's sight. He sent us here for a purpose. This is His will. It has to be."

The Abbot opened his mouth, but the King said, "Silence." Turning back to the Prince, "It was God's will for you and Yaif to kill two people?"

"It is God's will for His Name to be glorified, and his people saved, protected. Everything else is trivial. Make whatever reparations you need afterwards, as I will; do whatever penance, but for now you are the King. Save Marod. Make Nerranya Queen of the West, clean the cesspit that is Makkera and Vard, and praise His Name."

To Lida the world seemed to be rocking, and she had no idea what good and evil were any more.

The King glanced round at the other faces – Brother Jude confused, Kalla scared, Draider blank - and then at the ground. Back at his brother-in-law. "And against this the Abbot has only his old saws to quote, which he will, I suppose," he said. "*Thou shalt not kill. Thou shalt not bear false witness. Create in me a clean heart.*" He sighed, and gestured vaguely. "You can sit down. God help us. All this time. I thought I knew you. I thought we were friends."

"We are friends."

"No. Not now. I suppose all this means a confession, a boast, that you ordered Yaif to murder Jeppa, and lay a trail of lies against the Vard delegation. Against an old man who once fought against us because it was his duty."

"Jeppa would have been willing -"

"So you say, but we cannot know that, because you didn't ask her, did you?" His face was a snarl.

"The meeting," said Fillim, making everyone jump. "The purpose of the meeting the other night was so that invitations could be sent out, and that letter included."

"Yes, that pointless and absurd meeting," said the King bitterly.

"And it explains Yaif. You brought Yaif to serve you instead of your usual man, because he wouldn't know Jeppa. He would be less reluctant to kill her at your command."

Lida looked across at Yaif, who had been friendly to

her, and whose face was empty.

"Sit down, Braidoc," said the King. His face looked old. "I have to decide what to do with you."

The Prince didn't move. "You should speak to me alone."

"There is no one in this room I trust less than you. Why should we speak alone?"

"Because I saved your life." Their eyes met. "I did wonder why I had to. What was so terrible about being married to my sister, that four months after the wedding you didn't want to live any more? I wondered, and yesterday I was making conversation with Lady Madigam, and now I think I know."

Stillness. "Are you threatening me? I don't like being threatened."

"I am not. I am reminding you, Your Grace, that you are the Queen's husband, and our country is depending on you."

"Sit down."

The Prince sat. Fillim walked to the door, exchanging places with Draider, the only person present with a sword. He took up position between the King and the Prince, blade's tip pointing at the Prince's face. The

King met Fillim's eyes, and then stepped towards Yaif, who watched him come. "Look at me. What did you do to the man Gardis?"

"Nothing."

"You killed him."

Yaif turned to the Prince, who shrugged.

"I – put a pillow on his face."

Lida felt sick. She thought the King did too. "And you poisoned Jeppa."

"The Prince promised you wouldn't eat it, Your Grace. He promised you would be safe!"

"I was safe. She was not."

"What a great matter you make of one servant," said Prince Braidoc. "Anyone would think she was your lover." Several people gasped. "She was not, of course."

"I've heard enough from you," said the King. "And *you,*" turning to Yaif, "sit down, and put your hands on your head.

"Perhaps we should all sit." So the King and Prince sat on their chairs, and the old Abbot on the edge of the bed, and the others on the floor. Only Mistress Fillim and Master Draider remained on their feet, one between King and Prince, and the other with her back to the door.

"Your counsel, friends," said the King. "What do we do now?"

"The prisoners should be released. And the Consuls should be told. They're even now investigating Gardis' death," said Fillim.

"Released, yes. But this is my Queen's brother. And we still have a vote to win." Lida watched muscles harden in his hands as they clutched the chair's arms.

"If you told the Consuls you've dealt with the criminals, and those others are innocent," said Fillim thoughtfully, "might that be enough?"

"No," said the Abbot.

The King sighed. "No, I fear not. I'd like to think the Consuls would ask questions. And Haras and Antonos certainly will."

"Your Grace," said Draider shyly, "is Errios not entitled to know who accused him?"

"He would want to kill me. I am happy to fight him for you," said the Prince.

"You will be quiet." The King sighed. "I do not want – my wife wouldn't want – her brother tried and executed for murder in Vach-roysh. Vard will besmirch us all with this. He will smear the Queen."

"Yes," said Fillim. "He will suggest that we all knew of it. That your anger over Jeppa was a pretence."

"No one would believe that!" cried Kalla.

"They might." The King thought. "It's not fair to Yaif, but we can say we've discovered a misguided madman acted alone." He looked at his brother-in-law. "I suppose, if it were God's will, you'd let us throw your obedient servant to the hangman in your place."

No one ever knew what Prince Braidoc would have answered. Abbot Paul said, "This is not God's will, Your Grace. You know that."

"Yaif is guilty. We don't have to tell the Consuls everything."

"It's not only the Consuls. You spoke the other day about what the electors had a right to know. Without meaning to, Queen Nerranya sent a delegation that included a murderer. Do the electors not have a right to know that?"

"He's my Queen's brother."

The young man and the old one looked at each other. Then the Abbot said, "I see the difficulty, Your Grace. I am not the Queen's brother, and if it please you, I will confess to these crimes tomorrow."

"You! Don't be absurd!"

"The electors have a right to know that the guilt goes higher than Yaif. I am a delegate, and I will confess."

"But they'll hang you!" said Fillim.

"I'm a crazed old monk, with probably not many years to live." He stood up, very solid, but Lida thought he was trembling slightly.

"Wait." The King put his head into his hands. No one spoke. Abbot Paul sat down again, bending his head, and fingering his rosary, presumably praying.

God help us; why don't You help us? Lida thought.

King Barad raised his face. "We will tell the truth. I will talk to the Consuls. Then -"

"Even you cannot do this! Are you all mad?" Prince Braidoc jumped up. "You might as well hand Haras the crown on a platter. That may be what you want, Barad of Haymon, but in Marod we fight for our freedom."

There was a moment of thunder-tenseness in the room, and Lida thought Draider murmured, *"Yes."*

But Fillim strode three steps, swung her arm across, and struck the Prince hard in the face. He staggered and fell against his chair. Without bothering to straighten, he twisted towards the King, and said, "My sister entrusted this to you, and now you'll betray her. But then you always have, from the very beginning. From the very first. I should have let you die."

What? How?

As Fillim glanced for instruction, he stood up slowly. The King's face was expressionless. Then he said, "They're all wondering what you mean by that. Go on, then."

The Prince's eyes burned. Softly, "I found you lying in a pool of blood, and I bound your arms and stopped the bleeding, and called Jeppa and another, and swore them to secrecy. And I wondered why. What had my sister ever done to you? She loved you."

Lida saw the King flinch.

The Prince went on. "She told me, beforehand, 'Arranged marriages can be happy ones. Our grandparents proved it, and our great-grandparents.' She was ready to give you all the love a man could want. But you didn't want it. What did she say when you eventually told her what you are? A man who would never desire her, who'd rather be in bed with Draider here." Draider gaped. "Or Jude, or even me. Did you manage to father your own children, Barad? Whose are they really?"

"Hit him again," said the King, and Fillim obeyed.

"You will not insult my wife." He stood up. "Draider, your sword."

Master Draider passed it. The King curled his fingers round the hilt, jiggling it a little as if he were preparing for practice at home. Then he lifted the blade-tip to within an inch of his brother-in-law's face. "I should probably kill you now. It might be safest." He looked down to the right, at the floor. There was no sound but breathing. Then he glanced at the Abbot; and almost as one they shook their heads a little.

"But to kill you in this room would be murder. So - we could hand you over to the Consuls for their justice, Haymonese justice. Distracting everyone from what we came for. Or we could take you home, and try you there. I won't do that to her.

"Fillim, get him out of my sight. Put them in his room, with parchment to write a confession. Search them for poison, and guard them well. And tomorrow, brother, you can set off on pilgrimage."

The Prince stood up and bowed. Then he and Yaif walked out with Fillim and Draider. He didn't look at Lida.

As if they had spoken, but they did not, everyone shifted themselves, and flexed their legs.

"One guard in the room, and one outside. I've sent a message that you wish to speak to the Consuls," said Fillim, returning.

"Thank you. A long and terrible night, and not over yet."

Lida remembered the expression she'd seen earlier. "You guessed, Mistress Fillim! You guessed it was him, before we came here!"

Fillim stared at her, and so did everyone. "What d'you mean?"

Trembling, Lida said, "After the funeral, I heard you say, 'Not possible.' Wasn't that what you meant?"

"Be quiet. No, it was not." She glanced at the King, who looked back at her with weary curiosity. "I had many wild ideas, but that one was the worst."

"What could've been worse than this?" asked Brother Jude, and then looked shocked at himself.

The King smiled, a sad smile. "The worst idea was that I killed Jeppa, as Duke Haras suggested?"

"No. Forgive me, Your Grace, but something Errios said their spy said, and then when Duke Voros talked of bereavement -" Everyone was staring. "I didn't believe it, it couldn't be, but if the poison had been meant for you, for a moment -"

"For a moment you thought that the Queen might have asked someone to get rid of her tiresome husband for her?"

Fillim's face was answer enough. "Forgive me. I knew it couldn't be true."

"No, ah, if my wife wants to kill me, she would find it easier at home." He smiled at her, and the air seemed to lift.

But then the smile faded. "One more thing." He breathed deeply. "They are my children. Never doubt that. My wife has much to endure, but she didn't have to take a lover to father heirs for Marod. May I die this night if I'm lying.

"And now I need Fillim, but I think the rest of you can retire, and rest."

He picked up a goblet.

"Not that one!" cried Fillim and Jude at the same moment.

"Ah yes, this one would probably kill me, or make me sick again."

Lida bowed, and left with Kalla, the Abbot and Brother Jude.

"Come with me," Abbot Paul said to her. "You still have a penance to complete." They went into his room.

On this mad night, perhaps she could ask a question.

"Brother," she said timidly, "I didn't understand what the Prince said about the children, and their marriage."

He looked at her, pushing his lips out, and seeming embarrassed. "Did you not? In my day, squires were less innocent. It isn't your concern, or mine, Lida. But you know that men and women love, and marry, and have children."

"Of course."

"There are some men who don't wish to love women, would prefer to love men. And some women, similarly. It must be very – difficult - for such people when their duty, or their family, demands that they marry."

"Oh."

"Difficult, but not impossible. Your penance."

She had to think back a very long time, months of strangeness it seemed. Back to when her prince was not a murderer. But at last, "Our Father, which art in heaven -"

"I absolve you," he said, and laid a hand briefly on

her head in blessing.

The Debates at the Council

Errios struggled through battle-dreams, stinking of blood, ears torn by the shrieks of the dying. He woke in the hot darkness, cursed his enemies and his own fear, and at last slept again. Waking for the fourth time, he found it was morning. A man was standing by his bed.

"Sir? May it please you to rise? The King of Marod wishes to speak to you."

"Tell him to go and fuck himself."

But he couldn't stay in bed, as if wounded. He dragged himself up, dressed, and allowed the man to plait his hair. No one came to hurry him, to his surprise. So he had time to plan how to fling their lies back at them, and defy their hypocritical justice.

As long as they didn't kill him in a bedroom. As long as they let him die under the sun.

The man had tidied his bed. "Are you ready, sir?"

"I am ready."

He'd been standing by the window, but then he changed his mind and crossed to the chair. He sat down with his legs arrogantly apart, and his hands on his knees. Like a king receiving supplicants. He smiled grimly.

The King came in, followed by the Abbot and Mistress Fillim. They stood in a row in front of him, and they all bowed.

"Honoured sir," said King Barad, "we've come to release you from any constraint, and to ask pardon for our suspicions, which are now proved groundless. The murderer has been found, and we know it was not you, nor anyone from Vard."

He sat still, unable to understand. And then he did, and it was sweet. "Could you repeat that, Your Grace?" he asked, his eyes flicking gleefully to Fillim. "I'm an old man, and I didn't hear exactly what you said."

*

No one came to drag Talinti from her sleep, so plainly her fears had been foolish.

She broke her fast in the Hall, and learned from others' gossip that a man had died the previous evening, the Consuls and the King had been in discussions until long after midnight, and Errios and his attendant woman had rejoined their delegation.

So now she was free to be trivially nervous on her

own account. This morning, the beginning of this day, was her moment, or rather Upali's.

Talinti had never liked speaking to a crowd, although of course she often had to. When tenants gathered in her hall, Izzan used to pull her aside, squeeze and kiss her distractingly, and whisper, "If they give you any trouble, have them all whipped." Not very practical advice, even at home, and certainly not here with these great folk. The bread and cheese which were the simplest food she could find, lay heavy and congealed on her stomach.

Kariam was apparently helping Tormenas and his steward with some task, so Meriden was waiting in the courtyard alone. Talinti handed him her roll of parchment, almost learned by heart, and slightly crushed in her damp hand, and they walked towards the Theatre, entering the walkway that joined it to the main court. She glanced at him, and thought she caught again a moment of dislike and disapproval. But as the guards opened the double doors before them, he bent towards her and said, "This is what you came for, my lady."

It was.

But as it happened, she wasn't called first, after all.

*

Fillim Queensister read the document to the astonished company.

> *I, Braidoc, son of Dras, brother of Queen Nerranya of the Marodi, confess before God and in the presence of my brother the King that I arranged for the deaths of Jeppa, daughter of Anam, and Gardis, son of Ristor. I did this with the intention of laying blame on Errios of Girifay, or any other of the delegation from Vard, and thus to wrongfully influence the electors at the Council. I arranged for a forged letter discussing the murder to be addressed to Errios and placed in his room. My accomplice was my servant Yaif, son of Adam, and no one else. I confided my intentions to no one else. My sister and the other delegates would have rejected them, as they have now done. In the sight of God I repent of these deeds, and my other sins.*

Lida knew that the Vard people and the Consuls had been told beforehand. She stood by the wall, next to the confused Fric, and watched the platform. Archbishop Elizabeth shook her head bishopishly. Antonos looked solemn, but flashes of satisfaction tweaked out of his eyes. Errios stared above everyone's heads, expressionless. Duke Haras was openly grinning. The old Consul Jaikkad looked stern; the Consul Invildi smiled serenely.

It was she who stood up at the end. "Can you inform us how these facts were discovered?"

Fillim explained that there had been new evidence from two sources, and then added, "There can be no doubt. My King has ordered me to state as clearly as possible that all of us are fully convinced none of the Duke's people had any hand in the murder on Tuesday night, and to ask for the pardon, not merely of Errios himself, but of his slandered delegation, and also of all the people here, whom Prince Braidoc sought to deceive." Fillim bowed to the Vard delegation, and then to the hall. There was a murmuring everywhere.

For the first time, Lida felt the full humiliation of Marod.

She'd lain in bed last night, striving to think with adult calm of other things, reciting old tales; but continually jerked back to her prince justifying murder - insulting the King - being struck, and led away like a criminal. He *was* a criminal, and she was sick and cold.

And now she saw what it meant for the rest of them. Everyone stared at the three delegates, and the empty chair.

Duke Haras stood up. "Where is the man?"

"He has confessed," said Fillim. "We consulted with the Consuls last night. A reparation in money will be made to Gardis' family. Braidoc and his servant have surrendered their weapons, and have departed under guard, to travel to the holy city of Vachansha. There they will work out their penance for as long as Prelate Peter rules, as is the Defardi custom."

"And what happens after that?"

"Whatever God pleases. But the King and Queen and Consuls will order that their lives are forfeit if they ever return to Marod or Haymon. You may wish to ask King Osgar for a similar order for Jaryar."

"Hmm." The Duke turned to consult with the other delegates, and Fric pulled at Lida's sleeve, so that she could explain to him what the Abbot had explained to her.

"People who've killed someone without meaning to go to Defardu, and work there for a year to show their sorrow, and give time for the dead person's kin to stop hating them. This is like that."

"But he did mean to."

"I know."

It's an easier fate than he deserves. Or perhaps not – to be a prince, who could never come home. She shivered.

The Duke turned back, and said, not very graciously, "We will do as you suggest. The electors will doubtless notice that the Queen of Marod sent a murderer to Vach-roysh."

Fillim's bow was curt. She sat down. It seemed the matter was over.

*

I have to follow that, Talinti thought.

The Consul said, "God is gracious, and He cares for all of us. Not a sparrow falls, but He knows it. And it's possible, I say no more, that He has sent a divine message to guide you in your deliberations. I present to you Talinti, daughter of Malda, the lady of Lithermayg, in the county of Gard." Invildi's white-draped arm billowed out graciously.

Talinti walked down the central aisle, clutching her parchment, Meriden two paces behind. More than a hundred eyes pierced her.

She mounted the steps to the dais, and curtsied three times, once to each delegation, and once to the Consuls, turned, and curtsied to the hall.

Meriden waited stolidly at the bottom of the steps.

"A woman of Jaryari accent who said her name was Upali collapsed and died on my land on 1st April this year." She heard her voice crackle, and strengthened it. "She insisted she had words to be written down, words for 'the great ones at Vach-roysh', before she died. This is what my steward wrote. He and I will swear to it.

"She said, '*I saw their deaths. Abbos and Rosior. I saw it, and I spoke it, and they died. And now I have seen.*'

"These are her words:

'*To the hall with six flames* (People's heads were turning, counting.)

Call the great of the nine
For an heir to the King;
They will seek for a sign…'"

She curtsied again at the end. There was silence.

The Consul said behind her, "Thank you, madam. The electors may have questions for you. But I am authorised by the Duke to confirm that Upali, daughter of Galian, was exiled from Marithon after she predicted that King Osgar's brother Abbos and his son Rosior would die soon, and they were drowned seven months later." A murmur.

"We will pause now for a quarter of one hour for consideration and prayer. Then we will hear if the delegates wish to offer an interpretation.

"After that, the electors may question any here, and debate. In order to allow time for this, when we have seen so many unexpected developments, my colleague and I propose extending the Council by one night, and holding the vote tomorrow morning, instead of today. If it please you."

Talinti supposed that the Duke and the King were nodding behind her. She curtsied again, and stepped off the stage.

*

Some people had been scribbling, Lida saw, and many were muttering to each other. Few were praying.

Fric was balancing on one foot.

She saw a young man – that young man, Antonos' squire Justar – elbowing past spectators as politely as he could. He stopped when he came to Lida, and leaned against the wall next to her. "Good morrow, madam," he said politely.

People rarely called Lida "madam". "You, girl," was more common.

"Good morrow."

"So at last the heavenly message is out in the light. What does Marod say it means?"

She remembered Fillim's words. "It's hard to interpret prophecy at the time. It can often only be done years later."

She distrusted his smile. "Is that what you all think? We think the explanation is obvious." He nodded towards the stage. "You may have noticed the flower the Duke wears in his gown. He happened to pick it up yesterday, and took a fancy to it. 'A bloom from the mud,' you might say."

He'd spoken loudly enough for the electors at the back to hear, and one or two turned to listen. Fury gave Lida inspiration. "But in Haymon, a 'bloom' doesn't simply mean a flower, does it?" She was grateful for her Prince's instruction on the boat. "In all their ballads and songs, it means a lovely woman."

Justar's smile wavered. Fric giggled.

"This Upali wouldn't have known that. She was Jaryari, and this is a Jaryari election. Haymonese customs are not the point."

He was struggling. Lida shrugged.

And then someone rang a little bell, and their attention was called back to the stage. And Justar turned away, and once more he was smiling.

*

The Archbishop stood up first, clasping her hands before her. "We are all most grateful to Talinti. It is necessary to remember that interpreting prophecy is difficult, and no one can presume to know. But I have pondered and prayed over these words, and I think the meaning is clear. The electors are to choose the second." Her words were slow and processional. "Who is the 'second'? The man, whom we can assume to be Duke Haras, is named second. He is also the second by birth – three years younger than the Queen. And in a third way. As he reminded me yesterday, he was his parents' second-born. He had an elder sister, the late lamented Duchess Jilna." Heads were nodding around the hall. "I think there can be little doubt. God is calling on you to vote for the Duke."

Nonsense, nonsense. Lida willed the electors not to believe her.

The Archbishop smiled and sat down, and the Duke stood up.

Everyone saw him take a deep breath. "I am humbled by these words," he said, his hands hanging by his sides, and his gaze straight over everyone's heads. Like someone who has learned a speech very carefully, and doesn't want to be distracted. "It is a greater call than I had dreamed of, but I believe it is mine. And not just to be King of the nine provinces. The vote tomorrow means more than that.

"We all remember that other prophecy, King Asatan's Dream, a hundred years ago. Now God is calling us to make it real." A stir. "I swear to you, I had never met Talinti, or heard these words, before coming to this city, but God had already led me to make preparations. We have been in communication with the Kings of Ricossa, and we are planning an alliance."

Dizzy herself, Lida saw, everyone saw, the horror and fury of her delegation. They stared at him.

"You have -" the King exclaimed.

Fillim Queensister jumped up, but she didn't speak. She spun round, and laid a quick hand on the shoulders of the other two. Perhaps she said something. Then she turned back. "My apologies, my lord. Pray continue, and don't mind me. I think better on my feet." She began to walk up and down thoughtfully, gazing at him.

"Thank you." His smile was grim, and then slightly disconcerted. *Forgotten his words,* Lida thought with hate. But he cleared his throat, and went on. "Two hundred years ago, before their bloody War of the Three Kingdoms, Marod was three countries, and what was divided once can be divided again. The eastern part, Arbeth, is not truly part of the West. We will yield Arbeth to Ricossa, and they will help us to take what remains. We will discipline these wild people, whose princes lie and defame and murder. Jaryar has some vengeance to take for that, and for King Jendon's interference in our affairs eighteen years back. But this is not about vengeance. We have a greater future. We are the Lords of the West.

"Jaryar to the northern sea, as far as the Bay! It is ours, God promised it to us long ago! This was King Asatan's Dream, and we will take it at last!"

"Yes!" A plump young man jumped up from a bench near the back. And then a bald man in the middle. A woman on the right. Another man. *"Yes! Yes! Yes!"*

No! Lida wailed silently, through spilling tears.

Some people were applauding. Faces were excited.

Then the Duke sat down, and Antonos stood. "You came, my friends," he said, stretching out his arms, "to choose a monarch. But God has brought you here to choose Jaryar's destiny."

It was the old man's turn. He looked a little confused, after his time in prison. He hesitated, and then said, "Yes. I'm due some vengeance for yesterday. And for the Battle of the Lither. I have a long memory." He flexed his fingers.

There was a stir at the table on the right of the stage. The woman in the long plain purple gown rose, the Prelate's Secretary, Mary of Defardu. "This troubles me," she said. "Your lord, King Osgar, and my lord, the holy Prelate, authorised this Council, and brought everyone here, so that this matter could be settled peaceably. To *avoid* war." She turned to the Ricossan lady sitting beside her. "Is there such an agreement as the Duke describes?"

"Eh?" said the woman.

Reverend Mary spoke louder. "Is there an alliance between the King, or the Duke, and your lords in City Qayn? It seems very strange."

"Strange? It's all strange." The old woman didn't stand, but her voice was perfectly audible. "To a Ricossan it seems *strange* to call people from all corners to vote for a ruler they cannot know, the grandchild or great-grandchild of a someone dead for near fifty years. But you in Jaryar have your own ways." (Nobody knew, Lida remembered, how the Ricossans chose their kings and queens. Nobody in the world knew.)

"But the answer to your question is Yes." Lady Jeriet smiled. "I was sent by my Kings to bring their agreement to King Osgar's proposal, which the Duke has mentioned. You may have Rachonda and Qarath, and we will have Arbeth. We will bring the Marodi to civilisation, and true religion."

You scraggly old bitch! We're as holy as you!

"Thank you, my lady," said Antonos. "And there need be no war. To resist God's revealed will is defiance of God. The Marodi need only accept what has to be. As their friends in Haymon did, long ago."

The hall hummed as it all sank in. *Jaryar to the Northern Sea. Overlords of the West.* Lida heard whispers.

Reverend Mary sat down, looking shocked.

"Thank you, my lord Duke," said Fillim. She wandered to the front of the stage, along its edge to the right and back again, smiling with lowered head, silently quieting the hall, drawing all eyes.

"Alas, I'm only a simple warrior," she said at last, "and I don't presume to read the mind of God. If He has indeed ordained that Jaryar is to rule all the West, then it will happen, and if He's ordained that Haras, son of Massin, that wise, noble, Christian youth, is to be King in Makkera, doubtless that will happen. This is all I understand about prophecies. As my friend the Abbot said the other night, claims about the future may be from God, or from the devil, or merely some person's wild thought." She shrugged, and looked up, meeting faces. "But you are here to make a choice.

"I have a few thoughts about that choice, and about what Duke Haras has said, his boast that he will destroy us.

"I am a warrior. I've stood watch on our eastern border at Makaim. The nights there are long, wondering if this is the night the enemy will choose to attack; if it's tonight when I must die for my Queen and my country. Many of you will know such nights. Especially the electors from Lefayr, who know Ricossa, know Ricossa and its ways perhaps better than the Duke." She cast her eyes directly to one section of the silent hall.

"It's true that we brought a murderer into your midst, without meaning to. Last night I heard that murderer claim that his evil actions were God's will. You saw this morning how our King dealt with him.

"But the Duke - Duke Haras came here in peace, for a just and legal council. We also came in peace, believing in his good faith. He ate and drank with us, and all the time he'd made plans to rob his cousin of her birthright, to devour Marod, to sell us." Her voice wasn't loud. "To sell the east of Marod to Ricossa. Without honour a country is dead, however great it looks. Was this honour, clever statecraft, or was it an abomination, devised by the devil? Before anyone talks of 'true religion', as if the Marodi were heathen, ask if he and his friends consulted the Prelate, the Head of Holy Church? It seems not.

"And more. As the Holy Secretary Mary said, we all came here, you came here, so that Jaryar could avoid war. If you make Haras King, and he invades Marod, we will not go quietly. How many of your sons and daughters, nephews and nieces, will we kill? How many will the Queen's Thirty kill?" She placed a hand deliberately where her sword would have been, had she not surrendered it. "Is this your choice, that so many should die for the Duke's arrogance and greed? Is it truly King Osgar's choice? God preserve him, he's a sick man; who knows what goes on beside his bed? What evidence do we have that he agreed with foreign kings to throw your people, his people, into the cauldron?

"Lastly." She turned to face the Duke. "I don't remember your grandmother, Queen Igalla, and neither I think do you. She was born in Arabay, in Vard, but she became Queen of Marod, and we honour her memory. It's her people whose freedom you want to steal. If she were here, would she praise her grandson? Or would she curse you, and spit in your face?

"My lords, my ladies, you have a choice, of who is to rule Jaryar, and perhaps Marod too, two countries together. Who do you trust for this task? Who will care better for all their people? God has given this choice to you, not the Duke, nor this Upali."

She sat down. No one spoke. The King rose.

"I don't think I have anything else to say," he said. "Thank you, sister." He inclined his head towards the Duke. "Cousin," he said with contempt.

Everyone was looking at the last delegate, the old Abbot. He rose slowly. They had to strain to hear him.

"God have mercy on the people of Makaim," he said. "And on us all."

*

Dear God, Talinti thought, *what have I unleashed? What have I done?*

*

"If the Duke wins, there'll be a war!" whispered Fric excitedly. "Where's Arbeth?"

"All the eastern third of Marod," Lida managed to say. Her own home, Dendarry, was in the north. Which would be worse, to be conquered by Ricossa – people had been slaves there not so long ago - or by Jaryar? *But we wouldn't be conquered. The Thirty and our soldiers would fight for ever. I would fight.*

Electors stood around in the hall or the courtyard, eating and drinking and talking. They didn't mix carelessly, as they'd done in the last few days. They were in tight groups, gathered in their provinces; their talk was quiet and earnest. One woman fed her baby. Some faces looked eager, some joyful, some solemn; but she didn't dare to approach any.

The Abbot was standing with the Prelate's Secretary, and then the Archbishop joined them, and all three were silent. The King stood with Mistress Fillim, not far from Lida, smiling. Now and again he turned to the Queensister and spoke quietly and confidently. "Two and four and six-eight-ten, blue and gold for fishermen. Harn barn jambali scan -"

Nonsense rhymes. And Fillim nodded sagely, and replied, "The Great Synod of Makkera was held in 181 and decided for all time to come that -" Anything to be talking, to look unconcerned from a distance. The Prince had taught Lida that trick.

And then they were all called back, and it was time for the electors to debate and ask questions. Lida felt words and words wash over her. "Do we know if the woman Upali made any other prophecies?" "Did the Queen's birthing of the twins go well? Is all smooth with her current pregnancy?" "King Osgar didn't mention this alliance in his letter. Did he approve it?" "Why should we trust the Ricossans?" "How can we be sure the Queen didn't approve of her brother's plans for murder?" (To which the King replied, "If you think she did, vote for the Duke. And you may wonder what she will say to me when I return home," and there was nervous laughter.)

Several people stood to declare allegiance for one side or the other. "I am Desor of Naimatrai, a simple man, and the Queen is the lawful heir." "I am Duchess Palla of Vard, and I shall vote for my stepson. He is a man of great gifts and powerful vision, and he will be a great king." Lida hissed. But most kept their intentions behind their teeth.

One man – she thought afterwards he must have been very brave – got up and said, "I will vote for the Duke, because he is a man. Scripture says we should not permit women to have authority -" He was jeered down, of course. The Consul Invildi pointed out icily that that pernicious doctrine had been condemned five hundred years ago, and the penalty for persistence in heresy was –

"Flogging in Jaryar," said Antonos, "and death in Marod, I believe? They are severe there."

"In the most extreme cases," said the Abbot uncomfortably.

Talk, talk, *talk*.

*

If the vote had taken place by now, as originally planned, tonight would have been a feast, with a dance. Lida still hadn't had an opportunity to wear the rose gown. But nothing was settled, and so they had magnificent food, and uncertain rather dreary music, and no acrobats. And the High Table was quiet.

Lida and Brother Jude scurried to serve the three delegates between them. (There'd been a rapid discussion beforehand – Fric was too young to help, and Kalla too inexperienced.) The King ostentatiously made them taste every dish before he touched it, and his friends followed his example. The Abbot almost forgot several times, leading to a few fumbles, and a partridge wing landed on the floor.

Otherwise, there was silent dignity, which came naturally only to the Archbishop - and to Draider who stood behind them, hand on swordhilt, still and contemptuous. Fillim's fingers pattered on the table. Old Errios ate as if they'd starved him. Now and again, Lida had to dodge aside to avoid his servant, a big dark woman with a bruised face.

At last it was over, and the great people rose. "We'll meet tomorrow, then, for the vote. And after that, who knows?" Antonos said lightly, face to face with the King.

"Only God, indeed." King Barad shrugged. "I'm not a great swordsman. But Fillim here could kill any of the four of you with one hand tied behind her back."

"Indeed? Is that how you plan to cheer your soldiers? They'll need all the encouragement you can give them."

"My lords, my lords," said Invildi, lifting her white-draped arms, and frowning benignly; and for a moment both the King and Antonos looked like children.

As they turned away, Fric ran up to his mistress. "If there's a war, can I fight?"

"You're too young."

"Please, I want to fight for Marod!"

"I said, no!" and she boxed his ears, hard. Then, "Forgive me, Fric." Which was something Lida had never heard an adult say to a child. "We do not want war. I'm too tired to talk."

They were almost at the door. Lida peeped back at the Duke's party, watching Errios struggle to his feet. A nervous servant was handing the Duke a piece of parchment. She saw him read it, and scowl.

*

After supper at Tormenas', Meriden accompanied Talinti and Kariam back to the Palace.

"Are you well, my lady?" He hesitated, and then said, "It may be that King Osgar will recover his health, marry, and sire seven children for the throne."

She smiled, and it hurt her face. "It may be. But if not, I am alarmed. Marod cannot surely stand against two enemies at once."

"Marod is a name," he said, so quietly that she was unsure she'd heard. "They can change the name without changing who they are."

"And I hope it won't affect us," said Kariam.

"No." Talinti wearily dismissed them both, and climbed the stairs to the Chapel. She prayed for a long time, and never knew afterwards if her prayers made any difference or not.

*

The Vard delegation stalked to the Duke's chamber. Once again, Illi darted into the back room as they came in. Duchess Palla and her maid walked in after them. "You can leave us," she said to the guard at the door, and he bowed and went out. "Are these trustworthy?" she asked, indicating the other four attendants – Errios' woman, Antonos' squire, the Duke's plump and fastidious man, and the Archbishop's quiet nun.

"Of course," said the Duke, insulted. The others nodded.

"Good." She gestured to invite Errios to sit down, and he did so gratefully. "You seem distressed," she said to her stepson, in a voice without kindness.

"The electors of Tell and Exor have returned my gold. And Lady Relda sent a message saying we should feel no obligation to keep our promises to her daughter and son-in-law. They're all turning against me!" He banged his fist on the wall. As Errios had seen him do as a child. *I promised his father to protect him.*

"Not all," said Antonos. "Many are excited by your promise of conquest, especially the young. But a few are saying that if Nerranya becomes Queen, we're all one anyway - and that way Ricossa doesn't get Arbeth. And," he sighed, "Fillim spoke well."

"The bitch. The *bitch!* The Marodi are murderers, and they're still going to win!"

"Sit down, Haras, and be calm," said the Duchess. She herself sat in the most cushioned chair, and arranged her skirts delicately. Everyone found their eyes pulled to her.

The Duke dropped heavily onto the only remaining seat.

"Listen to me, son. You are going to win." Her voice was authoritative, as one might speak to a child.

"How am I going to?"

"Tomorrow morning, every elector will be given a piece of parchment. They'll each write a name, and place their vote in a basket. The baskets will then be removed by the Consuls for counting." She smiled. "The Marodi thought they were being very clever at the beginning. A secret vote!" She smoothed her already smooth skirt. "Look at me. You are King Osgar's rightful heir. The vote is secret, and the Consuls count the votes. So we don't bribe fifty-one people. We bribe two."

I don't like it, thought Errios, as soon as he realised

what she meant.

Antonos cackled. "Ah, yes. Clever woman. But d'you think we can?"

"I don't know what you've spent the last six months doing, but I've been acquiring information. Invildi and her husband have been spending a lot of money on grand buildings lately. He's a gambler - and their son's newly betrothed to a high-ranking woman, Lady Madigam of Adgor, they say. They're planning the grandest wedding the city has ever seen. She needs the gold. Jaikkad will do whatever she tells him, and also wants to help his grandchildren buy their future.

"I've arranged a meeting tonight, in a secret place. They want to meet the four of you, and they want five hundred gold pieces."

"Five hundred! Of course, we have what Tell and Exor brought back -"

The Duke looked up sulkily. "I want to win because I win."

"Winning is winning."

"My friend," said Antonos, "is it so different? Paying people to vote for you, or paying people to lie about the result?"

"It is different. It's not for the Consuls to choose!"

"The Consuls don't choose. We choose, as God has chosen," said Antonos. "The Haymonese will accept what has to be. As they do."

"I might win anyway," muttered the Duke.

"You might," said his stepmother. Her voice was like a whip. "It's true that you've done everything possible to lose from the beginning. Anyone who's returning our gold is doing so because of the mess you've made of this Council. For once, Haras, don't think only of yourself, and your childish feelings. You owe it to your father, who was a great man; you owe it to your sister, rest her soul, not to throw this away. What did you say to me, when Jilna died? 'I swear I will be worthy of her, and of Vard.' Be worthy. Take up Vard's destiny, Jaryar's destiny. Or abandon us all to the barbarians."

Errios opened his mouth, but before he could speak, the inner door jerked, and the woman Illi ran in, ignoring the Duchess' disapproving expression. She was very pretty, dressed now in silver and rose. She took her lover's face in her hands, and said, "You will do it, my lord. My love. Listen to her." She kissed him quickly, and said in a soft voice, "I want to lie with a king before I die." Or that was what he thought he heard.

The Duke embraced her tightly, eyes shut. Then he stepped back, straightened his shoulders, and faced his stepmother. "Yes. We will meet the Consuls, and do this."

"The Marodi may suspect," said Antonos.

"Of course they may," said the Duchess. "But we came here because the Haymonese are fair and unbiased – it was their idea. And Barad is Haymonese -think what a terrible insult it would be to suggest any doubt. If they do, we accuse them. We say that plainly they never intended to accept an unfavourable verdict – that they're seeking an excuse for war. While denouncing us for the same thing. Surely you can manage to say something like that?"

"Indeed, Duchess. I could. Are we agreed, then?"

"No, my lady, we are not," said the Archbishop. She turned to Errios, almost the first time she'd spoken to him since leaving Vard. "What is your opinion, sir?"

He didn't like being looked at, but he growled, "We didn't come here to let the bloody Haymonese choose our King. For money."

"You're right. I certainly did not. I came here to support the Duke, but the Jaryari church is not his creature, nor yours, lady." The tall dark Archbishop towered over the small sitting woman. "I do not like the way you've behaved, you and your paramour." Errios saw Antonos' mouth and hands grow taut at that. He remembered that the other man's wife was the Archbishop's cousin. "I don't like the way you have presumptuously planned war. Two weeks ago I was sitting by King Osgar's bed. He can barely speak. He may have signed a letter that you thrust before him without the Chancellor's knowledge, but if so he didn't understand it. You have taken advantage of his sickness to do what he would never have approved. I should have said so in the Theatre, but loyalty restrained me.

"And I do not like this. If the Consuls need the whole delegation to agree, then they don't have it."

The Duke opened his mouth, and shut it again when Antonos put a hand on his arm.

"A high-minded and holy response, as I would expect from you, Your Reverence," said the Duchess, looking upward. "How much gold was it that your nephew stole from his diocese, when he was priest in Frin? What were the other crimes he committed – the list is too long for me to remember at present – before you and your sister bribed everyone to silence, and had him moved on? Oh, I know, so many priests abuse their power, and we all conceal our kinsfolk's sins - except that *you* sent out that noble decree two months ago, did you not, *De Ira Dei,* against nepotism and corruption in the Church? I may be dishonest, but I'm not such a hypocrite. The Prelate might be interested, and so might the King, and so might the other bishops in Jaryar. They're not all fond of you."

The Archbishop had frozen - still towering, but like a dead tree. "You spy on everyone, do you?" she said.

"I seek information and then I use it, yes. You will support King Osgar's decision, and that of your future King. And you, sir -"

Errios wondered, really curious, which of his sins she was going to use against him. But she simply turned her head and smiled. "You swore allegiance to Duke Massin thirty-two years ago. You will obey his son." She raised an eyebrow in the direction of the Duke.

Who said, "Errios."

"My lord."

"You don't like it, but it's necessary. You will come to the meeting, you will not argue, and you'll speak of this to no one."

Errios hesitated, remembering the little boy, now grown up. And he thought of that morning, when the King of Marod had bowed so humbly, and apologised to him. He'd planned for that to be the most glittering memory of his life, and now it was tarnished.

"On your allegiance to me."

But the Duchess was right. "Yes, my lord. I will obey."

"Come," said the Duchess. "You're all needed."

*

King Garayn lay in a garden. It was a strange thing, a space set aside in a city, for plants to grow and be pretty, and people to idly walk. And for a tomb. The King's Garden was perhaps quarter of an acre of low hedge mazes, mosaicked paths, a few trees, and squares of pretty bushes. High walls were scribbled with climbing roses, not yet in bloom. White flowers glowed, sending out sweet April fragrances. In the centre, on a bed of heather, were a raised slab of stone and a cross. Four carved stone animals, a wolf, a lamb, a lion and an ox, stood at the four corners of the heather, facing inwards.

Meriden sat alone on the back of the lamb, looking at the tomb. By now it was too dark to see the carved words, but he'd read them earlier.

Garayn, son of Arator. The last King of Haymon. 465 –

521.

He accepted what had to be. You who pass by, forbear to judge.

Not many people did pass by. The Garden was beautiful and immaculately kept, serene in the grey moonlight. But there was no one else here.

He remembered the other tomb, the one on Stranger's Hill.

Gormad Kingsbrother from Marod.
Born 560, died 601.
He won the Battle of the Lither.
He came from the east, to a land not his. He fought for strangers, and died for strangers, and saved our people. His deeds are known from Marod to Lefayr, from Qasadan to Ricossa.
We will not forget. May God bring him to everlasting joy.

Whimsically, Meriden wondered what King Garayn and Gormad the Lucky might say to each other when they met in heaven. If they met. Garayn had committed suicide, and perhaps forfeited salvation. He could ask a priest.

He tossed a small pebble from one hand to the other. The vote was tomorrow - the murderous Marodi or the bloodthirsty Jaryari. Meriden supposed it was only decent to hope there wouldn't be a war, but otherwise he still didn't care. A failing in him, probably a sin.

So many hours spent in that bloody Theatre, his mistress' bodyguard or witness, standing at the back with her and sometimes Kariam; feet aching, and hands itching for something to do, even folding linen. But they had to obey Talinti's maddening sense of duty.

The event hadn't exactly been dull, certainly not today, with all these people's humiliation: their glee; their anger; their triumph and confusion and distress. Talinti's distress had been very great. Perhaps she was blaming herself. So many passions swirling about the hall.

Passions were for other people.

He was ready to go home, to dance at Sametta's wedding, and continue with his unimportant life. *Vanity of vanities, says the preacher, all is vanity.*

Again he looked at the Last King's tomb, the only thing in Vach-roysh he'd wanted to see. Perhaps he'd hoped that it might hold some answers; but it seemed it did not. There were no answers to the contradictions of life in Haymon.

"He accepted what had to be."

But, *"If my King tells me Haymon is worth dying for, then it is."* Gormad, the hero.

But, "*Haymon is a <u>name</u>!*" Malda, his first lady.

The Jaryari had killed both of them, by the Lither.

It was all a muddle. But one thing he thought he'd decided. Talinti was a good woman, and a kind mistress, and it was time he forgave her for walking away from the battle eighteen years ago. She had obeyed her mother, and come back to care for Lithermayg, and behind her back so many people they both loved had died.

He had hated her for that for so long.

And this also was confusing, because of course as well as hating her he also admired her, respected her, impudently desired her, and even sometimes pitied her. Her husband had also died, and two of her children; and she'd had to go steadfastly on.

It was hard to let go of the hate, but King Garayn's quiet garden seemed to be telling him that eighteen years is too long to hold a grudge. He smiled, and looked up at the sky, releasing bitterness to the deep dark blue, and to the moon.

And now it was time to be getting back.

But standing up, turning, he saw yellow light by the single gate. A man came in with a torch, followed by several other people. A slow-moving but straight-backed person and a large one waited by the torch.

There was no crime in being here, and yet he paused. For several breaths he paused. And more people arrived – he thought about eight. One of them was carrying a heavy box.

The two groups faced each other, unsurprised. It was too dark to distinguish features, but then the large person said, "God be with you. We are met, then," and the sleek voice he knew. The Consul Invildi.

"Indeed," said a man.

"All four of you. Good. We assume your servants are secret. The Duchess spoke to me earlier today. Do we have an agreement?"

"Yes. We have the money." The man – Antonos of Tayn – gestured, and the box was laid down. Antonos bent to open it, and put his hand inside. Meriden couldn't see, but he heard the chink of coins. "Let's think of it as a guest-gift."

"Very good. You understand that we cannot declare an overwhelming victory. That would look suspicious."

"Of course."

"I want to win by at least ten votes," said another man, gruffly. "I am the one prophesied."

"Very well. You shall."

The box was shut.

And so it was for him – Meriden, son of Andor – to decide what to do. If he wanted to do anything. If anything could be done.

And to do it quickly.

Talinti would say he had a duty.

What should I do? Help me, he'd murmured before he realised what a dangerous prayer that is.

He thought he'd decided, and he took a step forward.

There was an angry rustle. A shape, a man, stepped fast from behind a tree, and put a sword's point at his neck. Meriden's body jangled with fear. "Stop there, my friend." There was a woman on his other side. Guards' red livery. "Who else is here with you?"

"No one else," he croaked.

"What's going on?" called someone from the gate.

"Take his sword," said the man. To Meriden, "People only come here to fuck on summer evenings, and you expect us to believe you're alone? You *must* be a spy." A hand thumped his back, pushing him forward.

Over to the little group, staring with hard faces in

the torchlight. The Duke, the Archbishop, Antonos, Errios; their several servants; the two Consuls and an attendant. And the Guards who'd been prowling around to keep the meeting private.

"A Marodi spy," said the man.

"*How did they know?*" exclaimed Antonos.

"No! I'm not from Marod. I came here to see the tomb."

"What tomb?" asked the Duke; but the Consul Invildi raised a gracious hand. She and her colleague were not in togas tonight, but wearing ordinary dark cloaks, like everyone else.

"Who are you?" she said.

He swallowed. "Andor, son of Adam. From Thrahada." *As far west as possible.* "Visiting the city."

"*Sounds* Haymonese," muttered the old man, Jaikkad.

"Yes. You came here to see King Garayn's tomb?" Her eyes bored into him.

"Yes, my lady. But, please -"

"There's no need to be afraid, my friend." She smiled, and then turned to the others. "I will deal with this." Back to Meriden. "You've accidentally strayed into something beyond your expectation. I promise you, you needn't fear. Come to the Cathedral, and then we can talk." She nodded courteously to the Vard delegation, and walked over to the gate. Her attendant went with her, carrying the box. The other Consul followed. Then Meriden, with Guards either side. Their swords were sheathed but they carried his.

The streets were quiet. Invildi paused at the edge of Cathedral Square. "I'll meet you at the shrine," she said, equally to Meriden and the Guards, and she walked across the emptiness alone. Jaikkad and the servant disappeared. The two Guards nudged Meriden under the eaves of the houses round the huge space, until they came to steps leading down to a little door in the Cathedral's north wall.

The sanctuary itself must surely be open and occupied day and night, but this room was dim and empty save for a single monk, who bowed and left by an inner door - and a third Guard, who didn't leave. It was a low-ceilinged chamber, built around a pair of tombs side by side, two women carved in stone repose, each holding an open book. Skulls and bones, and more books, were carved at their heads and feet. Fresh flowers were heaped at their sides, grey and unalive in the dark. The saints Jaddi and

Lumia, the Translators. In a niche in the wall, below a single lamp, sat a casket all of gold.

This was the place that Talinti had stood in line to pray in, while he and the others waited outside, and Tormenas tried to bribe him. The air was heavy, and silence crept around the walls.

The Consul entered from the sanctuary. She'd removed her cloak. Her plain gown was dark-blue, but gold edgings winked from neckline and cuffs. She swished over to him. "Your name again, sir?"

He bowed. "Andor, son of Adam, my lady."

"Why are you in the city?"

"I – I came here with my master. He thought he'd find more customers, with all the visitors for this Council."

"What does he sell?"

"Toys - wooden playthings for children," he said, thinking as hard as he could of Brod's little stick figures.

"And why were you in the Garden?"

"I - the other night I was - a woman told me the story of the Last King, and I was interested. And I wanted somewhere peaceful. My master shouts, my lady."

"I'm pleased that our whores know their history," she said, smiling. "I hope you haven't been hurt, Andor?"

"No, my lady."

"And what are your thoughts, as to who should rule Jaryar?"

Meriden said slowly, "I don't care who wins the vote."

"Of course you don't. It's not something that need trouble any of us in Haymon. Please accept my apologies – the Guards can be over-enthusiastic in protecting me. You may go now, and tell no one what you saw and heard. And take this for your trouble." She held out a small bag, pulling the drawstrings apart so that he could see the money. "Ten gold pieces." He heard an intake of breath behind him.

"No, thank you, my lady."

She raised eyebrows. "I didn't mean to insult you, sir. You needn't take it, although there's no reason why you shouldn't. I merely need you to swear an oath of silence." She stepped back, and gestured royally to the casket in its niche.

"And keep it, if you know what's good for you," said one of the Guards behind him.

"Dard!" She smiled at Meriden, as if they shared secret knowledge. "Andor will keep it because oath–breakers go to hell. And if he broke it, there would indeed be trouble for him, and for his family. But mostly because he's an honourable man." She inclined her head, waiting. "Do we understand each other?"

"I will not break your oath," he said.

"No."

Deep breath. "I won't break it, because I will not swear it."

Her smile deepened, but her eyes were startled. "I cannot be certain of your silence if you don't swear."

"You won't have my silence. Don't do it. Don't take their gold."

"You said you didn't care who wins the vote."

"I don't care who rules Jaryar. I care that you don't let them cheat."

He watched her puzzlement. "What - *why?*"

"Because – because -" He wasn't an eloquent man. Staring at the floor, he stumbled, uneloquently, with what he'd just realised – or decided - he thought. "Because you're the Consuls. You're the rulers, like kings, kings of Haymon. Kings should do justice, and right. Should be honest. This is wrong. The vote – whoever wins, the vote should be fair. You should give them that."

"Honest? What do such as you know of honesty?"

With contempt, "I suppose you mean you want more money."

"No."

She stepped forward, staring at him intently. *Please don't know me. Don't remember seeing me in the Theatre. Talinti, her children, Brod, Kariam.*

He was concentrating so hard on this, and on not showing his fear, rapidly rising to terror, that he heard nothing from behind. Till abruptly his arms were seized and held behind him. The first Guard walked in front, and hit him in the stomach. He doubled over, and was pushed to the ground, to his knees. His head was thumped forwards, so that his forehead scraped the stone, and then dragged back up. Several different kinds of pain. Bearable pain, so far.

The Consul loomed above him. Clumsily she knelt, and took his chin in her hand.

Moments passed.

Clearly and deliberately, "I do not wish to waste any more time. I want you to swear an oath, Andor, for your own sake.

"But I do not need you to swear it. I only *need* to be sure you won't tell anyone. I'm sure you understand."

He understood very well.

"I feel fear, I see Death," Upali had said.

His death.

Oh God.

The Vote

"Bring him over."

He was dragged to his feet, and over to the hollow in the wall. Blood dribbled past his eye, tickling. Beside him, the Consul crossed herself, and opened the casket.

The ancient holy book, older than the Cathedral, bound in leather studded with gold and pearls.

"Listen, Andor. People die in this city. They get drunk, and then they get into fights. Almost every week. Is that how you want to be remembered?"

He'd been drunk before. Talinti would remember. The truth was so much less believable.

"Now. It's your choice. Swear, and go home, take some money if you like, not if you don't, and live. Or don't swear, and die. But it'll make no difference whatever to who wins in the Theatre tomorrow. We have decided what's going to happen, and it will."

She lifted his hand, wiped the palm hastily on her sleeve, and placed it on the book.

"Your oath."

"No."

He half expected a long pause, but she immediately tossed his hand out and back at him. "Don't make a mess in the Cathedral, Dard." Almost as fast as that, she was gone.

There were three of them. They put him on his back, and the two men held him down while the woman shoved a ball of cloth into his mouth. Terror, choking terror - but it was only to stop him making a noise as they stretched his leg out, and twisted it to the side, and the first man, Dard, took out a stick, and hit the foot.

He hit it again and again, until they all four heard a crack.

Then two of them pulled him up and to the door. Every glancing step sent pain screaming up through him. He couldn't run, or fight, or call for help.

Up the steps. Outside the door the cloth was removed just long enough for a skin to be put to his lips, and wine poured in. He spluttered and swallowed, and Dard poured the rest down his jacket.

"They get drunk, and then they get into fights."

Gagged again, he was dragged along the street. There were a few torches at corners. The younger man walked ahead, carrying Meriden's sword; Dard and the woman had their arms around his shoulders. They were two Guards carrying a tipsy citizen home. It was an ordinary Friday night, and most people were already in bed, preparing for work tomorrow. They met no one.

He was a child again, five years old, staring at his baby sister's body, learning that Death took people away.

His father falling from a roof, his mother grabbing at a sudden pain in her chest, his elder sister in childbirth, his middle brother and his friend in battle. Meriden in a tavern in Vach-roysh.

"His deeds are known from Marod to Lefayr." "If my king tells me Haymon is worth dying for, then it is."

Don't let Talinti blame herself.

Please, no! Please, I'll be good, I'll -

Would they let him change his mind? Was it possible?

They wouldn't. He wouldn't.

Oh God, please, the blackness. Everywhere was dark, and his foot hurt so much; he seemed in hell already.

A building that looked like a tavern ahead - muffled music and voices, light framing shutters. An alley ran down beside it. The youngest Guard handed the sword to the woman, and waited on the street.

The others startled a cat as they went down. The woman jerked her head at the building. "Machos'll support our story?"

"I'll tell him what to say."

The alley was not entirely clean. Mud and worse underfoot.

They pushed his back against the wall. It was at least hard and real in the nightmare. His mouth was stuffed with slimy linen, and saliva he couldn't swallow. His own sword pointed at him. *Talinti's father gave me that sword.* The big man Dard took out a knife, slashed through the laces, and reached slowly, grinning, inside Meriden's jacket. His body tensed, flinching inwards. *Saviour, Jesus, please.*

But it was only to cut a string, and the hand withdrew holding his money pouch. "Now. Let's see. You're drinking too much. You play dice with some low folk. You cheat - no, you're the fool from the country, you accuse one of them of cheating, and he hits you." Dard paused, and turned a little. Then he swung the pouch in hard at Meriden's face. Numbness in his cheek, and more blood trickling. "He and his friend walk out laughing - you're a mean git, and you're angry, and you draw, and run at them.

They knock you down, drag you out here, smash your foot and take your money to teach you a lesson. And then you annoy them, it's your *face* maybe, so they decide to finish -" He was placing the knifepoint, below Meriden's breastbone. He breathed, and smiled.

Smiled.

There was a thump, some yards back. Rapid steps. "Hey!" said the woman, and her sword wavered.

Someone was running towards them. "What?" Swords clashed in the dark. Dard thrust Meriden back, and turned to switch knife for sword, and Meriden seized what chance he had, and lurched forward to grab at him. They went down together.

Dard kicked out with the other foot. Meriden jerked away, and the boot landed on his ear. He sprawled, clinging to Dard's ankle, rolling to avoid more kicks. Above their heads a fight continued. Through a haze of pain and blood, Meriden thought there was a gurgling, and someone was slumping down to the ground.

Dard struggled away and up, and now he was fighting the stranger, a stranger too good for him. While Meriden was pulling the cloth from his mouth, and gasping, and blinking blood, in that short time, Dard was killed. He fell over backwards, almost on top of Meriden, throat gushing blood.

"Get up." A woman, dark; no one he knew.

He was sick on the ground. He tried to stand, and almost shrieked.

"Fuck you, get up!" She dragged him to lean against the wall. "Anything of yours here?"

He strove to understand. "My sword. My pouch."

She found them for him. "Lean on me. *Move.*"

They left the two dead people by the wall, and a third slumped figure by the alley entrance. He let her pull him on, not caring where.

*

"I promise you need not fear."

Errios and the others watched the Consuls and Guards leave with the Lowly man. They gave them a few moments' start.

"The Cathedral," Antonos murmured. "How do the Consuls 'deal with' eavesdroppers, d'you think? A pocketful of gold, or a sound thrashing?"

No one answered, but the Guards had a reputation.

Errios was tired, at the end of such a complicated day, and he was feeling unfond of all his fellow delegates.

"Poor bastard," he grunted to himself.

The servant on whom he was leaning heard. Quietly, she said, "Sir? The man in the garden?"

"Poor bastard," Errios said again. He didn't like it, and he remembered the little room where he'd been humiliated last night, and the Guard there.

The others were a little ahead.

So, "They went to the Cathedral. Have a look what's happening."

"And -?"

"Let me know. I don't care, short of murder."

She was gone. Leaning heavily on his stick, he made his slow way back to the Palace, and up the stairs to his chamber. There he sat down, a little dizzy, and started to wonder what he'd given her permission to do.

Half an hour later, she came back, cloak wrapped round her to conceal bloodstains beneath, and he found out.

"I stood by the door next to the Translators' shrine, and opened it to hear. They told him to swear to keep silence, and he wouldn't -"

So there were now two dead Guards and one unconscious one in the city. And a stupid *stupid* cocky over-virtuous Haymonese commoner was lying injured in a shed in the Palace backyard.

"They'd done something to his leg."

Errios hit her, just once, to relieve his feelings, and chose between his few options.

They went slowly downstairs. "She's worrying my horse is sick," he muttered to the Jaryari guard in explanation. And out. She carried a candle. Guests do not normally see the backyard: privies, stables, storerooms, he supposed. They pushed into a dark shed with large chests and barrels. The youngish man was lying on the floor, blinking up at them in the sudden light. Errios didn't know him, but he knew Errios, and his face jumped in weary terror. There was blood on him and his jacket and cloak, mixed with mud. He stank of wine and piss. And the foot was twisted.

"They were going to murder him, and pretend he'd got into a fight."

"So you said. Huh. Hold the light. Long time since I've done this." With difficulty he got down on his knees. "This'll hurt."

The man nodded. He clenched his fists, and grimaced at the darkness, but he didn't scream as Errios probed and shifted. Old evil memories of battlefield surgery swam back to him. "Give me the wood. Now the cloths." He bound and strapped the foot as well as he could. Then he stopped to pant, and catch his breath. "Listen, fellow. Andor, huh? It's broken. If you want to live, make sure the bone doesn't tear through. It hasn't done yet. It's the open wounds that let in the poison and the fever, only God knows why. And if that happens, someone has to saw it off you, or you'll die screaming in your own shit. If they do cut it off, you may still die screaming.

"So keep it as still as you can. Except for getting out of here, early tomorrow. People may want to kill you, and I don't blame them." The man winced. "Tidy him up, and give him some water," he said to his servant, "and find him a blanket."

Andor seemed to be about to speak. Errios got in first. "We will not talk about it. Not at all."

A pause. Then, "But - in the Garden, the Consuls -"

"Fuck it, no."

"Then I can only thank you, my lord," he said shakily.

"Huh. Errios, son of Broxos, no lord."

"Thank you, sir. Errios. And you?" looking at her.

"Amidral."

"Thank you, Amidral, for saving my life."

"Try to sleep," Errios said, and she helped him up. They went out. He chose again. "Get him - what he needs."

She nodded.

Back in his room Errios for once took the trouble to pray – that she'd be able to do whatever was needed without alerting anyone; that he would be forgiven; that God would sort out this mess. *I'm a plain soldier. I don't interfere with politics.*

"You will come to the meeting, you will not argue, and you'll speak of this to no one."

Creep down again, and use this knife. Shut his mouth forever. It was probably his duty, after all.

He was too tired.

*

It was a lengthy and painful process. Amidral fetched warm water and cloths, a skin of ale, and a blanket. While Meriden took off his filthy outer clothes – he couldn't manage to remove the hose – and cleaned his face, neck and shoulders as well as he could, she shifted boxes and barrels, and helped him to drag himself into as hidden a corner as possible. Then they shared the ale.

He snatched looks at her, his enemy rescuer. As dark-skinned as the King, with similar very short hair, black tinged with grey. The candle-light found fresh angles on her face. A high forehead, and a forward-jutting jaw; fresh bruises. Long powerful fingers, curled around the skin.

"Why did you -?" he began.

She shrugged; angrily, it seemed.

Tormenas' people might wonder where he was; might be worried. But that couldn't be helped – Amidral had no reason to take her suspicious blood-stained self into the night for him. People might even now be finding the bodies, and ringing bells, or whatever they did. Besides, he hadn't told her his true name, and didn't want to. At all costs, he must keep Talinti and the others clear.

And he was beginning to see that he still had a decision to make. He was alive, but that wouldn't stop them. He had to tell someone. Go to the King.

More fear.

He thought of the Marodi anger in the Theatre that day. He thought of his news multiplying it ten-fold. And of the long lines of bodies, after the Battle. *"The sheep, they all wait – for mild peace or grim war."*

Amidral got up. "I'll find you some bread?"

"No. Thank you. I ate earlier. I'd be sick again."

She grunted.

He said, "I want to stop them. The Consuls."

"You can't. He'd like it stopped, though." Meriden stared at her. "The Duke ordered it, and he does what he's told, but he'd rather fight people than bribe them. Gruff old troll."

"What do you want?" he asked cautiously, looking up at her.

"Me? I don't care." Then she slowly drew her sword, and he felt fear rush back, a cold wind. "I'll get you out of here first thing tomorrow. And, Andor, you tell no one that we helped you. No one ever."

"No one ever."

"Swear it. On your mother's grave."

There were other graves that meant more to him, but this oath he was willing to make.

"I swear."

She sheathed her sword, and bent down.

"Please leave the candle."

"Huh. Don't set fire to anything."

She was gone.

He took deep breaths, thinking. Then, with a

grimace, he picked up his jacket. From its inside, he removed the parchment and pen that a good steward should always carry, and flattened the writing surface on the floor. There was just enough space, huddled behind boxes. He brushed some mud off his cloak while he thought what to say; and tried to sponge the wine off the jacket. Picked up a few bits of straw and put them in a neat pyramid, and jerked a box more into line with the others.

"Meriden, son of Andor, to the Most Noble Consul Invildi, greeting."

Perhaps not.

At last he wrote, *"I am the man that Dard did not kill. People died for Haymon. Do not betray them for gold."*

He blew out the candle, and tried to sleep. And strangely, blessedly, sleep came.

*

To Lida's awe and Fric's delight, the room Prince Braidoc had left behind had been allocated to them. Fric eventually tired of rolling around and bouncing on his knees on the magnificent bed, and fell asleep in a wide-armed sprawl. Lida slept on a pallet by the fireplace. Now she woke to a feeling of disconcertedness, and for a few moments couldn't remember why.

Her Prince had had to flee to Defardu, and she would never see him again.

And today was the vote! Today! She rolled at once out of her blankets, washed her face, and opened the shutters to look out at the courtyard, which a single servant was crossing with a bucket. And up at the fresh pale tingling blueness.

Chilly blueness. She shivered as she stood there in her smock, and grabbed for clothes. But excitement galloped up and down her veins, all through her – surely the Queen would win. Wouldn't she? *"She is the rightful heir."*

The delegation and their servants ate together in the Flowery Hall. As Lida and Fric entered and bowed, the King was cutting the rind off a piece of cheese, and smiling grimly at Mistress Fillim, sitting opposite him. "You should eat something."

"Yes, Your Grace." She turned her head rather slowly towards Fric. "Fetch me a large bowl of water – cold or warm, not hot."

Of course, all the delegation had been out late last night, trying to talk to electors in inns and taverns. Lida looked down to hide her smile.

"How much did you have to drink, sister?" the

King asked. Fillim grimaced, and he turned to Kalla on his left, or rather to the parchment she was writing on, with names in three columns. "Yes. Indesandu are still ours. I could hardly get away from old Voros. Lefayr?"

"Three of them," said Fillim, closing her eyes. "But that young idiot Marni seems eager for a holy war."

"Shit. I thought we could count on Lefayr. The clerics?"

The old Abbot rubbed his forehead tiredly, and cleared his throat. "Many of them were made anxious by what they heard yesterday. They prefer peace to war. But others were impressed by the Archbishop's arguments about the prophecy. They don't want to offend her. Or the King."

"King Osgar, who barely understands who it is he's talking to any more!" Lida's King tossed down his knife.

Fric came back in, edging past Draider in the doorway, and carrying a pretty bowl and a towel. He put it before Fillim, and she dipped in her hands, and placed them against her face. Then she dipped the whole face in, lifted it out, leant back, and covered it with the towel.

"Better?" asked the King.

"Mm. Your Grace." The cloth fluttered as she

spoke. "The Vendor party were arguing. Lady Dyallit's nephew over-praised my speech, and asked me to marry him. He knelt at my feet and gave me this." She fumbled at her side for a tall-stemmed purple arbinna flower lying on the table, and lifted it, twiddling the stem.

"Ha. Which he picked up from the mud? Is that what that line means?"

"But the 'bloom' is the Duke's sweetheart," said Fric suddenly.

Everyone turned to stare at him. Fillim took the towel off her face, and sat up straight. "What did you say?"

He grinned nervously. "The Duke brought a woman he loves – and her family's very poor. She comes from a street in Vard-town called 'Muddyhooves Lane', a groom told me. So that's what it means – 'a bloom from the mud.'"

His smile faded as he looked from adult face to face.

The King stood up. "Fillim, what is your squire's name?"

"Fejederic. Fejederic, son of Santos."

"Fejederic, who else have you said that to?" His voice was very cold.

"N-no one."

"Who else?"

"No one, Your Grace! I only thought of it just now."

"If you repeat it to anyone outside this room," said the King deliberately, "I'll have your tongue cut out, as they do in Ricossa to keep servants silent. Do you not understand that we need to win?"

Fric stood frozen. Lida felt unbearably sorry for him.

"Bloody hell," said the King, dropping back onto his chair. "Braidoc was right, you realise. He told us they were planning war."

No one spoke.

"Ahh. And in an hour or two it'll be over." He leaned back, staring at the ceiling.

Master Draider put out a hand and squeezed Fric's shoulder gently.

Then they made ready to leave. The Abbot stood, and formally asked God to bless what they did. The delegation smoothed hair and clothes. Either the prayer or the magical power of grown-ups seemed to calm them, and make them again grand and strong. King Barad was wearing a simple circlet on his mossy hair, a long red gown, with wide sleeves patterned in blue, and a gold belt. He looked fit to be King of Jaryar, or anywhere, Lida thought. The Abbot was much as ever, but Mistress Fillim's usual jacket and hose had been exchanged for an overgown of dark blue, with paler blue – like the sky - beneath. Her hair was plaited and coiled around her face, and topped with a neat blue cap.

The wretched Fric had spilt a few drops of porridge on his jacket front. The others were passing through the door, but Lida had to wait to rub at it with napkin and water, and assure him with cross pity that no one would notice. "Come on."

By now they knew the way to the Theatre well. There was a covered walkway to its entrance, and electors were trickling along it and in, nervously self-important. Fric and Lida had lost their delegation, which didn't really matter as they'd be standing at the back, but annoyed her.

A man leaning on a stick entered the walkway from the other side just as she did. For a tiny moment, she wondered if he'd been waiting for her. "Your pardon – it is Lida, I think? Lida from Marod?"

"Yes, sir."

The Lithermayg steward was very different today. He wore no cloak although the day was chill, his face was grazed and bruised, and his lower leg was all bound in cloth. But still he had a tidy look. "May I ask your assistance? I need to – to take a message up to the stage, and as you see I'm not very steady. Could you be kind enough to prevent me from stumbling?"

"Yes, of course, sir." So Fric scampered on, but Lida fell behind and took his arm. At least the man hobbled briskly, swinging the injured leg, pressing down on his stick, staring firmly ahead.

"How were you injured, sir?"

"Oh - I was in a fight. Some of the Guards thought I was being impertinent yesterday evening." He gave her a quick smile. They went through the doors, and into the Theatre, where delegates were standing bunched by their chairs, and electors were gossiping at their benches. Others were coming behind them. The King had wanted to be early, so it was still hubbub, business not yet begun. No one looked particularly at Lida and the limping steward as they walked down the central aisle, and then he leant on her to mount the steps.

The two Consuls were sitting side by side in their

togas, chatting together. The steward bowed. "An urgent message, my lady," he said, and when Invildi looked up, he passed her a small piece of parchment. It didn't look very clean, Lida noted disapprovingly. The man bowed again, and turned right, towards the Marodi delegation.

"Mistress Fillim?" he asked, a little awkwardly. Fillim Queensister inspired awkwardness in a lot of people. She managed to turn a polite face to him, interrupted in whatever she'd been saying to the Abbot.

"What is it?"

Quietly he said, "I – pardon my intrusion. My mistress was hoping that her message the other night was helpful."

"Yes, it was. Very helpful. Please thank her from us." Fillim dismissed him with a curt nod.

Lida felt a little sorry for him, but after all his message could have waited, and it was rather presumptuous at such a time. He let her help him back down the steps. As she turned away, she glimpsed the Consul's eyes move to Fillim, and then to them, as if puzzled. More than puzzled. Dismayed.

More than dismayed, Lida thought, but surely that couldn't be.

They made their shaky way to the back wall. "I'm very grateful. May God bless you, Lida."

"It was nothing, sir."

She edged along to find Fric.

Now nearly everyone was in place. There was an expectant buzzing along the benches.

The Consuls were talking together again. Jaikkad glanced nervously first at the Vard delegation; then at the Marodi. Then back to his colleague for another whisper.

What could they have to say? Everything was arranged yesterday.

"Hurry yourselves, can't you? We're to vote," Lida heard one of the electors mutter. On the stage, a little impatience seemed to be creeping into the formal serenity. For no obvious reason, the Consuls bent sideways, speaking to the nearest delegate on each side. King Barad nodded peaceably, but Duke Haras looked rather shocked. *Hurry up.*

The Consul Invildi stood. "Welcome, all. This is the time of decision. I will ask the Holy Secretary Mary to pray for God's blessing and direction for you today. Then a parchment will be delivered to each elector for their vote. Place your votes in the baskets at the front of the Theatre."

She lifted her head, and spoke to a place high up, where the wall met the ceiling. "And so that all can bear witness to the fairness of the result, we invite the Secretary, and the electors from this front bench here, to join us in the back chamber of the Theatre, to observe the counting."

That seemed sensible, Lida thought.

Two Guards stepped up to the back row of electors, each with a basket of blank parchment. The Prelate's Secretary moved to stand before the stage, and raised her arms formally to heaven.

*

Talinti sat still while Kariam plaited and tied up her hair, and then they went down to breakfast. The vote was today. And if the Duke won - "We shall take Marod."

Kariam ate fast and twiddled her fingers, a sign normally of pleased excitement.

The sunlight was bright in the courtyard. Bunches of electors were gossiping in varying tones, and none of them looked welcomingly at the foreigners.

Then Kariam squeaked as Tormenas bowed. "Greetings, kinswoman. I'm here because – well, it's historic, is it not? But also I'm a little concerned. You should know that your man Meriden didn't come home last night."

"Oh?"

"He ate supper, and walked out, promising to be back later – and we've not seen him since. I hope he's not in any trouble."

"Oh, I hope not." Kariam's voice was malicious, and Tormenas' was bland, and Talinti felt annoyed with both of them. Meriden was a single youngish man in the city, probably with money in his pouch, and if he didn't choose to sleep in his own bed, it wasn't hard to guess what he'd chosen to do instead. She didn't care for their plain desire to bring him into disgrace for it.

But it was ill-mannered of him to stay out all night. And he ought to be here now. Meriden had never before not been where she needed him to be. They waited for a little while, until matters had plainly started, and he didn't come.

"He will arrive shortly, I doubt not," she said at last, "and he can find us in the Theatre, and I will flay him."

She was surprised by how annoyed she was. She set out with Kariam and Tormenas across what was still a rather full courtyard. Many people who hadn't cared about the debate seemed eager for the result of the vote. And suddenly Talinti felt afraid and alone.

"Two killed by the sword, and a third attacked! Who would dare?"

She'd passed the gossiping couple before the words fully struck her. "Who's killed?" she asked Tormenas.

"I don't know. Someone said there was a fight last night by the ale-house in St Luke's Street. It happens sometimes. D'you want me to ask about it?"

"If you know anyone well informed, thank you." He disappeared back, and for some reason Kariam went with him.

There must be fights in Vach-roysh all the time. Perhaps some of the Marodi had lost tempers. Meriden wasn't an aggressive man, nor was he interested; he would keep out of trouble.

But her heart was banging, and her shoulders cold. Great holes were tearing open around and inside her. In her mind was a strange picture of herself telling little Mritta that Meriden was dead. But she kept walking, because there was nothing else to do, and a servant threw open the Theatre doors.

No speeches were being made, but there was a buzzing. The delegates sat very still and majestic, but the electors were wriggling on their benches, showing or covering small pieces of parchment to or from each other – borrowing pens.

Observers were three deep around the wall. Almost she didn't recognise him in the lines of intense faces. Then she did, and she marched furiously through the flurry.

"Meriden, where the hell have you been?"

He was alive. Her eyes took in bruising, bandaging, a stick. "And what the hell have you done to yourself?"

He turned to her a face so joyful that she gasped; it was so unlike him. *Surely no whore in the world could make a man look like that.*

She watched him try to pull on a mask more appropriate for addressing his mistress. Watched him fail.

"I am sorry, my lady. I drank too much, and got into a fight."

Not only joy, she thought, *but triumph, and glee*.

"Come out of here. Now. You have explaining to do, and you need to see a bonesetter."

He glanced at the stage. "They're just voting -"

"I will hear it later, and you don't care."

So he limped out with her, and neither of them learned the result for some time.

*

The Consuls and their chosen witnesses were in a back room, counting. In a little while - So many people, Lida included, stared at the stage, where the King smiled, and the Duke rubbed his thumbs on his belt, and the Archbishop gazed serenely ahead, and Fillim – unbelievably – played cat's cradle with a piece of string.

Even Fric was silent. Lida recited the only two psalms she knew by heart (the 23rd and the 51st), and waited, fiddling with her jacket hem. Someone on the benches belched, and there was a general titter. Otherwise, nothing.

A future King or Queen of Jaryar. *(Overlady of the West,* Prince Braidoc had said.)

The door opened. They marched back in, and sat down, expressionless. One of the groups of electors stood up; then other scattered people did; then everyone. Their backs and heads blocked Lida's view. There was something large but non-existent in her mouth. *Please, please -*

It was Jaikkad's voice, thin and straining to be heard. And -

"The votes have been carefully counted, and re-counted. And the result. Is. For Duke Haras, twenty-two. For Queen Nerranya, twenty-nine."

"Hooray!" shouted Fric, into the silence.

A few people laughed, and more clapped, and then the clapping faded. Everyone sat down again.

Yes, yes, yes!

"But the Duke was second-born," somebody muttered.

"As was agreed," said Jaikkad, and Lida could now see his face, and thought he looked nervous, "the losing delegation will swear to abide. By the result."

And no one spoke. No one seemed to breathe. Lida looked at the evil Duke. He didn't seem to be there – as if someone had taken him away from the hall, and replaced him with a doll. He didn't look alive.

One of the electors rose from the second row, the little woman with a crimson gown and a long veil. The Duchess.

"No," she said. "Vard does not accept this."

Lida heard murmurs.

"Vard must accept it," said Invildi. "The chosen electors have voted."

"He was prophesied. Jaryar cannot have a foreign Queen!"

"I assure you, my lady," said the Holy Secretary,

"the count was fair."

"The count! Don't talk to us of the count. We are betrayed!" She stretched out an arm towards the stage – the Consuls and the Marodi.

Invildi, hands gripping the table in front of her, said, "My lady, you are an elector. You cast your vote, and it was counted, and this is not your time."

Slowly and deliberately, the Duchess said, "Treacherous, murderous, dishonourable, creatures of the devil!"

With a scraping of chair legs on the dais, the Duke stood up. "Mother."

"Haras, this is your right. Don't trust them, any of them, and their lies."

"Trust?" he said. His eyes swept over the hall. "I don't trust any person here." Back to his stepmother. "We have lost." To Jaikkad, next to him, "Give me the paper."

"Haras, you will not -" Her voice rose.

"Sit down, madam." He held out his hand, and Jaikkad put a parchment into it.

"Don't do this," said Antonos.

The Duke read, "I am Haras, son of Massin -"

"No!" the Duchess screamed.

He lifted his head. *"Sit down."* Someone pulled her to her seat.

"I am Haras, son of Massin, Duke of Vard, third of that title. I acknowledge and accept before God and this Council the verdict here given. I am, and will be, a loyal subject of King Osgar, long may he reign. If he dies without closer lawful heirs, I will -" (*Yes!*) "I will swear fealty and allegiance, for myself and my heirs, to my cousin Nerranya Marial, now Queen of Marod, and if she is dead, to her lawful successors. May God bless and guide her."

He bowed to the utterly silent hall, and then turned towards his blank-faced delegates. Lida suddenly thought she had never in her life seen anyone look so alone.

"You swore allegiance to me," he said. "Antonos. Errios. Do it."

The two men stood, old Errios stumbling a little. The Archbishop also stood, and took the paper.

"I am Elizabeth Maludi, Archbishop of Makkera. I acknowledge and accept before God and this Council the verdict here given." She passed it to Errios.

"I am Errios, son of Broxos, of Girifay, owing allegiance to Vard. I acknowledge and accept before God and this Council the verdict here given."

And finally, "I am Antonos, son of Borosin, of Tayn, owing allegiance to Vard. I acknowledge and accept before God and this Council the verdict here given."

The Duke turned to his left to meet the man who had risen to greet him.

"Kinsman, amen," said King Barad, and they awkwardly clasped forearms.

Lida felt tears pouring down her face. She heard cheering.

We won, we won, we won!

The triumph was written on her heart forever.

The Return

As the sky darkened, Meriden sat with his leg propped before him on a stool, staring at the ceiling and listening to Brod snore. The rebandaged leg hurt – bearably - and *un*bearably when he shifted position. And he was a little worried about Talinti and Kariam. They were attending the feast at the Palace, and it would be so easy for the Consul to remember who'd been standing by her side all the long days.

So there was pain, and there was anxiety, but otherwise he was happy. He hadn't been happy for many years.

Happiness was something that stopped when you grew up. You replaced it with jokes, and occasional fornication, and you did your duty, cheerfully, forever. So it had been for him, at any rate; and Talinti's way of seeming to greet each day as a gift had puzzled and impertinently irritated him.

Last night and this morning had changed that, and he was trying to understand why. It wasn't only that he was alive, when he'd expected to be dead.

He'd discovered that the rulers of Haymon were utterly ruthless and corrupt, which should be no surprise; and at the same time had discovered that the *honour* of Haymon was something for which he was – preposterously – willing to die. And – preposterously again – he had not died, but had been able, had been allowed, to do something, to make a tiny change in the way things were. No one but God, perhaps, would ever know. But he had done it.

He sat running his eyes along beams above his head, and noticing a spider-web that someone had missed, and the world was terrifying beyond understanding, and beautiful beyond belief.

So many years, when adventure and marriage and fatherhood and love had been things for other people to seek. He was no longer hurt that Sametta, and others before her, had wearied of him, and kindly but firmly set him aside, out of her life. He only wondered that it had taken her so long.

Was he still young enough to have another adventure?

He was healed of an illness he hadn't known he had, and the room faded as he sat there, enjoying being alive.

*

Errios and Antonos stood in the Jaryari meeting-room, painted with gigantic birds, waiting for the Duke. The Council was over, and so the delegates and electors were to come together for a celebratory feast and dance. An excellent plan, for the victors.

But *they* would have to face a Marodi delegation not merely triumphant, but also angry - justifiably angry and contemptuous. "They've found out, so we cannot do it," the Consul had whispered on the stage, and that had been the end of that. Five hundred gold pieces had been quietly returned.

Errios hadn't needed the whisper. He'd known as soon as he'd seen that ungrateful bastard limping up the aisle. So now the name of Vard was at the mercy of all King Barad's insults, and he himself was a traitor. Andor might have mentioned him, or the Marodi might guess. The Duke would not forgive it. To be in danger of hanging twice in two days - He stood as erect as he could.

Antonos said nothing. The Archbishop swept in and joined them, with a stiff bow. Then the Duchess.

And then the Duke; and at his side was the young

woman they all recognised, but none of them had spoken to. In a gown of deep green, her short hair concealed under a peaked hat except for a few fluffy curls, she curtsied very low and carefully to the Duchess. "Stepmother," the Duke said with rigid courtesy, "may I present to you Illi, daughter of Yenilda?"

The Duchess' sallow face paled. She stepped forward and slapped him hard on the cheek. Then she walked out of the room.

"Madam," said the Archbishop in the silence, "thank you for joining us."

"Thank you," she whispered.

The delegation and Illi crossed the antechamber in military formation, and met the Marodi outside the door of the Great Hall. The High Steward opened the door, and all marched in, past electors and their spouses and servants, to the dais where the Consuls awaited them. The Duke must have sent a message ahead, for there was an extra place at his side at the High Table.

"Your Grace," between gritted teeth, "may I present to you Illi, daughter of Yenilda?" And perhaps everyone at the table held their breath.

"I am honoured," said King Barad. "I hope my

cousin can spare you for a dance later, madam?" As they sat down, "And I've not forgotten that Her Reverence has promised me also."

The Archbishop stared; almost simpered; and Errios blinked. He thought even the Consuls seemed disconcerted. Fillim Queensister said, "This is a most impressive hall – but I understand the Great Hall in Makkera is even bigger?"

"Big enough for King Gissrin's chariot races, in our ancestors' day," Antonos managed to reply.

Such pleasantries were not at all what they'd expected.

Music started up, and tonight the musicians played loudly, and sang their best songs, and people were expected to listen. This was a relief. Errios found that after all he was hungry. His unwilling admiration for the Marodi king increased.

During a pause between songs, the King said idly, "And the streets of Makkera are really green?"

"Yes," said the Archbishop, and "Not all of them," said the Abbot, at the same time.

Antonos raised an eyebrow. "You've visited our capital, Brother?"

"Many years ago," said the old monk. He lifted his eyes, and awkwardly lowered them again. "When it was first proposed that King Jendon – *Prince* Jendon then – should marry your Lady Igalla, he – the Prince – visited Jaryar, so that they could get to know one another. My master went with the Prince, and so I was privileged to go too."

"You knew Queen Igalla?" Errios heard himself ask.

"That would be too great a boast. She was kind enough to speak to me once or twice."

Everyone seemed fascinated. "And they became friends?" asked the King.

"I believe so. They spoke together frequently, and it seemed with pleasure. They, er, he asked her to show him the city in the evenings, and they roamed across the river – we were told that was the less pleasant district, and her attendants were shocked. Not alone, of course – she took a maid, and my master and I were there, and guards." He smiled. "We were in a tavern, when someone mocked the Prince's stutter. He grew out of it in later years, I heard, but when he was young it was very noticeable. A rude fellow imitated him. Lady Igalla ordered that the man be whipped through the streets, but the Prince said that was too harsh, as his little sister laughed at him all the time."

"And when she came to Stonehill, and they were married," said Errios carefully, "did all this pleasantness continue?"

"I was sent to Defardu for my training not long afterwards. But they were said to be very devoted. They practised swordplay together."

"He was most grieved when she died," said Fillim. "He ordered two locks of her hair cut off, and plaited with two of his, so they could be together even in the grave. So they say."

"But he made war on her country a few years later." Amazingly, it was the young woman Illi.

"Come, madam," said Invildi, "let's not re-fight all the grievances of the Second War of the River."

The silence was a little awkward, until Antonos said to the monk, "He must have been a very devout young prince, to take priests with him into the Makkeran backstreets at night."

Errios had been thinking the same thing. The Abbot looked puzzled, and then, "Oh, I see. My master wasn't a priest; far from it. He was Kai Kingsbrother, and I was his squire."

"You did say you had a warlike history. And that you almost committed murder in your youth, did you not?" The King leaned forward, laying down his knife. "Forgive me, but that sounded like a story."

"I'm not a storyteller, Your Grace." But everyone was looking at him curiously, even the sullen Duke. He picked up a nut from the neat pyramid in the centre of the table, and fingered it. "Master Kai wasn't my first master. When I was a foolish lad, I was sure I was going to be the greatest warrior Marod had ever known." Errios and Fillim both smiled. "My parents were fortunate enough to squire me to one of the Thirty. He was said to be – and he was – a great swordsman, very much admired, and he was kind to me. What I felt for him was idolatry. Not less." He stared at the nut. "A few years later, he was hanged for murder and other crimes." He looked up, directly at Fillim.

"Ferrodach. My mother's brother and sister," she said, nodding.

"Yes. I knew nothing of the children. But later he told me the King had sent us on a secret mission, and I believed him. He told me this mission meant we should disobey orders, and assault a soldier, and run away, and I believed him. He told me to distract the leader of our Six when he gave me a sign, and I did - and that gave him time to kill her.

"When they hanged him, some said his name should be taken off the wall – the Table of the Thirty is carved on the north wall of Stonehill Cathedral," he explained. "But King Arrion said, 'We cannot deny the truth.' So his name remains, with the words 'the Cursed.'"

"And what did they do to you?" asked Errios.

"I was given a small penance, and a new master, and told it wasn't really my fault. I was - 'bewildered' is the best word. Everyone was very kind to me, and I was ungrateful and troublesome. And then at last God showed me that worship and prayer were what I was made for, not fighting, and that I'd never been as skilled as I thought, anyway.

"But such things stay with one, which is perhaps why I was so bold the other night, Your Grace."

"Thank God you were." The King grinned suddenly. "When *I* was sixteen, I ran away from home, and lived in the woods with a friend for four days. My parents told me I was the wildest, most depraved youth in the west of Haymon, and a disgrace to their name. But I haven't such a story as yours. And now look how respected and wise we both are. All of us here." He waved a hand vaguely, including everyone, and Errios couldn't detect any sarcasm.

The feast ended, and the servants and squires were feeding themselves at the back. People rose and flexed muscles and straightened gowns, trying to catch the eye of those who might be willing to dance with them. Younger people, anyway. Errios' servant helped him turn round on his bench, so that he could watch, and then assisted the Abbot similarly.

The two old men were silent together, a friendly silence, until the lines had been made up, and the skirts began to swing. "How long are you planning to watch, sir?" Errios asked. His back was aching.

"Eh? I shouldn't stay long. It's a snare and a temptation to me. Beautiful women." His mouth wriggled.

"Even a monk can look, surely?" Errios' eyes had found the woman Talinti, crossing hands and skipping down the line with some elector from Marithon. As before, he thought she filled her clothes out nicely, and would have looked even better without them, and he saw no harm in an old man looking.

An old man who was not after all going to be hanged.

*

"Tonight we will dance with them all, not on them," the King had told everyone earlier. "No triumph."

"We do not take pleasure in torment," Fillim quoted, and grinned.

This was being the absolute best day ever in the history of Lida's life. A Palace maid had been provided for her sole use – something that had never happened before. She had bathed in scented water, and had put on her white undergown, which she'd managed to keep perfectly creamy and clean, and had such a prettily scalloped neckline. (One day, when she was enormously rich, she would have real Ricossan lace, but this would do.) And then the rose gown was laced on round her, and the maid did her hair, and Lida was handed a real silver mirror that she could hold and watch the process in. Mirella – that was her name - plaited it up in a smooth ring, with loops that swung down by her ears, and pinned on her rose cap.

Lida turned her face this way and that admiringly before her reflection, and thought that even Jeppa would have found nothing to criticise except the vanity. There was a pang at the thought of Jeppa, who hadn't lived to see her master's triumph, but that had to be put aside, and she went down to serve and eat.

And now the King was lining up with the Consul, and next to him the scowling Duke with his lady, and other couples, and Lida hastily brushed crumbs from her mouth, and wiped her fingers on the cloth. For Fillim leaned across smiling, and said, "Lida, daughter of Arrada? Shall we prowl?" The two of them left Draider standing still serious and suspicious on the dais, his eyes following the King. And all the young and not-so-young men looked up hopefully, knowing it wasn't for them to approach anyone as great as Fillim. It was for her to choose.

But perhaps it was also inevitable that she stopped in front of Antonos. "Do you dance, sir?" And he smiled, and they stepped away, and Lida was face to face with a youth a little taller than she was. Justar.

"Do you dance, sir?"

He disconcerted her by pausing while his eyes flicked up and down. "Only if I like whoever asks," he said incorrectly; but then he smiled also, and gave her his hand.

They squeezed into the line of couples, and swung and clasped and unclasped each other and other people — and by the time the dance was finished she'd learned that he wasn't merely Antonos' squire but also his wife's cousin's stepbrother. Justar seemed surprised that in Marod it wasn't necessary for squires to be related to their masters or mistresses, or even to be highly-born. She had to throw in a reference to inheriting Dendarry some day to reassure him that she was worthy of her place. And then they poured themselves wine, and gossiped a little about the fact that Antonos was afraid he might not see his children again because of the adultery – "not that he sees them often as it is" – and agreed comfortably about the absurdity of a city like Vach-roysh, built so flat, and without proper walls.

They drifted out of the hot hall into the antechamber, and found a pillar to stand behind. He gently touched her forehead and cheek, and as she'd three-quarters hoped, he wrapped his arms around her, tilted his head, and put his lips on her mouth.

This first kiss – and the second and the third – were a very interesting experience for Lida; and also very pleasant, except for the spice on his breath. And he stroked the loops of hair, and murmured, "How long would this be, let down?" and she blushed with pleased horror at such an indecent question.

His smile curved in a way both excited and smug, and he ran his fingers over her bodice so that she tingled;

and said softly, "I was wondering, Lida, daughter of Arrada, if you know where -"

"I was thinking how lovely it is to dance," said Lida brightly, and she took his hand and led him back to the Hall. "In Stonehill once, I danced with the King himself."

She didn't dance with the King that night, except in passing in the line, for he was very busy. After the Consul, he danced with the Archbishop (slow and stately), the Duchess (stiff and silent), and the Holy Secretary Mary (enthusiastic but clump-footed). And with Fillim (sprightly), and with his sister, and with several of the electors and their wives and daughters. And even with the woman Illi, which no one else could except her lover. The Duke flouted all protocol, and ignored every other woman in the room.

Lida danced almost every dance, including another with Justar, and whenever her hands met King Barad's in the line, he lifted his eyebrows and smiled at her. And at last, when people were beginning to drift away to bed, she leaned panting on a table, and saw him near her wiping his face.

"I think I've done my duty," he said cheerfully. "A hard night's work. D'you remember the dance in Stonehill?" She nodded. "It hasn't been quite what either of us expected, I think. The Consul thanked me for my forbearance and generosity. I have no idea what she was talking about. Ah, well. To ship tomorrow."

"Will you miss it, Your Grace – your home?" she dared to ask.

"I never lived in Vach-roysh, except for a few months when I was a squire. I come from the northwest. Stonehill is my home - for the present. And in time, I suppose, Makkera." He looked around, sighed a little, and turned back to her. "And are you looking forward to going back?"

Suddenly it struck Lida that she'd come to Vach-roysh as the Prince's squire. That was her place in Stonehill. And now he was gone, and she had no place. The adults would decide what to do with her, and where she should live; and it might be back to Dendarry, or somewhere duller.

But she smiled up at the King as bravely as she could, and said, "Yes, Your Grace. Of course."

"We're both going back without someone we came with, you and I. The Marshal will find me another servant, but you?" He was grinning at her, and suddenly her heart leapt.

"I haven't had a squire since I lived in Haymon, but I think one might be useful. A squire who knows how to fight, and obey, and laugh - and think for herself. What d'you say?"

*

Talinti had been honoured by a summons to attend the feast, and she went down with Kariam. She ate and drank and smiled and danced – but after a time the music was just noise, and the bright clothes and candles just glare; and she slipped away through peaceful shadowy corridors to the Chapel.

There was no one there. Only the candles on the altar, and the Reserved Sacrament in a niche in the wall to remind her of the constant presence of her Saviour. Talinti walked forward and knelt.

She intended to pray sensible, appropriate, calming prayers. To thank God for averting war; to ask for healing for Meriden and Brod; to beg protection for all the visitors from Lithermayg, Jaryar and Marod on their long journeys home. And for Kariam, who she strongly suspected didn't intend to go home. And then to reflect, as she should, on her own sins and mistakes and confusion.

But instead she put her face in her hands, and burst into tears.

She couldn't pray sensibly, for nothing made sense.

"The second will rule, when the counting is done." The second?

And Meriden. *"I went to the King's Garden, as I told you I would, and sat there for a little, and then I went to a tavern and had a few drinks. Perhaps one too many. There were some big fellows there who took something I said as an insult to the Consuls, and decided to teach me respect. So there I lay in the gutter, and a couple of Good Samaritans passed by, who bandaged me up and let me sleep in their shed. It's absurd, my lady, but I was too confused and, I fear, too drunk, to remember their names."*

Or where they lived. Or which tavern.

None of it was believable. But he'd served her faithfully for many years, and she didn't like to accuse him of lying to his face. Two of the Consuls' Guards had been killed that night, and a third bashed on the head. Talinti had checked his sword, and it was clean, but that proved little.

He was not a murderer. She knew this. *Oh dear God.*

Of course she'd realised months ago that she liked Meriden better than was wise, or even proper. And – to be honest, as she must be – she'd brought him to Vach-roysh, not just because he was a witness, and very useful, and to cheer him up, but because she couldn't do without him. She could not do without Meriden to stand by her side; to dare to criticise and tease her; to effortlessly read her mind.

So now. She'd sowed the wind, as the Scriptures said, and she'd reaped the whirlwind.

He is my servant, whose duty is to obey me in all things, and I took shameful advantage of that five years ago. I have forfeited any right – any chance – to speak honestly to him, and expect an honest answer. About anything.

(Five years ago. She had snuffed out the candle with one hand, and laid the other on his arm. So lonely. And had stood very close to him, clothes touching, until he kissed her. "Yes," she had said, and he'd carried her to her bed. And no more words at all had been spoken until morning, when she said, "You should go.")

I'm in love with him, she thought now, madly, tears spilling through her fingers and onto her best gown. *And I cannot marry him because he's my steward, and anyway he dislikes me.*

I cannot marry him because he dislikes me, and anyway he's my steward.

She couldn't even talk to him about it. She could do nothing but wait for the weeks, or months, or years that it might take for this feeling – this desperate yearning affection – to go away.

She had never been in love before, and she had no idea how long that would be.

*

So they rode home.

The first time someone edged his horse up next to Errios' Hercules and whispered, "Sir - are you for the Duchess or the Duke?" Errios had simply glared in silence until the man sidled away. But then he thought about it. The second time, he allowed the enquirer a single glance, before saying quietly but distinctly, "I have honoured the Duchess, and I do so still. But my allegiance will always be to the Duke, as is my duty. Is it otherwise with you?" And the woman looked ashamed.

It wasn't a very clever reply, Errios thought, but he repeated it steadily when asked or hinted at, and after a day he heard someone else saying it. Being wrongly accused of murder had enhanced his prestige. Otherwise, he said little, and kept away from the whispering, and the anxious huddling into two groups.

The Duchess' secretary had left for Vard-town - or was it Makkera? - early on the morning after the vote. When this was pointed out to the Duke, he sent his younger brother and another friend to follow at once. It is useful to tell your version first.

Everyone else departed in the early afternoon, hardly sorry to leave the city. Errios remembered just in time to order his servant to buy sweetmeats for his grandchildren.

Now they were over the river, back in Jaryar, and parties of electors were bidding them a warily courteous farewell, and peeling off due south or southeast. Errios was looking forward to his home. It seemed unlikely that he would ever travel so far away again.

On and on – straight back, aching joints, impassive face - splintered mind. Talking to nobody.

He heard hooves behind him, and ignored them. But the other rider came alongside and didn't move on, so he had to look up. The handsome young man with small neat beard and overly-calm face.

"My lord."

The Duke nodded. He said nothing for a little, as they rode side by side. None of his servants joined them, which must be by his order. Therefore he had something to say.

At last, "Errios."

"My lord."

"That day, in the Theatre, I said I trusted no one in the room. You should know that I never intended that to apply to you."

"Thank you, my lord."

"You've always been loyal. And you advised me well." The Duke stared at his fingers, gripping the reins whitely. "When I woke that morning, before, I wished I'd listened to you and the Archbishop, and chosen honour.

"And now I've lost everything." His voice was raw.

You are still Duke of Vard. That's not nothing. But you've been the Duke for some time, and no songs have been made about those years.

"You remember my sister?" the Duke asked, and now tears were squeezing out from his eyes.

"Yes, my lord."

"She would have laughed at the thought of me as a King."

That was true. Duchess Jilna hadn't been the kindest of sisters.

"And now everyone will laugh."

"No, my lord."

Errios wondered if the Duke wanted him to provide comfort – some wise saw from his grizzled years.

But he'd never had time for that crap. People do what they do, and learn what they learn.

The quietness at last perhaps became a good quietness. Duke Haras wiped away the tears that no one else had seen, and looked up. He said, "I will not abandon Illi."

It was not, Errios thought, the most important decision he had to make. Nor perhaps the most sensible one. But it was a decision. He bowed stiffly, and the Duke rode on and rejoined a little group consisting of the Archbishop and two electors from Vendor.

Errios turned and jerked his head at the woman who'd been riding a few paces behind him all the time. As she approached obediently, he said, "Give me the wine."

She had served him for eighteen years, ever since he'd saved her life in the Battle of the Lither. She would go on serving him until he became so decrepit that it was indecent. When he needed a man to wash him and put him to bed he would provide for her somehow. As he unstoppered the skin she handed him, he asked, "Why did you do it?"

There was no one else within hearing.

"You ordered me, my lord."

"I ordered you to go and see. Not to kill two Guards!" *And ruin our mission.*

She said nothing.

"Look at me. Why did you?"

Because I know you, my lord. Because I know that you hated the Duke buying a throne, you like battle to be open, and you love tales where heroes rescue the innocent. Because that man's murder would have haunted you, and you would've feared it would bring bad luck to Vard, and Jaryar.

All true, and all making it his responsibility. He knew he didn't want to hear her say it. But he'd asked the question, and her hesitation was an affront to him, so he glared threateningly, and said again, *"Why?"*

"Because -" She turned her head away, and spat into the grass by the road. "I didn't like those Guards."

"Explain."

"I've heard things about them. And Asor told me how they made him talk."

Asor? Errios had to think back a long way to his incompetent spy. "That Fillim thumped it all out of him."

"She hit him a few times, but all that got was his name and his village. Then she went off to the debate, and the Guards took over. They knew where he lived, and they said they'd send people there. He cried when he told me. The things they promised him they'd do to his wife and children. So he talked."

"Oh."

Perhaps that was the reason. One of the reasons.

He handed back the wine-skin, and grunted.

"Do you need anything more, my lord?"

"No. Thank you." He hesitated. "Thank you, Amidral."

*

Slowly the city of Vach-roysh emptied. The Vard delegation had been the first to leave; then the Marodi, and the first of the electors. Beggars were permitted back on the streeets, and the prices in taverns and shops fell back to what Talinti supposed were their usual levels.

And Kariam came to her meekly, and asked to be released ten weeks early from her current quarter's service. Tormenas had offered her a place in his household, caring for his child and helping to run his business. It was very plain that Tormenas also had other things in mind - and that Kariam was aware of this, and pleased about it. Talinti attempted a clumsy warning, which was not well received.

"Thank you for all your kindness, my lady. I'm not afraid,

and he's a respectable man - and I know where the herbs grow." So she agreed.

Meriden's foot was healing well enough after a week for him to ride if someone helped him mount and dismount, but Brod was still in bed. So Talinti had to arrange for her groom to be cared for in the city, and then transported home - and meanwhile to hire a professional guard, on Tormenas' recommendation, to escort two people back to Lithermayg. This journey had turned out terrifyingly expensive, but her steward kindly refrained from pointing this out.

So three of them rode away from Vach-roysh on a cloudy day. The guard, Affrai, was silent, and rode in front; and Talinti and Meriden rode behind. They also were rather silent. There were no songs, and no jokes.

She wondered how much his leg was hurting.

For two days after his accident, despite the pain and inconvenience, he'd glowed with his mysterious joy. Then one morning it had disappeared, and it hadn't come back. His face wasn't bored; his voice wasn't flat; but he was glum.

She wondered why, and wished she could do or say something to cheer him up. But such thoughts only brought danger.

Sometimes she caught him looking at her, and hastily away. Perhaps he was expecting more questions. Or perhaps he was waiting for her to admit something. As she should.

Her uncle said one should never permit a servant to criticise, even by a look, and that had also been Izzan's opinion. But not hers, she hoped. So after a few hours, and to Meriden's obvious surprise, she asked, "How long have you been in service at Lithermayg?"

He thought. "Since I was ten. Twenty-one years."

"A long time." She smiled, teasing. "A very long time to do everything I ask, and endure all my strange whims."

"I haven't always done that," he said, smiling back.

"Not quite always. But still. There are things that are hard to say." *Many things. And especially hard for me to say to you.* "But twenty-one years gives you the right to scold, so I'm ready to hear anything you want to say."

"To scold, my lady?"

"Of course. You made it plain you thought this journey was a foolish waste of our time, and so I see it was. I was arrogant enough to think that God had a special use, a special message, for us, and we could be important. I didn't ask why He should choose to speak at Lithermayg, or through that woman Upali. 'Cursing Upali.'"

It did humiliate her to say it. Meriden was staring at her with unhelpful blankness. "You think the prophecy was mistaken, my lady?"

"Of course it was mistaken! Upali must have been deceived, or deceived herself." Talinti made her voice go on. "She described the Theatre, and the meeting, but nothing else was right. Only one person died; there was no blood. And 'the second' should have meant the Duke. It must have meant him."

"Because he had an older sister?"

"He had an older sister, he was younger, he was named second. And also - no one mentioned this, but he and his people arrived second, a full day after the Queen's delegation. It wasn't a prophecy, it was deluded nonsense, and I led us on a useless errand. So far you've been too courteous to say this, but I give you leave to say and think these things, and anything more I haven't mentioned."

"It wasn't useless." His mouth twisted.

"No, you're right. Worse than useless. We spent a great deal of money, we annoyed a lot of people, and you and Brod were almost killed. We should have stayed at home, as you said."

He burst out laughing.

It was perhaps the most unexpected, and the most hurtful, way he could have reacted. And he plainly understood this, for almost at once he was trying to stop himself, and to apologise, but he couldn't. He laughed, and she waited. Affrai looked back a little curiously, and then forwards again at the road.

"Forgive me, my lady," Meriden said at last. "Kariam wouldn't agree with you."

"Kariam has a new place in the city. She may still be glad of that in three months' time, or she may not."

"And we were helpful to Mistress Fillim's enquiries," he said. "You and Kariam were. So she found the murderer."

"I think she would have done that anyway. She seemed an able person." Crossly she asked, "Why can you not admit that you were right and I was wrong? I am wrong sometimes."

He stared at Leo's ears. He seemed to be thinking hard, and she wanted to slap him. Meriden had criticised her with eyes and silences so often; why couldn't he find the words now? "I don't know," he said at last, "if God spoke to Upali or not. But whatever her words meant or didn't mean, I've changed my mind. I think we were right to go. It was good for me, in any case. I was blessed in Vach-roysh."

"*Were* you?" she asked. *What the hell happened to you that night? Did you fall in love, and that's why you're out of sorts, that you had to leave her behind?*

"Whatever it all meant, you did what you believed was right. And so you should. You told the Council, and left them to decide."

Talinti shrugged, feeling oddly unshriven. She sensed them both awkwardly casting around for something else to say.

"My lady, did you know it was him? Prince Braidoc? You said – I don't remember when – but I said it must've been the Jaryari, and you said maybe not. How did you guess?"

He had no right – there was no one in the world she needed to tell. Everything was very quiet; two ducks squawked and splashed at each other on the river beside them; and then it was quiet again.

She heard her voice saying, "I've never fought in a

battle. And neither, I think, have you."

"No."

Talinti went on jerkily. "No, but people say - I've heard - that when men have fought and won a victory, have killed people, what many of them want afterwards isn't rest, as you'd think, but a woman. A whore, or one of their battle comrades – or some other available woman."

She stared at her reins. *Was he watching her? Would she be able to feel it if he did?*

"The night it happened, the murder, I was afraid. I thought there might be more deaths, and I went to the Palace chapel, and so did other people. Prince Braidoc came and prayed, and we left together, and walked back to our chamber, Kariam's and mine. The way he looked and spoke, and what I learned he did afterwards, made me think that was what he was seeking."

Now she glanced up, and he was looking away. Perhaps embarrassed. "It seemed an odd way to act, on such a night, and for a prince of his reputation."

"They should have killed him," said Meriden, after a moment. That was all.

They rode on, back to silence, and her soul felt very sore.

*

The streets of Stonehill had been full of cheering crowds, ignoring the drizzle. And now Lady Meril the Marshal presented the returned delegation to a more high-born dry crowd in the White Hall, and the King stood before his wife to report on all that had happened.

Of course messages had arrived before they did, and none of it startled the Queen. She knew the good, the bad and the terrible; and she didn't flinch as those around gasped. King Barad gave full credit to Fillim Queensister, to the Abbot, to Draider, and to Jeppa; and he was interrupted several times by cheers.

He finished, and kissed her hand, and the Queen smiled.

"I thank you, my love. The Council and I approve and endorse all your actions. You didn't set out for war, but you've achieved a great victory. Marod had to win, for everyone's sake. Sooner or later, something like this was bound to happen. This way, it's without fighting. We can now hope there will never be another Jaryar-Marod war."

She sat down, and he sat beside her. Lida and the others rose from their knees.

Lady Meril handed the Queen a parchment.

"I grieve for the crimes of my brother, and of the man Yaif, son of Adam. By this order, which I now sign, they are both condemned to exile from Marod, never to return on pain of death. If any are aware of debts they leave, or further crimes they have committed, such information should be laid before the Marshal." She signed the parchment, and set it down.

"I am grateful to your companions also. Every one of them here -" her eyes scanned the group - "every one, was given a sacred trust, and has fulfilled it with honour. The chronicles of three countries will recall these few weeks, and I intend to be sure that the Marodi ones at least give credit to our friends." Lida's heart swelled with pride, knowing it was true that she at least had been useful.

"And one in particular."

She half-turned to her husband, and King Barad nodded. 'Fillim," he said, "how can we praise you? At every turn you saved us with your sword, your wits, your eloquence and wisdom. You saved us from the Prince's perverted schemes, and I believe and pray you have saved us from the Duke's monstrous war. I don't want to count the men and women who might have died, but for you. We owe you everything." His merry face was solemn. "I can think of no reward great enough for what you have done."

"I did only my duty, Your Grace." Fillim smiled, bowing.

The King and Queen exchanged glances, and the Queen said, "Hmm. You wouldn't care for our eldest son's hand in marriage?"

"Alas, Your Grace," said Fillim. "My siblings know that I am not a patient woman. It's a failing in me, but I cannot wait – sixteen? – years until he is old enough to be a husband."

"Fifteen years would be sufficient, surely. Many are married at seventeen."

"And besides, if I married Prince Achad, I would be in danger – a small danger – of living long enough to become Queen some day. I would never wish that. My brother finds it troublesome enough, merely ruling Ferrodach."

"We'll have to think of something else, then. And now we'll rejoice. The feast is being prepared, and will soon be ready."

It was a happy evening of reunions. Lida gave all her friends traditional Haymonese flower-badges, which they didn't know what to do with. Fric showed off the little wooden figure with movable arms and legs, that the injured Haymonese guard had made for him. Draider sat with his siblings of the Eastern Six, taking a drink every time anyone asked him if he'd met any beautiful women in Haymon. Kalla danced with her husband. Fillim did not dance, but strolled happily round the room with her friend Lady Yaffet, waiting for the moment when they could slip away together. And the King presented his proposed new squire to his wife, and subject to her parents' approval all that was agreed.

Lida had already been present at one of the happiest reunions of all, when King Barad walked into the nursery, and little Achad and Raidor ran to him with shouts of delight. They clamoured to be put on his shoulders, and to play with his hat, and he sat on the floor with them and with Lida, and took off his shoes so that they could become warships on the River Vay.

But the new squire had said good-night and gone to bed when at last the celebrations were over, and the Queen and King retired to her private chamber. The King sat on the bed where generations of Marodi royalty had been conceived, born and died, and watched her maid brush out her long black hair. And then the maid left, and she beckoned him to join her on the cushioned settle before the fire, and the Queen didn't quite weep as she remembered the brother she would never see again.

"He was always jealous, I think. Ever since he realised what it meant that I was older. But still we were children together. I remember one time he smuggled me food when I'd been sent to bed without supper. He did love me."

"Of course he did. That was why he did it. He wanted to make you Queen of Jaryar."

Her mouth twitched, and he wondered if the tears were coming. "Yes. He wanted to make me Queen of Jaryar. And when you and I went south to Makkera, he wanted to rule here in my name. Alone. He would have been the obvious choice. I'm sure he told himself it was all for me, and for God."

"That was what made it so horrible, that night. I think he really believed it was justified, a holy murder, and God would approve. Commit any crime, do anything, and holy words and looks will make it all acceptable. Abbot Paul said it was some heresy with a long name. And, ah, he was right about Duke Haras' ambition, after all."

"Hmm." The Queen shifted a little, rearranging her

mantle, and smoothing the folds of the nightgown beneath. "Someone said to me once, that holy people are the most dangerous, if they aren't also humble.

"I did love him, and he did love me. And he was friendly to you, when you came to Stonehill, was he not?"

He looked grim. "Yes, he was helpful and friendly. He saved my life." The fire crackled. "Which he now regrets doing. And he has the rest of his life to spread whatever lies he chooses about us, and about Achad."

There are few rumours so damaging as those about a prince's legitimacy. They both knew this, and that they would have enemies enough in Jaryar.

"Another reason for you to hate me," he said. She cautiously put a hand on his, and he didn't move it away. They both knew her answer, which she had made him before. *"I do hate you sometimes. But never for long, because I like you too much."*

"Should I have killed him?"

"No. *No.*" Her mouth twisted again, and now the tears began to trickle. "It was so monstrous. But I keep remem-remembering playing together on the tables, and *under* the tables, in the Great Hall when we were tiny. He'd be a squirrel, leaping through the branches up above, and

I'd be a rabbit, burrowing underneath."

She laid her head on his shoulder, and he put an arm awkwardly around her. He wished, as he had often wished before, that she could have had a husband able to comfort her properly. Such had not been their destiny.

After a while, she said, "And what was all that about a prophecy?"

"I don't know what that was about. It made no sense at all."

"Hmm. I pray King Osgar lives many years more."

But he will die, she thought, *and we will become Queen and King of Jaryar. We will travel south, and live in that huge green city. When I die, I'll be buried far from home. And however hard we try to keep Marod distinct for our children, in a few generations it will just be 'that bit in the north that we also rule.'*

After a little, he stretched out his legs, put his head back, and said, "I'm so bloody tired. Being sensible and charming day after day. It's good to be home."

They sat on for a little, and then they went to bed, and slept.

*

The Sword and Ploughshare Inn had forget-me-nots and primroses growing attractively under the front windows, but inside it was a squalid place. Two basic dormitory bedrooms upstairs, one for men and one for women, and a better one for travelling gentry, already occupied; and downstairs a horrid square box of a room, with a chimney that needed sweeping, lit by an assortment of stinking rush-lights and tall candles. The candle-sticks were finely-carved but unpolished, and the table was sticky with over-slopped ale. Talinti sensed Meriden's disgust.

They shared the fireside that night with local and travelling drinkers. Stories were told. Meriden narrated the victory of the beautiful Queen of Marod, and the crimes of her devil-inspired brother, and they heard in return about the sacrilegious theft of silver from the church two villages away. And after a time people drifted away to their homes, or, like Affrai, upstairs to bed.

Meriden went to the stables to check the welfare of Dragon and the other animals, plainly not trusting any hired man to have done it properly. Talinti sat at the table alone, polishing her sword, and wondering if she could bear another day of awkward silence like today and yesterday.

When he came back in, she said, "Is your foot hurting?"

"I'll manage, my lady." He shook his head

vigorously, spraying raindrops, and walked over to warm his hands at the fire. The candles flickered.

"I suppose that means 'yes.' Well." It was time for bed. She half-rose, but then, made foolish by longing, asked, "Did you pick up any other ideas for the Christmas entertainments, as Mritta suggested?"

He looked round. "I heard that while we were all being questioned, there was a pageant in the market-place, on stilts. Araf might try that."

"Excellent. I wish you a good night."

She made herself turn towards the stair, but instead of the expected "Good night, my lady," he said behind her, "But I won't be with you at Christmas. I'm sorry if it causes difficulty, but I must leave Lithermayg at the end of the quarter."

"You too?" Talinti sat down again, rather suddenly. It was a solution, of a sort. "Why – to do what?"

"To seek my fortune," with a twisted smile.

There was complete blankness, and then she was angrier than she had ever been in her life. "I see." She didn't speak loudly, but he flinched. "That was what you meant. I think after *twenty-one years* you might have given me the chance to match the offer, whatever it is."

He looked awkward. "No, I, I haven't an offer. In fact, I was hoping you would be kind enough to give me a letter that I could show, of recommendation -"

"You don't have another place?" So perhaps she'd been right. He'd said he'd been blessed. "Did you meet someone in Vach-roysh? Are you to be married?"

"No."

She clenched and unclenched her teeth. Slowly, heart thudding, "*Did* you do something terrible in the city? Are you in danger from the Guards?"

And surely he was considering whether to use that as an excuse. Her bewilderment grew. "I don't think I am."

"If you want to go and do something, climb a mountain or some such, Sister Salome could manage for a few months."

"That is good of you, but no."

I had enough of mysteries in Vach-roysh. "So. You insist you must leave, although you have nowhere to go. Have I wronged you somehow?" She stood up, bench scraping harshly on stone, and slapped her hands on the sticky table. "If you must go, you must, and of course I'll give you a letter recommending your work. But *you owe me a reason.*"

"Because -" He stood in front of the fire, tall and

very pale. He swallowed, and shrugged a little. "Because I woke up four mornings ago, and found that I was in love with you."

Her heart thudded steadily, and there was no other sound.

"So I have to go. I'm sorry, my lady. It's not convenient for you, but it would be a worse problem to have me stay. And I can't, can't sleep two doors away from you and not - I can't go on pretending not to want to kiss you every time you walk into a room.

"God bless you, and the children."

"But you don't have to," she whispered. She turned away from the table, a little towards him. "Please don't leave. Stay. Please."

There were tears on her cheeks, and her arms were held out. He walked into them.

This time it was not dark, and she was not ashamed.

They kissed with wondering joy, and they murmured each other's names, and then they sat down on a bench by the still-glowing fire to kiss better, and to ask and answer.

"How long have you -?" he asked. "Less than a week. The morning of the vote." "Oh. I didn't kill anyone," he said, reading her mind again. "I know that. And you – four days, did you say?" "Yes - or perhaps all my life. I don't know." They went on looking at the faces they'd known for so many years, and she kissed him again, slow and long and happy.

Then his face changed, and he drew back. Quietly he said, "You have to let me go."

"No." She stroked his cheek. He lifted her hand gently away.

"What else can we do?" he asked.

His eyes held hers, and they both stared at what they were. Mistress and servant. As they always had been, and always had to be.

Meriden said, "Some rich ladies take lovers from the hall, or the gutter. But that's not you, and it's not what I want either. Everyone we know would despise us both, and you'd never be able to take the Sacrament honestly again."

"What do you want?" she asked, and watched his face grow miserable and angry, as it had been for three days.

"What I can't have."

Her head buzzed, as she said, "There is nothing you can't have."

He looked angrier, if anything. "Don't do this. The lady of Lithermayg cannot marry her steward."

"The lady of Lithermayg will marry whomever she damn well pleases," but it felt empty.

"It's impossible."

And she felt all her ancestors for generations back agreeing with him.

"It might be impossible in Jaryar," she said. "Not in Haymon."

"Do you really think so, Talinti?"

They looked at each other in the quiet room, and she thought of what her neighbours would say, her liege lord, and her uncle. Worst of all, her son, Lithermayg's heir. And however hard it would be for her, it would be worse for Meriden.

But if she didn't marry him, she would be lonely for the rest of her life.

They both seemed to be waiting.

"All these years," she said at last, "I've given orders, and you have obeyed them. This time, you decide. You decide, and I will abide your choice."

She sat still as Meriden got up. He walked over to the shuttered window, and touched the wood with one finger. Then he opened the shutter on the dark, and the cool spring air blew in and extinguished one of the candles.

He turned back, and he was smiling. "I choose, then," he said, "to be impossibly happy."

With his arms around her, and tears flowing once more, she said, "Now will you tell me what happened to you in Vach-roysh?"

Meriden laughed. He told her the story, leaving out names - the story that would never appear in any of the chronicles of Jaryar or Marod or Haymon; and then he kissed her again.

THE END

ACKNOWLEDGEMENTS

Thank you again to the Early Readers: Katie Attwood, Clint Redwood and Eleanor Wallace-Howell.

I am also grateful to all those who read "We Do Not Kill Children", liked it, and told me so, and especially those who told others! There are too many to name, but your encouragement was very welcome. Katie Attwood (possibly Ragaris' number one fan) and Annelise Arnold-Tetley asked me to start reading the book aloud to them, and didn't change their minds until the whole thing was done. Jem Bloomfield interviewed me online, which was fun.

Mandy Stanton is responsible for the naming of the River Angan, on which the city of Makkera stands.

John Wallace-Howell said something in a tavern while I was working on this book that confirmed to me that I might be on the right track. He doesn't know what, and won't until he reads it.

As before, thank you for technical advice to Jonathan Batchelor and Gina Hall. All mistakes are mine.

The map was expertly drawn by Stephen Hall. The cover illustrations are by Ian Storer (http://scipio6.wixsite.com/scipio-designs)

Thank you again to everyone at Mightier Than the Sword UK Publishing, and especially its guiding spirit, the charismatic businesswoman and prolific author C S Woolley.

In the Acknowledgements for "We Do Not Kill Children", I mentioned Katherine Kurtz. Marion Zimmer Bradley's "Darkover" novels first gave me the idea of a series of connected-but-stand-alone books set at different places and times in an invented history. Others have done the same thing, but for me she came first, and feministically.

Thank you again, and again, and again, Mark.

Coming in 2018:

The Servant's Voice

The third tale from Ragaris

In the powerful eastern land of Ricossa, rich people use brutal and permanent methods to protect their secrets.

An eccentric pauper is knocked down and killed in a tavern. Drunken manslaughter, or deliberate murder? The victim's niece is determined to find out which.

As an investigator, Hridnaya faces many disadvantages. The case has already been closed; she's an insignificant servant; she can't read or write.

And she can't talk.

Many years before Gormad the Lucky was a national hero, he played a small part in someone else's story.

We Do Not Kill Children
The first tale from Ragaris

"Dorac Kingsbrother, I find you guilty of the murders of Ilda, aged twelve, Gaskor aged nine, and Filana, aged five. From this day, and forever, you are exiled from this land."

Dorac's life is over, and so he heads to the Old Stones, the place where Death will come for those who ask. But he's not alone – a troublesome ten-year-old insists on following him.

"Why are you here?"
Gormad said, "I want to be your squire."
"I am an exile. I have no use for a squire. And I do not like children."

Dorac has a few friends who believe him innocent. But

even if they can prove it, can a verdict be undone? And why would anyone want to kill the treacherous Lord Gahran's children anyway? How large a conspiracy lies behind this murder?

About the Author

Penelope Wallace has lived in St Andrews, Oxford, Aberdeen and Nottingham. She is a pedantic bibliophile, a sometime lawyer, a not-completely-orthodox Christian, a wishy-washy socialist, a quiet feminist and a compulsive maker of lists. She has practised law in England and Scotland, in the fields of employment, conveyancing, and marine insurance litigation.

Her favourite writers include Jane Austen, Agatha Christie, Nancy Mitford, George RR Martin, JRR Tolkien, Marilynne Robinson, JK Rowling and the Anglo-Catholic Victorian Charlotte M Yonge.

She invented a continent where the buildings and manners are medieval, but the sexes are equal. This continent is Ragaris, and the concept is Swords Without Misogyny.

To find out more about Penelope Wallace's work please visit:
www.penelopewallace.com

and

www.mightierthanthesworduk.com

or connect via Facebook:

www.facebook.com/swordswithoutmisogyny

or

www.facebook.com/mightierthanthesworduk

Printed in Great Britain
by Amazon